Stumbling toward Love

Oct 20 2019

To Michael & Hilda
Please be friends - what does
it doesn't work for you...
My very dear friends here.

Bill

Other Books by W C Stephenson:

The Inward Journey, (Harcourt Brace, 1970)

*Can't Stop Falling, a Caregiver's Love Story
(*Amazon, 2019)

*Rowdy and the Javelinas (*Amazon, 2019*)*

ISBN-9781076954435

Cover design by Sandra Baenen at <u>artwerks@got.ne</u>t

Stumbling toward Love

a novel

W C Stephenson

The old poem we learn by going where we need to go

Holds true for those who need to understand the what,

The when, the where, the why in the mystery called life

To learn that way, outgrow the need to keep control:

Dance, stand tall, and watch life grow the way it grows.

In a dark time, light may shine.

PART ONE

CHAPTER ONE: DESTINY OR DESIRE?

YOU'VE BEEN DRIVING WEST, up and down hills all morning since leaving Asheville. Now at the top of the tallest hill a small sign announces the crossing of the Appalachian Trail from Georgia to Tennessee and parts northeast. Since you're energetic enough and the day is young, you park and decide to hike ten miles to the summit of Siler Bald, from which someone told you that other balds like Tusquittee, Walah, Round, and Rabun can be seen.

You're not sure you still like to hike, and certainly find this trail challenging. It's manageable, if not well maintained; studded with rocks and roots. Tall trees and dense thickets of rhododendron hem you in; it's good you're not claustrophobic because the sky is too far away to be seen. The path is so steep that you have to stop every fifty feet to catch your breath. After an hour it finally straightens out, then takes a sharp curve right and drops into a bubbling creek. You want to drink but know you shouldn't, so settle for splashing water over your face and into your hat.

By the time you make it to the top, assuming you've found the barely-marked cutoff, you're worried about making it back down. But up there you'll smile broadly, turning in circles to take in the beauty stretching fifty to a hundred miles. Spectacular! You are finally not hemmed in by trees; can breathe. If you've brought your handy I-Pad, you might Google to learn why the hilltops are called balds. Did the Indians burn off trees for grazing or was it just to mark a trail? Google doesn't know, will give variant answers, so don't bother. You probably can't get it up here anyway.

Since the better part of a day has been spent hiking up and down, you need to hurry to make it where you've got to go. Yet when a scenic turnoff presents itself for parking to survey the Tusquittee Valley below, you can't resist, so get out, stretch, swat a fly, and wish you'd brought your binoculars. Were they super strong, you might see two older guys stepping out of their cart on the Ridges Golf Course down at the edge of Tusquittee Valley.

The one on the right is tall and still in pretty good shape. He stretches his arms into those crazy golf maneuvers to loosen up, and hits. Good shot, if not very far. He has a gray mustache, but his hair is still brown, medium cut. He washes it every day; confesses to being a little vain about it, especially since it still has color. You guess he used to be handsome enough to qualify as a lanky cowboy-looking guy, maybe someone who'd try to sweet talk a bar woman. You wouldn't know that before that time, back in high school, he grew up skinny, shy, and afraid of the world. Being bullied took away self-confidence, but he managed to recover it in mid-life.

His golfing buddy Frank is shorter and more muscular, with easy confidence. He hits his drive almost twice as far, and today's shot predictably slices right--out of sight for both him and you. You hear him cursing and trying not to throw his driver. Some might say that his head is a bit too big for his body and his mouth too small. He would never have thought to grow a mustache to disguise it. Few men would want to get into a fight with this muscular guy who has continued to work out in gyms ever since his high school days when he was the school jock poised to take on the world. The main difference between the two is not which one is stronger, has a mustache or the biggest head, but their eyes. Bert's green ones have a far-away cast, and Frank's brown-black ones bore directly into a person, issuing an immediate challenge. Bert remains the dreamy romantic he's always been, and Frank is still the let's get it done kind of guy--let's figure this out right now, not tomorrow.

Two women have unexpectedly joined you for the drive down to the Tusquittee valley. One looks to be around 30, the other, 50. Maybe mother and daughter. They beg you to stop at the golf course they've recently seen pictures of. Not to approve the lush fairways or rustic clubhouse, but the impressive rock wall...three hundred yards of stonework from three to fifteen feet tall, protecting the clubhouse and inviting guests to enter. The two ladies and you can almost overhear the older guys you spotted from the scenic turnout. The ladies aren't interested in them, rudely dismiss them as dinosaurs hitting silly white balls.

You disagree, maybe because you're a male or more likely because you're older and wiser. In fifteen years, you'll be retired and you will be them. There's no need to correct the ladies' hasty judgments; you have your own opinions; so does everyone, and it doesn't really matter now.

It's time for you to leave, but should you stay to learn more about the two old-timers? They could be the soul of America you've been looking so long for. You haven't found it in the younger set; they're too busy getting and spending. Could you find it in men who've lived in two centuries, stubbornly rooted in the elusive past yet successfully enduring the troubling present? Maybe but now you have to go. Maybe south to Atlanta, west to Chattanooga, or north to Knoxville, all equidistant from this Hayesville place. We'll never know because like the two ladies, you don't really belong to this story, in fact don't even exist. The two golfers do. We'll stick with them.

The two are shouting and complaining, first about their game, next about something more personal. They're pretending to be very angry.

"Yeah, how many times have you told me you love her?" Frank snarled his best ferocious snarl. "We both know that's not true. You don't even know her!"

Bert threatened him with his putter but settled for harsh words. "Hey, bumblehead, don't go there. You think you know everything just because you've got this degree complex, but you don't...."

Frank jumped in when Bert couldn't come up with a good conclusion. "Don't bumblehead *me*, bumblehead. How long *have* you known her? All of two months?"

"Does it matter? I guess you wouldn't know, being incapable of loving anyone but yourself."

Frank threw a fake punch. "Lay it on thick, as usual. What's really bothering you?"

"You—telling me I'm on the rebound!" Bert jammed his putter back into his bag. "You, you …know that's not right."

"Do I? You just said I don't know her! Make up your mind."

"Are we going to talk or just shout?"

Frank tossed his putter in his bag and climbed in the cart. "Let's get a move on, looks like someone coming up behind."

Bert and Frank rarely get angry at each other for anything important, but sometimes their banter can push them close, as today. Bert was upset over Frank's insistence he was using Brie to replace his lost wife. "That's the dumbest thing I've heard," he started to say but stopped, thinking instead to go on the offensive. "Are you ever going to invite us over to meet Marsha?" He knew Frank must know Brie rarely gets out, and needs female friends. And he also knew Marsha could use an ally against her stubborn husband.

11

Frank waved his arm the way he does when conversations take a detour. "Well...yeah, maybe so." Their banter coming to an end, they agreed to a time for dinner and opened another conversation.

Frank's surplus of self-confidence came from his high school days when his physical prowess made him the unspoken leader of the in crowd. Despite being shy, skinny, and the brunt of class bullies who'd grab his thin upper arm and shake him around in circles, Bert regained his self-confidence in seventh grade when he suddenly blossomed into the class Romeo, dating all the girls. Then something happened when he hit tenth grade, causing him to derail. He slipped into a cocoon, staying there until half-way through college, again afraid of the world, when Frank magically appeared to pull him out.

Frank attended the same college, joined the same fraternity, and helped Bert come back not by counseling him but by believing in him. He was not only the first of his family to attend college but went on after graduate school in psychology to became a successful shrink. Bert, meanwhile, stumbled around in the business world for ten years until he finally bumped into the career he was made for, being a real estate appraiser. Along the way he got married, and his first wife helped him spot, buy, remodel, and sell enough homes to amass a small fortune.

Both men went through the predictable first divorce. Frank sailed through, eager to start again with the prettiest divorcee he could find who wanted to be the mate of a successful shrink. Bert didn't; when Eileen left him for no reason he could think of, he crashed, falling back into his shell again and losing all the hard-won confidence that his career and marriage had produced. Fortunately, Eileen and he had successfully raised two confident kids, the male of whom grew up and took father under his wing, teaching him golf and nursing him back into life the way Frank had done earlier. All this in a space of two years, after which Bert got married again, this time to the woman of his dreams.

He and Suzanne stayed together for more than 30 years, a perfect love match, until she contracted a rare disease and succumbed. Frank meanwhile married Marsha, a beautiful woman who turned out to have a brain after all and became a perfect wife for him except for being extremely compulsive about keeping a spotless house. Frank can't tolerate neatness.

Nowadays the two friends don't take themselves as seriously as they do golf. They've been playing together off and on for three years, but Frank and Marsha just recently returned from a long European vacation, so the two friends are reconnecting. They've developed a strange routine of starting the game fast and quiet but ending slow and noisy. On the eleventh or twelfth hole, the talk starts—not about the game, but about life. This affects their score the way inattentiveness always does, but by that time they don't care, having lost interest in keeping scores to lower their handicaps.

"Ok, let's start over," Bert said slowly. "I said I'll admit to being in love."

"Again, how many times have you told me that?" Frank replied. "For what--two, three months now?"

"What's today? Oh yeah, July." Bert counted on his fingers. "It goes way back...four or five months now. I'm in deep shit."

"What goes back, being in love or just meeting this raving beauty?"

"I met her in January but didn't start falling for her until May. We didn't do anything but talk and play card games. You know...."

"I do, you're a real fast mover. Most guys would have had her forty or fifty times and dumped her by then. But you, you finally got as far as holding hands."

"Stow the teenage language. I said it was love, not lust."

Frank gave an obligatory nod and told Bert he was probably just confused. "You can't see what you're looking at, just like golf. It's not love; you're just trying to replace Suzanne."

Bert scowled, started to speak, but Frank interrupted. "Sorry, I know it's still tender. But what I meant was you're still missing Suzanne too much to be in love with this new one."

"Hey, Frank," Bert said, "You don't know the woman, have never met her."

"Quiet down. I'm not talking about her, just you. Maybe she was on the rebound too, but I think you said she hadn't had anybody for a long time. You, however...."

"Yeah, I'm always running around looking for some new woman."

"No, but you know the standard wisdom. And there you went, charging after this woman a couple months after. If that's not being on the rebound, what is?"

"Care to stop a minute to hear the real story? Can you listen with an open mind?"

"Only if you don't pour it on thick."

Bert took a gulp of water, took off his cap, and splashed water into it. "I didn't go looking for her. I've already told you we met in church. It wasn't just an accident."

"Yeah, yeah, the old church story. How many times do I have to hear it?"

"Listen up."

"Ok, so you met her in church."

"Out of nowhere she walked into our tiny Presbyterian church. And, yes, it was only a couple of months after Suzanne died. I didn't see her sitting in the back row until someone behind me spoke and I turned. She was wearing this gray baseball hat and scarf thing that covered her forehead and ears–in church, of all places. Just another newcomer to our small church, but much younger than most, and with an unusual taste in headgear."

"The story's coming back. You asked her for a date."

"No, I didn't, I was just doing my church thing and stopped to greet the newcomer. You know me, I'm no church fixture. I never entered one for the first forty years of my life until Suzanne begged me to go with her."

"Ok, so the now-but-not-before-faithful church guy walks back and greets the good-looking newcomer."

"Hey, that headgear covered her up. I didn't know she was a looker."

"Aren't you a deacon or something there now?"

"No, I do maintenance and make blueberry pancakes for our monthly breakfast. Sometimes lead a Wednesday lunch session on literary topics. Didn't I invite you to the one on the medieval poem, 'Sir Gawain and the Green Knight'?"

"I might have spaced it. You know, it was still inside a church. Keep going."

"We exchanged pleasantries and I think I remember asking her if she'd like to go for a hike. I don't call that a date. I couldn't see much of her face but couldn't

16

keep my eyes off her blue eyes. Anyway, I was still grieving for Suzanne; certainly not ready for something like this."

"And when did you go on the date--er, hike? How soon after?"

"She came back the next Sunday, and I think we went Monday or Tuesday afternoon."

"Ok, hold off on that one. I still want to know what was so special about your meeting in church. You aren't telling me you think God put you two together?"

"Well, it is 'sorta crazy where we met."

"Not at all. A better place to meet than in a bar. It happens all the time. Hell, guys surf churches looking for someone like Brie."

"But I wasn't. I was just sitting there...."

"Come on now, this just happened to be the place where this horny guy meets this lovely woman who's what--ten years younger?"

"Ok, ok, I won't say it was meant to be...although after things got going for us, we always talked that way."

"Sure, love talk."

"Well, I'll drop it. But I still can't believe she just happened to appear when she did, when we both needed each other. There's no way it could have been an accident."

Frank smiled. "Why don't we just use secular talk and say it was meant to be. I might go that far."

Bert took another swig of water and motioned for his friend to be quiet so he could concentrate on his drive. Then, the minute Frank stepped up to hit, Bert smiled and shouted, "I can't help it if I'm attractive to younger women...even in church."

Frank immediately miss-hit, waved his club threateningly, and scowled. They went looking for the ball Frank had sliced toward the lake. Bert kept smiling while driving the cart; Frank kept scowling.

Two holes later Frank had simmered enough to go back to their talk. "So, aside from the question of whether God put you together with this fantastic looking woman or you just happened to notice her one day in church, what else is new? You going through another mid-life crisis?"

"Don't you think I'm a bit old for that?"

More than a bit. You're another mid-life past mid-life. It was so long ago you can't remember coming out the other side."

"You told me a person never comes out."

"So you do listen. You said you never believe anything I say."

"I don't. Who can believe a shrink? You're all crazy as hell."

"True, but...."

"No buts, so what crisis you talking about? Or are you just playing the advocate again?"

"*Devil's* advocate," Frank corrected. "No, I was referring to a spiritual, not emotional, crisis. Assuming, of course, you're advanced enough to manage that."

"Uh, oh," Bert said, looking back toward the foursome who'd left the green and were climbing into their carts. "We'd best push on."

But instead of hitting their drives, they sat watching. "Shit! I thought August was supposed to be slow. Let's wave them on," Frank said, not waiting for Bert to agree, but signaling them to play through.

When the four younger golfers came up, Frank and Bert small-talked and pretended not to watch them drive from the black tips thirty yards behind their white tees. Frank lit one of his cheap cigarette-cigars while Bert wet his towel at the water tank to clean his irons. Two holes later Bert brought them back to their earlier talk. "I thank you for your *objective*, impartial, and of course misinformed counsel about my love life." He stopped to wipe his sunglasses. "And who knows, you might be right about the rebound. It was too quick, and that could be what's causing the rocky ride now. But I'm still convinced I came along at that time to help her. And she, me."

"Isn't that what we're all supposed to do, help each other?"

"You're just arguing. Of course, that's true generally. But this is true in a special sense."

"Seems to me everything is special to the person it's happening to."

"Ok, maybe true again. But the question is whether something just happens or happens for a reason."

"God."

"Maybe so, maybe not. I didn't say 'happens for a reason we're supposed to know.'"

"Destiny."

"What's that Shakespeare quote I keep forgetting? 'Hanging and wives go by destiny.'"

"Seems to me I remember a different one. 'Not in the stars comes our destiny but in ourselves.' Something like that."

"Sometimes you do surprise me, Frank."

"Can't help my own brilliance...."

Before Bert could gather his thoughts to counter with something brilliant, the cart lady drove up. Frank bought four beers and an ice pack. They were on hole 15, an easy three-par, 145-yard shot across a pond. Both got across, but Bert's landed far left, while Frank's hit two yards short, directly in front of the pin.

"Go for it," Bert said. "Three dollars if you make the birdie." Which he didn't.

After moving to western North Carolina, Bert started playing twice a week at the nearby Chatuge Golf Course, a municipal course with well-maintained and watered fairways and greens. It skirts one inlet of the lake, where a sign reads, "Golfers will be fined for hitting balls toward distant homesites." Bert had no way of knowing Lake Chatuge was to become the center of his life a few years later with Brie. He liked the course, especially the dogleg fourteenth which he finally mastered with a four-iron shot up to the landing area and seven-iron over the gulley to the green 150 yards away.

The Ridges course differs dramatically in being less wooded and less crowded, with spectacular mountain views. Being an expensive semi-private course, it has no old-timers dallying over the green—putting and re-putting, gabbing and joking, ignoring impatient foursomes behind. From almost every hole a person can look up to see blue or violet mountains hugging the peaceful Tusquitte Valley. Bert came to like the course well enough to join, partly because it allowed him to walk with Rowdy. Unlike Chatuge, for some reason that Bert never understood, the Ridges had no squirrels…only one small lake that his dog chased ducks into, even though his doggy mind must have known who would always win.

Bert enjoyed all golf courses for their beauty and peace. More than once he found himself giving unvoiced thanks. He always encouraged Rowdy to roll in the deep grass, guessing that the dog appreciated life on the course as much as he. Everyone at the clubhouse recognized his friend, and against club rules let him join his master. They'd made an exception for him because his church friend who lived on the second hole told the club pro that his friend needed the help of his faithful dog to get over the death of his wife.

Frank hadn't played much golf before joining Bert at the Ridges, but characteristically began with several months of lessons. George, the club pro, told him not to worry; he'd shown lots of older guys how to hit it straight and true. Almost immediately George spotted Frank's problem: right-arm dominance. He tried unsuccessfully for ten lessons to drill it into him to take the club back slow and wait until the last second to hit hard…but Frank couldn't seem to get it. George switched to teaching him how to handle the irons, and even got him to be a decent putter, so Frank was happy; he'd straighten the drive one day.

Golf not only renewed but cemented their friendship. Frank needed time out from Marsha, whose obsessive neatness drove him nuts, and Bert needed to talk first about his difficult caregiving life and more recently about the new woman in his life. Frank grew up in the East, the only one of his large Portuguese family to attend college. Bert came from the West, his dad having attended Harvard for one year, whereas his mom went to an extinct Midwest college also for a year. His sister went to several colleges and finally become a somewhat famous actress off-Broadway about the time he enrolled in the University of Minnesota, where he met Frank when they both joined the same fraternity.

Off and on the two relived their undergraduate days. In many ways, they couldn't be more different. Recently they starting sharing secrets and aspirations, which brought them closer. But they hadn't suffered together on some battlefield, hadn't covered each other financially, hadn't come to blows on a prolonged camping or driving trip. And because Bert's wife was confined to a wheelchair for such a long time before her death, they never socialized as families, just played golf or hit bars together.

They never talk about the same things the guys on Bert's pickleball court discuss—sports, movies, cars, fishing, hunting. They can get heated over politics, but since both are on the same side of the fence, they rarely waste time agreeing. Mostly they discuss books. Frank likes American history; Bert prefers old-fashioned literary novels but will go along with historical novels that are well enough written. Once both bought Will and Ariel Durant's eleven volume *Story of Civilization* but agreed it made better shelf decoration than everyday reading. On occasion they become a two-man book club, reading the same study of current affairs or environmental problems and lecturing each other on and off the golf course. They rehash the same things people all over the county rehash: people becoming uprooted, narrow-sighted, apathetic about working for the better good. They worry over world hunger, mayhem, disorder. They hate it that everyone belongs to some tribe with its ideology ruling their lives. They worry about ideology starting to govern not only political action but all the nation's activities. Unlike some old-timers, they refuse to glorify the good-old days but harp on contemporary political correctness and the furious pace of today's life. When they run out of things to disagree about, they try to talk each other into reducing their eating and drinking intake. At this they never succeed.

One of Bert's preoccupations is making sense of how to relate to deity, if deity really does exist, whereas Frank sometimes wonders if he should try to outgrow his behaviorist mindset.

Two holes left to go. Frank grinned, walking up to the murderous 510-yard seventeenth hole knowing his super strength would pay off. But the golf pro George hadn't been able to convince him the road to winning wasn't through his powerful right arm. When he smashed the ball 280 yards, his outside-in swing caused it to slice out of bounds. Frank had a hard time connecting his hooks and slices with his inner personality.

Bert smiled while walking up to the same tee box, thinking not about Tiger but Freddy Couples. His personality told him not to conquer but to dance. He'd learned long ago to perfect a graceful inside-out swing and settle for a modest 180 yards to the middle of the fairway. Another two gentle hits would bring him next to the green, and then it was just a controlled chip and gentle putt for par. Bert loved golf when it rewarded his patience.

Frank fumed after finding his lost ball and counting the penalty, but since his third shot brought him fairly close to the green, he could at least tie his partner. Could, if he'd remember to relax and hit down on the ball, not muscle it, which he couldn't. He had to settle for a bogie. That's ok; he muttered, there was still one hole left to go. They tied it. After the eighteenth they dropped off their clubs and went into the clubhouse. Bert ordered a beer for himself and root beer for Frank.

"How long we been at this?" Frank asked.

"Drinking? Golf? Living?"

"Golf, dummy. Three years now?"

Bert nodded, "Something like that. One of these days you'll learn how."

They sipped their drinks in the clubhouse, empty save four noisy men in the corner. They replayed the day's golf for a while, then fumbled around for something interesting to discuss. Bert smiled mischievously, a stray thought popping into mind. "I've noticed something about you, Frankie Boy."

"What's that, Mister Observant? "

"When I came over to your house that time Marsha was gone you cooked a meal for us…."

"Yeah, maybe the only one. I don't cook much."

"I watched you search through all the cookbooks, open one and methodically follow the instructions, down to the last one-quarter teaspoon of salt."

"So?"

"So I guess you're a 'follow the instructions' kind of guy."

"Yeah?"

"I think there are two kinds of guys—the followers and those who play it by ear."

"Play it by ear?"

"You know, make your own rules, don't automatically follow what some expert has decided is the best way to go."

"You're telling me I'm a follower?"

"Yeah, sort of. For cooking anyway. It might extend to other aspects of life. Ever try painting by the numbers?"

Frank snorted, put on an ugly face. "Good news, I bow and scrape whenever someone tells me how to do something."

"I knew you'd blow this out of proportion. Go back to the cooking example."

"Ok, I do follow there because I don't know what the hell I'm doing with cooking. That makes me a follower?"

"We both know your golf routines."

"Such as?"

"You always tip your cap, wipe your brow, and wag your ass before each shot."

"That's called waggle, you moron!"

"What about not starting the cart up until all the bags and clubs are lined up exactly the way you want-- always the same. Very methodical!"

"Impressive examples."

"Well I'm hard-pressed here. But don't think I'm belittling your natural disposition, just looking for examples of it."

Frank scoffed loudly. "You've reached a new low, Bertie Boy. I've endured your idiocy for years now, but this doesn't even reach the level of nonsense. Are you just trying to start a quarrel?"

Bert smiled sheepishly. "Well, I...."

"Let's at least quarrel about something meaningful. We can find lots of differences in people, but the one that interests me is the dividing line between you and me."

"You mean high IQ—low IQ," Bert chuckled.

"No, idiot. This has to do with the way we process things."

"As usual, I'm all ears."

Frank waved his arm, ignoring him. "Some people unconsciously look for similarities," he said. "They find correspondences and correlations. People who do that all the time can end up in la-la land, believing in things most sane people consider delusional. When two things happen together one after another, they assume it's not an accident, but one caused the other. *This* looks a lot like *that*, so probably caused it, or vice-versa. Correlations and correspondences, not differences.

Bert nodded even though he wasn't sure he understood.

"That's you, my friend. But me, I'm the opposite. My disposition makes me look for differences. I don't assume anything, because I see everything as separate, different, and unique.'"

Bert shook his head, getting his drift. "You're an Aristotelean, I'm a Platonist."

Frank started to agree, then stopped. "Maybe, or it might be I'm just a little autistic—I look at the details, not the big picture. I don't know. But hear me out." He coughed and started again. "People who look for similarities to explain everything can not only be delusional and superstitious, but can end up in

28

conspiracy land. Especially these days where you can find whatever you want on the internet. You want to believe our government is responsible for everything? Then you look around and immediately learn that our air force is salting clouds, causing chem-trails."

Bert nodded. "I think I'm a far cry from that, Frank."

"Absolutely! I'd never accuse you of any kind of delusional thinking. But I do think you habitually look for similarities, whereas I look for differences. That's the different way we think." Bert started to reply, but Frank said he wasn't done yet. "A good example of you looking for causes is your insistence that God must be behind you and Brie. After all, you met in church, and you both believe in God and want to make your sex life respectable."

Bert snickered. "Ok, maybe, I'll have to put some thought to that. But where would the person who thinks like you tend to go wrong?"

Frank scratched his chin. "Hmm, hadn't thought about that. How about relativism? If I think we're all totally different and separate, I can end up in the land of solipsism. People can't really communicate because there are no absolutes, no shared truths. Everything's relative, period."

"I get it. And for once I won't disagree. You're saying I look for confirmation, and when you see something that I see as causal, you just let it be a coincidence. Right?"

"Right. Sometimes your mental acumen astounds me. I mean you can follow me and even summarize my brilliance. So yes, our brains are wired a little differently. Yours is wired to believe that a correlation is also a cause. Maybe that's true for other animals. You put a bird in a cage with a key that lights up before food appears, and pretty soon Mr. Bird will start pecking the lighted key to get food."

"Baseball pitchers spit or rub their bellies before pitching in order to get a strike."

"Yeah. We all do a little of it. It might help us learn. But in my statistic course I was taught that a correlation isn't automatically a cause. I think it's called the post hoc ergo propter hoc fallacy."

"And then there's the fact that you're a shrink, trained to disagree."

"Yeah, maybe I've trained myself to be wary of easy answers…settle for coincidences and happenstance."

"So again, I'll have to admit you're talking a little bit of sense. I used to say our difference was just that I was more of an idealist, you a realist. But this could be rooted scientifically, in the brain, not just philosophy."

Bert started to continue but the bartender interrupted with another round of drinks. When he left, they mutually decided they'd explored that topic enough and sat sipping their beer. Frank asked if they'd totally finished their former talk.

"You mean about Brie?"

Frank nodded. "Yeah, I guess you really do think your affair was divinely appointed. Why? There's got to be more to it than your meeting in church."

Bert smiled. "Maybe some of my divine interest had to do with sex."

Frank laughed, couldn't stop for several minutes. "The truth comes out. You know, *in vino veritas.* Sex! Good! Yes, I'd suspected as much. You told me you never got back home until midnight. She'd kick you out, never let you spend the night at her place."

Bert smiled. "Well, it really was intense. You know me, I'm not going to talk about that, but it really was intense."

"Intense, I gather."

"Come on, egghead."

"Hey, it's not uncommon for us guys to attach great importance to healthy sex. So much importance it balloons into something spiritual."

"Neither of us had ever experienced anything like it. I can't explain what I felt when I looked into her eyes. But it was way beyond lust, way beyond sex."

"As I think I've told you before, consider it a blessing. A big one. But *spiritual?*"

Bert sensed their talk coming to a good stopping place. "Thanks for listening," he said.

"I won't charge my usual fee for listening."

"Good, and I won't charge for letting you listen."

They finished their drinks and Frank went home to a spaghetti dinner cooked by Marsha, while Bert stopped at the Mexican fast food place for a final beer and enchilada before driving back to his empty house.

At home Bert wondered if he'd spoken too candidly about his love affair. He couldn't explain it well because he hadn't pieced it together himself. Frank had helped a little. But how in the world could he convince Frank that Brie and he had very unintentionally and very gradually fallen in love--and known it to be love, not just physical attraction? Not that it really mattered; he knew now he was in so deep he couldn't back out. Nor could he admit he always need to be in love with someone. Or that both of them were trying hard to believe God was in charge.

But if God was love, then God must have put them together. That part still confused him, made no sense. It obviously made no sense to Frank, but that was because he didn't believe in God. But Frank was very smart, and a good psychologist. Bert appreciated his friend's different orientation; didn't want confirmation, just clear thinking.

He tossed around in bed, visualizing Brie, knowing he'd wake planning projects that she needed or places they had to visit--things they had to do. They might get together only three or four times a week, sometimes for only a few hours, but after they discovered the lake everything changed.

He couldn't get to sleep, decided to give it up for a cup of hot chocolate. Took it to the computer, which these days he always left on. He'd never done any creative writing but had taken to keeping a journal while caregiving Suzanne. It helped keep him sane. After she died, he revised it and showed it to a close friend, who encouraged him to publish it in order to help other caregivers through their ordeals. He knew he was no author but said he'd consider it after several more revisions. He enjoyed revising more than writing.

Opening the file, he saw he was almost halfway through his fourth rewrite. Yes, he'd get it done sometime. But he was more interested now in the other thing he was writing. After he and Brie met in January of 2014, he bought three spiral notebooks and started keeping notes. The journal remained very personal; he never mentioned it to Frank or anyone, but eventually began transferring journal notes to the computer. He opened the file he'd started in May or June, the month he knew he'd fallen in love. It started out to be just a casual account of his early encounters with an interesting woman. Then he'd started rewriting it and giving it a title, "The Mermaid of Penland Isle."

Recently he felt it influencing his daily activities. As he told Frank this afternoon, life with the woman had moved beyond the innocent stage. Had reached the point where almost every day he'd rush home to jot something down. He liked replaying the good times and correcting the bad...sometimes anticipating what might happen next as well as enjoying or regretting what had just happened. But were life and art starting to get hopelessly entwined?

As he opened the file, a loud noise interrupted his reverie. Someone shooting his way this time of night? The hillbillies on the other side of Town Mountain again, blasting away with their shotguns. Probably aiming his direction, not caring if their pellets found their way to the courthouse or school–if they missed his hillside house, that is. He thought about dialing Roger again, but the last time the sheriff had come, he'd just shook his head, saying the rednecks lived outside town limits. Bert turned the radio on and looked at the file. He'd lose himself in that other less noisy and maybe more real world.

Rereading what he'd written a few months ago, he found the tone too studied. It was starting to look like it was written for someone else, not just him. Had he revised it too much? Parts he still liked, even though he noticed that five of the six first paragraphs started the same way, with the first-person pronoun. Oh well, he'd get it right one day, not that it mattered.

THE MERMAID of PENLAND ISLE

I know how, when, and where I met her but not why. This is hardly surprising since the first three involve facts, the last, conjecture. The sort of thing that distinguishes novels or news specials from obituary columns.

When most people enter the land of *why* they start using destiny language: "It was meant to be." "There's no way this couldn't have happened." "Thank you, God, you planned it all along. I just had to learn to trust you."

I too happen to believe we need to learn to trust, and have no problem adding the deity word as direct object instead of leaving the sentence properly generic: "trust the powers that be;" "trust whatever was to happen;" or, yes, "trust what was meant to be." But all this destiny talk bothers me, whether it includes real or pseudo spirituality. I suspect most people who address the spiritual dimension have come a long way from their forefathers' serious belief in predestination. It's hard for post-moderns to take predestination, destiny, or fate seriously...yet also very easy to get caught in a maze of contradictions.

I don't exempt myself from this dilemma. For instance, I want to say that Brie didn't just happen to walk into my life; "there's no way" this could have been an accident. But I'm not going to add that it was meant to be, even if I secretly think so. I could list a host of specifics to talk myself into believing this...but it might be better to just call her arrival at that time and place more probable than improbable.

I not only subscribe to the impossible, improbable, yet also hard-not-to-believe-in power behind religion, I sometimes think this force controls my life when I let it. And ever since my Suzanne died her hard, tragic death, I've tried my best to let it be controlled. I know I can no longer control it, and in fact have lost all desire to try.

Brie came to our small Presbyterian church (which these days does not believe in predestination) in January of 2014. I didn't see her sitting alone in the back row until someone behind me spoke and I turned. She was wearing a drab baseball hat with a strange grey scarf covering her forehead and ears. "Well, this newcomer hasn't gone to great lengths to make herself comely to strangers" flitted through my head, but then Rhonda started the service, so I had to face forward.

Church, therefore wasn't just the *where* behind our story, but even impinges upon the *why*. For Brie didn't just happen to enter our church. No one can even find it tucked behind the bigger and more popular Methodist and Baptist churches, and we don't advertise or even have a phone. Here's how it happened. Only a week or so after she'd settled upon our western North Carolina town as the best place for her to relocate, she started looking for a place to worship in. She didn't care at all about the denomination, just needed a church without fluorescent lights, loud music, electric organs, microphones, or most especially, wi-fi. Such places are hard to find, even in a small, backward town like ours.

She'd visited and rejected several, including the smallest church around, a primitive Baptist on the edge of Lake Chatuge. You'd think that one, with a congregation of seven or eight, wouldn't be filled with the electrical charges that hurt her, but the minister uses it to house his radio or television ministry, so it's wired to the hilt. And I can just imagine what our area's megachurch over in Hiawassee would do to her head were she to walk inside...even wearing five or six of the special hats and headbands with silver wires to help keep out harmful electrical charges.

How then did this stranger find our place, if she couldn't go into grocery stores, restaurants, bars, courthouses, hospitals, or churches to ask people? I've heard the story so many times it bores me, because she has to tell it to everyone. But then she's still busy meeting everyone, and everyone is curious about this mysterious condition that's afflicted her. It goes by many names: electro-sensitivity or ES; electromagnetic hypersensitivity or EHS and sometimes EMS; and VDT, used in Sweden but I don't know what it stands for. I prefer EMS.

She was sitting on the porch outside the popular deli, asking a couple where she could safely worship, when Roger happened to open the door and walk by. He heard, stopped, and gave his predictably curt reply: "There is one. Ours, the Presbyterian past the old courthouse. Try it; no fluorescents, no microphones. You'll like it." What's really strange about this encounter is the fact that Roger never talks to anyone, even friends sitting next to him in church.

She did try it, and that's when I met her. I guess our church building was more tolerable than most, and after she became a regular, Rhonda and Bob, our pastor team, went out of their way to make sure all electrical things except a few lights were turned off, including organ and air conditioning fans.

If Roger hadn't happened to walk out the deli door at that particular moment, Brie and I never would have met; that's a clear fact. She doesn't get around much, and I certainly don't drive around looking for another woman to replace my recently deceased Suzanne. It's that kind of coincidence that makes most believers reject the notion of coincidence...although I realize that even coincidences great enough to be called miracles still don't convince non-believers. Paradoxically some will still keep saying "it had to be," even though in their minds nothing has to be.

Throughout January I saw Brie only in church; she always disappeared right after closing. Most of the older ladies went to the Pig Palace for lunch, while I went home alone to read, write, or weather permitting, go smack golf balls. I was still rewriting and revising the journal covering the last several years' difficulties with Suzanne; crying a lot.

All winter I'd told myself I was not going to start looking for a future possible partner, although I guess I was. My experience losing Suzanne had pushed me closer to attaining the kind of simple trust that good believers are supposed to have...but who can actually believe God's one desire is to make life joyful for us humans? Especially when your picture of joy includes the worldly stuff most of ours does.

It surprised me, then, when I found myself asking this strange newcomer if she wanted to go on a hike sometime. I'd never mastered the art of small-talk, let alone verbal come-ons, because for 34 years, with no reason to be interested in another woman, I'd completely forgotten how to put on nonchalant masculine appeal. But I said it anyway, and she nodded.

It wasn't my masculine appeal which prompted her to accept my sudden invitation; I'm over the hill. It might have been prompted by the spirit of the place where we met. As I guess I've already said, I don't think it accidental that Brie and I met in this particular church at this particular time. I was grieving alone since family members lived far away and friends had already endured enough of my ordeal. Brie was new to the area and needed a helping hand, and also quite obviously had her own strong emotional needs. And as we were to learn, we were both on similar spiritual journeys.

But before we learned all that about each other, we took our first physical journey, to Fire's Creek a few miles west of town. There she discarded her scarf and hat for a reason that neither I nor anyone could understand or believe: because there, away from all electric lines, wi-fi towers, and cell phones, she was safe. She no longer needed protection against the electronic radiation that sent her head spinning and, when strong enough, threw her unconscious to the ground.

Which happened a couple of months later, strangely enough in church, after a new family with three youngsters ignored the sign, "Please turn off–don't just mute--all cell phones. They physically harm one of our members." That incident helped some of us believe she was telling the truth, even though we couldn't understand why these harmless devices that all of us carry could pack such a punch. To be honest, it took me a long time to stop doubting her mysterious condition; there's nothing in the media, social or otherwise, warning that electro-magnetic radiation can hurt people who are for some unknown reason susceptible to it.

But I shouldn't jump ahead. Looking back on our pleasant afternoon walk along Fire's Creek, the first thing I noticed after she discarded her strange scarf was how beautiful this woman suddenly looked. Her blue eyes immediately transfixed me.

Bert thought he liked the opening of the story. Noticing that he was already having trouble keeping dates and events straight, he told himself he needed to take Suzanne entirely out of it. He couldn't bring himself to do it since she'd been such a big part of it for him, not her...having met Brie only two months after his Suzanne had died. He scanned the narrative again. Before reading any more, he needed to admit the last paragraph about the blue eyes was incorrect. They didn't transfix him from the start; he didn't fall into them until much later. He thought about making another start, eliminating what he guessed he'd written a few months ago to make things sound better. "I'm trying to outgrow my need to keep control," he told himself, then mentally added: "The reason I haven't junked the first attempt to make sense of what happened to us is because I couldn't leave out the unimportant detail about the ugly headgear. Yet that part makes no sense without going on to talk about her eyes." He talked to himself a lot while sitting at the computer. Eventually he scrapped his idea about giving the truthful date for noticing the blue eyes. That kind of truth mattered not at all. It was much better to elaborate on them. Which he went on to do.

Since I've made such a big deal about her eyes, I should perhaps elaborate, maybe give vent to my penchant for waxing poetic, to use a phrase I never use. Like her Gemini personality, her blue eyes shadow forth five or six different people. On a calm day outside, they magically blend into the light blue of distant skies, especially early afternoon skies. I look into them, then up, marveling at the same color.

Inside a building, like our church or her house, or sometimes even on the porch while we small-talk, her eyes deepen into a neutral, non-committal, but still quite attractive blue. The generic blue of a Crest toothpaste tube, not the up-in-your-face blue of shiny Mexican tiles or fast food walls. A person looks into this shade of blue, nods pleasantly, and enjoys an everyday conversation. But let's be honest; even this non-threatening blue can be dangerous.

When something comes over her, whether a fright or a fancy, the slightly darker irises suddenly explode, deepen, and start shining. This happens when a police car or ambulance sirens by, or outboard motorboat on Lake Chatuge zooms in too close, not to mention when the crazy pilot who lives near Fire's Creek dips his biplane trying to scare the daylights out of people below, like Brie, innocently walking the dam road or paddling her kayak.

Whenever Brie and I play Scrabble, Texas Hold'em, or Skip-Bo, whether inside or outside, her eyes sooner or later deepen into the darker shade of blue that lets me know she's relaxed but paying attention. She never plays to win, like me, but always has to be in control of what she considers important. Like mastering, not necessarily winning, the game.

Then, maybe an hour after dinner on the porch and card games, when late afternoon skies turn dark, her eyes deepen even more, especially after we go inside and head toward the inner room, where I need say no more. Except, to say this, as circumspectly as possible: at some point her wonderful, beautiful, unbelievable blue eyes become limpid, shiny pools of dark that pull me deep inside, much like the lovely water-dwelling Irish silkies who come ashore to lure a man into distant watery depths. I think these silkies might be kin to mermaids, which is what Brie turns into when she puts on her green flippers and jumps into Lake Chatuge.

Once again, I keep rushing ahead. This account of Brie's magical eyes takes me far ahead of our chronological narrative. I must learn to go slow.

One Sunday back in early February I stopped at her church pew to talk longer, and then found myself driving to her place only a mile or so from my house or the church for lunch. I think I made sure I told her about my situation, and that day she explained more about hers, going so far as to lend me several books about EMS plus her personal testimony, a moving piece that almost convinced me she wasn't making things up--as so many believe, since this disorder is so rare and sounds so improbable. We had something in common: a great need for inner healing.

We had other things in common too: both being open and for the most part positive people, both trying to serve the same God, both loving the outdoors. In her case, she had to, since inside places, including her own house, contained too many dangers. She showed me her electro- magnetic monitoring device and I walked around inside watching its needle jump. She'd had an electrician remove, rewire, and shield appliances and fuse boxes; had replaced her fancy electric stove with a stripped-down gas model; had moved her refrigerator into the garage. She'd grounded her bed (and car); bought an expensive sauna to advance the detoxification process (a sauna built of poplar wood, not cedar, which would release more toxins); and had purchased several helpful items like a special telephone from the EMS catalog that predictably charged exorbitant prices for everything, including things that were obviously bogus. In the process she'd all but depleted her nest egg, already greatly diminished by an expensive and thoroughly exhausting trip from the eastern coast to Dallas to visit the country's only EMS specialist.

All this greatly impressed me, reminiscent as it was of my own attempts to make life more comfortable for my Suzanne–who'd also contracted a mystery disease--PSP, or progressive supranuclear palsy, an evil cousin of Parkinson's with the difference in its being fatally

43

progressive. I'd known almost from the start that there was no praying Suzanne out; PSP's typical duration was at best seven years, and our last four progressed faster than doctors had led us to believe.

Brie's condition, although serious enough to send her slumping to the floor on occasion, was neither progressive nor fatal. Even before I knew much about it, I found myself telling her she would get better. "You will heal." She said I was only the second one to tell her that, but in weeks to follow many others repeated the encouragement. I don't think she believed any of us, since the literature on EMS--what little there is–calls it a permanent condition.

As February progressed, I'd gotten to know Brie well enough to think she might profit by a prolonged association with Rowdy. He'd finally started getting over his shyness to her because I always took him on my lunch or dinner visits. Toward the end of the month I'd be hooking up with my son Jed for a week's golfing trip to Destin, Florida. Normally I would place Rowdy with Doggie Do, but something told me he could be as good for her as she for him. She agreed, thus cementing our relationship around the dog. Rowdy replaced church as our focal point.

Our friendship ripened slowly, revolving as it did around this black and white half-cocker, half-bichon frise whose single mission in life is to chase tennis balls. We alternated fixing dinners, and occasionally I'd take her to the lakeside restaurant where we could sit out on the patio far from the wi-fi. Being as nuts as I about fire, she'd long wanted a proper fire pit, which

I helped make possible by lugging in six big hickory stumps. She had already found a good metal ring, and her neighbor Little Joe brought a load of white stones for the fire pit's apron. Little Joe is a kindly older man who'd taken to watching her back (plus, unfortunately also her front).

Occasionally Brie and I held hands on our walks around her lovely four acres. Once or twice I had to put my arm around her lest she fall. (My last two years had gotten me almost permanently conditioned to helping Suzanne walk). Needless to say, I liked that part, and she didn't seem to object, even though she obviously needed no help. But we never hugged or kissed.

Sitting on her big porch during our first long afternoon, we exchanged histories. I learned more about EMS; she learned what Suzanne and I went through with PSP. It wasn't until much later, however, that we discovered how similar the ordeals had been–at least in duration. Both hers and Suzanne's mystery conditions stretched back to sometime around the turn of the century and remained undiagnosed and untreated for many years.

By 2008 Suzanne and I knew something was definitely wrong but didn't know where to turn. For two years we went to every doctor, quack, and psychologist we could find in the boonies of western North Carolina. We scratched out repeatedly. Everyone blamed her anxiety, fear, and confusion on female hormones, age, or depression, and could do nothing more than prescribe antidepressants and hormone replacements.

One reputable neurologist cleared her for Alzheimer's but forgot to consider Parkinson's. The stress of not knowing took its toll on poor Suzanne. It wasn't until late 2010 that we finally located a neurologist who said she definitely had some form of Parkinson's -- "hopefully not PSP."

During the same time period Brie was still working in the computer-dense environment that had for years been zapping her brain. The headset she had to wear produced chronic earaches, and unknown to her, all the computers, fluorescent lights, and radio waves kept storing their radiation inside her body because EMS bodies can't drain electricity like most people's. As with Suzanne, she lived daily in great stress and anxiety. No matter how many physicians, specialists, dentists, and psychologists she visited, no one suspected what was wrong.

The regular medical profession has never heard of PSP or EMS. If they have, they automatically defer the PSP suspect to a Parkinson's specialist--most of whom don't know much about the mystery disorder that's said to affect only around 5,000 in the US today. The same is true for EMS only worse; most everyday doctors refuse to touch it, saying it can't have a genuine physical component...even though some respectable researchers say it's now affecting up to 10% of the population. The best Brie's team of experts could do was prescribe antidepressants and psychological counseling–exactly what Suzanne's doctors prescribed.

Both Suzanne and Brie suffered spiritually, emotionally, and physically. They couldn't understand how the God they loved and trusted could let them down and sometimes began to wonder if he'd ever been there for them. They became emotional wrecks. Without family support, they would have given up. Many serious EMS patients see no light at the end of the tunnel and take the wrong way out. Most PSP patients end up in nursing homes where that option isn't available. Predictably, their physical bodies take downward spirals. And here I'd been put together with two of these special mystery cases.

Suzanne had already given up driving, and we both watched her handwriting shrink to tiny scribbles. Soon she gave up cooking, answering the phone, and going out, except when I forced her. Her voice reduced to a whisper. She blamed me for being deaf, while few people could make out anything she said. All Parkinson's patients similarly "shrink;" in fact one physical therapy involves shouting and waving arms and legs in an attempt to "get bigger." Eventually she started falling, even using first a cane and next a walker. Toward the end, five different falls took her to three emergency rooms for head and body stitches. One doctor who'd stitched her head before pulled me aside the third time and said it was time to start considering other less dangerous living arrangements.

Brie's physical disorders were quite different but just as serious. In early spring of 2010, she began feeling like she was going to derail, disconnecting without knowing what was wrong or how to stop it. The earache she'd had for some time continued to get worse and might have been responsible for the frequent nausea. She'd previously had a dentist check her teeth and been sent to a specialist to check an old, deep root canal.

In mid-March while at work using her computer and headset, she experienced a sudden electrical storm inside her head, feeling currents and spasms race from her brain to the back of her neck and skull. The intense pain shot down her left arm, causing her to crash unconscious to her desk. She revived immediately, but the panic took her immediately home. She was not to return to work; they gave her no severance and told her to stay away.

Whenever she was exposed to electronics or loud noise, parts of her face fell asleep. Eventually her long blonde hair turned silver-gray and three toenails popped off. Yet, as with Suzanne's head scan, an EEG showed nothing conclusive. In addition to problems at her electronically-rich work environment, she could no longer watch tv or the radio, use her cell phone, or finally, the home computer. Night driving became a huge problem, plus often regular daytime driving. Her normal life came grinding to a stop, although she still didn't comprehend the magnitude of her sensitivities.

Things progressed until she finally learned about an environmental health center in far off Dallas. At the end of June, 2010, she decided to gamble on making the long drive southwest from Asheville, North Carolina. She survived the ordeal and settled into a two-week outpatient routine in the Dallas facility to undergo extensive testing. The doctor told her how to modify her activities and living conditions and of course made prescriptions, including one shot which she took four times a day for the next two years.

In 2011 Suzanne and I finally found another neurologist down at Emory who actually specialized in Progressive Supranuclear Palsy. My heart jumped when he announced she undoubtedly had it. Unfortunately, all he could do was fiddle around adjusting the dosage of Sinemet, the Parkinson's pill, and speculate with other unknown prescriptions. Like EMS, there's nothing that can be done for PSP, and unlike regular Parkinson's, it's always progressive and fatal.

There is one thing that can be done to help EMS sufferers–change the physical environment or make the place safer to live in. That meant Brie had to move to some remote farm or cabin to begin the long process of detoxing. Fortunately, one of her brothers had that exact place, a fifty- acre farm in New York. After selling her Asheville condo and most of her possessions and saying goodbye to her friends of ten years, she packed up and headed north. Fortunately, her other brother drove her from West Virginia to New York because she was too compromised to make the journey on her own. She lived a hermit's life on the quiet farm from the spring of 2012 until the fall of 2013.

Now comes the critical year for both Suzanne and Brie, 2013. Suzanne and I theoretically know the end is near, for she'd had so many falls we decided to move her into a nursing home. We're both in denial but recognize what's around the corner. That corner will literally dead-end in November.

Brie has also come to know the worst about her condition, but even though she's detoxing and theoretically forward-facing, emotionally and physically things haven't changed much for her. She fiddles around with playdough, sits quietly on the porch all day, moves to the grass where she can ground while sitting barefoot. The books have told her grounding always heals. But of course, some tell her all kinds of things; she never knows what to believe, so believes what fits in with her religious outlook and common sense.

It was beautiful in New York, but she was all alone and felt it was time to move on. She couldn't stay forever in the middle of nowhere living an empty life. Could she can find some kind of safe place elsewhere? She needed to worship with other believers; needed human contact and a place to call her own home...hopefully a place without much electricity.

Whereas Suzanne's journey ended at the start of that winter, a month before Christmas, in a sense Brie's just started when she left the north to travel back south, staying in a tent she'd purchased because motels or buildings were no longer an option. As she tells everyone, at this time she simply had to make a choice: give up or do something to stay on this side of the grass. Move forward...with God leading the way, as she tells everyone, always including God in her story. She got in the stripped car she'd bought that had roll-up instead of electric windows and no GPS, and arrived in western North Carolina in October of 2013. I met her three months later.

Bert pecked away at the computer, changed a sentence or two, tried to make it sparkle. Then read it from an outsider's perspective, which caused him to worry about its believability. Two women with rare neurological disorders? God put him with these two? The more he revised, the more he wondered whether Frank was right about his trying to elevate his attachment to this new woman to some supernatural level. The newly-found writer in him said he talked too much about his struggle to believe in a god who set bad things in motion for both women he loved. If he ever did make it into a book, which of course he wouldn't, readers wouldn't be interested in that. But at least he'd written it out of his system; he could hit delete later. The good thing about computers: easy in and easy out.

He kept staring at the computer, wondering if Frank was also right about his being on the rebound. Hmm. Again, he reminded himself to omit references to Suzanne because this was Brie's story.

So why did he write it? he asked himself. And he knew the answer; even before Frank's objection, he'd heard it inside. It was simply to convince himself about the purity of his motives. Damn it, someone had to stand up for Brie! Even her two brothers and mother didn't believe her, and everyone's eyes would cloud over whenever she'd tell them about this dreaded disease that modern science rejects. She needs my support, Bert told himself. Needs my love. Needs me. Yes, God put us together for her healing, he told himself for the umpteenth time.

Yeah, but what in the world does that have to do with Suzanne? Oh, yes, there's a connection--telling the world that diseases like EMS and PSP are not to be dismissed. He'd been writing it not for himself, but for the world and for Brie...not that he'd ever show her either story. He must have been writing this one in order to convince himself, or maybe her. Yeah. And maybe trying to convince Frank and the rest of the world about these mystery diseases.

Can't the world see that even if Brie's EMS is more emotional than physical, it doesn't matter? She thinks she has it, so things will bounce around in her head whenever she sees she's near a cell phone or gaggle of high wires. She's going through her private hell, and probably thousands like her. Maybe grabbing onto the physical diagnosis is some kind of perverse reassurance it's not all in her head.

He and everyone he talked to knew Suzanne, by contrast, was not making it up. Hell, the famous Emory doctor even wanted her to become part of their on-going PSP research. And yes, he, Bert, had helped make it possible for her to live graciously to the very end. And yes, God was the driver in that picture, no doubt about that. Even if he hadn't fully believed, she did because she needed to. Just as he'd done everything for Suzanne, he could do the same for Brie. Had to, since they both believed God had put them together, first in the church, then slowly, week by week, bringing forth love from somewhere deep inside both

52

of them. Brie, the woman who'd given up on love between humans, thought it only possible between her and Jesus.

Ok, so it was important for him, that's obvious, he told himself. But now he just needed to stop. Before shutting down the computer, he asked himself again why he couldn't talk freely with Frank about Brie's neurological condition. He'd started to bring it up several times, but Frank had always shut the door. The scientist in him would never believe a word, couldn't. He pushed 'save,' turned the screen to sleep, and took himself to bed. Maybe in the morning he'd reopen it.

From the start Brie and I were both convinced we'd been placed together to be just friends. We didn't talk about that, just acted out friendship. We enjoyed being friends. Close friendship doesn't confuse. Friends, not lovers.

Nevertheless, we both started getting confused. We tried hard to stay good friends, doing the kinds of things good friends do together. But of course, friendships often morph in different directions. The part of the story where we graduated from holding hands to kissing comes a bit later, but I mention it now because we–or at least I–had already started thinking about it.

It didn't take me long to recognize Brie was a woman capable of doing just about anything for herself–build a solid firepit; find the right kind of non-electric gas lawn mower to use; find contractors knowledgeable about shielding wires in her house, plus other things to make it as safe as possible for an EMS patient. When she decided she needed a kayak, she miraculously found a good used one for a song...and then another one for me. She'd never owned a sleeping bag or tent yet camped out all the way from the east coast to western North Carolina. So yes, Brie is capable of handling things herself. That being the case, I still have to offer masculine help on occasion.

When she told me she needed a sanctuary, I had to provide the cross and six sturdy seats, plus help her locate the perfect spot. Well, that almost popped out at us, a private place next to the horse pasture, surrounded on three sides by trees and invisible from the house, road, or just about anywhere. It should have taken us a week or more to find and build the place of worship, but it flew up in two or three days. She had the hard part, clearing, weeding, and digging in the seats. I just provided the materials and screwed things down.

When we weren't building sanctuaries, firepits, kitchen pan racks, clotheslines, or a rope swing for her stroll down to the cross, we explored Lake Chatuge in our kayaks. Everything we did fell immediately into place, including Rowdy's being willing to ride behind her on her kayak.

Brie and Rowdy eventually proved to be good for each other's spirits. When I asked her to watch over the dog for a couple weeks back in February, she hesitated. She didn't feel she had enough energy–something I stupidly failed to recognize. Then she relented. At the start of her dog-tending ordeal, Rowdy totally ignored her, looking away whenever she'd draw near and refusing to participate even in ball-throwing. The cocker spaniel part of him made him hard-wired to be a very stubborn one-master dog. Brie took the situation in hand: "You, Rowdy, settle down. You're just grieving for Suzanne and missing Bert. But she misses you too, and he'll be back soon."

Rowdy wasn't convinced, so she got down on all fours, face to face. "Ok, Rowdy, we have a couple of weeks together; you can be miserable, ignore me and call it a day. Or we can have an awesome time together. Your choice." He listened, maybe understood, but still wasn't convinced. He kept to himself, refused to join.

The next morning while Brie was busy doing her yoga stretches, the dog sat on the bed sneaking peeks (he'd compromised the night before by sleeping at the far edge of her bed). By the second week he was dropping his ball on her and lying on her belly during her leg lifts. They went on like this daily. Rowdy swam at the lake on his long leash–but Brie still didn't trust him enough to let him off. The only time she left him alone in the house was to attend church. He took his frustration out on her stuffed rabbit and bear, ripping out an eye and nose...but jumped for joy when she returned. They had more long talks. At one point when the dog got the blues, she knelt down to him. "Your mommy didn't leave you Rowdy; if it were her choice, she'd be here right now. She loves you with all her heart and wants you to be happy."

That apparently convinced Rowdy, or maybe it was the way Brie walked, fed, and bathed him. She renamed him Rowt Man for his demanding demeanor. They played together for hours on end. And then he started becoming overprotective, something he still is. Maybe he was afraid to lose her as well. By the end of the long dog-sit, the other half of Rowt Man–the quiet bichon frise–kicked in and helped calm him down. But most of all, Brie simply loved Rowdy into submission. In turn, he did his part by helping restore her broken spirit.

We continued to meet three or four days a week to play card games, cook over the firepit, and talk. Meanwhile, as usual, I spent my time alone at home. Back in March of 2011, when I knew something was wrong with Suzanne but still had hopes for recovery, I'd begun surfing the internet seven or eight hours a day. I love to do internet research almost as much as drawing house plans. Before Suzanne's condition worsened enough for me to consider a nursing home, I spent an entire spring researching places to move to in Mexico or South America. Places offering a full-time nurse and companion for Suzanne plus a part-time cook for me. Where I could sneak away occasionally to sip beer on a sunny afternoon at some lazy tree-lined town square with its sixteenth century historic buildings. (Back then I wasn't preoccupied with golf.)

The place I settled on in Mexico was Lake Chapala, southeast of Guadalajara. The lake was Mexico's biggest freshwater lake, unfortunately very polluted, but still pretty to look at from a distance. I spent two weeks checking out rentals, land purchases, churches, places to go, and things to do. Sending and getting e-mails. At first, I'd been leery of crime, but that area sounded safe enough. And still fairly inexpensive.

When I told my daughter about an impending move to Mexico, she gasped. "Dad, do you remember how old you are? Do you speak Spanish? What about hospitals? Meeting people, making friends? Think about it, Dad!" In other words, stop thinking about it, you fool. And she was probably right.

Still, I couldn't get the full-time nurse and companion for Suzanne out of my mind. And I wasn't *that* old and infirm. So I started reading about Costa Rica. Alajuela in the Central Valley near San Jose looked just right. I spent another two weeks on it, finally deciding I was a dozen years too late. Ten years ago, my son Jed had encouraged me to buy the bed and breakfast he and Frieda had stayed at. That move would have changed our lives drastically, probably for the better.

Well, two down and one to go: Mendoza in Argentina. Of all the places I'd imaginatively visited, this wine-growing region struck me as the best. And once again my world traveler son had been there twice. Only one problem: it was too far away for people to visit. We'd really be stuck. And by the time I'd gotten around to applying Lynn's advice to Argentina, I'd also come to realize that as much as Suzanne said she was ready for the new adventure, it was just too much for her. By the time we made the final move she could be in a wheelchair. I closed the door on more internet research.

Now, several years later, without the love of my life and while Brie and I were still just casual friends, I reopened the research door. Maybe I could find a safer place for Brie—assuming of course that she and I might eventually be together. This research led to a much closer place, the American west that still haunted my dreams: Colorado, Utah, New Mexico, Arizona. The four corners I'd roamed so often. All EMS victims know that part of the country is the safest; in fact, they have colonies in Arizona, where wi-fi towers aren't found every mile.

It hadn't taken much for my son Jed to convince me how nice it would be to live somewhere warm enough to play golf all winter. "Hey, Dad, I'll drive down to play with you two or three times a winter." Then I could drive up to Colorado to be with him and the new grand-kids in the summer. Sounded good to me. First, I had to research which area would be best to build in. Behind my thinking was the possibility of finding a remote place without dangerous wi-fi towers.

My home state of Colorado was just too cold. I'd lived there half of my life and would always carry it in my soul. That left Utah, New Mexico, Arizona. After ruling out crowded and overpriced places like Sedona and Santa Fe, or cold places like Provo, it came down to three or four. The first two in Utah: Cedar City or St. George. I immediately fell in love with the idea of St. George, and Jed said he'd golfed at most of its six or seven courses; all good and affordable. The small city was close to Colorado, and much warmer. I spent three weeks checking it out on the computer and called him to say it was currently my first choice.

I couldn't rule out New Mexico or Arizona, however. I remembered visiting Silver City with Suzanne many years before and falling in love with it. It was beautiful, the right population, and near the Gila Wilderness Area. But once I started researching, I couldn't find good golf courses, and noted the place was almost 6,000 feet--higher and no doubt colder than Denver. Hell, I might as well stay in North Carolina; it was warmer.

That left Arizona, the state that had always been first in my thinking anyway. For five years in the late '80's Suzanne and I had lived in Payson, a small unknown town just below the Mogollon Rim. We liked it immensely, though it was dead and had only two golf courses, one being a private course that I didn't fancy joining. Phoenix down in hell was so hot you could fry eggs on car hoods in August.

Tucson? I'd never been there, but it was probably just another big city. Suzanne and I had always avoided big cities, which made it difficult finding work in some idyllic mountain village. But having just retired, I didn't need much work now, and below Tucson was a small artist community that an old friend of mine, a suitemate at college, had just moved to. I needed to call Ralph to find out more about Tubac.

Ralph convinced me the whole area was worth checking out, with seven or eight decent golf courses, so I called my son Jed to make plans. Ralph had invited me to stay with him and his partner Hamilton for a week. Then Jed, Freddy, and Gil would join me at the Best Western up in Green Valley. We made reservations for at five different courses. It sounded perfect...so perfect that I decided to scrap St. George altogether.

Now the only question was what to do with the dogs. Danny, the lovable Lab in his nineties by human measurement, was a self-keeper. He still walked the road down from my Hayesville home to the mailbox every day, causing the three neighbors above to patiently wait until he moved aside–or didn't move. They all loved this big black dog who'd ruled Town Mountain for nine years. He'd be ok; they agreed to feed and water him.

Rowdy was something else. I certainly couldn't ask Brie again; she'd get the wrong idea about my intentions. And I couldn't tell her I'd mentally included her in my moving plans. But I remembered her other dog-sitting venture and concluded this bundle of joy might again lift her spirits. When I hinted toward the subject, I saw her mouth close a bit. No, she wasn't up to it. I dropped it quick and we went out to start a fire at the new firepit.

Two days later, however, she told me she wanted to take care of him. I'd already gotten to know her well enough to know she was one never to make snap decisions. She'd processed and re-processed it, and really meant it. I agreed and prepared for my trip to Arizona, everything fast-forwarding.

The golfing vacation zipped by, as it always does, and I was distracted every day by thinking of Brie too much. I came back to a long, late, and unusually cold spring. The retirement house I'd lovingly built was empty and cold. Worse, when I drove to her house to tell her how much I'd missed her, holding her tight for the longest time, she appeared guarded and remote. I didn't understand. She tried to smile but couldn't fake her confusion. We ate dinner and I took Rowdy home.

During the next week I continued to visit her regularly, always finding her guarded. When we tried to talk the subject out, I finally got the point. Her healing was her first priority, and this new development threatened to short-circuit it (to use an inappropriate electrical metaphor). I tried to understand but couldn't conceal my disappointment.

Eventually I came to accept the fact that I was the one who'd initiated confusion. When I came back from Arizona so enthralled with that part of the country, I immediately started telling everyone my new plan for life was to sell my house and move there come fall. I would live in there in the winter and in Colorado near my grand-kids in the summer. Or something like that; of course, I didn't tell them it might be Brie and I doing the moving back and forth. I'd tried to tell Brie about the possibility of building an EMS-safe house, but she had turned a deaf ear.

Without thinking, one afternoon I asked her to come to my house to help me pack everything that needed to be moved out before I could sign up with the realtor. We packed twenty or thirty boxes of household goods that I'd eventually give to Suzanne's sister down in Texas, and then she helped me prepare the yard by raking and burning leaves for seven hours. The result of all this activity being that now, and invariably at the wrong time, people kept asking me when I was moving away. No wonder she was confused, especially when I'd come back from Arizona greeting her with a giant bear hug and telling her how much I missed her.

I never suspected how angry she'd gotten. One late afternoon without calling me she threw tent and sleeping bag, but no food, into her kayak and started paddling toward the closest island. Setting up camp was automatic for her, and she had remembered to tell at least one other person where she was headed. She'd even called 911 to let them know where to find her should they receive a mystery call in the middle of the night. Later when she told her brother about that, he suggested, "Sis, usually you call 911 afterward, not before."

Knowing her as I now do, I can hear her jumping up and down on the shore: "Hallelujah! Hallelujah! Shiitake mushrooms! Shiitake! You @#$$$## you!" Praising and cursing.

She made it through the night without all her rejoicing and cursing attracting campers from Jackrabbit campground across the water. No doubt they'd heard and wondered what in the world this mad woman could be doing waving her arms and jumping up and down. She stayed for two days, fasting and in some strange way healing. No doubt swimming nude in the middle of the night.

Two days later, when she told me about her unusual nighttime visit, I didn't know what to think. Had I been that bad? But alternate cursing and praising made sense with this woman I'd come to know.

After letting things simmer for a week, I eventually decided it was time to confront my foolishness. I apologized for confusing her, and she almost apologized for whatever it was that was bothering her. We started sharing dinners again, and occasionally held hands on the way down to her sanctuary. Time passed.

Unfortunately, friends kept asking in her presence when I was moving to Arizona. I wanted to shout, "Forget it! I'm not moving!" but feared they'd cast suspicious eyes on what could be happening between us two. Which I knew she worried about anyway, especially with some church friends. They couldn't have missed our Sunday morning smiles; church ladies always manage to know what's going on with people they're curious about. At any rate, I apologized to Brie, making a big point of telling her I wasn't going to get a realtor, was putting off selling.

Meanwhile I found myself missing her whenever we weren't together. I couldn't admit it but suspected I might be a little jealous of the time she spent with old and new friends, despite the fact that I welcomed everything that could help her heal...and that obviously included being loved by as many people as possible. Around and around we went, all the time circling closer and closer because no matter our confusion, we nevertheless enjoyed each other's company.

Could it be that I was by degrees falling hopelessly in love? In love with a woman who didn't share my infatuation—whose love was the kind Apostle Paul talked about, not the kind Petrarch, Shakespeare, and all the poets celebrated? In love with someone who'd still never kissed me without reservation or used the love word that occasionally popped from my own mouth; sometimes--gasp--even in her very presence?

Was I becoming love's fool? Stopping at roadside gravel beds to search for heart shaped rocks; scribbling love notes like I did back in seventh and eighth grade; calling her at odd hours just to hear her voice; bringing her flowers and silly presents; imagining elaborate love fantasies in the middle of the night?

All I knew was that she needed time alone to do things like take her evening two-hour oxygen rest (not for better breathing, but to increase the oxygen flow to her brain); relax after a long morning detox session in the sauna (sessions which could sometimes knock her flat for a couple of hours); and eat only the kind of foods the doctors had recommended (gluten free and all organic), not the kind I liked. I also knew that I can be demanding, capable of making her guilty for not joining me in whatever I want to do. I could be a stumbling block.

One week in early spring Brie joined my backgammon friend Jim and me on a four-day camping trip to nearby Jackrabbit Campground on Lake Chatuge. We two men stayed in his oversized tent and she in the smaller one she'd used so often on her way down here. She got hers erected in five minutes whereas it took Jim and me--with the help of a campground attendant--almost two hours, rain drenching us the whole time.

Brie loved the camp-out, Lake Chatuge being one of the main reasons she chose western North Carolina to settle in. Chatuge is the first in a series of TVA lakes that ultimately join the Little Tennessee downstream. It's fed by a host of small rivers and creeks leading into the Hiawassee valley, especially the Hiawassee River itself that tumbles from the Georgia mountains. Like almost everything in this forgotten part of the world, it's unbelievably beautiful.

Nothing very memorable happened during the camp-out; Jim had so many chores and outside duties that I saw him only during breakfast and dinner hours, and I had my pickleball events, plus golf. But we all enjoyed our evening meals and sitting next to the fire after the sun had set.

On the last two days the rain fell harder than before. It pounded so ferociously the last night that Brie had to sleep in her car...while Jim and I held our breath that sudden gusts wouldn't dump us into the lake. Our tent got flooded, but the rain stopped long enough the following morning for us to break camp.

Because we all did different things during the day, Brie and I didn't get to know each other as well as I'd anticipated. But we had our new kayaks to try out--when the rain wasn't pouring down. The first venture was a paddle across the lake to the small island Brie had identified as her special camping spot. "I've been wondering about it ever since camping in that cute place across from it when I was waiting to close on my house."

"When was that?"

"Back in October, about a month after I got to Hayesville."

Would we two ever camp out on the island?

As we paddled close, there was something I immediately disliked about the place. It was too small and too close to the mainland. We beached and immediately learned I was right. The raucous sound of weed eaters and lawnmowers across the way almost brought her to her knees. Huge power lines loomed on the distant dam, and when we started looking around, we found mounds of trash. Apparently, locals had used this spot often enough to erect makeshift tables and benches...but thought nothing of leaving all their refuse behind. Disillusioned, we headed back toward Jackrabbit.

After fifteen minutes of paddling we came to what could be a large island...something we'd speculated about while looking at it from our Jackrabbit camp site. A small sign at the edge of shore read "1." We circled around looking for established campsites and finally found one on the far eastern side. It looked perfect: level ground next to the lake, two good firepits, and no trash--well, a fair amount of broken glass which we later removed. No poison ivy anywhere in sight, beautiful sassafras shoots taking root everywhere, and small paths leading into the woods for firewood. Facing east, the site captured the morning sun and gave shelter from the hot afternoon sun. Best of all, it was tucked into a small cove, which meant the stupid ski-dos and motor boats wouldn't come zooming by. And, as everyone knows who's spent any time in western North Carolina, all lakes there are spectacularly beautiful.

We both smiled. "Look, that's the cleanest water I've seen in this lake," she said, and I agreed, adding that the cove also captured the gentlest breezes.

After leaving the future campsite we learned we'd guessed correctly: the island on its south side faced directly toward Jackrabbit–less than a half-hour paddle away. We shot across to our campsite and dragged out Brie's lake map. Number one was Penland Island, the largest in Lake Chatuge. We checked all the put-in places to use on our next trip; the closest turned out to be at a small picnic area she'd often visited with Rowdy when dog-sitting. It looked to be about a fifteen-minute paddle and would be a safe place for parking cars overnight. We couldn't wait for our first camp-out to Penland but would have to since we were both busy the rest of May. Neither of us discussed the possibility of intimacy. I thought about it a lot. The test would be if she asked me to bring my tent also.

May passed and in early June a close friend of hers from Asheville arrived seated on the back of a flashy motorcycle. The rain had still been falling so consistently over western North Carolina that I'd long ago abandoned any attempt to plant a spring or even summer garden. I just scowled and watched weeds take over my built-up gardens. But the constant rain didn't stop me from driving over on a late afternoon to join Brie for drinks and hopefully supper on her comfortable outdoor porch. And this afternoon was when Juli arrived with her sugar daddy.

Juli, Brie had told me earlier, had a lifetime of making mistakes choosing men, and the new sugar daddy looked to be no exception. Rolf had the bulk, swagger, lingo, and personality of male bikers everywhere. The leather jacket covered with metal objects and patches told the world he wasn't to be messed with. I tried to be knowledgeable, asking him which club he rode with, and he turned to show me the big patch on the back of his jacket. "But hell, I ride with everyone. They know me from the Keys to Charleston. I'm a lone wolf." Now a little over the hill and overweight, this lone wolf could still probably drop someone like me in a minute without qualms.

Back in the 1970s my parents surprised me by driving from Denver to Minneapolis to give me a huge graduation party. We rented a warehouse north of the Twin Cities in an area known to be controlled by the BPM gang (Beer, Pussy, and Motorcycles). It was the only place available, and back then I was still young enough to be immune from danger. Just another college dude slumming it. The party was a huge success, almost a hundred attending and the band ringing the rafters. They called themselves the

Roaches, which told everyone but innocent me what they smoked, and we let them play whatever they wanted. Like everyone else, I got wasted on Scotch long before midnight but do remember walking down the stairs carrying a plate of leftover beef. My friend Bob walked in front and was stopped at the bottom by a monster wearing the colors. The monster made remarks about my wife behind me, and Bob said you don't talk to women like...when he was flattened with one blow.

I picked Bob up, apologized profusely, and we miraculously made it past the monster and his four buddies with no further ado. Later the beef steak ended up on Bob's right eye. Ever since that night, plus another time when at some bar I'd watched similar creatures devour ten shots of Black Jack followed by a tall beer, and disappear after leaving a $20 tip, I've learned to ask no questions of roaming bikers.

Remembering that, I breathed deep as Ralf dismounted and Juli rushed to hug Brie. It was 6:00 and they were two hours late. Brie had outdone herself preparing a fantastic dinner. I overcooked the steaks on the fire pit grill, but what bothered me more was the fact that they decided to spend the night in her spare bedroom.

Rolf surprised me by being polite, even to the point of sparing us rough talk and congratulating Brie on the gorgeous table she'd set, but I knew he hadn't missed Brie's beautiful blue eyes. I couldn't leave her alone that night, no matter what she said.

When I whispered in her ear that I wanted to sleep on the living room couch or maybe even on the far edge of her king size bed, she breathed a sigh of relief. She too had apprehensions. The die was cast by a visiting biker.

Unexpectedly, this would-be couple who'd done nothing more than snuggle standing up suddenly found themselves lying next to each other on the big bed. At 8:00 in the evening, with eight long hours stretching in front. Well, we still had clothes on.

I'd told Brie before that I hadn't thought about another woman for 34 years, let alone kissed one. And here I was in bed with one, a very pretty one. She'd told me how she had vowed long ago not to let another disappointment interrupt her healing process. The man she'd been with several years ago had walked away after finally realizing she couldn't go to rock concerts or even movies with him. Both of us had processed our past problems and present needs many times, and no doubt she too had pondered what might lie ahead. But neither had expected the unexpected would happen so soon.

Surprisingly, what immediately happened was a bad case of the giggles. "What do they think...?" "Can you believe...?" "Rowdy, what in the world are you doing there at our feet?" "This is impossible..." "Can they hear us giggling like kids...?" "What in the world...?"

Giggling is fun, especially at night in bed, but snuggling is better. Nuzzling is better. And what about smooching? Dared we go there?

We did and the night held pleasant surprises.

The following morning Rolf turned out to be more civilized than he looked. He'd worked many regular jobs and even run his own home inspection business. When Brie explained how she'd had to modify her house, he asked to see the electricity monitor and proceeded to spend several hours checking house and yard.

In the afternoon friends from church came bringing a surprise birthday party, and Ralf disappeared to make notes on all the electricity outlets, phone hookups, and possible sources of trouble. Later he gave her the sheets explaining his suggestions for improvement.

Juli's and Rolf's visit turned out to be a boon for everyone, especially for me. It even prompted a poem:

A Late Night in June

This I have been given,
walking a dark road
slowly lest I stumble
while Rowdy rushes on.
Given more time to grow,
unlearn what has to go.
Rowdy never stumbles,
always sees or smells
exactly what he needs
to make his way along.

And I've been given time
to learn what I must do.

On this sunny June day Brie was singing in the rain.
No, dancing in it. Dancing in the spirit in the rain.
Scary, but wonderful to witness.

We'd gone straight from the church supper to the lake,
stopping to change into bathing suits and pick up
Rowdy plus two kayaks. We had to wait 30 minutes
for the mid-afternoon downpour to come and go.
Sitting in the car, we watched black clouds swarm out
of the east, dump their load, and retreat west. Just as
we started to pull the kayaks out, the rain circled back
east to keep us inside, where we watched for another
fifteen minutes. Then the sky cleared slowly from west
to east, blue poked out of gray, and we counted once
again to a hundred and pushed our kayaks off shore to
venture into unexplored areas of our lovely Lake
Chatuge.

An hour later we returned with sore arms to the put-in
place to swim. Another hour later, we packed kayaks
and Rowdy into the Element to return home. As soon
as the car doors closed, the rain came back, turning
into a gully-washer. Unlike the first one, this second
storm whipped up inside of minutes with absolutely no
warning. Had we been paddling out in the middle of
Chatuge, the thunder and especially lightening might
have taken its toll not just on Rowdy, but on Brie. It
even waited for us to pull kayaks up the hill and into
the car. Discussing that minor but maybe major

miracle, we both smiled. I love to see Brie smile. Have I ever mentioned her blue eyes?

Now we're safely back home, rain still pounding down. Wet swim suits still on, she pulls me toward her backyard and starts jumping up and down in the rain, waving her arms and laughing. What a free spirit, I marvel, and shiver. Unlike her, I'm starting to go cold.

I walk inside for a hot shower, leaving her to cavort to her heart's desire. Fifteen minutes later, when I walk out onto the covered porch, the rain is still pounding, and yes, she's still jumping up and down on the grass wearing the same huge smile. She's singing, shouting, smiling, jumping, waving, and dancing all at once. Later, after the rain finally stops and she mounts the porch stairs dripping water, she explains she'd been praising and dancing in the spirit...something she'd done only one other time in her life, maybe fifty years before when she was seven. Dancing in the spirit was something I thought only whirling dervishes did, but this woman is ever capable of surprising me.

Brie had attended a Pentecostal and charismatic church in Asheville, and I was that staid Presbyterian. But Suzanne and I had also had our own charismatic moments when I'd learned about the movement of the Spirit. There was a period in my own life many years before when I was spiritually where Brie was now, if not as demonstrably. We finished the day preparing a pizza. First, we talked about it, and then while I sat down to relax, she prepared a strange monster involving Shiitake mushrooms and summer squash. I sat on her couch watching her rustle fifteen feet away while Rowdy kept pushing his ever-present ball into my lap.

Life can't get much better, I muttered.

But then, later on, it did get much better...even better than before.

June has become our month of love. Here I am, spending the better part of a week composing and revising a full-blown love poem. June's always been Brie's *bete noire*; she's never allowed anyone to see or visit her during her birthday month–for reasons she's refused to disclose. I hope the poem will cheer her up– and silently thank her for letting me be the first to be with her throughout her troublesome month. She's never received a love poem; doesn't know she is to receive many more. I will call the poem "Love Burns" and one day get around to revising it properly.

Prologue

White daisies bloom o'er the yard,

midsummer dreaming looms a pace.

Past June, I come upon a woman

of stubborn will and saucy face

reigning beauty unseen by all.

Oh my, will Spring spring into Fall?

[Three acts to come. Curtain, rise]

Act I   Can you trust me?

You know I'd say most anything

to keep alive our magic nights,

prolong idyllic daytime flights.

I'd tell the world I love you true,

always will, as lovers always do.

Come, Brie, let's dance until the dawn.

Act II   Can I believe you?

You might say love burns too hot,

too fast, behooves a slowing down

lest love outstrip your healing soul.

Or do you worry when others talk,

heap guilt upon love's wild disport?

Remember, please, love conquers dread.

Act III   Confusion in the middle.

God knows how some lovers try

to hear the voice outside their two.

Is the bed we share our bed alone?

When summer ripens will we know?

Late spring's still here, and daisies too.

Dear Brie, let's strive to keep love pure.

I'm pretty sure Brie has read no poetry, never attended a play, and never had anyone write crazy love poems to her. But I'm also sure she'd appreciate mine. I've come to believe she doesn't fake her condition but still wonder if its intensity isn't governed by years of living with it. Her mood swings confuse and thrill me--the first stanza. My own fantasies scare me--the second. And I've never understood her worries about what others think, or worse, her fear that the intensity of our loving might inhibit her healing–the third stanza. I've always believed love can do nothing but promote healing, especially when it's put in service of something higher than lust–the last stanza. And, needless to say, the poem ends before the play ends; we're still caught in the middle.

CHAPTER TWO: HEALING WATERS

I DO NOT ACOMPANY BRIE to her Tuesday night healing sessions at the local Episcopal Church but she tells me what goes on. Actually, I'd gone to one myself shortly after Suzanne died, but because I wasn't overly receptive, nothing much happened. Brie, however, is overly receptive; the ideal candidate for results. On her first visit she met a young man who'd been cured of stomach cancer the year before. But she didn't need that kind of verification; she came expecting transformation. Of course, I hoped she'd get it. I hoped it would produce a shining new human, someone who has finally forgiven herself as well as others; who has learned what to hold tight and what to release.

Secular America has no clue about what goes on in such advanced spiritual healing sessions. Their expectations are based on television evangelists' thumping and shouting. Given that, they've good reason to equate spiritual healing with seances and flying saucers. What happens at this local Episcopal church, however, is a far cry from hocus-pocus. It's also a far cry from the circumspect laying on of hands or anointing with oil that's so common in fundamental churches but produces mainly a solemn nodding of heads.

Unfortunately, I can't begin to explain how it works or if it works since I have no idea. I remember back in

Colorado when I unexpectedly became a believer after being atheistic all my life, my mentor Bill Hedrick told me their prayer team would assemble four or five hours beforehand, praying continuously until the person walked into the padded room. Team members would stand behind or in front; hold shoulders, head, or hands; and look him or her in the eye or not, all depending on the Spirit's leading. Their job, which they'd perfected over time, was simply to follow a lead they knew nothing about. In those sessions, if I can trust Bill (and I thought I could trust this scientist who played a role in the early days of the space program), what happened was truly amazing...people getting bounced around the room, falling down and rising a different person.

Brie told me pretty much the same, although her sessions weren't so wild, saying each was different because different healers showed up. One time she fell asleep, another time she cried for two hours. She said touch was always present from the start; in fact, was essential, just as between mother and child...or lovers, for that matter. Words weren't important, but sometimes happened. They came from the person submitting to healing, not the prayer team members, who always remained silent. One time she started shouting so loud that the three other participants were asked to leave. This was to be her hour.

Since she's never shared specifics with me on what inner wounds were brought to the surface, I can only guess at the process. Bill told me that spiritual healing, like psychological counseling, dredges disturbances from the distant past to the present. It surfaces deeply buried subliminal messages that keep replaying, unseen. Bill said that the Spirit helps the counselors conduct the dredging...which Brie says can be quite painful. The theory is that each time the old hurt replays, the emotional hurt gets less painful. If so, the Spirit must know traumas have to be handled little by little, not miraculously in one fell swoop, as most people guess.

Of course, I'm just repeating what I've heard and read about. But I do know her healing sessions are so emotionally draining that she comes home totally exhausted, sometimes sleeping through most of the next day. The other place where she gets healing, Lake Chatuge, delivers it more gently.

Bert looked at everything he'd written, decided it was pretty good but again thought about deleting parts. No one wants to be preached to. He'd done enough writing to get it out of his system, now just needed to let go of it. Except he wanted to save the three-act poem; it was good enough to revise. What the hell, he was writing this thing for himself, not the world. There was no big hurry. He'd just keep on writing and watching what was happening. He laughed to recall the shotgun shooting incident in the middle of the night back at the beginning. The following week he'd read in the local newspaper about two guys getting arrested for shooting illegally. So long ago!

How do I describe the beautiful woman I feel myself falling for? I've never been good at describing anyone. In fact, I know myself to be unobservant–unlike Brie, who immediately recognizes something out of place or in place.

She's tall. Almost all my women have been tall, but she, at 5-foot-8, maybe the tallest. She's thin. Maybe 135 pounds, just right for her body. She has wonderful silky hair: light silver on top to darker gray half way down to tan and light brown where the color is slowly coming back. I guess it might all return golden brown eventually, but I do like the silver. And it's always smooth. She has an unconscious habit of stroking or pulling at her hair, and when I get close, I like to run my fingers through it, gently smoothing it over my face.

She doesn't have just long hair, but long legs, long arms, long fingers. Most anyone would say she looks great in tight jeans.

A person's face is always hardest to describe, especially when this Gemini can wear two or three very different expressions. The shy face is matched by awkward, shy body movements of an eight-year old girl. Well, that's not quite right: she walks like all woman are supposed to walk but few do, not like a child. When no one's looking, she has a half-smile, unconscious half-turned head, and eyes that appear fairly normal, despite their beautiful color. Oh yes, I guess I've described those light blue eyes already.

But the other Gemini face, the one with the darker blue eyes, the face that comes on when she gets worked up--bouncing up and down shouting hallelujah! or kick ass!--is one that leaps out at you, challenges you, demands you to pay attention. It calls across the room, Here I am! Ready for anything!

Get closer to that face once it settles down as it always does after its brief outburst; study it. The smile natural and relaxed. A smile that could launch a thousand ships, as Homer said and millions repeated. The smile perfectly matches the eyes. In fact, the mouth and eyes smile together, laugh together. Have I mentioned that they draw strangers in as well as potential lovers? That, plus her habit of broadcasting spiritual love, get her in trouble because most men can't tell the difference between being loved in the spirit and in the flesh. I'm lucky to get both.

I might as well come right out and say that this woman is beautiful in so many different ways. Saying this is something, coming from a man who considered Suzanne the prettiest woman he'd ever met. Unlike a lot of guys, I like the fact that she's not top-heavy. She doesn't quite fill out her bathing suit, and sometimes she's just average looking, but even then, I find her striking. When she's on stage–which she used to be literally and still is mentally–I suspect she's drop-dead gorgeous, to use the term I hate that she uses too often to describe friends, her mother, her sister, her daughter. When she's totally with me, which happens only when we're alone, never when we're walking the dam or sitting in the back pew of our church, her beauty overwhelms me. It causes me to tell her too often how beautiful she is.

The funny thing is that I know her parents or men rarely told her that. I doubt if they ever told her they loved her, let alone wrote silly poems to her, but she doesn't seem to fall all over herself when I do. I must be using the wrong words or talking too loudly. Or maybe she is taking it all in.

Once or twice a week we kayak back and forth across the lake, using our waterproof lake maps to search out hidden coves. Every island, and there are only four or five big enough to be considered islands, has one or two camp sites to be investigated. Most haven't been used for years. "Why doesn't *everyone* want to come out here?" she always asks. I explain that ninety percent prefer to camp in expensive air-conditioned campers. Out here, there's no water, potties, tables, or trash receptacles.

Resting on a large rock on one of the smaller islands, we skirt the subject of when we will actually come camping. That involves a commitment. Also, it involves hauling all the necessary camping equipment, not to mention water and food, to an island with nothing but trees on it. What is a fastidious person to use for a toilet? How would we bring water? In plastic quart or gallon jars, but they'd bounce around in the kayaks and wouldn't leave enough space for sleeping bags, tent, and air mattresses. Fully loaded for a two or three-day outing, each kayak would threaten swamping, but we could paddle slowly. Fortunately, it's only a fifteen-minute paddle to our favorite island-- no problem unless waves from a kamikaze motor boat overwhelm us.

On our day trips our biggest risk is always Rowdy jumping ship, deciding he wants to be captain of a different kayak. Pulling him out of the water risks tipping coolers, floats, and stuff sacks. Since Brie's kayak is flat on top, it's possible to pile things up, whereas mine is closed off except for the seat, so I have to stuff everything either behind me or next to my legs--which I can sometimes manage to stretch out in front.

Today Rowdy rides with me, which has to be on my lap; with Brie, it's directly behind her, in front of a cooler, or sometimes at the tip of the kayak, like some animate figurine. Either way, he provokes smiles and shouts from passing pontoon boats. The red pancake life preserver on his back turns him into a cartoon character. "He's just a kid in a red dog suit," Brie laughs.

After our practice venture, we decide to return home before the afternoon swells build. Back at her place we start a fire in the firepit and settle into cooking hamburgers. I try to talk her into trying bakery buns: "Burgers are no good on gluten-free bread." She nods but means no.

While I cook, she reminds me to keep an eye out for Klepto, the neighborhood collie. "He could nab that burger before you could count to two." And sure enough, whenever I'm gone, he shows up to perform his stealing act. One time, Brie found a garden glove, paperback book, and two wooden kitchen forks in a hole outside the garage. But he respects the fire, unlike Rowdy, who always sniffs around it too close.

I poke the fire and pour myself another glass of wine, this time not the sweet Muscadine I've been buying for Brie, but a dryer Pino Grigio. She doesn't like it, so I make a mental note of picking up a big box-wine of Muscadine for our next trip to the island. After dinner she asks if I've had too much to drink to drive home safely. I laugh, saying I've been driving slightly drunk for years, never had any problem. "Not that I'm a drunk, of course." Her eyes darken; she doesn't laugh back.

Here comes July, the busiest weekend of the year. July 4 with fireworks, loud boats, noisy people, all kinds of hell breaking loose. Why in the world would we choose this weekend for our first camp-out on Penland Island in the middle of Lake Chatuge? What could we be thinking?

Maybe because we'd waited so long for the rain to end. We finally decided to leave on Thursday, planning to stay through Saturday. It took us two hours to pack the kayaks and paddle out. The trip normally takes only fifteen minutes, but with both kayaks loaded close to sinking levels, we paddled very slowly. Singing most of the way.

Chatuge is no wild lake like Santeetlah fifty miles north, but we pretend it is. Until the boats start whizzing by, that is, which on a busy weekend like this usually starts around 10:00 in the morning and lasts until 10:00 in the evening. When she was back in Asheville searching for the ideal lake to relocate near, no one had mentioned Chatuge. They knew about Santeetlah and Fontana, but this unspoiled gem was too far away--and Santeetlah too remote. The realtor she'd contacted in Franklin tried to talk her into Fontana Lake near Bryson City--a lake that's more of a pregnant river. The realtor failed to mention Chatuge because it was out of her region. Eventually Brie dismissed that realtor and kept driving west.

So here we are on our favorite island–the biggest on the lake that she'd wisely chosen as her own. No one around. Well, maybe not totally accurate. Upon our arrival we immediately discovered a large tent just past the camping area which we'd weeks before designated as our personal place. I silently cursed and started paddling in the opposite direction toward the other campsite we'd found.

My camping companion, however, had different ideas. When we paddled to the other campsite, we found it occupied by friendly people. She asked about the large tent we'd just passed, and they replied they'd seen no one visit it throughout the week they'd been camping. She shouted to me to go back. Maybe the weekend would turn out to be ok after all.

She pitched her tent, the double-sized one she'd used while camping all the way here since she couldn't stay in motels, and we held our breath. No one came to stay in the ghost tent--until an hour or so before we left on Saturday, when an older man and his grandson rushed in to grab a few things and rapidly climb back into their motor boat.

Right away we had to inspect the ghost tent, which to our surprise was surrounded by low-lying monofilament fishing lines stretching almost to the lake and a third of the way toward our own tent. They were two feet off the ground to deter or maybe somehow sound a warning about approaching visitors. Spooky. For a second, I thought the lines could be wired up to explosives.

The other campers told us no one had come, so we concluded one of three possibilities: either they'd put up the tent to claim the area for a later visit; they'd simply abandoned camp for some unknown reason; or they'd been run off. The last seemed most likely, as they had left behind a hatchet and fishing knife plus a tent full of crackers, balls, baskets, and other things.

Worse, hidden behind a bush was the head of a bear. Had another bear or hunter done it in?

Closer examination showed it to be the head of a large stuffed bear doll—which the man and his grandson three days later came to recover.

It was time for dinner, so we decided to stop speculating about the tent and simply ignore it. I did pull down a few lines that encroached upon our territory, for by now it was ours, not theirs, while Brie strung up her hammock. Then I went about my serious business of rebuilding the shabby firepit and helping

Brie remove broken glass. The Fourth of July weekend had begun.

We'd been dreaming about outings to the island for weeks and were now finally here. She, of course, immediately put on her green mermaid flippers and went for a plunge. I went the other way, deep into the woods to find a supply of firewood, enough to keep a campfire continuously burning, even smoldering during daytime heat. Later I was to regret all these firewood excursions, as the woods were swarming with chiggers.

Then followed two days of lazy swimming, paddling, and fire-sitting. Boats, especially noisy ski-dos, raced around the lake, and occasionally one of the bigger launches would send her hands to her ears. At night we watched the boats form a slow parade from opposite directions toward the fireworks place. Which we heard but never saw. Eventually we settled down into the comfortable tent, Rowdy at our feet. Well, we sort of settled down...hours later.

I'll always remember that night. The moon peeked into our upper screened window around midnight-- transforming a mere human into a glowing goddess. I rose and held the goddess once again in my arms, gently running my fingers through her long hair. She settled down upon me, murmuring.

The following day I woke from a Saturday afternoon nap on her hammock wondering again what Brie and I had been placed together for. I stoked the lazy fire and started looking everywhere in vain for her. Worries surfaced but something told me to just keep walking down the shore; she'd be floating on her raft. Which she was, a good two hundred yards away. Asleep, about to bump into an anchored pontoon boat. I bawled her out for being careless.

Before leaving for our island escapade, I'd told my daughter about my new friend. She said it was good we had each other to lean on. I wanted to say that was just part of the equation. The bigger part has to do with joy. We'd both been denied it for some time and were now getting paid back in measure. Laughing, smiling, just being silly happy. Look at the two kids and silly dog frolicking on the lake! She with her green mermaid flippers sticking up out of the water; I splashing away on the $4 kiddy raft I'd bought at the dollar store; Rowdy dog-paddling toward me, red life preserver strapped to his back. Far across the lake, kids and their parents cavorting on the swimming area. Brie laughing. I laughing. July Fourth. Joy.

"Just bring it on," she shouted after another bass boat droned by, sending hands to her ears and tears to her eyes. "They can't take away my joy!" The deep wellspring of joy she's already started sharing with me. Much later that night I fell asleep composing an untitled poem:

sometimes a moon pours inside

or night birds call outside the light

sometimes a goddess gives her love

while night birds flit around the lake

CHAPTER THREE: ELECTRIC SHUTDOWN

THE THIRD SUNDAY OF JULY Brie suffered her first major setback in over a year. Everyone at church had been discussing how good she looked; surely she was making a remarkable recovery. The texture of her skin so creamy and clear; sparkle of her big blue eyes so remarkable; sheen on her shoulder-length silver-tan hair so touchable; infectious smile so sweet; confident walk so comforting since it that told the world she knew she was going to win the struggle. Well, maybe not everyone else was seeing those things.

Then out of the blue, eight minutes into the service when we stood up for the first hymn, wham, she collapsed to the floor. When such things happen, she doesn't have time to give the simplest warning to the person standing next to her. Fortunately, I was that person, and was able to prevent her head from banging on the wooden pews. Then I had to get her on her feet and outside to the grass. That took three of us. She couldn't move arms or feet. In fact, she was unconscious, and when she came to, she still couldn't move them for another hour.

As she'd so often instructed me, the only solution was to remove her immediately from the offending source. In this case, six or seven kids five rows in front busy texting--visitors who'd ignored Rhonda's polite but firm warning from the pulpit to turn off, not just mute, all cell phones. No one thinks cell phones capable of any damage; today's life blood for youngsters can never be shut down.

Someone else might have called 911, but I knew that was utterly out of the question. Even the fingertip monitors they use, let alone the cab full of whirling electronics, siren blasting, careening ride, would all push her over the edge, possibly do her in. And what would happen once they arrived at the wired-up hospital? Hospitals are one of the most dangerous environments for a person with extreme EMS.

We lifted and dragged Brie to a spot on the church yard half-way between power lines. I babbled feeble reassurances into her ear while Mendy massaged her hands and Jill applied pressure to the bottoms of her feet, saying it would send pulses up her legs. It worked; within minutes Brie started coming to. Later in the week I told her I'd feared she had died, she was so still. She said she felt her spirit had flown to what she took to be heaven...where she was disappointed not to meet her master and was refused entrance because it wasn't her time. I'd just been reading C.S. Lewis's *Great Divorce* about a fantastic bus ride from hell (earth) to heaven, and her words registered, but I still didn't believe her.

We kept her stretched out on the grass for only a few minutes until the fire ants I saw heading our way moved me into action. I drove her 4x4 up the lawn and we bundled her into its back seat. In five minutes, we were driving down her backyard lawn toward her private sanctuary, a quiet grassy area where she could recover unseen in peace. There she remained on the blanket for three hours, sometimes feebly smiling, mostly dozing.

Jill stayed the rest of Sunday morning, and after church Rhonda appeared. She helped move Brie to the house and change out of her Sunday dress ("My, it's been a long time since I've seen nylons worn to church") and get into bed. Before falling asleep Brie kept apologizing. We told her not to and eventually everyone left. She slept off and on throughout the afternoon while I read on the porch and Rowdy tried to get me to play ball.

Thus began our long, stressful but also blissful week, the last week of July, 2014. She knew that she couldn't stay in her bedroom; it was too close to the electricity meters on the back of her house. So, my dear Brie very predictably went into the garage to fetch her tent and erect it near the sanctuary. There we would spend six long yet very lovely nights on the uncomfortable ground. At first silent, then slowly giggling, laughing, and gurgling as usual. Our sweet sounds of love. So sweet to stressed out ears. But we didn't expect fast recovery; she couldn't use the house except for brief periods.

On Monday morning I went home to feed and walk Danny, leaving her asleep in the tent. I checked my e-mail to see if my nephew Collin had written telling when he and his family were coming for their vacation. Then I went back, amazed to find her seemingly well on her porch. (How my heart jumps whenever I drive down the long driveway to see her sitting beyond the porch railing.) She'd made it, maybe even recovered.

The next three days remain a blur: sleep, feed dogs, play pickleball or nine holes of golf, fix dinner on her firepit when it's not raining, go to the tent for an early bedtime. And then more of the same, always fretting. Sometimes visitors came; everyone loves Brie and worries about her. By now it was pretty obvious that people knew we were together, yet it didn't seem to bother her anymore.

On Thursday I finally heard Collin would be arriving on Sunday; Brie and I had only a few days left to be together. Is this good timing? Would she recover before I had to leave her alone? Could I find someone to stay with her?

Thursday night came and she was feeling better. We talked; dug even deeper into our wildly different pasts. For the first time I told her of my stomach problems, the strange bumps I'd gotten all over my back (I still didn't know they were gifts from Penland's chiggers), how I wanted to eliminate some of my prescriptions, and finally how I'd been trying for two years to cut back on alcohol. She didn't say anything but gave me a troublesome look.

Had I gone too far? If we were to keep going forward, we had to get everything out. No secrets. She'd told me more than enough about her past; too much it sometimes seemed. I didn't have spectacular misadventures to share, just minor problems with too much wine and beer. If anybody had been fortunate enough to lead a normal life, it was me. If anybody hadn't, it was her. Men especially had a habit of doing her in. It didn't matter whether they were pastors, psychologists, or a friend's husband; sooner or later they'd start hitting on her. But why, since she didn't lead them on?

I certainly couldn't answer why but was happy she'd finally started trusting me. I wasn't one of them. The more I opened up, the more she responded. We'd already processed hard issues: former lovers, present expectations, our uncertain future, different styles of worship, secret fears and worries. But then I had to bring up booze, confessing it wasn't easy for me to slow down. I knew I could, the same way I'd stopped smoking thirty years ago, but just didn't want to. "What's wrong with a little wine at happy hour, not all day?"

She said nothing but her expression told me it wasn't just a little bit. Who was I trying to kid? Then I had to remind her: booze never tips me toward anger or violence, just sleep. Before I get crazy, I just fall asleep and sleep it off. Again, she said nothing. No judging; Brie doesn't judge.

From her expression I guessed the issue had to do with things beyond me. In all our talks she'd skirted some childhood issues; no doubt this was another big one. Had I thrown her right back to the problem she'd been trying to deal with for years–first with psychologists, now with the prayer healing team?

We finished our chicken dinner and headed for the tent. Tried hard to ignore the stress. Tried hard to giggle but ended up with no snuggles.

On the next day, Friday afternoon when I returned from a brief visit home, something had drastically changed. Myrna was there visiting, so Brie's face didn't show emotion, but in my spirit, I could tell even before I reached the porch. "I'm ok, but maybe you should let Myrna and me talk," she said. I considered driving home but settled for sitting on the porch. After Myrna left, the fireworks began.

She'd been mulling it over, all night and most of the day. Wouldn't say what she was mulling, but I knew somewhere deep inside it had to do with my "problem." If I knew, then why in the world did I have to go to the refrigerator for that bottle of wine? And offer her a glass?

My indiscretion on any normal day would be bad, but this was the week of the meltdown she'd yet to recover from. All EMS literature says its symptoms are difficult to distinguish from ordinary stress–which is probably why so much of the medical community downplays or simply dismisses it. Brie also knows the parallels and knows she can't always distinguish physical from emotional. We both should know that emotional upheavals aren't good any time, let alone after a physical meltdown.

I certainly wasn't ready for this upheaval, though part of me must still have been feeling guilty. At first, she tried to stay collected, avoiding eye contact and keeping the proverbial stiff upper lip. My stomach tightened. What had I unleashed? I can't begin to remember her words; they just kept tumbling out. Fast and furiously, some heading off into unknown directions.

All I remember is her mouth. Such a beautiful mouth, the bottom lip fulsome like a movie star's. Yet now twisted, hard, angry. Driving nails into me. But some words I do remember: "How could you do this to me? Just when I was finally–finally starting to trust you? How…."

How indeed could I have, at this critical junction? Her words, her mouth, her hard eyes reduced me to tears. They kept flowing and flowing. I couldn't talk, was choked into silence.

She wouldn't look at me. No tears on her part. Wouldn't listen or respond, said nothing. I couldn't control my words but was trying with all my might to make amends, bring things back to where they were. All I could do was cry like some mad fool. I haven't cried like this in years, maybe never. I couldn't stop.

Time didn't stand still, it just ended. I looked around to see her calmly sitting at the porch table while Rowdy was busy trying to garner attention. I was over here, far away, suffering. She wasn't. She was boiling.

Minutes passed, maybe hours. A small part of me tried to tell me everything would pass. And it did, eventually. She finally talked. "You're not going to change. It was wrong of me to want it. It's my problem, not yours. Mine."

It all came into focus. It wasn't just the alcohol, something more. Something deeper. But what?

I needed to say something to get more words from her, which finally came: "You're not bad. But we can't go there together. *I* can't."

"Where?" I lamely asked, fearing the answer but not knowing what else to say.

She didn't answer, just said she'd been praying for me every day and now knew it wouldn't happen.

"But I can stop any time I want to," I protested. I reached for her but she pulled back. I went to get a tissue.

"He was the same," she started, then stopped, and I knew not to ask for a finish. Enough! Maybe it *was* her problem, not mine.

Then a blast from the blue. "I saw the answer in the sky. Four rays--perfect rays of light shooting out of the black cloud." She pointed off toward the eastern sky, now just filled with milky clouds.

"When?"

"Just before you got here. There they were, answer to my question. Time for cooling."

That did it for me, quickly brought me back. Rays! Is that she wants, corroboration for her nightmare? What's happening? 'Time for cooling'? She wants me to leave, go away? Who is this person, anyway? I couldn't believe it, got so angry I couldn't think straight.

We stopped talking. Time stopped. Her mouth relaxed. We sat quietly. Birds chirped and the universe returned to normal.

I knew us to be so different in everything. But many or maybe most couples are. Male, female. Extrovert, introvert. Nothing wrong there. The big difference: she was used to listening to a voice from God she wanted or maybe just needed to hear; I was learning that deity speaks a different language. She was tied to fear and anxiety; I to hope and faith.

I tried to forget the differences and concentrate on the similarities. Before, both of us had luxuriated in laughter and giggles. Who giggles that much? Laughs in the middle of a kiss? Delights in small things like frogs in the window shutter, horses neighing in the far pasture, bumping knees while walking...or bigger things like spirits vibrating together, feeling a perfect union, becoming one, disappearing into each other for hours at a time, naked and unashamed. Adam and Eve. They can't take that away from us. Hey, there's no *they*. *You* can't. *I* can't. *We* won't. Will we?

So now the crying has vanished and my anger passed but I still worry about her rays coming out of clouds. They're simply His beauty--no warning or message.

Time passes as we sit quietly on the porch in the late afternoon. No lawnmowers or frogs croaking. Her eyes grow mild. I reach for her again and she lets me cradle her arm. I lift her hand to my head, pray silently.

After an eternity we rise and hug. I know this will take time. Nothing will return to what it was; we've taken a giant step backward. I dismiss the rays and ask if she'll forgive me. She says she already has. I ask how I can regain her love, and she replies such love can never be taken away. That's the first time she's said something like that–and after such an outburst!

Later when I went inside to go to the bathroom, two opposite emotions hit me: relief and apprehension. Relief knowing the crisis was over; apprehension as I looked around the living room, kitchen, bath, and bedroom. Everything that had spoken only of Brie before now spoke also of me. Looked familiar--too familiar. I had indeed crossed over the line without knowing it.

Could I do anything without her? Maybe cooling *was* in order.

Cooling would be in order, wanted or not. In two days, my nephew and his family would arrive for a week's stay. I'd be without my Brie for seven days and nights. No dinners together. No afternoons on the porch watching hummingbirds fight or listening for a horse's neigh. No debating what to do about bumblebees burrowing into the eaves. No snuggling or laughing.

Later in the afternoon we pretended nothing had happened. We discussed dinner, settling on cooked chicken from the grocery. These days we bought or prepared our food one day at a time. The refrigerator back at my house contained practically nothing. I drove a mile to Ingles for chicken and when I returned, she'd set the porch table.

We sat at the table and asked a blessing for the vegetables and chicken. Suddenly her face clouded and she whispered, "Something's not right. Up here," pressing her hands to forehead. "Not enough oxygen! Got to go inside to get some oxygen."

We threw up a fast prayer and went inside, settling her into the leather living room chair while I turned on the oxygen unit behind the bedroom door. "Can't take another meltdown," she said, and I knew these would be her last words for a time. But she surprised me. "Go outside and eat. I'll be ok. Go." And I went, reluctantly.

I gobbled my food faster than usual and returned, expecting to find her face more relaxed. But it wasn't. She was off somewhere very far away. I called Myrna, her closest neighbor, and Rhonda forty miles away near Franklin. Myrna said she'd get dressed and be right over.

Myrna stayed for more than an hour, holding Brie's hand and whispering to her. I fumbled around in the kitchen, cleaning up and putting food away...leaving them alone. And worrying.

After what seemed like a long time but wasn't, Myrna came in to tell me Brie was better. Managing a wee smile and squeezing hands in reply to questions. The worst was over; another meltdown averted.

I walked Myrna out to her car and she surprised me by giving counsel. This person whom I barely knew, almost a perfect stranger, asked if I knew what I was doing. Asked not in an unfriendly or demanding way, but confidently, as if she knew something I didn't. "Are you sure you two are going where you want to? You've fast forwarded beyond being just friends. Are you moving too fast? Have you thought out what's ahead?"

She looked earnestly at me, forcing me to return the look. "You know her condition; it may take time to improve. Worse, it may never. Can you live that way?"

I stood uncomfortably next to her car, not knowing what to say, so saying nothing. She continued. "Do you really care for her as much as you think? She's told me how you're recovering from your wife's death. I know that one. Bob died only last year; I know how long it takes. She also told me you were planning on selling your house and moving to Arizona."

I finally opened up to this stranger because I sensed she was talking without judgment, was talking for my benefit not hers. It was almost as if she was willing me to say what I'd wanted to but couldn't. I told her how much I really did love this Brie. Not just needed her–that too, but more. I loved her, not just my idea of her or my need for a warm body. I knew this was true because I had submitted my desire to God, asking for Him to let me know whether we were still good for each other and should stay together, asking that He'd let me know if I needed to back off.

I never talk like this, especially to strangers, but couldn't stop it from coming out. I told her I didn't worry about the future, explaining that I'd long ago given up the idea of moving to Arizona. I told her I didn't worry about not being able to do things with her like going out to eat or to the movies. I just wanted to be with her, even if it only meant sitting together on her porch.

I told her everything except my big worry that it was becoming difficult for me to recognize the difference between love and dependency. Then Myrna must have read my mind, for she said, "You two are becoming very dependent on each other. Is that ok?" There it was, apparent to the world and last of all, to me. How dense was I? And what were we to do?

One thing we were to do was relax and sleep. The minute after Myrna left, I helped Brie walk back to the tent, where she, not I, immediately fell fast asleep. She slept throughout the night, some of the time my arm tight around her. Of course, I had to rise five times to pee in the plastic coffee can, not only because of those three glasses of wine I shouldn't have had, but more especially because I'd left my BPH pills back at my house. Getting up was not unpleasant, however; it gave me a good chance to work off sore muscles from sleeping on the ground. It also reminded me where I was, for the present. With Brie, in her tent, Rowdy at our feet.

Light shone in the dark.

Water. We sit on picnic table benches at Fire's Creek, kids splashing in the creek behind. I ask her why water always makes her feel safe. She doesn't appear to be in a good mood to talk, but answers my questions.

"It grounds me."

"That doesn't make sense."

"No, nothing does. All I know is what works. Water never gives me hits. Does it somehow reject electricity?"

"Well, we all know it *conducts* it. Is it a good idea to throw a toaster into your bathtub?"

"Yeah, ok. I wish there was some expert somewhere who could answer all my questions."

I tell her I've been doing a lot of internet research on EMS. "There's a bunch of stuff out there," I explain, knowing she can't use a computer to find it, "but it doesn't answer big questions-- whether water really helps; whether battery d.c. electricity is better than a.c.; whether LED lights would be better than incandescents. If I could get these questions answered I'm pretty sure I could build a safe house somewhere, maybe all solar, with electricity stored in batteries isolated outside rather than flowing around the house. But I'd have to convince the building inspector we have different electrical needs... and that's probably impossible."

I finally realize I'm talking mostly to myself. Back in Colorado, I start anew, the building inspectors made me wire our little mountain cabin for both a.c. and d.c. And that was a cabin so far off in the wilds that no one could find it. No one except the inspector, who eventually red-tagged the house even after I'd done both wirings. I was just lucky to sell it. I ramble on.

She nods; I can tell her mind is elsewhere. I keep rambling anyway and eventually stop to give her a firm look. "But then you don't want to talk about that."

She turns toward me: "About what?"

"About my building an EMS house," I say, annoyed at her lack of attention. "One down south, maybe Arizona or New Mexico, somewhere off in the desert away from wi-fi towers. I could build one there, and we could spend winters in that safe house and come back here in the summer for your lake. This house of yours will never be safe enough. I know, you've spent thousands and done a wonderful job, but it's still a manufactured home."

She's finally starting to pay attention without frowning, so I continue, repeating myself, but it may be necessary. "We've talked about this before. We could spend winters there, come back here in May, stay until November. Six months there, six here. Summer here is ok at your house because we're outside so much, like right now. Think about it."

But I know she wouldn't. Too independent. Too much at stake. I decide to drop it and return to talking about water. "Is it better for you *under* water, or just as good floating around on top?"

She doesn't want to answer. Maybe we get should get back in the car and drive ten miles above our picnic area to the horse camping place, where trails extend thirty miles out in all directions. It's rugged country, bear sanctuary country. People get lost in it and die. Rangers don't patrol it the way bears do. Stay Alert! the forest service signs say, and could add, like the bears.

But we don't go up above, just get up to walk the stream here, where it's perfectly safe. Picnic tables, bear-proof trash cans, portable toilets. Not my kind of place, but if you go at the right time, you can find a picnic table far enough away from all the hubbub. If you're really lucky, a table that has a view of the small but beautiful waterfall. We've been lucky today, and have enjoyed a nice quiet afternoon.

After a while I get up to wade the stream and take waterfall pictures. Wading isn't easy because the rocks are covered with moss. Before crossing, I watch three youngsters slip and fall. I manage to make it over, take pictures, and return–to find an elderly man handing me his camera and asking me to take pictures of the waterfall for him. I don't want to, noting his very expensive digital camera, but he keeps encouraging me, and he and his wife steady me for the first half of the wade.

The whole time I'm busy taking risks, Brie is calmly grounding her feet in a shallow pool, watching kids and adults frolic. Later, when I go to get the cooler, she strips to her bathing suit and starts splashing around in the freezing water. She talks me into trying it, and I manage to float in ten inches of water for almost a minute, to her five. Then I snap pictures of her smiling while stretched out floating.

Walking back across the bridge, we stop to peer below. Whoosh, my cheap sunglasses tumble into the water and float away. We laugh, and immediately know that every time afterward when we'll stop at the same spot, we'll look down for sunglasses parked on some rock.

The afternoon still being young, we decide to drive to Chatuge, where she can get in a brief swim. As soon as we park, she jumps out and jumps in. I watch her swim out too far; too close to incoming ski-dos. I shout and she waves. And then I start wondering if her affinity for water is largely psychological. Maybe stemming from the positive experiences she'd had last October after her dismal and frightening drive from West Virginia. She'd arrived ragged but breathless, immediately finding the deserted Park-and-Rec campground, where she could swim every day. She got to camp in it for three weeks, but then it closed half way through the month. She said she prayed hard and found perfect sleeping quarters at a local conference center. Although October can be cold here, that fall was pleasant, allowing her to swim off the pier, alone and safe. She always talks about that time, the safe time before she found her home–the one that's turning out to be not so safe. We all have these secret places tucked far away inside.

Watching her swim back and forth, it strikes me that she prefers being alone. Even if I wanted to join her, which I don't, I wouldn't be particularly welcomed. I go back to wondering if she just thinks water is physically healing. I certainly can't test the suspicion with her; she violently rejects all inferences people make that her problem could be psychosomatic (what she calls 'mental'). But whether her relief comes from somewhere hidden deep inside her head or deep inside the blue waters of Lake Chatuge makes little difference. For being in water always makes her feel better. Even thinking about it. Take away that possibility, as happens all winter long, and she's in hell.

I know that feeling well; the winter months alone drive me toward my hell also, depriving me of my own water fix–the golf course. I try to silently recite the platitude that we're all called to trust and be thankful. Maybe paying attention to that call is what causes healing. But how hard that is when you're trapped inside day after day. Fortunately, I tell myself, those cold days are a long way off. It's still summer. She's safe inside the lake and I can go anytime I want to play at the Ridges. I look out to see her rise from the water laughing. She removes her flippers and walks toward me. She's so pretty. I hand her the big towel. What a strange day.

She joins me for twenty minutes on the lawn, then excuses herself to rejoin the lake. I rejoin my internal reveries. The winds starting to blow off the lake carry strong memories. Soon enough, whitecaps will start to build up and bring her back to shore. But that will be in an hour; right now, I sit alone, my mind wandering away from this still-peaceful lake to our country's biggest lake, Superior. I see Jed and me paddle our rental kayaks, always hugging the shore, wondering if we dare paddle toward the closest of the Apostle Islands a mile away. I certainly didn't want to, but knew he did. Superior is no calm inland lake. Six-foot waves can loom unexpectedly, as they threatened to that day. Neither of us had tried to master the Eskimo roll–didn't even have the kayak skirts for it. We kept hugging the shore.

And now my mind drifts farther back, before Jed was born, to when my high school buddy Edward and I portaged the twenty-foot aluminum canoe across Minnesota's Boundary Waters on another part of Superior. We were 18 or 19, having planned the trip for weeks but inevitably coming up short and having to rent heavy pots and pans. It was on this trip, in the middle of a calm day, that we set the small island on fire. And almost lost the car keys, which would have stranded us a hundred miles from Minneapolis...but found them while beating out the fire with what was left of my Levi jacket.

Brie eventually returns, beaming. We gather our stuff and go to her house to cook over the firepit. I remind her my nephew is coming in two days, and this might be our last time together for a week. After we finish eating, she doesn't suggest we go inside, so I take the hint and bid her goodbye.

The following day I play nine holes in the morning and then call her saying I'm going to visit the lake. She tells me she'll join me after the knitting ladies go. Ladies from the church come by once a week to teach her.

I wait for her, enjoying the gentle winds blowing off the lake and recalling last week's strange event. I'd lost Suzanne's wedding ring on the golf course after finding it a few months before on our driveway–where it had miraculously appeared after a friend pressure-washed down the entire drive. I got Brie to come with me and we walked the course for two hours, but of course were trying to find the proverbial thimble. The ring twice lost.

Now I'm peacefully happy, waiting for Brie to drive to the park after the knitting ladies leave her porch. Rowdy sits at my feet; we've just dried off after a very short swim. Rain clouds form and it tries to thunder, but I doubt it'll do much. Brie will arrive in time for a swim, when Rowdy and I will just watch.

She finally gets here and we sit alone on the small circle park of Lake Chatuge. No one's around; it's totally peaceful. She's relaxed and appears quite normal, being in a safe place surrounded by water instead of electricity or wi-fi--unless a ski-do whizzes around the corner too close, then she suffers a minor setback. We're both young kids again. I'm not doing caregiving here, just giving honest love. I remain relaxed.

After my nephew and his family left, I went to be with Brie. She was busy with her new porch sport, knitting. She hoped to finish a baby blanket, shawl, and something else for her upcoming trip to the family reunion. We talked but failed to connect. We spent a leisurely afternoon on her comfortable porch, she knitting and I throwing the tennis ball for Rowdy. The horses snorted and frolicked in the far pasture. Her yard was abloom in flowers, especially the huge Rose of Sharon bush that was trying its best to cover the firepit. I drank ice tea. We talked, but not about us, about the people we'd come to know together.

I asked her when we'd be going to Penland together. She didn't know because the weather was still a problem. It rained almost every afternoon, sometimes came pounding down. Not good for her to be paddling in the middle of the lake, especially with thunder. Rowdy, sitting behind her, would freak out and what could I do if she had a meltdown? We talked about emergencies. I learned more about her condition. We skirted the problem area.

And I studiously avoided bringing wine or beer. But didn't avoid it at home.

The next day I called her to tell her I'd be coming over to pick up her garbage. Since she lives outside the town boundaries, garbage has to be taken to the dump, where they'd recently installed a digital counter that predictably gives her a jolt. It gives me great pleasure to do little things like this, like going to pick up the groceries she'd ordered at Ingles. When I don't do it, Pat, a supervisor there who also happens to be a part-time pastor, picks and bags the groceries she calls in. I'm sure he's never questioned her sincerity about EMS like everybody else. The first time I explained her condition to my son and daughter, they politely questioned why, immediately after caregiving for Suzanne, I tried to hook up with someone who thinks she has a debilitating disease. I couldn't come up with an answer that would sound good to them.

We all know it's impossible to have perspective on something you're in the middle of. I haven't been able to this summer, the one I know I'll look back on as the summer of endless love. Endless and timeless. I wake, eat, walk Rowdy, play golf or pickleball, work in the house or yard, and call her at noon to see if she wants to go for a paddle or a swim, walk the dam, or drive to our old spot up on Fire's Creek. Maybe just sit on her porch throwing the ball for Rowdy and counting the horses. Doing nothing with her is something.

The hot August dog days this year have been pleasant— or maybe I've just been too happy to notice the heat. We've been seeing each other three to four times a week, sometimes staying together from noon to past midnight. I've been writing more love poems, buying sweaters, socks, jeans, dresses, blouses, and even a dressmaker's mannequin for making her costumes and outfits. I bring her special ice tea drinks, ice cream, and fruit. I deliver or pick up things from the grocery store, pharmacy, dump, or post office.

We play six or seven different card games at night before moving into the bedroom. We've even devised a crazy dictionary game. The days have blended seamlessly into each other. We have no interest in what's happening in the news–wouldn't watch the tv or computer if she could. Sometimes, however, I do miss listening to music and visiting other people.

At home I'd been rereading the *Odyssey,* and one day tried to share it with her, knowing her father had deprived her of the higher education she wanted so much. When she asked who wrote it, I swallowed and went on to describe how my love affair with the early Greeks had led to two trips to Greece. The following week I brought her Cahill's excellent study, which she returned after a while with a reasonable excuse for not getting into it. I gave it one last try, describing Circes' turning Odysseus' men into swine and him into a reluctant lover. She perked up on this, so I went on to describe that better lover, Calypso, after which she immediately asked to borrow Homer.

The local bookmobile stops by every three weeks to drop off a box of modern romances. I once gave her an older quality romance, Seton's *Katherine*, which she devoured inside of a week. All this led me to believe there was hope; she still wasn't too old to enter a community college. But of course, her disorder would prevent that. Nor could she take courses on line; she still refuses my offer of building an EMS-proof computer enclosure that I'd read about on line.

Nonetheless, we always enjoy our Scrabble and dictionary game. We sit leaning against her living room sofa while one of us searches the dictionary for a word the other couldn't possibly know. Despite her lack of formal education, Brie does pretty well, and enjoys the game.

It bothers me how her father had raised her to be the family slave; her life could have taken a different direction if she hadn't had to tend home base until getting married to a man whose only interest in her was showing her off to his chums. And then she had to end up in a call center answering phones for a miserable collection agency.

I always feel stymied trying to help her. When I offer to go shopping at Safeway for her, she usually reminds me her pastor friend who works there does that. When I bring by clothes, books, or even food, she accepts them unenthusiastically. She wants to do things herself, and this I respect. But I still want to help. Maybe I have crossed a line.

Now it's almost September, too early for the trees to start losing their leaves, but not too early to drive around checking them out. We keep our afternoon drives short and come back to sit on the porch looking out toward the horses.

Nothing in Brie's behavior prepared me for what was to come.

Well, maybe one thing did: the fact that I still didn't know what she really felt about me. My poems, presents, and behavior told her what I felt, but I had only her lovemaking to convince me...and even it often seemed more oriented toward her pleasure than mine. I guess I needed reassurance that she really did love me. I used the love word daily, and she rarely.

Moreover, always being someone who has to look forward, can't live simply in the present, I knew I needed some inkling of what she saw in the future. I'd been doing a lot of looking, wondering if we'd still be one in spirit a dozen years from now. Basically, would we be a bona-fide couple, if not married?

I did note her talk about wanting a pontoon boat and a lake front house. The two often come as a package; pontoon boats are too troublesome to drag to the lake, so you need a dock. And to buy a house with a dock on Chatuge takes a million dollars. I could do that but thought it much better to find a good site and build the kind of EMS-safe house we need. That site would be hard to find since everything's wired up around the lake.

I started driving my little blue Metro convertible around day after day looking for the perfect house site. It's enjoyable, with the top down, even though Rowdy thinks he has to hide under my feet. I drove for two weeks up and down every side street. Needless to say, I didn't tell her what I was up to.

One day I found two treeless half-acre sites with grass sweeping right down to the lake, one with a decent dock. Both surprised me by being listed at under $150,000. But both were unsuitable for us because of close power lines and houses jammed on either side. I had to find a hidden place without immediate neighbors, and hopefully, one with lots of trees. This for me as well as being a necessity for her. For if I were to live on this lake–a noisy lake most of the summer–it would have to be somewhere I could kid myself into thinking I was out in the wild–-like most of the lake land up in Minnesota or better yet, the UP of Wisconsin, where you can still purchase spectacular lake land for under $50,000.

When I was about to give up, I found my ideal place at the end of a long dirt road, isolated and surrounded by old trees--a very old cabin with a decent lake view, if not immediate access. It looked like a dock might fit out there, and the hand-made sign did say "lakefront." I figured I could offer $100,000; for maybe another $400,000 I could tear down the cabin and rebuild.

When I called, I kept getting no signal, but on the third try found myself talking to someone far away. He said he'd sell me the place at a rock bottom price, $310,000. I laughed and hung up. And stopped driving around the lake. If Brie and I were ever to have that pontoon boat, we'd probably have to keep it on one of the lake's docks, which sort of defeats the joy of jumping out of bed and into the boat. The funny thing is that I don't even like pontoon boats.

We continued tiptoeing toward talk about the future, but she always stopped short. One evening back at my home, like a fool, I decided to put my concern into a letter, telling her what I saw fifteen years from now. I all but insisted that she tell me what she saw. "No hedging replies," I think I wrote, suggesting several alternative living arrangements I'd mentioned to her before, like moving back and forth from a warmer climate to North Carolina. Toward the end I might have come right out and asked her to tell me how much she cared for me.

Less than two days after I'd dropped it into the mail I wanted to rush over and get it back, and even thought about calling, telling her to tear it up immediately before reading it. But she read it, and my doom was sealed. Brie, I would one day learn, was not one to make firm commitments. She moved up to them, but once she got too close, backed firmly away.

The leaves don't start turning here in early September, but I thought they might higher up. I wanted to go for a long drive to find out, and talked her into taking a country drive to the Cherohala Skyway above Robbinsville–a handful of miles past the Joyce Kilmer old growth forest with its 300-year old poplars fifteen feet wide and 100 feet tall. We took her car, safer for her than mine, and came prepared with lunch and drinks. I knew the trip would encompass most of the day and worried if that would be too long, but also knew it was a remote enough area to present few difficulties.

Everything went wonderfully: no cars, no high wire lines, in fact nothing but a beautiful, empty road with turn-offs every few miles to look toward distant peaks and balds. She enjoyed it as much as I, and eventually we found the feeder road to White River Falls. You can drive right up and almost into this spectacular waterfall. Last time I'd been here, years before with Suzanne, after leaving the waterfall we kept on the dirt road south toward North Carolina instead of turning back to the Skyway, and eventually made it home.

This time, however, after almost an hour of driving on dirt roads that kept getting smaller and smaller, we discovered the road had been closed without notice, so had to waste another hour getting back to the blacktop.

Then instead of returning the same way, I decided to continue to Tellico Falls, Tennessee, which was a big mistake. When I got there and pulled off to examine a map, Brie groaned and I looked up to see a huge electrical generating station looming across the road. She suffered the rest of the way home, as I did with guilt. I should have been on a better lookout. I shouldn't have even tried to take her out for such a long drive.

I carried the guilt home with me after dropping her off and trying to get her comfortable, and foolishly drank three beers and then four glasses of wine, predictably suffering a huge blowout later in the night, a monster headache, and needless to say, more untold amounts of guilt. The following day she must have noticed my debilitated condition, and asked if I was ok. I told her I'd had too much booze, which was a big mistake; I still hadn't internalized how much she objected to my drinking.

If this wasn't bad enough, the guilt made me confess that my drinking habits might be worse than she'd thought. She listened and told me to attend the talk the

Episcopal church was holding on Saturday on how to ask for God's blessing.

I went, reluctantly but obediently, to listen to the speaker from England explain a good way to ask for a blessing. Eventually I confessed along with everyone else and told the couple at the table with me that I needed to stop drinking so much. They didn't share their problems but we all asked for my blessing. I went home and gave thanks.

The next day, Sunday, I met her in church to tell her how confident I was that I'd received the blessing. I knew it would produce the needed change. She wasn't impressed; in fact, was angrier than before. She carried on about how I wasn't trying, how alcohol changed the way I behaved around her, and how I'd probably never give it up. I protested, even retaliated by asking her why she didn't also go to the event to learn how to ask for her own much needed blessing... which she simply ignored. I had to leave without her saying goodbye.

She wouldn't see me for almost a week, saying she needed time to process. Things were looking bad. One day she finally agreed to an afternoon kayak tour of the lake. She kept paddling ahead, wouldn't wait for me, and when we were all done complained about my not keeping up. I knew what she was thinking, wanted to tell her I hadn't had a drink for over a week, had made it over the hump. But I knew she wouldn't listen. We packed the kayaks into my Element and drove home, where she immediately disappeared inside, not even offering a perfunctory goodbye.

My favorite month was half over–my birthday month. But the beautiful September days were already losing their luster; I couldn't fully appreciate the golf course splendor. One day I awoke to the realization that I wasn't controlling events; they were controlling me. My birthday approached. Would it become some kind of dividing line between untroubled and conflicted love? Brie's apprehensions worried me; not just her fixation on my booze problem, but her occasional distance...and contradictory behavior. One day talking about buying a pontoon boat together, the next day turning a deaf ear to the future. As I was soon to discover, however, she'd done everything she could to make my birthday memorable. She'd been preparing for it all month, must have pushed my foolish letter, the dangerous drive, and then my unnecessary confession to the back of her mind. She almost made my 67th the best ever.

This time our Penland outing was to be a very quiet one; no Fourth of July nonsense. We paddled to our second site, the one with better water and view, arriving late. By the time camp got set up and we ate the special meat-vegetable-pasta dish she'd prepared at home and reheated over my fire, we fell almost immediately into sleep. I woke only once, to the sound of lazy whippoorwills who insisted on leaving off the "whip" part of their mournful call.

The next morning my built-in clock told me it was probably around 6:00, full morning light. I reached over to make sure she was right next to me, still naked, half on her pad, half on mine. Long hair covering her neck and shoulders. Sound asleep. Beautiful.

And what day could it be? The 30th of September. I unzipped the flap and peeked out to see if the fire I'd stoked at midnight still had coals. Maybe. But there was no hurry; I re-zipped and pulled the thin blanket up, trying to find some part of my body that wouldn't hurt to lie on. Later I woke to the smell of eggs. She'd snuck four into the crowded kayaks and was busy frying them with sliced potatoes. I poured a cup of coffee and wondered what surprise Brie had prepared for me--but wouldn't discover it until later in the day.

As usual, she went for her long swim in the lake. After lunch and my brief nap in her hammock I woke to my big present: a pair of flippers to play blue-footed merman to the green-footed mermaid. I couldn't guess where she bought the big flippers and matching snorkel goggles; she had no computer to order from and couldn't enter a sports store. She must have made the long trip to Murphy, 20 miles each way, and ordered from their front door. She found them, wrapped them, concealed them on her kayak for the trip over, and surprised me the day after our arrival on Penland.

She'd also managed to bake and conceal on the kayak a huge chocolate cake, complete with candles. "How in the world did you stow it in your kayak without my seeing it?" I asked, beaming.

"Easily, right on top of the red cooler. You never looked. Maybe too much other stuff." The other stuff being twelve water bottle gallons, box-wine, cooking gear, sleeping gear, living gear, and food. It all got somehow packed inside and on top with Rowdy, both kayaks riding so low in the water that if we hadn't paddled in early, the wakes from passing pontoon boats could have swamped us.

We stayed three days, and the first two were heaven. Off in the distance, the Appalachians, forest after forest covering high-rolling hills. Waves of green marching over hills, filling valleys, leaving nothing bleak, eroded, or arid like throughout the West. Leaves murmuring, water rushing, bees attacking trees and bush blossoms. But over on the slopes of those distant hills, danger lurked: not just wild hogs or panthers, but rhododendrons so dense that you enter at risk of never returning. Here on the island, you can safely walk throughout—except for the invisible chiggers.

Brie spent all her time in the water; that, after all, was her main reason for coming, to let the water protect her from offending electrical impulses. I read, collected wood, lounged in the hammock, and tended the fire all day--even though it was too hot for one. On this trip I added wine to my relaxation. I knew it was a stupid thing to do, but it was my birthday.

It took me a long time to recognize something going wrong. She concealed her smoldering discontent, which I couldn't recognize because I didn't want to. Everything would have remained heavenly had I not brought that three-litre box-wine. She never said anything; probably didn't want to spoil the event. On the last day, however, I did spot trouble. When I donned the flippers and flapped like a madman out to the buoy, congratulating myself on the return trip, she barely smiled...just nodded and looked away.

I did my best to ignore the bad ending to our Penland outing, the longest we were to ever have. We made it home before the late afternoon winds came up. A wonderful but damaged birthday.

In early October Bert read what he'd transcribed into the computer from the yellow pad he'd been scribbling in during their Penland visit. He frowned. What in the hell was he doing keeping this stupid journal that pretended to be some kind of novel? It had made good sense to maintain a journal while caregiving Suzanne and maybe some sense to continue writing afterward, but not now. It was time to stop. The only problem was he didn't want to, he enjoyed writing too much. He knew how to handle things: one day he'd stop using the first person, switch to third. Sooner or later.

CHAPTER FOUR: NATIONAL DISASTER?

FRANK, LIKE MOST PSYCHOLOGISTS, had his own demons to battle. Mainly he was bored to death. Bored with not working and having nothing important to do, yet not in the least interested in returning to consulting, as he knew would be so easy. He didn't need the money; didn't need the stress. What the hell did he need?

He knew he needed his friend, Bert; spent too much time complaining to him about Marsha's compulsiveness. Hell, Bert knew he cherished her, even if she drove him crazy with her constant need to put this here, not there; clean this, move that; put it over there.

And there's always golf. Used to be tennis, but now this ridiculous tennis elbow. Book club, poker once a month. But this whole area has nothing else to offer. Why did we ever move here? Oh yeah, she wanted the view. Not the ocean but the mountain view–plus a sliver of the lake. Wonderful. Well at least there was a lake for a boat. Should we move? Could we ever sell this house that's not right for us, plus the other lot we stupidly bought?

What's there to do here, really? Walk the dog Trouble, play golf, and once in a rare while take the boat on another tour around Lake Chatuge. Or once in a while make love to Marsha, but not like it used to be. Was anything like it used to be? Would anything? Shit and double shit.

All July he'd been thinking about what he'd said on the golf course to his friend–or hadn't said. He hadn't been open, honest. He knew Bert was going through some private hell with his crazy girlfriend who claimed to possess strange electrical sensitivity, or something like that.

He'd openly dismissed his friend's claims, but in the back of his mind something kept triggering what a former girlfriend had told him...so many years ago. How many? What in fact was her name? Judy, Judy with the honeydew melon boobs. Judy who had so many hang-ups none of the other interns wanted anything to do with her. But it was hard to stay away from those boobs.

She'd pushed her way into his life. Into his superbly single, free-ranging, no complications life. Everything had started out innocently enough. Friday afternoon at The Club. Dancing, drinking, and then of course, more. She initiated it, didn't she? Told him she needed to talk to someone. Of course, she wanted free consultation from the psychologist. He should have walked away.

He remembered telling Bert one day about his adventures back in Gainesville, all the women flocking to the interns. They didn't have to go searching, the women came to them--nurses, secretaries, grad students. And he, the bachelor who'd never been married, attracted more than his share. Judy was just

124

one of them, one who didn't last any longer than the others.

She'd walked right up to him that Friday afternoon at The Club. All five-foot six inches of her, one inch short of him, daring him to kiss her in front of everyone. Her eyes some shade of green or maybe turquoise. Beautiful, absolutely beautiful. So of course, he welcomed her with open arms. Kissed her with bravado.

"I think you're the one, baby," she'd said, or something like that on their second date. He tried to stay cool, maybe said, "You know I'm him" or something even less cool. Anyway, he let her know he would be the one; who could refuse? And they did get it on.

Toward the end–maybe half-way through their time together–he started noticing something wrong–not just her hang-ups, which he could tolerate, but her evasiveness. She wouldn't look into his eyes, just gaze off into space. She'd oblige his desire but never meet it openly. She'd smile, coo, and urge him on with rehearsed words: "Oh, oh, do it, do it, come in me now." Which turned him off, not on. He wanted to get to know the real her, not the fake one.

He'd stopped dating others but didn't know what to do about her. Should he just walk away? One night he got her totally sober and demanded they talk.

They talked and talked. Or rather, she talked and he listened, amazed at the transformation. Once the floodgates opened, she dropped pretenses. No, her father hadn't abused her; neither had her two brothers. Nor had her first boyfriend...or second. What was bothering her didn't have anything to do with them— let alone him. She was just hurting for her sister. Becky was dying right in front of her eyes, and there was nothing anyone could do.

Frank saw it coming, didn't want to let it swamp him, but he'd asked for honesty, had to listen. The two had been close right up to the time her sister had gone to college, when they'd lost touch. She'd gotten married and started her own life back east. Judy stayed in St. Louis, taking night classes. One day she got a desperate phone call; Becky was coming to visit her, would in fact be there in two days. She'd lost her job, left her husband, and was sick--extremely sick. She stayed with her older sister for eight days.

Becky had been the picture of health all her life– skiing, sky-diving, running marathons. She jogged before and after work every day. Had to because her work kept her cooped up in a small overcrowded office jammed with thirty people wearing headsets, all hunched over their computers. Phones, computers buzzing all day long, five days a week. One day she just fell over, smacked her head on the keyboard. Her supervisor yelled at her to stop sleeping on the job, but she was unconscious and had to be rushed to the emergency room.

The hospital didn't admit her, couldn't come to any conclusion about what was wrong. Once out, she realized she couldn't return to her job; the place started her head spinning the minute she walked in. She was fired of course, with nowhere to turn. The whole story went downhill from there. Frank couldn't remember the details but did remember that just before Judy and he separated she'd given him a copy of a long newspaper interview with Becky. He'd read it back then, maybe, but remembered almost nothing. Now might be a good time to give it a closer examination.

After two hours of looking through his storage shed, he found it tucked away in one of three cardboard boxes labeled Cases. Back at the University of Florida he'd gotten so used to extreme cases that were much worse— bipolar and schizophrenia--that he must have minimized Becky's, yet he'd somehow managed to save it.

The first two pages of the interview entitled "A Strange Kind of Allergy?" had been lost; what was stapled together started in mid-stream.

*Would you please describe your physical limitations in detail.

I can use anything not wireless: a computer, a landline. But I need a screen over my computer monitor to reduce electric fields. My keyboard and mouse have wires. And I put the cable transformers in a metal bin to reduce magnetic fields. I don't use a cell phone, not even for emergencies. I've never used a smartphone. I'm sensitive to Wi-fi, not technology in general.

*When did this all start?

July, 1990. I was so excited to go buy a new laptop, because I love computers. But when I opened it, something didn't feel right. The left side of the mouse pad was vibrating and made my fingers tingle. I've been working with computers forever so I knew there was a technical problem – maybe too much static electricity. I exchanged it, and the store confirmed it was defective. But when I turned on the replacement computer the screen was jumping, and I felt pressure in my heart. I felt hot when I was by the computer, but it calmed down when I moved away. I took that second laptop back and got a different model from a new store. Then everything got weird. I couldn't understand what anyone was telling me, it was like a brain disconnect. And my heart was jumping. My face felt like it was on fire. I was nauseated. All this would start when I was near the computer.

* Had the computer really caused it?

I have no idea. I did an internet search: "heart jumps when using laptop," and saw so many complaints. I'll never forget one from a pregBriet woman saying that when she was using the laptop the fetus would kick. I decided to go to the actual Apple store to confirm that there was something wrong with the third computer because this was just too odd. The woman said, maybe your body doesn't like Apple computers? They checked the laptop and confirmed it was defective. I went back home and then same thing happened – this was the fourth laptop. I returned the computer. I hoped it would work, as I love computers and need them for my work.

* Did you go to doctors?

The scariest symptom was my jumping heart, so I went to visit a cardiologist. I was fit and active — I swam and did two or three spin classes each day – so why would I have chest pains? There's no heart disease in my family. When she tested me, the Wi-fi was off, so it's not surprising that they didn't find anything wrong. She called the occupational clinic to get their opinion. They said they'd heard people say they feel sick from using the computer but there's no scientific evidence to support it.

* How long had you been using computers?

I was always into gadgets and electronics and computers. Both of my parents are computer people who met at a computer course. I started learning computers at school in ninth grade, but I didn't really like it and all my parents did was talk about computers. So, back then, I actually hated computers. When I joined the army, I thought it was a bad joke when they put me on the computer track. I ended up commanding the computer center for the army's headquarter and for the operation center, serving more than 600 users with computers networks including the prime minister and chief of staff. So I spent two years sleeping in a room that had dozens of wired routers and monitors and computers – but this was not wireless. It was one of those jobs where you don't want to remember everything. When I finished, I forgot everything I'd learned about radio frequencies and antennas.

* How did the illness progress?.

Weird things continued to happen. For example, I was on one side of the bed in my apartment and I'd get this really sharp pain in my head. When I moved to the other side, it stopped. I noticed there was an electric socket there and I asked the mainteBriece guy to disconnect its electricity. I didn't really want to use the computer so it was difficult for me to research what was going on. I took two tests — an EEG, which detects electrical activity in the brain, and an EMG, which sees how your nerves respond to electric currents. They couldn't find anything wrong with my body unless it's exposed to wireless. When I live in a radiation-free environment I do not have symptoms. My heart is fine and my nervous system is fine.

* What was that like, not knowing what was wrong at the time?

I hoped it was a bad dream, that I'd wake up and the symptoms would have vanished. But I couldn't be anywhere and couldn't sleep. One day I ventured out, saw a shopping mall with a white strip on the roof. I asked someone what it was, as I could feel the pain was coming from there, and she told me they were cell-phone antennas. I started crying. That's when everything collapsed. I was just laying on the floor. We went to buy radiation shielding materials for the windows. I couldn't stand up in the house.

* What happened next?

I couldn't think properly. I went for a month without any sleep. Someone wrote me that there's a place in Green Bank, West Virginia, where nobody is allowed to use wireless signals. I contacted her and she said I should go stay. I drove nine hours there that same day. But I felt ill in her house because I was so sick at the time I was reacting to any electricity, not just wireless. Then I met an intelligent guy from California who'd gone there with his mother because he was so ill. These were my first encounters with other people like me. I put a tent out on her porch and was flooded with clarity. It was freezing cold, but it was like my head was finally quiet. I cried and cried.

* Why were you so sad?

I met these people who were so sensitive and most of them had been in that state for years. I didn't identify as electro-sensitive, I just felt like I was having a short-term problem. But that night I knew I was in a different reality, this wasn't a bad dream. I could not return to society. I didn't know how I was going to survive in the world but knew I couldn't do it there. Sometimes I wanted to commit suicide.

* What did you do during the day?

Desperately searched for spots where there was no radiation. I borrowed books from the library and would sit and read in the car by a park. Every time someone came near I had to leave if they had a cell phone. I wondered if this would be the rest of my life … the world felt so hostile. I heard of a conference about electromagnetic sensitivity and I found a list of speakers and called one who was electro-sensitive herself. We really connected. We're around the same age and both used to be really successful career women. She lived in an isolated place in South Carolina. She said, Why don't you come here? I packed my bags again.

* What was it like when you got there?

It took time for my body to calm down, but I do think I started sleeping after about the fourth week and it was great. After six weeks, I went back home, still wanting to find a house I could live in safely. Eventually I found a farmhouse and asked the neighbors if they'd turn off their Wi-fi.

* Were you sure it was Wi-fi that was making you sick?

My theory is that once you become affected by the radiation, something happens to the nervous system and it recognizes the radiation as a threat and then reacts to warn the body that something is wrong. So while the first reaction was to wireless, I then started to react to anything with vibrations, anything that the nervous system detected, so I started to be affected by electricity, then light and sound. Something in the first computer caused the appearance of the symptoms. I think something was defective and might have created a strong electromagnetic shock to my body. It may be that the accumulated use of wireless technology and the fact that at the time I was sleeping three feet from a circuit breaker weakened my body, and then that laptop may have been the "last straw." I will never know the definitive answer to this.

* So, back then, what kind of a house could you live in?

It had to have a gas, not electric, stove. I could not tolerate a fridge, lights, a dishwasher, microwave, washing machine. I was still reacting to all electricity because my electrosensitivity was so bad. Mountains block radiation and I couldn't have neighbors so I had to look around hard. I must have examined 500 potential houses, only 60 of which I went to see and only one of which fit. For months I just lay in bed sleeping, and even then, I was still feeling the electricity. I'd leave the house and go into the woods when I put in the laundry.

* How did you keep in touch with people?

Even a regular phone hurt my ear so I used a speakerphone. The future didn't look so exciting. I had to create a life there. I met a woman who became my best friend and then started a book club. I missed getting dressed in the morning, feeling beautiful, and going to work. When I could make it to the supermarket I'd chat away to the cashier just to have some interaction. I created a pretty interesting life there: I grew vegetables and I had beehives, but I just couldn't live like that.

* Did you tell people that they had to leave their cell phones behind when they visited?

I'd put up a big a sign on my door. Nobody was allowed in my house with a cell phone.

* How did you keep warm?

I couldn't use electric heat, just a wood stove. I'd sit under lots of coats and wear snow pants.

* Did you feel better there?

After a few months my body started to recuperate. I could tolerate electricity again so I could work on the computer. I began to dedicate my time to expose the harmful effects of wireless signals and work towards the recognition of electrosensitivity.

* What's your life like now?

You know, nowadays there are huge cell towers all over, and there's open Wi-fi on every street, so finding a house is impossible. I can't drive for two hours on the roads without feeling like fainting. I fall asleep and I become very weak. For five years I've been dreaming of water, which is the one place where I'm safe. I don't go anywhere. It's like being in a prison cell. I haven't been to the movies for five years.

* How do you spend your days?

Working on my computer, my computer that's been made safe, sometimes for 14 hours a day.

* Do you have much of a social life?

I have friends but haven't been in a relationship for a long time. Many people don't really believe me. I'm crazy, making it all up. I might look like a ditzy blonde, but can explain the science behind everything, so I haven't encountered total doubt. But whenever someone says I should see a psychiatrist, I made a big scene. I'm very intolerant of people who deny my situation. How can people say that the electro-sensitive are crazy? How many of them could live in such an absurd situation and keep their sanity? I just don't think about the future. Whenever I think about all the new wi-fi towers I go insane — how can I live in a wireless world if it makes me so sick?

Frank had counseled too many cuckoos like the woman who thought ants had invaded her brain to get alarmed at the account...except for the fact that the parallels with Bert's girlfriend Brie were truly remarkable. Almost the identical story. What should he do? He should probably support Bert and Brie by giving them the article. But it would be best to wait until he knew more; take time to do the research, find out if this electrical sensitivity thing really has any validity. But right now, he needed to be there for them. He called Bert and invited them both for that boat trip around Lake Chatuge Bert had hinted at before. Now was the time; he'd bring Marsha along to put Brie at ease.

As boring as Bert thought it would be to motor around a small lake in a large, over-powered boat trying to avoid thirty other over-powered boats, a couple dozen ski-dos, and an occasional sea plane, the boat trip went better than Frank had planned, Marsha had dreaded,

Brie had worried about, and Bert had hoped for. When you're boating or fishing on Lake Chatuge, you can look up from anywhere to see mountains to the east, south, and north. The lake is the first in a series of TVA reservoirs that stretch into Tennessee, has more than a hundred miles of shoreline that's mostly coves and finger projections, but also hundreds of expensive houses, invisible or clumped together where feeder roads lead in from Hayesville, North Carolina or Hiawassee, Georgia. ("We're now in both states," Frank shouted to the women in back when they got to the middle of the lake, and a second later, "Oops, now we're in Georgia.")

Frank, used to boating and fishing off the coast of Florida, could have piloted blindfolded, really didn't enjoy it much since fishing for small-fry was something he'd never try and he took little pleasure pointing out the same mediocre sights–islands, dam, public or private docks, expensive houses--although he did enjoy it every time the grand-kids came to water-ski. Still, he tried to be a jovial host. He'd arrived early to unwrap the boat's covers. Marsha was seated inside reading a magazine. Standing next to the boat, Frank watched Bert steer Brie down from the parking lot. He was surprised to find her tall, graceful, and elegant. He'd expected someone closer to Bert's age and demeanor. Bert had been both wrong and right about her: she looked the picture of health, not sickness, and she was indeed sexy as hell.

When the two reached the pier, Brie released Bert's protective arm and scrambled in, greeting Frank with a generous hug that lasted longer than usual since the

136

boat lurched. Then she climbed in back to join Marsha. Bert sat up front with Frank and they pulled out. Once they got going, it was too noisy for all four to communicate, so the women in back talked about recent activities while the two men discussed important things like whether the Ridges would fold or find another banker with deep enough pockets to keep the course going.

Bert had packed a cooler of sandwiches and wine, and they dropped anchor off the biggest island–Penland, named by or after a large local family who still lived nearby in both states. "This is where I camp," Brie said enthusiastically. "Over there, you can almost see where the place has been cleared. It's got the best fire-pit you've ever seen...but of course you can't see it from here."

Bert kept quiet. She'd used "I," not "we." Well, maybe she didn't want them to think she was promiscuous; she had no way of knowing what Bert had told them about their relationship. Penland was his favorite place too, but maybe for different reasons than hers. He was always looking forward to the evening, especially after dinner when they'd disappear into her tent.

Frank asked about the island, and Bert explained how anyone could camp on any of the islands since they were public land, sort of like Forest Service land but owned by the TVA. They didn't have official campsites, just makeshift places which locals had obviously appropriated. Officially it was always first come, first serve, even where someone had tied canvas and flags to trees trying to make it look like an occupied private campground.

"The first time we came," he explained, "I saw this big tent set up beyond the firepit. It was a regular tent, not stretched canvas, so I started paddling off to find another place. Brie told me to wait a minute, she'd paddle her kayak over to the site a few hundred yards south, ask the campers there."

Everyone looked where he was pointing.

"She returned, saying they hadn't seen anyone come to the ghost tent for the three days they'd been there. We went ahead and took the site; ignored the empty tent." He laughed, and then added, "That's Brie for you, never the shy one." He looked over to see if she was angry he'd mentioned their camping together. She was busy talking to Marsha.

After they finished eating, they climbed back in the boat. Once when Frank checked to see if the women were comfortable, Brie surprised him with a broad smile and wink. They finished the tour and headed back. It was 5:00 and boats were starting to thin out. "This is my favorite time of day," Brie told Marsha, and went on tell how she and Bert had bought maps of the lake and explored almost every cove in their kayaks. Brie didn't know it, but this was probably the first time Marsha had enjoyed boating on the lake. The two of them hit it off from the start.

After Frank docked the boat, he helped the women disembark. Marsha scrambled out, but Brie went slowly, holding tightly to Frank's arm. She thanked him warmly and gave him another hug, then joined Marsha, already headed up the hill. Bert and Frank stayed behind to put the covers on. As they got close to the cars, they both noticed Marsha was having to support–almost carry–Brie. Bert rushed to help. After he got her into the car, he went back to thank Frank, who asked him what was wrong. "The cell phone," Bert answered. "You must have forgotten to turn yours off." Frank started to apologize and Bert told him not to worry, it happens all the time. "She'll get over it later tonight," he said and patted Frank on the shoulder.

It took Bert almost an hour once they got back to her place to get her comfortable sucking oxygen in the living room chair. She hadn't said anything, but eventually started coming around. He asked her how she liked Marsha. He didn't want to talk about Frank's error, which she didn't bring up either. She said she and Marsha got along fine. "It was good to talk to someone again...I mean another woman," she corrected.

Bert didn't pry, and decided she didn't need to talk much now, so he got out the Skip-Bo game and talked her into quietly playing. Then after an hour he went home.

Back at their home Marsha chastised Frank for not shutting off his cell phone. "How could a small thing like that hurt?" he asked. Uncharacteristically, Marsha didn't back down. "Bert told you she can't take wi-fi. Maybe you'll believe it now."

Frank didn't reply, didn't want to start an argument. Instead he maneuvered the conversation toward what they had talked about, huddled so close together. "Women secrets?"

She didn't smile, was still huffy, but answered, saying they talked mostly about Brie's problem. "I told her how brave she was. She said Bert sometimes called her Superwoman. We talked about whether it was safe for her to be camping alone on the island, like the first time. We talked about all kinds of things."

Thinking of the article he'd just read, he asked if Brie had explained how her electrical sensitivity started up.

"She said she was working in this computer environment in Asheville. Her company back east had asked for volunteers to relocate and she'd accepted. Lower pay, but a better place to finish bringing up her daughter and son. Anyway, after a couple of years she just keeled over at her desk. They had to call an ambulance."

Frank nodded. Yes, it was the very same story, "Keep going."

"She had to quit and go live with her brother in New York, or maybe West Virginia. Anyway, way up in the mountains in a remote cabin. She stayed there for almost a year, then got stir crazy."

"Did the new environment help?"

"Maybe, she was talking so fast I missed a lot. Anyway, she decided to come back to Asheville.

Unfortunately, she ended up selling her house and going to Dallas to this expensive doctor who was supposed to be the world's authority on her condition."

"And then moved here to Hayesville?"

"I'm not sure of all the dates, but yes, she bought this four-wheel car without computerized gadgets and slept in it all the way down here. In fact, she might have used it to get to Dallas–I know she can't take a plane. I don't know how she does all this by herself."

Frank scratched his head. "Did she get any healing from this Dallas doctor?"

"I don't know. She said he charged a lot–maybe $20,000. Which of course Medicare doesn't pay for, and she wasn't on it anyway since she's too young, and she'd lost her insurance after they fired her. There went most of her nest egg."

"What about her kids?"

"What about them? I just told you, she has two, a girl and boy."

"Do they, uh, think she...I mean do they..."

"You mean, do they believe her? I don't know, didn't ask. But *I* do."

"What do you think she'll do?"

"I have no idea, but she did talk about visiting Santa Fe. Lots of people with her condition live out in the desert."

"What about Bert?"

"Hey, what we talked about is private. But I know she doesn't want to hurt him, appreciates what he's doing for her."

Hell, he loves her to death, that's why he's doing it, Frank almost said.

"She seems to think her healing has to come first. But for God's sake, don't tell Bert that."

Frank fell silent, pondering her strident tone. Had Brie opened a sore spot for Marsha and him? Something about the way the two had leaned upon each other coming up the boat ramp....

Frank and Bert had been talking about an extended golf trip for some time, decided now was that time. They made reservations at Callaway Gardens, packed everything into Frank's van, and took off, vowing on the way not to talk about three things: women, God, and current events.

"Exactly what my dad warned me fifty years ago," Bert said. "The only fatherly advice he gave me, except to brush my teeth twice a day, was to never argue over sex, politics, and religion; leave them on the table...which left a literal minded 14-year-old wondering how they got up on the table in the first place."

Frank snorted. "You made up wondering about the table, unless you were a very dense teenager." Bert laughed and confessed.

The three-hour trip to Columbus was uneventful. They mostly listened to bad country music after fifteen minutes of trying to hear a scratchy tape on the Vietnam war. When they arrived, they were pleasantly surprised to find they'd magically qualified for a mid-week special, getting two nights and three days of golf for only $150 each. They had time for an afternoon round and the skies were clear. Life couldn't be better.

Out on the course they small-talked, avoided any challenges. This was to be a time to relax, leave worries behind. But having made the pact, Bert found it difficult to keep, had to fudge a little. He couldn't help telling Frank that one reason Brie wanted to hurry up and get healed was so the performer in her could come out.

"Performer?"

"She's always liked to dress up, act out. Was convinced she'd grow up to be a comedian. In fact, in her early twenties she got up on a stage in some bar and brought the house down. And she's always spent weeks designing and sewing costumes for her kids and her. Once she walked sideways on another stage and the audience saw a ragamuffin boy. Then she turned around the other way and they saw a pretty woman. She won first place." Bert smiled, then added, "I guess why that's why I bought her a dress-making mannequin and foot-powered old-fashioned sewing machine."

That night they decided to eat at the Gardens, even if it was too expensive for what it offered. It was crowded and they had to sit at a small table hidden behind a column. Into their second beer a young woman– probably still a teenager–pulled up a chair next to Frank. He shot a what's up look toward Bert, who rose to go to the bathroom and stopped on his way back to sit at the bar.

After a half hour Bert noticed Frank signaling him to come over to join them. Frank introduced her, saying she'd just gotten in town and found herself in this crowded place. A late-blooming runaway? Bert thought. Or maybe an early-blooming prostitute. Or both.

Bert nodded occasionally to their talk, and eventually she rose. Before leaving, Frank slipped a twenty-dollar bill into her hand and said good luck, stay clean.

"What's up?" Bert asked.

"Well, that's what I wondered. Seems she's peddling her wares. Offered to satisfy me any way I wanted for $100. I told her I wasn't interested but wanted to know more about her. Why a young thing like her had decided to give her life away."

"Bold of you."

"Hey, I'm a psychologist, remember. And I wanted to let her know she wasn't going to score with me, but maybe she needed someone to listen for a while."

"What was her story?"

"The predictable one. Ran away from home three years ago. I think she's around 19. Father abused her, boyfriend got her pregnant, next an abortion. The old story."

"She's so innocent looking."

"What I thought too. It's sad, and there's nothing you can do. She'll be wasted in another ten years, no doubt before 30, with nowhere to go."

"Maybe she'll find a man who wants to marry her."

"I hope so. Though he's just as likely to be the kind of man who beats her."

"A nice world we've created."

"And it's here to stay. Let's change the subject. Get back to golf, something cheery."

The second day's golf went well, and that night they decided to visit a brewpub in Columbus. Unlike the Gardens restaurant, this place was almost empty--too early. That was good because they had something important to process. First, they had to warm up to it with a little sparring. Bert working on his second Dos

Equis, Frank finishing his first and announcing a switch to Diet Pepsi.

"You know, that stuff's worse for you than beer. Sugar! You should stick with Dos Equis, the real stuff."

"Maybe, this Pepsi sucks. They need to get root beer here. But you–you need to switch to kombucha. That beer makes your stomach pooch."

"Yeah, I know, have considered it. I could add some vodka to it."

"Kind of defeats the purpose of drinking a non-alcoholic fermented drink, doesn't it?"

"What's wrong with a little poison?"

They carried on until Bert got to the real poison. "I'm not just playing the advocate here."

"*Devil's*. Go on."

"Ok, sit tight. We all know lots of things can take us down. Used to be atom bombs, Nazis, Commies, huge meteorites. Then aliens, epidemics, terrorists, computer failures, financial crashes. So many bad possibilities."

"Not to mention dictators, drugs, and universal disorder."

"A lot of d's there."

"Yeah. Go ahead to the other one that no one's thought about. I sense you getting serious here."

"You catch on quick. Most of what people worry about these days are environmental disasters. And ninety percent of the time that means natural environmental disasters, not man-made ones."

"Uh, huh."

"Let's assume lots of people started developing a strange skin disorder, maybe due to some kind of unexpected solar radiation or genetically engineered food–it doesn't matter. They can't go outside–can't stay outside for more than a few minutes."

"Horrible! No golf!"

Bert chuckled. "Well, this example isn't the 'let's assume' I have in mind. I've another one, more realistic. Already some people, still a very small minority, have started developing a toxic reaction to something we can't remove from the environment. Something we humans can't get away from, are virtually surrounded by."

"Like air."

"Like air, yes, invisible, and everywhere. It's something that didn't even exist a century ago...and it's not part of the natural environment. It's man-made."

"I'm all ears," Frank started to say, then suddenly added, "I get it--electrical radiation."

Bert nodded. "Like we've talked about, no one believes in it because not enough people have shown the symptoms. it's probably under one or two percent, though some people talk about eight or ten. But what if–just what if–that number increased to fifteen percent? Would science pay attention then?"

"Of course, maybe even ten percent."

"I've got your attention. I doubt if more than one person in a hundred right now could believe in what I'm about to say, but it seems to me it could easily happen."

"You're about to say something happens to trigger massive EMS in the population. But what? The Zita mosquito?"

Bert smiled. "No, nothing outside the system, something inside it. Just constant exposure. Over-exposure, over a long period of time. More and more exposure with heavier doses."

"Electricity's been around a long time."

"True, and also true that as its prevalence has increased, so has the human tendency to adjust to it. We always adjust to any new environmental threat."

"So...."

"So think about it. We've had a bunch of strange new diseases these past twenty years. Diseases, disorders, conditions, each with its proper acronym. So many acronyms we've probably run out of them, may have to revert to abbreviations. You know, AAS, ABCD, ACC, ACS, ADEM. The other day I Googled the list, found more than thirty in the A's alone."

Frank laughed. "Yeah, it's ridiculous. I have a hard time believing in all of them."

"That's not all," Bert continued. "I read somewhere that it takes the human body around ten years to adjust to a new environmental situation. Ten years or more before negative symptoms start appearing. That right, doctor?" Frank nodded. "So how long have cell phones and wi-fi been around?"

Frank smiled. "Ten, fifteen years!"

"Unless we're just making all this up, we humans are getting less healthy, even though we live longer. Something's affecting our immune systems. In fact, I bet half the new disorders are immune related. Anyway, our new generations could be coming into the world carrying genetic disposition for all these new disorders."

"I see where you're going."

"Do you? I haven't reached the main point yet. It's not just electricity–at least not electricity as we all picture it, wires overhead, outlets in every room. That's not the problem; as I said, it's been around long enough for us to adjust to it. And we've already learned to avoid massive exposure–you know, it's against the law to build a house anywhere near a bunch of high voltage transformers."

"If not electricity...?"

"A certain kind of electricity, actually one with the most minimal, not maximal, voltage. One that hasn't been around long enough for us to adjust to. *Wi-fi*. It's everywhere--cell phones, computers, television, cars, houses, businesses...you have to look long and hard to avoid it. Used to be we'd search for restaurants to find free wi-fi; now it's everywhere. Show me a kid who isn't carrying wi-fi in his pocket, right next to his gonads; who doesn't sleep with it next to his bed; who isn't hooked up to it at least ten hours a day."

"And yet not everyone's coming down with the symptoms."

"Right now, but not tomorrow. The key word again is exposure–over-exposure, over a long period of time. Remember, we haven't had wi-fi for that long; wait another forty years and see what happens."

Frank started to speak, then decided to let Bert continue. "The few individuals who've come down with it could be like the frogs on the pond who die when the water gets too polluted. Or the Pacific coast abalone; I hear they're disappearing. I think the term is species indicators. Harbingers of impending doom."

"You think those who suffer from EMS today are harbingers of what we'll all be experiencing, given time?"

"Maybe not all. Maybe only ten to fifteen percent. My point is, it could be coming, but science may ignore all the signs until it's too late to do anything."

Frank remained silent, thinking. Bert continued. "Right now, we haven't built up enough of a critical mass to be worried. It took fifteen years of constant bombardment for Brie to build up to her collapse, and she had other emotional and physical contributing factors. Today's teenagers will grow into their twenties and thirties, and by that time–say 2035–we'll know whether their mega-exposure to electromagnetic radiation causes or doesn't cause them to develop severe cases of electromagnetic sensitivity. Well, it could take longer, but I think the outside date would be 2050."

Frank nodded. "Yeah, maybe we should take it more seriously."

"Sweden does, plus other Scandinavian countries. Don't ask me why, but they do."

"I vaguely remember reading that. Yeah, I have done a bit of research. But yes, my mind was closed at the time. I'll try to do better."

"You're the scientist. Is there any way of studying the matter now?" Excited, Bert couldn't wait for an answer, so kept talking. "I can think of one obvious way, but I might be the only one in the country to think of it. Make a carefully controlled study of a thousand Bluetooth wearers--the things plugged into your ears that keep you connected sixteen hours a day to the internet so you can talk and listen to music at the same time. These devices next to your brain should be the most damaging–if electromagnetic impulses do cause damage."

"Over how long a time would you make the test?" Frank asked, then Bert answered, "The experts know all that, and of course know how to manipulate the conclusions. But let's assume they didn't rig it, and it turns out only ten percent develop severe symptoms. Maybe no big deal. Twenty percent would definitely create alarm. Wouldn't it already be too late? Besides, what could we do?"

Frank waved his here-goes arms and picked up the talk. "Ok, I'll go with you. Let's assume these studies, conducted before 2025, definitively prove mega-exposure a causal agent. Within ten years that knowledge would be released--after a big-time lag produced by the electronics lobby. By the middle of the century the country might have decided to do something. As you just said, what could we do? Eliminate cell phones? Regulate them? Rebuild them so that they don't use wi-fi? Tear down the hundreds of thousands of towers now installed throughout America so pervasively that there isn't a square mile that isn't totally wired-up?"

"My point exactly. Nothing to do, it's already too late right now."

Frank went on with his scenario. "It would take another twenty-five or more years to come up with some kind of solution–although I can't imagine what that could be. By 2075 half the population would be disabled. Couldn't work because they can't survive in a wi-fi intensive atmosphere. What'll they all do, move to Mexico? By then it'll be all wired-up too, if it isn't now. What happens when we lose even ten percent of the working population, let alone twenty to thirty to forty percent?

"That's why this is one health crisis that could prove fatal to the entire country. We'd have to junk everything it took us the entire century to build up, and no one's willing to do that."

Frank shook his head. "Right now, it sounds unlikely. Let's hope the scientists who hypothesize an electro-magnetic personality, not the actual waves, are right. That's far-fetched, though, unless they mean something more like a predisposition. Anyway, given how the electronics industry keeps burgeoning, I guess you're right, within forty or fifty years, people will be experiencing a couple hundred times their exposure now. There'll be no way to escape massive doses of electromagnetic radiation. We'll just have to hope it won't predispose everyone."

Bert ordered another Dos Equis and some tacos to split. "Well, we might have just predicted the end of the world. But you sound like you've done more than a little casual research. What's up?"

Frank scratched his nose, didn't know whether he should tell his friend what he'd learned. "Well, I put off telling you about this article I found. I wanted to tell you right away, started to several times, but just didn't feel the time was right. Don't ask me why. Anyway, now might be the right time."

Bert got a puzzled look and Frank told the long story, ending by saying as soon as they got back he'd give him a copy of the interview.

"You think it's just a coincidence that your friend's sister's symptoms were the same as Brie's?" Bert asked.

"That's the scary part. There's no way either one could have heard about the other; no possibility of collusion or influence. It's just too unlikely. For two people to get slammed from the same computer environment-- experience identical etiologies...."

"I guess you do believe after all?"

"Hell, Bert, I don't know what to believe. My head still wants to tell me it's got to be psychological. But then I think about the chances of two people suddenly dropping unconscious onto their computers after the same continuous exposure. Zero chances. And you don't fake going unconscious, especially when you know you'll get fired. It makes no sense."

"How many cases like this would it take to convince you?"

"Maybe only these two, given the impossible probabilities. Unless, of course, Brie had heard about Becky–but there's no way she could have. You decide after reading the interview."

"Where does that leave us? Does it lend any credence to our apocalyptical scenario?"

"I don't know, still need more time to digest it...and do more research. But I will say it's scary."

They finished their drinks and returned to the hotel.

The last day's round of golf cheered them up, and they left for home. Unfortunately, half-way back they got so engrossed in current events that they failed to check the speedometer. The police woman didn't, and the siren wailed. When she pulled them over, she said it was too bad her radar registered 86. Had it been 84, they'd be below the line. The line that turns a $200 ticket into a $400 ticket.

CHAPTER FIVE: UNEXPECTED REVERSAL

BERT SAT STARING AT THE COMPUTER. He hadn't written much new since the boat trip that he, Brie, Frank and Marsha had taken. His mind drifted back to his birthday on Penland. Was that some kind of turning point? Were bad things coming? Nothing in his life had prepared him for this volatile woman...not even the novels he'd read about worse things. Maybe they hadn't been meant for each other after all...he'd just been misreading the signs. One day he'd know, but that was little consolation. Now he had no idea what to do. He decided to reread what Frank had given him.

As Frank had said, the similarities were amazing and scary. He was particularly taken by Becky's theory about EMS: "My theory is that once you become affected by the radiation, something happens to the nervous system and it recognizes the radiation as a threat and then reacts to warn the body that something is wrong. While the first reaction was to wireless, I then started to react to anything with vibrations, anything that the nervous system detected, so I started to be affected by electricity, then light and sound." That explained what had always bothered him—how she could be affected not just by cell phones but also by sirens, bright lights, loud noises, motorboats. Of course all the trouble could be coming from her head, not to her head.

The week after my blissful but damaged birthday on Penland, I tried to talk Brie into staying overnight at my place. "Why not, it's much safer than yours, the walls aren't paper thin, they shield electricity better, and I can turn off all the appliances, even the fridge at night. And if you're worried about neighbors knowing, they won't. I'll be picking you up, so it'll only be my same car parked there."

No answer.

"I don't understand. It's ok for us to sleep together in a tent–on an island or in your backyard–but not in a house. What's with that?"

Again, no answer. Then, finally, "Ok." But a reluctant ok.

The previous time we'd come to my house for dinner, not the night, I had carefully unplugged everything except the microwave–and then, horror of horrors, since microwaves are one of the worst offenders for EMS, I'd flipped it on for a quick coffee zap while she was sitting ten feet away in the dining room. It hit her immediately, and I felt terrible. Our whole day was ruined.

So today I went ahead of her, unplugging everything except the fridge, which I put on high until she arrived, when it would get unplugged. I changed all my squiggly florescent bulbs for incandescents, unplugged the radio next to my bed, and made sure all fans were off.

We had a good dinner, having cooked the flank steak outside and then spending most of our time sitting quietly on the porch. Night came and I coaxed her into visiting the bedroom. Our lovemaking activities, whether at her house, in a tent, or at mine, always seem to include Rowdy. We can never keep him off the bed, but at least he always hugs the far side, never moving close the way he does with me normally. And what's much stranger, no matter how many times we've made love, we always start the same, saying it feels like we've never known each other yet a couple of hours later saying it feels like we've never been apart. Is this common?

We had an amazing time from nine-thirty right up to midnight, when she got up, took a shower, and got dressed. I had to do the same and drive her home, returning to an already cold bed.

Two weeks after the tumultuous birthday event and one week after our first night in my house everything suddenly reversed direction again.

The news hit like a ton of bricks. Our night together had convinced me we'd stitched things together. But then along came another problematic lake cruise. Brie insisted we kayak to the last unexplored place on the North Carolina side of the lake. It was a long five hours of continuous paddling, but on the most beautiful October afternoon imaginable.

My arms were killing me by the time we stopped on Penland for lunch. She appeared unphased by the long paddle, immediately started walking the beachfront. I tagged along behind, lost in thought. Why didn't she go to the campsite to look around? Why didn't she respond when I carried on about how good it was to come back? I finally caught up with her and spoke more loudly. "It seemed so long ago we were here, but really wasn't that long. Does the place feel different to you also?" No answer, just a head nod.

While I went to gather firewood for a lunch fire she disappeared up the beach. When she did return, she declined putting on her fins for a swim out to the buoy. I didn't want to; the lake would have turned cold by now. But I screwed up my courage, put on my new birthday fins, and swam out 150 yards and back. Had to show her again I didn't need to wait for her lead; was no longer shy about making that cold plunge. She smiled faintly when I got back but said nothing. Later, during another brief stop on an unnamed small island, she turned away when I spoke. I knew she'd heard.

Dragging the kayaks up the ramp into the Honda, I noticed her scowling, not at me but at nothing in particular. She'd been glum all day, maybe hurting physically. More than once she'd complained about being cold; maybe that was why she hadn't jumped in the lake and was acting so distant.

When we got back to her house in time, hopefully, for a cup of hot chocolate around the firepit, she turned away again. Kept examining the horses in the far pasture. I didn't volunteer to stay, said something about getting together maybe tomorrow or the next day.

"Not tomorrow, I have too many things to do."

"Wednesday?"

"You're busy then."

"Thursday? Friday?"

"Maybe. We'll see."

Ok, so it wasn't her catching a cold or feeling bad from EMS. I drove home perplexed and worried late into the night. We hadn't held hands, let alone kissed for what seemed an eternity. I couldn't get her to smile; her bright eyes had turned dark.

When the call came the next afternoon, I wasn't surprised. Her rare phone calls had always been hard to decipher because she had to stand so far away from the speaker. All I heard was a strident tone and the words, "Kayak I've put outside the garage door."

"What, you want me to come pick it up?"

"Yes, now. Klepto's outside and could run off with one of your bags."

Pause. "And that's it? Pick up my stuff? It's over?"

160

"You just need to come and pick up your stuff."

"I can't make it right now, maybe in an hour or so." I looked off toward the fourth hole. No incentive to finish nine holes now.

"Klepto's roaming around outside."

"I get it! I hope you have some note of explanation. This is sudden, to say the least."

"I do," then the phone going dead.

I finished the nine holes, expecting to muff every other shot, but didn't. The late afternoon sun was shining golden in the blue sky as I tossed the bag into the Metro's trunk. I couldn't bring myself to go over to her place alone, so drove over to the storage shed where poker and backgammon buddy Jim would be cleaning and repacking.

It was already 5:00, past time for the place to be closed, but thankfully Jim was still at it. He'd been kicked out of his rental when they had to sell it and was trying to get organized. Sometime soon he'd be moving in with me.

"Can you go somewhere with me for a half hour to help me pick up some stuff?"

He immediately recognized my strained voice and put down the box. "Let's go." Then glanced at his boxes and said he'd have to put them inside before the place closed. He'd meet me at my house in half an hour.

I changed into some long pants and sat down at the computer. Had to leave some kind of note at her place before reading what she'd probably written. Since she has no computer or cell phone, we have to communicate the old way. I wrote my note and revised it twice.

Dear Brie,

I write this before reading your letter–before reading it, obviously, since this is typed. After reading it, if you did leave one, I know I'd have too many things to say. So here goes.

In case you might have forgotten, I'd like back four things: *Narnia*, my other two books, the love poems, and my chair. Maybe they're there now with the kayak. I will stop by tomorrow afternoon to pick them up: you could leave them on your porch swing. I won't knock.

When Andrew calls about the praise songs, I'll give him your phone number. You'll remember, he's the one I drove all over to find for your outdoor worship. I thought you'd appreciate that, but apparently not.

I'm still totally baffled–I do hope your letter explains things. I can only assume it has to do with the drinking: maybe you can't believe God can change me, but the blessing has already made me strong. I hope you share your blessing request with someone. You need to do that; it can't be done alone.

162

I will not get sentimental here; I'll eventually overcome the shock and loss. I know you well enough to know that you've decided what you think is best for you. Your health is the most important thing to you right now, and apparently you thought I was getting in the way of it. You must have thought love gets in the way of healing.

I'm guessing your letter will close by saying that you will continue to pray for me. You know I continue to seek your full healing and ultimate EMS ministry. I've been praying that you would get stronger day by day. Now, as always, I have faith in your total recovery.

I close as you always do, in God's love, and asking if I have done something wrong, that you will forgive me. Maybe even take the time to tell me what it was.

Always, Bert

While the printer was busy printing, Jim arrived, saying he was taking me out to dinner. "To the Orient Bowl. It's the best." On the way there we talked about his upcoming move.

First, we had to pick up my stuff. I tried to explain what had happened, reluctant to use that ugly phrase, "she dumped me." Jim didn't know much about our relationship, but said he wasn't able to believe it. He probably still remembered her only by the camping trip to Jackrabbit--although since then I'd told him a thing or two about her ups and downs.

163

We found the kayak and bags carefully stacked in her driveway, loaded them into my car, stopped at her mailbox to deposit the letter, drove home, and threw all my stuff into a corner of the carport. Then left for the restaurant.

Later that night Jim gave me a long stare. "I hate to say it, but you might be lucky."

"Lucky?"

"It's probably better this way."

"Do you think something's wrong with her?"

"Do I. Looks like she's a little bi-polar. You know, one minute on fire, then another, glum. It's not right. It's not normal what she did. I've never seen you dead drunk, no one has. You know, isn't a guy allowed to drink? So long as he doesn't hurt anyone?"

I tried to smile and utter a platitude about men never being able to understand what women want, but instead found myself prodding Jim to say more, wanting him to paint her black.

Later that evening I screwed up my courage to read the short letter she'd put with my stuff.

"Dear Bert,

I can no longer sit by and watch you self-destruct. You are in denial and I can't be part of that process. Its your choice whether you admit it to yourself and seek help.

I'm fighting with everything within to get well–it is too stressful to try to rescue you and me. I can't do it.

I will see you at church on Sunday if you are there the Sundays I'm able to attend–I will wave to you if I see you on the lake. I have nothing farther to give.

I will continue to pray for you. I pray you will choose life and sobriety. But again, thats your choice.

I don't wish to have further contact at this time.

In His name, Brie

P.S. As you know I'm an all or nothing person–I gave you my all and it simply wasn't enough. Time for both of us to heal from lifes happenings."

CHAPTER SIX: SELF DESTRUCTION

AS SOON AS FRANK BROACHED THE SUBJECT, he knew he'd made a mistake but couldn't go back. Marsha pulled her chair closer to his tv chair and said nothing, anger in her eyes.

"I don't know why I didn't tell you earlier. I don't know why I didn't tell him earlier. Hell, I wish I'd never read the damn article."

"But you did. And that should have told you something, Frank. Something about being too stubborn. I thought you were supposed to be his good friend."

"I was. I mean I am. It was no big deal. We went on to have a good talk about the whole EMS scare; about what could happen if lots of people start getting it."

"Of course they'll get it. I know nothing about it, just what Brie told me. But she's no kook. If she got it, others will. She's just more sensitive than most. But that's not the point, Frank. The point is that you didn't use your head. You, the psychologist."

"You're making a mountain out of a molehill. It didn't bother him in the slightest; in fact, I know he appreciated the news. It just bothers you...and I can't for the world understand why."

"Because it will bother Brie, remind her of what she's going through. That's who I'm worried about."

"You've got it backward. She'll love it--it'll convince her she's not alone!" Frank tried to keep his voice down.

"I don't, *don't* want to argue, Frank. That's not good for either of us. But you don't always know what you're talking about."

"Ok I don't want to argue either. Let's just talk, quietly."

"Much better. Quietly. Where were we?"

"We were talking about the article—the interview with an old client of mine." He scowled, then corrected: "with the sister of a client."

"I'm thinking about Brie. Look at her, don't just look at her condition, look at her. She's suffering."

"Here we go again. That she's suffering is pretty obvious. Hell, it's the main reason Bert hooked up with her...to help her. He really loves her, you know. In fact...."

"I believe you. But just the same, he's not helping her get over her suffering any."

What would you know, he almost said, but changed it: "So how is he not helping?"

"She told me about two times. The first was when he did something to get her mad enough to paddle over to the island and camp alone, for maybe two nights. She could have gotten in big trouble. There are lots of rednecks out there, men who think nothing of bashing women."

"I doubt it. But he didn't cause her to go; she reacted foolishly."

"But her condition...."

"You can't blame everything on the electromagnetic thing. She's unstable."

"That's my point, she needs help, not provocation."

He held his breath. "You said he hurt her two times. What was the second?"

"He took her on this long drive to the skyway that goes over to Tennessee. They ended up parked next to a huge electricity plant. And it took them hours to drive back. It was very thoughtless of him. Thoughtless!"

Frank was having a hard time staying patient, wondering why she was reacting so strongly; wondering what this all had to do with them. He tried to bring her back, gently and quietly. "I understand, Marsha, but still don't see what this has to do with us. Don't get me wrong, I'm not...."

"Everything to do with us!" She rose, walked around her chair, then sat back down. "You're his best friend, and now I seem to be *her* best friend. Maybe her only really true friend. We have to be thinking of them, not us."

"I am, Marsha, I am. And *you* are. What are you really saying?"

She took a few minutes to answer. "I'm saying that she needs space. Like me, I need it too." She paused, then decided not to continue.

Frank wanted a cigar but wasn't allowed to smoke in the house. He asked her if she wanted a glass of wine or anything and went to the kitchen. He needed time to cool off; time to find a way of bringing her back to reality.

"Ok, now we're getting somewhere," he said when he came back ten minutes later bearing a tray of crackers, cheese, and two half-full wine glasses.

"Thank you, dear," she said, offering a polite smile.

"What you're really wanting to discuss, I gather, is me. I'm doing something wrong...or not doing something."

"That's the psychologist in you speaking. But yes, you're right."

"I've noticed something not quite right for some time now. Even before that boat trip, which I know set you back just like it did her."

"You're always so observant, Frankie dear."

"Please don't Frankie me, you know I hate it. Just when we were starting to talk...honestly."

"I'm sorry. I guess I have been on edge. *Am* on edge. Maybe it's that time of the month."

You can't go there, he thought. Those times passed long ago. But how to bring her around?

"Maybe we should consider going to counseling," she volunteered.

That was the wrong direction. "Why? Is it that bad?"

"It might be. For us."

"Not for me. I still love you just as much, Marsha."

"And I love you. But it might help to clear some ground, ease some tension."

They continued talking into the night, getting nowhere.

Bert hadn't seen Frank since their boat trip, and Brie since their self-destruct. At his home, dog sleeping underneath his computer desk, he was confused. Before, there had just been Suzanne and him. Then Brie and him. Next, he'd confided in Frank, rehashing his problems with Brie, as if those problems existed in another space and time. And more recently he'd started writing about what was happening in the present, not re-reading or revising something written in the past. Sometimes referring to himself as "he," not

"I." What was happening? Was he trying to write some kind of novel about someone else? Why had he kept it up? Well, now he'd have to stop; she'd thrown him out. Maybe he needed to throw her out. But right now, he had to write something else to get it out of his system. A letter that he hoped she'd read carefully. Before starting, he reread her letter one last time, getting so angry he passed right over the poor grammar.

Hello Brie,

"No more contact now; maybe I'll see you in church when I'm able to go, or wave to you if I see you on the lake." I guess that also means you want no letters from me. You don't have to read this but I have to write it.

Your brief letter, certainly not written in haste because you'd been processing your decision for several days, maybe weeks, was most cruel. Not the Brie I've come to know, which is why I asked for my poems back. They were written to another of your many Gemini faces, the loving and caring Brie I thought I'd come to know so well these past five months.

That Brie would have waited another three weeks to see if I could hold true to my promise of cold turkeying for a month. Or at the most, just told me we both needed to cool things for a spell...as we did before during that other spat.

Instead, this harsh Brie, like some angry landlord, simply evicted me, piled up all my stuff outside her garage. I guess this act symbolically assured you that no part of me would ever get close to you again.

It was hard enough seeing all my camping, hiking, swimming, cooking, and kayaking gear carefully bagged up (you always said you were, if anything, anal), but that final bag I opened really hurt. Inside were Rowdy's food, biscuits, life preserver vest, and four balls. It's one thing to cast aside your lover but another to toss away your close doggy friend--the one who couldn't stop jumping up and down inside the car every time we approached your house.

I guess I'll never know how much you cared for me; you couldn't bring yourself to declare your love in words. I always thought your actions spoke louder than words. But had you really cared for me, you couldn't have written what you did, saying you can't sit by and watch me self-destruct, that I'm in denial and in need of help. I assume you were referring to what you call my drinking problem, not me in general. Your idea of my drinking problem, that is.

What you wrote is not only angry and mean-spirited, it makes no sense. You never doubt God; you're one of the few people I can say that about. For the past four or five years you've had to depend entirely on him, something that's cemented faith into your inner core. But here you're doubting God's ability to give *me* the help I need. His blessing of healing apparently means little to you. Or maybe you think I haven't asked for it or haven't received it and never will.

You know I didn't lie about asking for his blessing. Or maybe you think I lied about how easy it was dropping cigarettes, which I've told you many times before. Maybe you doubted that also; you probably think I'm just another man like all the other unstable ones you've known.

The fact is that I asked for the blessing from the bottom of my heart, one of the six steps Russell spoke about that I wrote down for you that night when I came back to tell you my good news. I guess the bigger question now is one I'm having a hard time asking because I don't want to hurt you...even if I am still angry over your hurting me. Have you asked yet for your blessing? I encouraged you to formulate it–down to the specifics, which I hoped would include something like this: 'because I still can't get rid of the fear associated with seeing mega-high wire lines, cell phones, or fluorescent lights, please make me physically and emotionally stronger each day that passes, so that my fear will gradually dissipate and I can ask for the blessing of full health from the very bottom of my heart, without reservations or doubts.' Why didn't you ask me to help you give the blessing? You know how eager I was to help you do it. You know you can't do the blessing step alone. It's pretty obvious you are the one in denial, not me. No, I shouldn't write those harsh words.

Well, I'm almost done. I'm not going to add a postscript like yours about my also being an all or nothing person. If you don't know that, you've never known me. But I don't believe the rest of your sentence: "*I gave you my all and it simply wasn't enough. Time for both of us to heal from life's happenings."*

That was exactly what we were doing together, dear. The proof of the pudding being the wonderful birthday card you made for me last month, a perpetual card of cut-out pictures of mountains, lakes, waterfalls, maps of western North Carolina, golf courses, hiking boots, life preservers, dinner tables, and candles, plus the best, a bigger cut-out of a woman's red lips saying "To Lord Bert. Love is contagious...I caught it from you. Lady Brie."

In addition to the sensuous pictures, magic words--four pages of 300 or more thin one-liners you'd clipped from various magazines you always save: what we found–mountains and streams; non-stop adventure has never been more relaxing; beaches uncrowded; back-packing; more camping; play in the center of it all; what's not to love; makes you smile; unlock your full potential; fire up the grill; laugh; the one and only, go for it! and dare to be happy.

Not to mention those private inner two pages: the thought of throwing on a bikini makes you...; Prince Charming; a nice balance of boyish and sexy; because we just want to; nibbles at; heart; you made it the best play date ever; now nudes come alive in the buff; love story; fantasy pants; and most telling of all, the two words on the back page--love to love and soul restoration. I'm still opening them and could be for another year...if I don't throw them all away.

The birthday card, the most personal, intimate, best one I ever received, hit everything square on the head: 'Healing play and healing love.' Don't tell me we weren't getting the healing we needed from life's happening!

So now I must stop. But I can't help wondering: perhaps your half-page letter of explanation (explanation?) is not to be taken at face value. Perhaps it was carefully calculated to provoke me to succeed in my vow. A challenge: "If I tell Bert he can't stop, he will." If this was your intention, I assume you'd be dropping me now only with the intention of our eventually getting back together. I'd like to believe this but can't; it's not in your personality profile. I'd like to believe it because I know I'll miss you dearly, and certainly don't need another grief added to my life. But I am human. Why would someone who's been thrown under the table want to come back asking for more?

Bert

Two days later he woke early to attend the boys' and men's church breakfast with Jim, meeting three new men he suspected he could get to enjoy, plus two he'd already known. He'd already discovered the Episcopal church has a reputation for being the friendliest in the area…this area being one with a church on every block. The same church she'd gone to for healing sessions and he'd gone to for his no-drinking blessing.

Later he rummaged around the house, delaying chores and trying to decide what else to do. At last he jumped in the blue car with Rowdy to head off to the golf course. As they walked up to the back nine, a through-cart pulled up. He drove back to the front nine...only to find five carts cued up. He had to settle for smashing balls on the range. Anything to push depression demons toward the back of his head.

While he was slamming balls, he conjured up a list of good things she did for him before breaking his heart. The list got so long he had to find a tree to sit under—after going back to his car for paper and pen.

You taught me to stand tall, walk proud, and kick ass.

You taught me to remember to say grace before eating, and to drink less.

Your good example helped me enjoy many things I'd disliked or ignored: swimming in a cold lake, sleeping night after night on a thin pad or four-dollar plastic float, keeping a relatively spotless kitchen, throwing out spoiled food or frozen food from three months back.

Your caresses gave me infinite pleasure and rejuvenated my tired body. Your feminine soul awakened, enriched, and challenged my masculine soul.

Your godly spirit charged my lukewarm spirit and helped me open up to others more; helped me think of others more.

Your habit of looking for good points instead of flaws almost taught me to stop judging others for being obese, rude, or careless.

You taught Rowdy to become more civilized, if not less rowdy and obsessive over tennis balls.

Your inability to watch tv or stay for long periods inside my house helped me need fewer modern diversions. Of course, that was mostly because I was over at your house playing Skip-Bo, talking, sitting around the firepit, eating, or smooching.

You educated me in the value of organic food and necessity of reading labels, not that I stopped buying good bargains on regular food.

Your compulsive and sometimes anal behavior made me more attentive to matters of dress; even got me to get rid of the bucket hat and purchase a nice macho Aussie hat.

Your enthusiasm prompted me to write a dozen pretty decent love poems.

Your unpredictable, at times distracting, behavior nevertheless kept me on my toes, always looking for new ways to please.

Your fear of bears and intruders, but not snakes, wasps, frogs, bees, or large pasture rats, taught me nothing in particular.

I could go on, but to what point? You aren't there to read this, and I know I'll never send it to you.

After he got home, he phoned Lynn to say he'd be coming early for Thanksgiving, and then blurted out his news. He could visualize her nodding while listening. When he got to the part about Brie's always being off and on, Lynn said it sounded like she had a borderline personality, quoting from a book she'd read: "I love you so much I have to leave you."

His daughter, a counselor, should know, but Bert wanted confirmation. He'd have to talk to his son Jed to hear what he said. But when he called, his phone went to voice-answer.

The next day he played pickleball for two hours, sweating out the poison. Many of the couples he'd gotten to know had already started drifting off to Florida. He looked forward to playing all winter in the new indoor rec center courts; enough full-timers would stick around. Fred, who'd partnered with him at last month's senior games, had invited him to kayak down a stretch of the Hiawassee, but called last night to cancel. Too many things to do before leaving.

In the afternoon he called Jed to unload his sad story and learn when he'd be arriving in Dallas for Thanksgiving. Feeling stupid all the time, an old-timer like him carrying on about a romance gone bad. Jed listened without giving advice or much response. Eventually they switched to their favorite phone talk, good and bad swing thoughts, whether or not he should purchase the new Bio-Cell driver and fairway wood, when the Steamboat Springs course would close, and what Jed would do to stay sane once the snow came, which would be soon.

Later in the afternoon Jim got back from something and they took Rowdy to walk the dam. The same walk he'd taken such a short time ago with her, laughing while pointing to the sun shining on the mountains and clouds piling overhead. All he could see was the same dam, the same sun, the same lake, the same trees, the same woman. And feel the same damn feelings.

He tried to keep up with Jim's talk, but could only hear the patter inside his own head. He'd tried to let go. How good it would be to be free. He'd call the realtor and tell her to reduce the house. Get away, get on with it. Go to the desert paradise. Not too old yet.

But how he missed her. Was that a yellow kayak out there toward Penland? How could she do it, be so happy to go it alone? Dear God, please take care of her. She's got to be as confused and hurt as I, even though she's the one who brought it on. Or is she smiling and talking to strangers, happy to be independent again?

He could forgive her, if only to watch her smile and step into his arms. He could put up with her anal, if not compulsive behavior, if only to feel once more her body press down upon his. But could he put up with another slam?

No. Could he stay in North Carolina after selling his house? Where? Even had things worked out, she wouldn't invite him to stay in hers. He wouldn't want to step outside every time she got a family phone call or watch her enact her methodic routine of sauna, oxygen, and writing endless letters. Not to mention driving himself crazy looking for signs of improvement or listening to her bring up another repetition of her old EMS episodes.

What would they do during the long winter nights when they couldn't play outside? Sit on the floor playing Skip- Bo repeatedly? Listen to each other talk about nothing, now they'd run through all the important talk too many times already? Winter time demands good music, television for the sports events, and restaurants, not sofa sitting and chit-chat. It's one thing to wish back stolen pleasure and another to get realistic about the dangers of boredom and deprivation of modern conveniences and necessities.

Were they ever soul mates or were they kidding themselves? True, their bodies fit perfectly together, as they'd so often repeated while intricately entwined, but bodies are not souls. Was the focus really just on sexual pleasure?

The following Sunday, while kneeling at the altar after the 8:00 a.m. mass at the Good Shepherd Episcopal, which he'd decided to attend in addition to the 11:00 service at his Presbyterian church, he asked for two blessings: one for grief and one for forgiveness. To forgive her in case he hadn't, as he told himself he had, and to forgive himself for whatever he needed to. And for God to forgive him for continuing to be so self-absorbed. Most of yesterday afternoon he'd tried to pray for her, not himself, while out walking the golf course, but then before falling asleep he kept replaying his submerged anger at her for being so thoughtless and cruel.

He didn't want her to hurt the way he was hurting. It would be best if she didn't come back to the Presbyterian church. She probably wouldn't. Or did he really want her to hurt a little? If she really had acted callously, it might do her good to be snubbed by some of the ladies. No, they'd all go over to her side. Who knows? Leave her alone; she'll either come or not on her own.

He sat for forty-five minutes outside on his porch watching the fog lift and examining the leaves, now almost completely turned. After church someone had talked about how good it was coming back from Europe to these wonderful mountains. Yesterday he couldn't get enough of them, plus the trees. But now the leaves kept sending him back to last October's former grief–walking the dogs in the countryside while waiting for Suzanne to die. Crying, walking, sobbing while walking into God's beauty.

Jim returned after dinner and they sat down to another game of backgammon. Jim asked how it went in church. "She never looked at me; I never looked toward her, just sat in my pew."

"Better that way, buddy. Life's like that. I mean, you know…."

"Bert scowled. "I went there to learn something. Didn't learn anything. I still know nothing."

"Yeah, you did, you just can't bring it up. You want it both ways, guy. You want her gone so you can move out, get it on with your life. Move on out to sunny Arizona. But you also want her back. Natural, no one likes being lonely. But you can't have it both ways, dude."

He thought Jim right, and went on to beat him by more than 320 points–almost an impossibility. Tomorrow another day. More autumn beauty, more golf, more grief. It was very good to have Jim there. Too soon he'd be off to the orient; what would he do during the long lonely winter?

He woke late to find Jim in the living room announcing coffee was ready. They immediately pulled out the backgammon set, started playing, and kept playing most of the morning.

Next week the highlight of Wednesday was shooting three birdies on the front nine with Frank, putting him at even par, plus 41 for the back nine. Better than he'd ever done. Maybe he wasn't hurting so much after all. Maybe he'd become a man again. Then on the way home while driving past the road to her house he thought about turning in but immediately replayed his promise to let go. Instead, he stopped at Safeway to buy a good bottle of Riesling for the afternoon backgammon game, plus another bottle of red for cooking shish kebabs.

He climbed into bed at 11:30, feeling a little guilt over too much wine. But the anger and disappointment were starting to wear off. In a few weeks or months, he'd forget her taste, touch, smell, smile. Jim had assured him there were plenty of women out there waiting for a good man like him, but he just wanted the right one, and mistakenly thought Brie was it. He needed to know for absolute certain whether she was or wasn't. He turned the radio on to the PBS late night jazz station and sulked. Tomorrow a new day.

One thing Jim said hit hard. "You were trying to capture a wild bird. Just let it fly." The words didn't sound like Jim; he must have memorized them...but they spoke truth...if, indeed, she was some kind of wild bird.

Thirty members came to his last pancake Sunday at church, everyone raving about the blueberries from his garden. Afterward Mary took him aside and just had to know what was wrong. News flies fast in a small church. He changed the subject, told her about the recliner he'd found for her, suggesting they check it out. His affair affected so many people, including this older newcomer to the church who'd taken to both of them. And after the church session Mindy assured him she'd be visiting Brie in the afternoon and would call him. She'd find out what was up with Brie. All he had to do was wait.

She didn't call, but he called her, at 4:00. No surprises, Brie had told her the same thing she'd told him, that alcohol had changed him; she couldn't help him heal. He was a drunk like all the others. Shit! Examples? If she were rational, she'd have to give some.

Mindy, of all people, trying to recover from her own husband leaving her--her husband a bone-fide dry drunk. No help there, though Mindy was careful to say she hadn't and wouldn't side with either of them.

It is what it is, Bert mumbled: Brie grabbing at straws to make him into a villain. If not that, just a man she had to leave. Why? Because something deep inside told her she was getting too close; told her it was time to pull back.

And he was trying to hear something deep inside him telling it was time to thank the stars he was free.

Anything else? he asked himself. Remorse? No! No more excuses. It's over. Over. Tomorrow he'd reduce the house by another $5,000. Arizona beckons!

CHAPTER SEVEN: REPRIEVE

LIFE AT THE CONYERS, GEORGIA, Monastery of the Holy Spirit. Bert sat outside on the unmown grass, spiral notebook on his lap in case he wanted to start writing. He'd already fallen in love with this place his pastor Linda frequently visited. This time she'd arranged for him and two others from church to accompany her.

A quiet, calm, early November day. The weather, suburb fall weather, not winter. "If this place can't tell me what I need to know," Bert scribbled, "what I'm capable of, then nothing can. Such perfect, perfect timing. Thank you! And now I'm off to another daily prayer session."

Pray, pray. Hand it over. Write poems. Watch birds fly. Attend the sessions on Thomas Merton and Mary Oliver, even if the lecturer is too academic. Heal. Eat meals in the no-talking dining room. Relax in the monastery's sanctuary gazing up at the beautiful blue stained-glass windows.

What peace! Solitude. No talking, just walking around looking at the trees, lake, birds, sky, bonsai plants in the greenhouse where the monks grow and tend. Can you imagine living your entire life here? he asked himself, immediately answering he knew he couldn't.

After Vespers he went to his tiny bedroom to write a poem:

Silent November at the Monastery

vaulted arches march mute in line
hold bright glass stained blue and

solemnity enters into time
eternity appears, to disappear

listen! stillness spreads across the lawn
watch! night appears, robed men bow down

now hear! bells ring, love speaks again

Back in North Carolina, Bert fell easily into his routine. Morning pickleball, then saying goodbye to Jim--off for a few months travel in southeast Asia. Next, heading for the Ridges. After shooting six over par he thought about stopping at Brie's on the way home, not having seen or talked to her for a month. He wanted to share his monastery experience and give her the poem he'd started to like. He turned left on Meyers

Chapel Road and right on Brook Road, but before arriving, his spirit told him it was not time.

He waited a week and drove over to talk, but again something stopped him. He'd lost his anger but not his confusion. Thoughts about leaving for that magic destination Arizona hadn't left. If so, why was he so anxious to talk to her? And why did he keep getting stopped?

Sunday came and he finally decided church would be the right place. He went late and immediately headed toward the back pew. Something told him she'd be there. If she refused to acknowledge him, he'd have his answer. What if she was too sick to come?

He found her quietly sitting in her customary pew, tapped her on the shoulder and asked if it was ok to sit next to her. She nodded indifferently. Then Jill came over to talk to her, so he walked back into the entryway. When Jill left, he sat down and gave her the handouts from the monastery.

After a few minutes, he snuck a quick glance, to find her eyes watering. The music started and both looked forward. The music stopped and he looked back to her. She returned his look, revealing nothing. He put his hand gently on hers. "Is this ok?" She nodded, this time not so indifferently. Her eyes relaxed. His stomach relaxed. The guitar music started again. They sat together throughout the service, not talking or looking, but still holding hands. Is everything going to be okay? he wondered. Are we being brought back together? Is she going to become my Brie again?

The service ended and he asked her if she'd like to drive up to Fire's Creek for a picnic. She agreed, and he rushed home to fix sandwiches. When he drove up to her place, she climbed into the Element, Rowdy of course on her lap.

Up at the picnic table where they'd sat together two months ago, they finally opened up. Bert skirted some things but tried try to be honest, admitting how angry, frustrated, confused he'd been. She finally admitted her own hurt, saying she'd gotten mad at herself for shooting herself in the foot. She laughed, saying she was so upset that she started attacking the weeds in her driveway. Sitting on the ground with her gloves on, pulling and pulling weeds three hours a day for three days. Little Joe drove by shaking his head, convinced she'd gone crazy.

"Then I started missing you," she said.

Bert couldn't believe it. "I thought you'd given up on me entirely. You *missed* me?"

"Just because I was furious at you doesn't mean I stopped caring for you."

Tears. More tears and then hugs. Bert talked about the monastery. He told her how he'd finally given his anger and frustration to God and let go.

Then they hiked up the creek, holding hands and smiling. The creek? What creek? Later in the afternoon they went back to her house and made passionate love until midnight.

Shortly after their magical reunion, in spite of or maybe because of the flu shot he had in late October, Bert contracted an unmanageable cough. Was it the virulent form of flu that had been working its way around western North Carolina? He ignored whatever it was, as he tended to ignore all maladies, but eventually had to do something. He visited the doctor before leaving for the Dallas family reunion, so was able to bring antibiotics with him. Not that they'd do much good; he'd be consuming too much beer and wine during Thanksgiving week to let them work.

He took the hacking with him on the plane, muffling it with his sweater and explaining to the quiet lady sitting next to him that he was no longer contagious; it was just sinus drainage, not the flu. Which he hoped it was; his doctor didn't know. And then carried whatever it was to Dallas, where it went underground for a few hours, but resurfaced after dinner...driving him into his bedroom, unable to join the living room festivities. And kept resurfacing all week.

Even when you're not feeling well, it's always nice to join family for the holidays. Eating, drinking, talking, playing. Walking out to watch pelicans on the lake early in the morning while everyone sleeps, coming back for coffee. The usual games of golf, pretending the cough and congestion weren't there, although two frightening episodes of reflux didn't convince his son Jed.

Maybe because of his condition, maybe because he was able to spend only five days there, the time flew and he found himself driving from the Atlanta airport up the deserted Appalachian Highway at 1: 30 in the night as usual since he always managed to schedule night flights. Driving, moaning, coughing.

Eventually the congestion subsided enough for Bert to agree going with Frank and Marsha to Snowbird Lodge above Robbinsville, a quaint historic place overlooking Eastern Tennessee. Frank had talked about it for months. It was expensive, and had to be booked for three days, but they both considered it worth the splurge. The only problem was fitting everyone into the picture. They finally had to admit that Brie wouldn't be able to go, which meant it could only be the three of them. They went back and forth, Marsha dragging her feet, not wanting to do it without Brie.

Frank convinced her they couldn't wait until Christmas, when they'd never get in. When the lodge informed him of a cancellation in early December, he accepted and told her they were going. The three of them.

The lodge, known all over the Southeast, had been in business for 75 years and was appropriately rustic, remote, and upscale. It never cut corners on the meals-- considered gourmet by some--but certainly not all-- patrons. In the summer, when it was also full, people sat outside on one of the many porches, played tennis, went for hikes, or paddle-boarded on Lake Santeetlah.

In the winter, they usually remained inside, drinking and talking in front of the big fireplace. The rooms weren't all that unusual, on the kitsch side, but comfortable.

Frank took his chess set, and Bert his backgammon, in case they'd rather play than talk. They hadn't spent much time together since Bert's crash back in October and Frank's marital crisis--which Bert still knew nothing about. Frank had worried all the way to Snowbird about how to keep Marsha occupied now that Brie wasn't along.

Before dinner the three were the first to find choice leather fireplace seats. Soon after, the couples from Atlanta and then Raleigh arrived. It hadn't snowed yet, wouldn't in fact for another month. Everyone complained this wasn't the New England white winter they'd paid for. Yes, the views were spectacular, but no, the food wasn't what the reviews had said. This and that.

Bert wanted to get out the backgammon set. Frank wanted a cigar. Marsha wanted to go home. They tried to talk but needed a few drinks to loosen up. "All in all," Frank whispered to Bert, "an inauspicious start. There's still an hour to kill before dinner."

Marsha got immersed in a woman's magazine. Frank went to the bar to fetch two marguerites but when he came back Bert shook his head, saying he was going to close his eyes for a quick catnap. Frank snorted and started fumbling through a magazine. Then tossed it and picked up the only book on the table, a famous historian's recent search for the soul of America. He couldn't concentrate, wanted to talk, not read. He got up to walk around but scurried back when someone headed toward his comfortable armchair. Reluctantly he started reading, skipping the beginning. He immediately found the overall thesis predictable and overstated. America always swings back and forth from its good to bad angels. The inevitable backlash comes from bad ideology that the country can't get rid of. Well, this was something he and Bert always agreed on. He decided it was time to wake him, get busy thinking, not sleeping.

Bert shook his head and mumbled to let a sleeping guy sleep. Frank told him to stop grumbling and pay attention. He got only as far as, "This book I've been reading..." when the bell clanged announcing the opening of the dining hall and end of talk.

While they ate, Marsha, unpredictably, provided the entertainment. She told how she and her daughter had once spent a similar winter in St. Moritz.

"Back when you were married to your first husband?" Bert asked and immediately wished he hadn't. Frank had never talked about him; he only guessed because of the kids.

"Yes, it was a long time ago. Back in the '70s, when we were all much younger."

Frank stayed out of the conversation, so Bert felt obligated to keep it going, miffed at his friend. "Didn't you used to live in St. Louis?"

"I did." Then she suddenly fell silent and dinner talk ended. When no one volunteered to revive it, they ate silently, pretending to be absorbed in the food.

Waiting for dessert, someone had to speak. Frank ultimately filled the void. "Do you think it'll snow before we leave?"

Bert groaned silently, waiting for her to speak. She didn't, so they all got up to reclaim their fireside seats. The man from Atlanta was making for the big leather couch, but Frank headed him off. Marsha took the recliner closest to the fire, fifteen feet away, picked up a magazine, and started to read.

The two men tried to return to their earlier talk but were constrained by the rest of the diners coming to settle in. They drew closer together and Bert asked what was up with Marsha.

"It's that obvious?" Frank replied.

"To me."

"She's been giving me the cold shoulder for a long time now. I don't know what's wrong. Thought it had to do with her brother, always hinting at suicide, but then she finally admitted that was just his way of getting attention. So I don't know. But I do know she's getting more and more fragile, more and more remote. What's the problem? Anxiety? I got her an SSRI prescription, but that won't help much. It's unlike her to fret."

"Could be prolonged menopause?"

193

"Nah, that's over. She sits around watching a lot of tv, won't go for walks with Trouble and me. Doesn't want to eat out or visit friends. I see her retreating inside."

"This been going on long?"

"She's been distant for months. Hell, maybe a year if I'm honest. Goes to bed early, watches tv by herself, generally ignores me."

"Shoot," Bert said, not knowing what else to say. But then he got an inspiration: "Cooking too?"

"You know her well. No, she's stayed on top of that. In fact, maybe has gotten better--like she's trying to make it up for shutting the door on me.'"

Bert could tell he was very upset; he'd never opened up that much. But, not knowing what to say, he simply said, "Keep going."

"Nowhere else to go. I don't know what to say. Maybe she's stopped loving me."

Bert thought for a moment, then finally asked, "What about the bedroom?"

"That too, not what it used to be. Hell," Frank said quietly, "there's not a lot been happening anywhere these days."

"Have you two considered marriage counseling?"

"We have, especially her. But… you know...well...."

"The counselor doesn't want to be counseled."

"Sort of. I could, if I could find someone I trusted. But out here in redneck land...."

"It seems to me you're a counselor who lives out here in redneck land."

"Yeah, but I might be the only one."

"Have you checked?"

Frank started to protest, then fell silent. "No, not really."

"Hey, I don't believe a word anyone else tries to tell me about literature. But...."

"But if things are that bad for me, I should consider it."

"Don't you think so? I can't give any feedback–not even to you, let alone her. But feedback isn't what you need, you need interaction. Someone to open the disconnect. That someone doesn't have to know the human psyche. Just someone who pushes the right buttons. That's the way it works, right?"

"Right," Frank agreed. "Thanks, I'll see to it...maybe, before I go crazy."

Bert took a risk on keeping the ball rolling. "This couldn't be the first time you two have drifted. You've been married, what, fifteen years?"

"Sixteen. No, it's been an easy ride. Well, her compulsiveness, and my...."

"Your own strange personality, yes I know."

"But it's been such smooth sailing. That's why I'm so confused now. We seem to be in different boats."

The two sat silently for a while, then their talk ended. Frank thanked him for listening, adding, "I won't charge my usual fee for letting you listen."

They laughed and went back to safer topics, but Bert kept worrying about his friend. Like him, he had a lot invested in a woman...and like him, it appeared to be a woman no longer investing back.

Frank also worried, wondered if Marsha had been talking to Brie. Something about the way the two had leaned upon each other coming up the boat ramp after that fateful summer boat ride....

Bert tried to bring Frank back toward politics. At one point their voices raised high enough to attract attention, but immediately a louder voice erupted: "That's enough!"

Frank jumped up, rushing to Marsha's side. The stranger was too close, smelled of strong liquor. Frank made a threatening gesture, told him to leave, and the man got testy, moved toward him. Frank didn't back down but grabbed his collar: "You'll have the manners to leave this minute or I'll make you leave...in a way you won't like."

He left, and she moved closer to Bert and him on the edge of their couch. Now the men had to change their talk, find a way of involving her. Bert grabbed a random topic. "It looks like people here are pretty stressed out." The other two agreed, and Bert continued: "We grew up in a country that drove 35 miles an hour; now it's 85, and tomorrow, 125." Marsha smiled, Frank tried to smile, and Bert tried to continue. "Hell, I learned to drive going only 25. You can't get stressed out going that slow!"

His attempt to keep things going having failed, they all reluctantly decided it was time to call it a night.

In his room, Bert fell asleep to the television, while in theirs, Frank and Marsha never turned it on. Frank pulled a pint of scotch from his suitcase and found some ice in the mini-fridge. They toasted to a good winter vacation, Marsha smiling more broadly than he'd seen in a long time. She thanked him for the intervention, and they small-talked the possibilities of that happening at a place like this. After their second drink the two moved toward the bed, Frank thinking his action had solved their crisis, and Marsha still happy, but not so sure life would now be running smoothly. She moved toward his side of the bed, thinking it might run more smoothly if she cooperated. An hour later Frank fell asleep, and she lay there musing.

Early December turned warm enough for Marsha and Brie to sit on Brie's big front porch after the church knitters left. Marsha talked about the weekend at the mountain lodge--Frank's scuffle with the drunk who'd tried to soft-talk her. Brie started to congratulate her, then Marsha said he was just doing it to show off, be macho, not because he really cared.

"I don't believe that," Brie said. "You've got a good man there, need to keep him happy. Bert's told me how Frank loves you"

"Maybe Frankie does." She gazed absently toward the wall. "I guess he does, just hasn't learned to show it. He talks about golf when he's not out playing golf. He walks Trouble, complains about my house cleaning."

"What's new? Man stuff."

"I asked him once if we should consider counseling."

"How'd he take that?"

Marsha laughed. "What do you think? The counselor going to a counselor? He thinks they're all crazy." Then she frowned. "I've been wondering–know it's none of my business–but what's happening between you two? Is it all over?"

"Seems so."

"If you don't want to talk about it...."

"Maybe I should. Haven't had anyone to talk privately to. Except me, I talk to me a lot."

"Me too, these days. Anyway, you know I never share personal talk with anyone, even Frank."

"I know. I guess I don't know where to start. Things falling apart. Maybe they got too intense."

"Since when is intense bad?"

"Not bad, but not good." Brie paused. "I can't explain. Maybe the magic's gone."

"I can relate there. Mine's been going for some time."

"Don't get me wrong. I don't mean sex magic. There's too much of that. Way too much."

"Too much sex? Who complains about that?"

Brie tried to laugh. "I'd never experienced anything like it. He writes me love poems, brings me flowers, gives unbelievable back and leg massages that never stop. And then goes into front massages that *never* stop! Sometimes we go on for four or five hours, up until midnight or 1:00." She paused, then decided it was ok to continue. "I've never had a man know where to find me down there. Bert finds me with everything, can't stop finding me."

"Horrible!" Marsha giggled, eyebrows lifted.

Brie snorted. "I knew it wouldn't sound right. Doesn't make sense."

"Sorry to be snide. It's just...."

"I know, just unbelievable. Too good to be true, and yet..." She stopped, trying to find words. "I know any other woman would fight for what I had. Hell, *pay* for it!"

"So obviously there's something else. You still in love with someone else? Haven't gotten over him and get the two all mixed up?"

"No, nothing like that. Men dropped out of my life ten years ago. I drove them out, promised myself never again."

"I guess we need to talk about that sometime too, but you've got me riled up. How could you feel guilty about good love-making?"

"I don't want to. It comes up and then I try to drive it away. I can't tell you how wonderful he makes me feel. For the first time I've felt loved, really loved. And know he's not faking it."

"So how could you feel guilty about good love-making?"

"I knew I shouldn't have brought it up. You can't understand 'cause you don't know Jesus the way I do, can't see how it's wrong."

Marsha jumped. "Boy, I didn't know you were a Jesus freak!"

"I don't make a big deal about it. Don't worry, I won't try to convert you, but yes, I am."

"Sex is against your religion?"

"Not my religion, my God. The bible's very clear here."

"Maybe we should...."

"Yes, maybe we should change the subject, talk about something else. This is too hard to explain."

"Ok, but one thing, only one. What about Bert? Do you talk it all out with him, if not me?"

"I've tried to but we always end up in big religious arguments. We both believe, but he's a liberal and I take the bible seriously."

"And he doesn't?"

"Maybe, but my bible is very clear. He keeps trying to convince me the Jews back then were just interested in saving marriage faithfulness. But my bible, the woman's bible I've been studying for eight years, says all sex outside marriage is wrong, period."

"That's hard to get. Even for people over forty or fifty who've been married several times?

"That's what it says, in the notes at the bottom of the pages."

"Sounds pretty strict to me, especially for these days."

"See, I told you you wouldn't get it. 'These days' don't matter. We can't be changing the holy words to fit modern times, modern people. But you and I don't want to fight this out."

"Ok, we'll drop it. Still, I can't believe...well, never mind."

"Well *not* nevermind! What I've been saying is all true, but...well...there's a small possibility we might get back together."

Marsha laughed. "So that's got to be good news! Maybe I should get Bert to clue my Frankie in on what a woman's body wants. I thought doctors were supposed to know that."

"Maybe medical doctors. Not many men get it. Is there anything else troubling you?

"I don't know, I guess I just need space."

"Like me," Brie said. "To heal."

"And I need it to grow."

"That's good. You need space to grow, I need space to stop growing."

They laughed and switched topics.

CHAPTER EIGHT: CONGESTION and CONFUSION

BERT HARDLY KNEW WHAT MONTH IT WAS. Still December? His cold or flu had come surging back; the worst body-wrenching coughing he could remember, plus worrying he'd given it to everyone. Hell, it'd been so long since he'd seen Brie, he couldn't even remember where they stood. Eventually his cough and sinus condition eased enough to let him venture to the golf course. Afterward, he drove by her house, telling himself if she'd be sitting on her porch, he'd stop. If not, not. And there she was, knitting in the far chair facing the driveway. He took a deep breath and drove into the long driveway.

Rowdy immediately bounded up to the porch gate, but he found himself shuffling. She smiled weakly, and it took all his willpower not to grab her in a bear hug. They sat apart and talked...about nothing important. He finally got courage to ask her if it would be ok for him to go pick up a cooked hen at Ingles like he'd always done. She started to refuse, but he prevailed, whistling the mile-and-a-half drive to the supermarket.

While he was gone, she set the table and made a salad. They ate quietly, and then he helped bring in the dishes. How many times had he so easily and happily walked the same path past living room and bedroom?

He stood idly watching her put away the dishes, still wanting to touch her, but feeling her distance and keeping his since he wasn't sure he was past the contagion stage.

After he came back outside, waiting for her to finish the kitchen, he pondered asking her to play a card game, but was afraid she didn't want him to stay. Also, he felt the cough coming back so needed to go. He told her he had to leave but would love to meet again. Could he stop by in a few days, say Thursday? Her answer surprised him: a gentle nod. No smile but still a nod.

Back home, he was glad he hadn't pressed staying. The damn cold was still raging, despite all of his doctor visits and prescriptions. He lay propped up on the couch until late afternoon downing pills, hacking and spitting, fighting diarrhea caused by the fourth round of antibiotics, trying to get down some soup. He finally roused himself from the couch to call her at 7:00, saying he had a bad fever and asking what he should do.

She was concerned, telling him to consider the emergency room if it went over 102. Here she was consoling him, he thought, while his biggest prayer was for her: Please, God, don't let her get it. I can't have given it to her, of all people. I stayed far away, didn't cough.

He made it through the sleepless night and called again the next morning. She gave him the 800 number of a nurse who might give good advice, and he listened patiently, surprised to learn the woman was talking from Maine. "There's not a lot you can do except tough it out like everyone else. Go to the hospital if it tops 103."

The temperature finally dropped and he slept on and off for three days. He felt a little better, wanted to see her, but knew it was still too soon. He looked out the window at all the clouds. The sun had disappeared for the rest of the winter.

Eventually he decided it would be ok to call her on the phone. She had some good news: a friend she hadn't seen in years would be visiting in two days. But then she added she'd unfortunately gone through three boxes of tissues. He signed off and started a fire in the wood stove. Rowdy tried repeatedly to interest him in playing with a red, yellow, or dirty brown ball, but Bert declined, warning him that he desperately needed a haircut and bath. The last word registered.

Friday came and he called again to say he wanted to get together but still needed a few more days to recover. Then, in the third week of December he screwed up his courage to make a visit. He found her bundled up and sitting on her porch, not because it was warm enough outside but because she had to vacate the house while the washing machine ran. They played a game of Scrabble and talked. Eventually the topic of New Year's Eve turned up, and they decided to give it a go. Neither had stayed up to watch the big ball drop for years, let alone dance and shout, so they thought it was time to celebrate. Which, for Brie, meant dressing up and acting out...something she loved but he dreaded. Eventually he agreed to be Lord Bertram to her Lady Anne, and she coached him in how to make a respectable Elizabethan outfit. While talking about dressing up, she brightened. He tried to.

Visiting thrift shops and shopping online kept him busy for a week, and soon Christmas was almost upon them. Neither had made plans. Going out to eat was out of the question, but they finally agreed to cook a big steak out over her firepit--something they hadn't done for months. The cold snap had left; they'd be ok outside. The dinner was good, if brief.

Christmas eve came and they tried to be cheerful. The steak and potatoes were perfectly cooked, and sitting around the firepit was comforting. But something seemed to be missing: love, affection. Both tried to ignore the loss. Neither thought about kissing. He told himself it was still the ever-lingering flu.

A week later, the big New Year's celebration. Watch 2014 turn into 2015. The night came for him to pick her up and drive to his house. He wore his grand Elizabethan outfit of black pantaloons, floppy shoes, white puffy-sleeved shirt, black leather vest, floppy hat, and for good measure, red cape (probably meant for Dracula, but it added color). To his Lord, she played Lady, wearing a beautiful red dress she'd sewn, maybe using the dress mannequin he'd bought for her June birthday. "If there's one thing I hate to do, it's dress up--even for Halloween, let alone for nothing," he thought, shaking his head and trying to get the stupid hat to stay on. They politely kissed under the dining room mistletoe before Mindy and Don arrived.

Despite his care, she'd managed to contract his disease--which had come back to him once again with a vengeance, the throat congestion so bad he had to make an emergency trip to a throat specialist the last week of December. Pictures of the damage voice box were taken and he was taught exercises to bring it back. Even before their guests arrived, they knew the night was doomed. He sat across the table from her popping pills to control the cough.

He'd bought Cornish game hens and three different vegetables, plus red wine for Don. But by the time all sat down to eat he was scarcely functioning, and Lady Anne barely conscious. She took two or three bites, and he half-finished his, while Mindy nibbled and Don gobbled the rest of the asparagus and game hen.

Eight o'clock came, four hours short of the proper celebration time. It was already past time for the two hosts. They apologized and he took her home. A very bad ending to an otherwise spectacular summer of love. He couldn't believe it was about to become 2015.

January dragged, cold, miserable. He stayed in bed much of the time. His kids started worrying that his condition had turned into pneumonia. Lynn almost bought a plane ticket, but he kept telling her that sleep, water, pills, and positive thinking would do the trick. By next month they did; he was going to survive after all.

He waited until mid-February to call Brie, learning she'd somehow survived her own cold. Because the phone bothered her, she always had to put it on voice and shout across the room. He couldn't make out what she was saying, tried to say he'd come to talk in person, but then couldn't tell whether or not she got the message. They hung up.

He wondered if this might be their last conversation. Everything wonderful had come grinding to a ridiculous ending. Totally impossible that something so good could dribble out this way. Leaving him asking, as usual, what had gone wrong. Two years from now, he couldn't help thinking, I will still be twelve years older than she, and she still won't even qualify for Medicare, which I've been on for ...oh, shit, stop!

Already he was having difficulty remembering dates and details. The Summer of Love had slowly turned into the Winter of Discontent. Maybe he needed to get out the handful of handwritten notebook pages he'd stuffed in that box but stopped transcribing into the journal. He noticed the journal ended the same way he ended the short story his ninth-grade teacher had talked him into writing, with a big THE END!

I should get everything down right, the way it actually happened, not the way I wanted it to happen, he reminded himself. But he wasn't up to it; it was just too painful. He never would be up to it. Would February ever end, spring ever come?

February would soon end; March would come. He couldn't stay in the house any longer, so called Brie for an hour's quick walk. Meandering along Fire's Creek, they got to talking about the unmentionable–whether she was getting better or not. First the cold or flu, next, the condition. They couldn't hit it head on but circled. He tried to small-talk about the beautiful creek, and she smiled but held back. Eventually they decided it was time to drive home.

Back home, she said she'd gotten some small hits on the ride back. "Where they came from I'll never know. And what you can't seem to understand is that they never go entirely away. They linger."

"But you look so relaxed, smiling. Hey, we even got a little laughter in today! Sure haven't had enough of that lately."

She ignored his frivolity. "I still felt hits, all the way back."

"Was I driving too fast? I tried to keep it to a slow, steady pace."

"It's not you. Maybe just the car. And the power lines overhead. Who knows? Thank God we were in my car, not your little convertible. Either the canvas top–or worse, when there's no top–the lines overhead bombard me."

Bert hesitated, didn't know whether to protest, so tamed down his possible objection: "Was it this bad when you drove down from West Virginia?"

"I don't know. Don't get me wrong, I like going places with you, need to get out. I need to keep forcing myself to push the limits. Need to drive myself to the post office, where yesterday I got the added bonus of this older lady somehow appearing around the corner pushing a vacuum cleaner. It almost blasted me clear out of the building."

He tried to laugh politely but couldn't. Did he believe her? They started preparing dinner.

"I felt stupid but had to tell the guy next to me in line to ask her to shut the thing off before it put me on the ground. She did it, no questions asked. I got out, was able to wobble to my car and make it home. I never know what'll push me over the top."

He replied something and dropped the subject before it spoiled their dinner. Toward the end, when both were finishing their salads, the phone rang. She saw on the answerer it was her mother, so he threw on his jacket to take Rowdy for a walk.

She called him back inside in five minutes, saying her mother, whom she'd been worrying about, was ok. "She almost went under at the dialysis yesterday, her blood pressure dropping to almost nothing. I don't understand what keeps her going."

"She's been going for five years, three times a week?"

"Five years, unheard of! Big-Buddy drives her forty miles each way. Waits patiently in the car until it's finished. They're both amazing." Bert smiled: one brother is Big-Buddy, the other, Bigger-Buddy.

Bert thought about asking what she'd do when her mother's body finally gave out. The funeral would be up in Connecticut; she wouldn't be able to drive there herself. Would she even be able to drive to Big-Buddy's in West Virginia? And what about all the cell phones at the funeral?

Instead of asking, Bert decided to bring them back to the more pressing matter of whether she was getting better. "You were telling me that I still don't get it; don't understand that your zaps don't just come and go but stick around. For how long?"

"It seems like longer these days. I don't know if it's having to stay inside. It wasn't this bad last summer."

He said something to Brie again, trying to be Mr. Positive.

She tried to agree. "Yeah. But even so, you and everyone think when a cell phone gets me, it clears up after an hour or so and I'm back to normal. I'm not, never am."

He didn't say anything, but once again doubted her words, knowing how emotional she could get.

She continued. "Take Sundays. I get up, do my sauna, start the day ok. Have to drive to church; even though it's only a few miles, it's still driving. Then, you know, the church always takes its toll. We don't know if that's because someone's left the cell phone on, or whether the music is too loud, or what. By the time it's over, I drive home and stay exhausted for most of the afternoon. You've seen me. It won't be long before I have to stop going to church."

He nodded. "Then I have to come over and make things worse...."

"Then you come over, or maybe someone from church. And I always say it's ok, but my energy's going down fast."

"Today? I guess I was guilty of talking you into going for a hike when you were already compromised."

She said nothing, so Bert continued: "But you slept late, didn't do much of anything before I got here at what—1:00?"

"It sounds wrong. I know it's hard to believe. I hate it, hate it. Try not to admit it. But when this buzzing is circling around inside my head, it's hard to ignore."

"Do you think it's mostly the house?" Again, he wished he could convince her what a safe house he could build somewhere out in the desert far from wi-fi. But if he opened that hope, she'd turn a deaf ear. He wondered if she enjoyed wallowing, then immediately felt guilty for doubting.

He knew she'd experienced more in her lifetime than a person who's lived three or four times longer. A lot of pain. He'd known her long enough to know she's still keeping painful secrets from him. Judging from the ones she had shared, these had to be the dark kind you read about in suspense novels. She'd hinted at several more than mildly evil attacks, but he always stopped her. It wasn't that he wasn't curious, but he didn't want to pull her back; that was the job of her therapist. His job, he told himself, was to stay open and give positive reinforcement.

He knew she'd never provoked the physical attacks that invariably came from men, not women. Back when she was working, she didn't dress provocatively, in fact wore drab women's suits buttoned to the top. No doubt flirted, but never led a strange man on, like so many women do. And it's not clothing alone that attracts, it's spirit; as Bert had explained to many family members--she greets everyone in brotherly love with an unguarded spirit.

The following day Bert kept replaying her words about things getting worse. She wasn't complaining, just explaining. But was she also thinking their time together *always* took its toll? The only way I'll know is to ask her, he told himself. I'll call, saying I'll be over in mid-afternoon to play our new Rook game and bringing something to eat. She'll say she's busy cleaning after the knitting women left. "Don't worry," I'll say, "I won't be staying too long, I just want to see you." She'll say something about my driving a hard bargain; she's not ready but a short visit might be ok.

That was what happened. He went with cooked chicken, fresh strawberries, and yogurt ice cream. No wine. She cracked open the door and in rushed Rowdy, saying here I am, I own the place. She muttered something about needing more time to clean, being stressed out, everyone coming all the time, never giving her space, and didn't he hear her on the phone?

"No, I didn't," he said honestly, explaining his unpredictable cell phone in his back pocket--which he suddenly remembered he'd forgotten to switch off, so made an excuse to get something back in the car. We're off to a bad start, he thought after ditching the phone, but tried to put a friendly arm around her. She resisted. He quickly pulled back and said goodbye. The day is over. He returned home and stomped the snow from wet feet. Ate the damn chicken by himself.

Nowhere good to go, he muttered. Another five days of rain or snow predicted. Cold, almost thirty degrees lower than the norm. What could he do? Tend the fire, read, write. The dreadful winter was supposed to have ended but hadn't. Maybe he needed to open the wine.

He didn't know what he'd do if Brie closed her door again. Unlike her, he couldn't say all he needed is Jesus. He knew he also needed physical arms. Hers.

While eating his cold chicken, he swallowed his pride and called to apologize for storming out. She repeated that people are forever coming to visit at inopportune times, and he refrained from saying he's not just people. He tried to remind himself she needed time alone, time to detox and suck oxygen–everything he'd heard so many times before. He apologized again and wished her a good night.

He decided a late-night spin might clear his head. He drove to Chatuge Golf Course, parked, and told Rowdy to guard the car. Then got out to walk the first two holes. The night was peaceful; no squirrels or quarrelling old-timers, just the moon casting long shadows over the lush fairway. He sat down and stretched out on the grass. For no reason he could explain, except to remind himself that the mind is its own master, he found himself back on the Denver Country Club fairway at night, Sophie somebody lying next to him on a scratchy army blanket. They were fifteen or sixteen, not at all in love, but horny. This was their first and last date, one that he'd been thinking about for weeks.

He couldn't work up nerve to ask for a kiss. Maybe you're not supposed to ask, just do? They didn't want to small-talk. The moments passed slowly. He reached awkwardly toward her and tried to pull her closer. Her response was ambivalent. He looked up at the moon sailing overhead and said something about how beautiful it was. But the night wasn't particularly beautiful, just over. They rose, folded the blanket, and walked back to his old Chevy. It was a night he'd tell none of his friends about, and he hoped she'd do the same, but knew she wouldn't. Would blab it over the whole school what a pansy he was.

Well, enough of the past. How about the present? He wished he could convince Brie of why he needed her. Could he ever explain that sex played only a part of their deep relationship? Well, he knew that to be impossible, since while it's playing, it plays so profoundly. Anyway, he knew that what he needed most was someone to sing to, a love song like one by the Moody Blues or the Eagles. He needed to sing in her presence, watching him. So he wrote "A Poem That Sings a Song of Love":

You've told me what you need to keep you whole.
I've tried so hard to be with you,
hold you tight in body as in soul.
I know I ask too much and call too soon,
ask for what I know you cannot give.
For that, forgive; you know me well,
bear with this one who needs you so.
Have I told you what I really want,
do you know what it is?
You can't guess--it's not much at all,
it's there in the song I always hear:
"Nights in white satin, never reaching the end...."
you know the rest, I know you hear it too.
Now I simply need to sing this song of love,
and need to hear it whispered back.
Our nights may always end too soon
yet I can hope the words will never end.
"...And I love you, and I love you....
this song I hear and sing to you.
Are simple words of love too much to bear?

After the poem he added these words: "I write this warm poem to Brie in the middle of a cold winter that refuses to release its grip." He reread the poem, cringed at its facile rhyme, but still decided to drop it in her mailbox tomorrow morning and wait two or three days to call. What will be will be.

He waited four days and stewed. Ever since his birthday he'd been trying to brew an ulcer. When waking at 2:00 to go to the bathroom or throw another log in the fire, the black fog enveloped him. What's happening? he asked himself. Is she pushing me under the table again? Why am I so worried? Where's the old optimistic Bert?

His mind wandered back to October's breakup caused mostly by miscommunication. Then November, the horrid congestion keeping him up half the night and racking his body all day. By December the congestion had worked its way into his voice box, causing reflux problems. Maybe into his very soul. Also, he worried about giving the disease to her—which he ultimately did. By January he knew their relationship had deteriorated past return. They'd stopped laughing, giggling, relaxing together. He'd taken to holding his breath when calling, convinced she'd say she didn't want him to come over...which often happened. February didn't change things; by then he was convinced things had come to an end for them. Now it was March, and she was too worried about her mother's deteriorating condition to talk to him. They'd never make it to spring.

On March 14 both remained sunk in physical and emotional turmoil but reluctantly agreed to celebrate a late Valentine's day. The fact that she accepted his invitation to come to his house made Bert think enough time might have passed to make a new start.

He spent all morning taping small love notes all over his house, changed light bulbs, and turned off appliances for later in the afternoon, when hopefully they'd settle down to a quiet game of Scrabble or the new knock-off they'd never played, Horseopoly. Then even more hopefully, they'd stretch out on the futon in front of the wood heat stove. The temperature might drop to freezing in this most unpredictable season.

But first he had a surprise for her. He'd told her to bring warm clothing, hiking boots and poles, plus if she wanted, an overnight bag. But kept their destination secret. They arrived at Becky's farm at 11:00 to find her standing at the gate bundled up in red vest, coat, scarf, hat, and mittens. It was already hovering a few degrees above freezing.

He'd met Becky's husband Chuck at a Greek cooking class led by Nick the Greek from the Episcopal church. Chuck had found out he used to do wallpapering, and Bert agreed to paste up a large wall map of the world in his study. Afterward when Becky showed him her horses out in the pasture, he immediately thought of Brie...the woman mysteriously attracted to the horses she was scared to death of. One reason she'd bought her own house was its excellent view of 25 show horses that fed in the neighboring pastures. Those horses were anything but tame, but Becky had assured Bert hers were. "Well, Butch is, if not Red."

Brie was delighted but mystified and frightened. She had no intention of entering the fenced-off stable past the barn, stood frozen in place. Bert read her mind: "I'm not going out there! They don't have saddles, bridles, or anything on them. I'll watch you two from here."

Becky slowly put a halter on Butch and talked to Brie about the need to demonstrate mastery and lack of fear. Eventually she talked her into coming inside...slowly approaching the horse. Bert immediately knew it would go well. Inside of a half hour Brie was briskly walking Butch around the pen, firing question after question at Becky, who walked next to her, coaching what to do and not do. She told Becky what had caused her great fear of horses, a fall when she was barely a teenager.

Bert watched them and continued petting the semi-wild one, Red. He appeared perfectly tame, let Bert wrap his arms around him and blow into his nose. Bert had forgotten a coat and needed the big horse to warm him. Then Becky haltered Red and exchanged Butch for Red. Brie and he hit it off immediately, the quarter horse turning every few steps to give her his baleful stare. The two of them led each other back and forth around the stable for more than an hour, one smiling the whole time.

On the way to their next Valentine surprise, Bert tried to figure out who'd been more pleased–Brie, Becky, him, or Red. It couldn't have been better–except he really would have liked to ride the big Red.

Even before they turned off on Fire's Creek Road, Brie knew where the next surprise would be. They'd been to the stream's picnic area three or four times throughout the summer, always joking about Bert's lost sunglasses on a rock. Both the picnic area and the horse-camping area past it are favorites with locals because of the crystal creek and lush laurels and rhododendrons that bloom as late as July. They found a remote table next to the stream and spread out the lunch.

Already Brie was convinced this was the Valentine's day she'd always dreamed of, and it was only half over. Again, always the romantic, Bert pictured how cozy it would be on the futon in front of the fire. Especially after the lights were turned off.

After he shut off the refrigerator and lit the wood stove, he went outside to the porch to start up the grill. They had a glass of muscadine juice--pretend wine-- and avocado dip. Later, steak, potatoes, and creamed corn. Brie came forth with her usual: "That hit all the spots," and "It couldn't get any better." Bert cringed, lacking courage to tell her what he thought of platitudes left over from childhood or child-bearing. Instead, he gave her a bear hug and kissed her under the recently-removed mistletoe that used to hang from the dining room fixture. Leftover from the fizzled New Year's Eve dinner.

While she used the bathroom, he lugged the red futon in from the porch. It never got situated in front of the fire, however, because her expression told him what she'd been thinking. She'd experienced too much, needed to detox and hit the oxygen back home. He tried feebly to convince her to stay, but she said she had to leave before it got too dark, and thanked him for being such a gentleman, adding, "You are amazing." He had to settle for big smiles and the late Valentine's day that was good but should have been much better.

Three days later he received a beautiful thank you card saying "the planning, care, creativity, and love you displayed on our special Valentine's Day was heartwarming. Thank you for making an adventure with a surprise around every corner...You wear me out its true, but left me with a smile on my heart."

He told himself one day he'd get used to her poor grammar, and tried to convince himself he didn't mind missing the futon part; it was enough just to be with her. The next day he volunteered to drive her to the new doctor she'd found, a holistic practitioner down in Blairsville. Afterward they visited a country dry-goods having a 75% off sale, where she picked up a winter jacket and boots that he brought out to the car for her to try on. All in all, a fifty-mile drive that took its toll. She cried a little, then whispered, "It shouldn't be so hard to do a simple thing like that."

Bert was also having problems, having circled the nursing home he'd visited daily for almost a year. It was particularly hard driving past the places he and Suzanne had visited after she was admitted.

"I do hope it's the house," he said the following day when Brie told him about the new electrician who'd be coming to do his inspection with different meters.

"I hope so too. Do you think I'm getting worse?"

"That can't be true. What--four years ago you had to wear dark glasses at night as well as day. Had to wear gloves!"

"Yeah, but remember, I drove myself down here. I don't know if I could do that now. I certainly can't drive at night."

"Hey, that's not because you're worse, but because the environment's gotten worse. Back at the turn of the century, wi-fi hadn't even been invented, now you can't get away from it. You're getting bombarded at least ten to twenty times worse these days."

"And it'll get worse. And worse."

"We can only hope that your body will drain its toxins and win the battle. Recover enough resistance to stay ahead of all the cell towers and whatnot."

"We can. Hope, and hope."

Bert worried about this not being the Brie he'd come to know. Complaining and letting herself get down. Where did the Brie go? What was he to do?

The end of March was one of the coldest in Appalachia. Bert's book club that was supposed to meet to discuss *The Little Ice Age* was cancelled for the second time due to the cold.

It finally thawed and Bert worked up courage to call Brie. She told him to come over, and when he arrived, he found her dressed up, wearing lipstick and a smile. She snickered when Rowdy bounded past her, dashing around the house to check out smells. "I'm no traitor, I still love you best," she told Rowdy.

Maybe me too, Bert wondered. He embraced her, and she hugged back, if not as enthusiastically. Have I been wrong again, Bert wondered, thinking he was the problem when it was just her health?

"I can't understand what went wrong," she said, understanding his hesitancy. "But it seems forever now that I haven't been able to recover from a hit. I think it was when Bob came over with that fancy meter of his last week. He kept flipping it on and off, checking everything in the house, and I couldn't escape outside because it was under 20. I didn't feel anything, but like the book you gave me said, sometimes it takes hours or even days for it to build up."

Flabbergasted, he didn't know what to say, just listened. She looked vibrant--smiling and talking enthusiastically about her visit to last Tuesday's healing session. The only other one who came during that cold night was the mayor, part of the healing team. They sat there for a while, then she jumped up, announcing she was leading for the night, and proceeding to sing, wave her arms, shout hallelujah, and preach to the empty room. Then she stepped behind the mayor to lay hands on his shoulders and pray for him. Everyone laughed and when she was finished talking, Bert agreed to her conclusion that maybe a broken vessel could do healing after all.

They went outside to sit in the sun on the firepit stumps and examine the snowy pasture for horses. She told him about watching one of the bigger stallions raise up and kick another horse on his nose, hurting him and her so much it brought tears. He told her about being so demoralized by the winter snow and cold that his indoor pickleball game even suffered; he was unable to hit with power or confidence.

Later they went inside to fix a vegetable concoction, spilling flour and cauliflower while cavorting around the kitchen. Then sat down to eat, first giving great thanks. It was still early, but instead of playing the new Rook game they decided to do their religion talk. He was almost relaxed, ready to dispassionately discuss disagreement over sex. He'd brought sheets prepared from his own bible, and she went to get her woman's bible with its elaborate interpretations printed at the bottom. They were ready for battle.

Bert took the lead, giving his findings about sexual immorality--how the bible pointed it toward adultery, fornication, and other heavy matters, but never a failure to maintain chastity. He emphasized that purity was something much bigger than chastity or virginity. Purity involved inner intent and motivation, not just following a law. "A person can be totally chaste, yet still not spiritually pure."

She read from her bible's notes interpreting sex to be ok only for married people. He asked to see the book and cross-checked its references, noting they were to a lengthy passage in Colossians that talked about abstinence from fornication and adultery, not about unmarried consensual sex or purity. "And certainly nothing to do with marriage certificates."

They went around and around–but peacefully, sometimes even laughing while disagreeing.

The talk circled marriage. He had to agree the bible always promoted it, and sometimes seemed to advocate what her woman's bible made exclusive. "But we're really married, don't you see?"

She didn't nod. He pointed out that the root definition of marriage is being joined together. "And who joined us? We both agreed long ago we'd been put together by God. We've both been praying ever since for his guidance in our relationship. Would God allow us to go where he didn't want us to go?"

She didn't agree or disagree.

Bert went on. "We may not be legally married, but I believe we are spiritually."

Again, she said nothing. Maybe their talk hadn't been the impersonal, academic talk he thought it had.

By the time they'd exhausted the subject it was getting dark, and time for him to leave. He refrained from asking for a hug, yet went home relaxed, happy, and relieved...if a little confused. Have I done it again with talk of marriage? He wondered. Have I over-spoken my case? Should I have let sleeping dogs lie?

Before falling asleep he opened a devotional he used to read and found these words: "Keep your eyes on Me! Waves of adversity are washing over you, and you feel tempted to give up...you are losing sight of Me. Yet I am with you always..."

In light of all the true adversity and grief in this world, he asked himself, how can I be so petty to think only of myself? He tried to pray for forgiveness and being self-preoccupied. Asked to be steered back to sanity. And went to sleep.

CHAPTER NINE: THE BLACK HOLE RETURNS

BERT HAD READ TOO MANY NOVELS to think the river of love flows smooth. But he opened the letter to be smacked in the face. Not a phone call this time; a blast from nowhere.

Dear Bert,

This past year certainly has been filled with multiple learning experiences. We learned a lot from each other during the season we spent together.

The most important lessons are that we must learn to be true to ourselves. We met at a very vulnerable time, you mourning the passing of your wife, Suzanne, and me coming out of a year and a half hibernation and several years of unexplained illness. I wouldn't trade our paths crossing and our time spent together, but I recognize that it has served its purpose.

Looking in on the situation after serious prayer I see we're both starting to recognize you no longer need to be with me to fill Suzannes spot. Maybe that was done subconsciously–its time to release that need. By releasing me I believe you will be able to heal totally and completely leaving you available and ready to pull a healthy woman into your vibration.

You have multiple opportunities of fellowship opening up to you now which you need to explore. I release you and support you in this.

My prayer is that you get yourself healthy. I believe with all my heart that once you get yourself completely sober with zero tolerance, your memory will improve greatly. I saw proof of that during the months you applied yourself. I hope you will make and keep your doctors appointment to address your gastro issue–its treatable but shouldn't be ignored.

As for me, I'm working aggressively on wellness. The most important lesson I learned about myself is I can't take or handle stress of any kind. I'm sorry you got the brunt of that. I need to rid myself of the things I can control that stress me out.

I know you kid me about being a rule follower but thats exactly what I am. Problem is, I broke a lot of my own rules falling for you, I derailed. I've been told many times over the years that I'm the type you marry, the good girl. I need to be the virtuous woman God intended me to be.

We already discussed the reasons why we don't want to be engaged to each other. For you, timing, and I don't want to guess but I suspect the uncertainty of my illness. For me, I'm not able to live with your history of drugs and alcohol. It makes me feel unsafe.

It leaves me empty to know I compromised myself further with unnecessary stress resulting from poor choices.

I can't begin to tell you how painful it was knowing that sunrise services were all around me in churches everywhere–but I couldn't attend. Thankfully, after prayer, He led me exactly where He wanted me to be– the praise and worship was off the charts. The joy he restored in me overwhelms me at times.

We can never be on an even playing ground since I can't tolerate the environment in public. I've had to stop going to our church. I will always feel left out– that's just the way it is. So, for now, I choose to stand alone. Jesus, my homeboy, has my back.

I say we leave ourselves open to what God has in store for each of our lives. Continue to open yourself fully to Him and let Him guide your path.

It may be too difficult to try to maintain any kind of friendship at this time; the wound is too open to add salt to it. They say time is a healer; I guess we'll find out.

I pray God blesses you always, all ways.

With Love in His name,

Brie

Dear Brie,

I just received your letter. I hope writing things down helped you; it usually does...although therapists say all important relationship matters should be handled face to face, not by letter or phone. Anyway, here I am also using written words because that's the only medium you leave me. And don't worry, I'm not going to answer you point by point or try to convince you my side of the story is the right one. I see this as an opportunity for both of us to learn and grow, no matter what happens to the relationship. Just relax and read.

The book I'll be referring to is one Rhonda lent me for the upcoming church session, *The Enneagram Made Easy*– maybe if quotes from it perk your interest, you can borrow it from her, since you can't go to the sessions (or could you convince her to hold them on your porch?). I find the book fascinating; we always like to read about ourselves, discover what makes us and other people tick. I won't be attending the sessions, however, since I'll be gone all of May.

Before getting started I'd like to thank you for so many things–things that are still evident in your Dear John letter–like your concern over my reflux problem (which I hope will be helped by the doctor's visit I'm now scheduling), or for encouraging me in my writing, not to mention so many other smaller things you helped me with before, like walking tall, eating and dressing better, learning to enjoy swimming. I could go on and on. When you say we've been good for each other, you're right.

But as you know, we've also hurt each other. I think much of that comes from unconscious areas, something I've learned from the enneagram book. It identifies different personality profiles and helps a person come to terms with good and bad sides. So when I talk about what went wrong with our relationship, it's not just me talking.

Back in October, following that mostly wonderful birthday party on Penland, you decided to throw me under the table. You never told me why, but we almost recovered, despite the terrible winter when we were both so physically sick. Now here it is spring, and you've thrown me under the table a second time. Again, without really explaining, although this letter isn't quite as angry and bewildering.

Maybe I should admit to being selfish and blind to your deeper needs; maybe you should admit to being fearful and controlling. That's just me speaking; here's what the book says. It clearly sees you as a Number One, the Perfectionist, and me, a Number Four, the Romantic. Understanding these different personality profiles might help us understand what's happened to what we used to have.

First, the Perfectionist: "at its best is ethical, reliable, productive, wise, honest, orderly, and self-disciplined. At its worst, judgmental, inflexible, dogmatic, obsessive-compulsive, critical of others, overly serious, controlling, anxious." (Page 11)

Father Bill and I have both told you these words describe you, and this is also what your church healer Anne meant when she said you need to stop obsessing over EMS and start obsessing over healing. I don't think she meant you don't have EMS, just that you obsess over it, and perhaps unconsciously use it to attract and control people. It's really a shame that you've decided to dump her healing, plus Father Bill's. Who's next? (Well, of course, me.)

Next, what does the Enneagram say about me? I'm at my best when I'm compassionate, loving expressive, creative, intuitive, and supportive. At my worst when I'm depressed, self-conscious, withdrawn, stubborn, moody, self-absorbed.

The Romantic hurts himself and maybe others when he thinks he doesn't deserve to be loved; when he feels guilty disappointing people; when he feels hurt when someone misunderstands or doesn't appreciate him; when he expects too much from people and life and longs for what he doesn't have (p.56).

What's hard for a Perfectionist (Page 14) is being disappointed with herself and others when her expectations aren't met; when she feels burdened with too much responsibility; when she thinks what she does is never good enough; when she obsesses about what she should or shouldn't do; and overall just being anxious, tense, and taking things way too seriously.

Well, enough quoting from the book. I found it helpful in understanding what I need to work on.

Finally, I can't help responding to some very stilted, hard-to-believe words in your farewell letter:

"Releasing me, you will be able to heal totally and completely; leaving you available and ready to pull a healthy woman into your vibration. You have multiple opportunities of fellowship opening up to you now which you need to explore."

Such strange, mechanical words! Where is the healthy woman I used to love being around for all the small stuff: playing Scrabble, cooking, walking, quietly hanging out? Laughing. Did you never treasure the small stuff the way I did? Maybe you thought I was always thinking of the big stuff–the physical feelings you came to fear? Maybe you just can't relax? I thought that was what my magic fingers were good at–helping you relax, helping you let go, helping you heal.

Do you really think I suddenly want to "pull a healthy woman into my vibration"-- whatever the hell that is? Are *you* not healthy? Have you not re-read my poems about what I really want?

Where in the world is your heart? The most important thing in my mind has always been what's most important in yours–your healing. The small stuff is where healing comes from, not from six-hour noisy prayer sessions. Things like bocce ball, or just throwing Rowt Man his tennis ball. The small stuff! That's where our spirits connected. And yes, they did connect. It wasn't just another "opportunity of fellowship." It was love–pure physical, emotional, spirit love.

Why do you have to bump everything up to some impossible, unobtainable spiritual level? Can't you see that when our spirits connected, it automatically promoted healing?

233

LOVE ALWAYS PROMOTES HEALING.

Love heals. Love... not friendship or fellowship.

Please don't tell me I'm now free for "multiple opportunities of fellowship." I've always been free for that. Or by "fellowship" do you mean "love" (the word you have such a time saying)? If so, I've never been interested in multiple opportunities.

Nor do I want to be told I need a different healthy woman. Let go of me, if you must, but do it honestly. Don't make it sound like you're doing me a favor.

I needed and found *this* woman, a healthy woman...perfect in every way except one--her obsessive need to tell me what I do and don't need, should and shouldn't do.

Oh, how I would love to hear you thank me for loving you...not for being a timely friend whose time now ends.

You are the woman I'd prayed Lord God would bring into my life. We both knew our meeting was not accidental. We both watched it grow into love. Despite what you said in your letter, you do know how deep that love became. You also know how it helped heal both of us...because, again, love always heals.

But now you call our time together just a passing friendship...something that has "served its purpose" or come to its "appropriate end." Such cold, cruel words. You can't really mean them.

Such love, I know, cannot come and go so easily.

Now I must say farewell. I will always remember you and hope one day you'll lay down your need to control. Then you may be able to find and keep another perfect lover to replace this one.

You concluded your letter by saying "time is a healer and I guess we will find out." Right now, I doubt time could ever heal the deep hurt you've given me by refusing to acknowledge and honor the depths of my pure love. But I will continue praying for God to bless you, and more particularly, for you to accept his blessings and stop saying "I will always feel left out." You needn't feel that. You need to accept healing.

Bert

Bert was upset, confused, angry. Time to call Frank to ask what was happening. They arranged to meet at El Cancun after Frank finished his weekly spin around the lake in his big motorboat. Before they met Bert had a few more things to process, so started talking to her in his head. I've always been confused by how you choose to relate to deity. You never talk about God or the Holy Spirit, only Jesus. You call him your homeboy. I haven't heard the term; maybe it's like house boy? Your servant, someone who runs errands for you; someone who watches your back? Ok, so I'm being ridiculous; it's probably just your term of endearment–something you could never find for me. Whatever, I've always admired how faithful and serious you are in your worship. Even if I never understood what being "prayed up" means, I've learned from you how necessary it is to be serious and consistent in worship. You and I were always able to pray successfully together, no matter how differently. You always asked me to initiate the meal-time prayer, then followed with your coda about blessing our bodies to His service. In your private prayer time, your practice is to hold up your entire list–as many as a hundred–whereas I always find it necessary to form pictures of specific individuals. But, again, no matter how differently we worship, we both honor and love the same God. Like my neighbor Anna, you use the word *prayer* a lot. You automatically add it to most of your high-sounding sentences: "after serious prayer, I think that…." Like Anna, you need to convince people how serious you are about God. Merton's prayer, where he confesses that he doesn't know who God is or what he's up to in his life but tries his best to believe and to please God, is foreign to your strenuous belief, although I'll admit you did say you liked it.

Bert tried to stop his infernal internal patter. He knew he'd never learn what went wrong. He also knew they'd never have made it for the long haul. Playing Skip-Bo all afternoon, drinking ice tea, taking a walk on the dam, having a quiet dinner, and then settling down to another quiet game of Skip-Bo? Never going out, watching tv or listening to the stereo, never enjoying happy hour at the local bar. No, no, no.

Try as he could, he couldn't push away the nagging thought that she'd dumped him this second time again for *his* sake, not hers. Those sentences she wrote: *By releasing me I believe you will be able to heal totally and completely, leaving you available and ready to pull a healthy woman into your vibration. You have multiple opportunities of fellowship opening up to you now which you need to explore. I release you and support you in this.*

If she really was consciously setting him free to live a normal life, that meant she'd pushed him into a moral, not emotional, quagmire by acting altruistically, not selfishly.

Bert pounded the table. But that's *my* decision to stick out an impossible situation! *Mine*, not hers!

He picked up the yellow notebook. Maybe writing things down could help.

"Did you really cut me loose for my own good? Or was it just the nun in you winning? Were you afraid of getting more addicted to sex? Is that what drove you away? I remember you saying that your first husband put you up onto a pedestal to worship, reserving his love–really just lust--for lesser women. Now why have you put *yourself* back up on that lonely pedestal--so that God can worship you?"

Bert shook his head, dropping the pen. He doubted she could suddenly change her mind about what God wanted for her. That meant changing her mind about God, which she'd never do.

He picked up the pen again to give writing another try. This time to someone else. "Would you change it for her, God? For me? Well, give it a thought. After all, you know I'm right that our love has always put you at the center. You know it has. Go on, put us back together. Yes, I'm serious, God. If I thought for one minute that you had whispered into her ear that she needed to stop–to become more 'virtuous' for you–I'd never have written or sent the letter. My purpose was always to convince her she was controlling you as well as me."

Writing calmed him down a bit, but not enough. He threw the notebook away and headed for the car to drown his sorrows in drink before Frank arrived.

After they got to El Cancun Bert immediately started talking about Brie.

Frank asked what was wrong, and Bert said Brie kept pushing him away. Frank asked why.

Bert snorted. "She won't give any good reasons, just lame excuses about sex, religion, and alcohol."

"Are you sure she thought you two had a true love relationship?"

"Absolutely. She didn't spend much time telling me she loved me but I know she did. The first time after dumping me she said, 'It was never about love.' But of course, refused to tell me what it *was* about."

"And you kept probing?"

"Yes, in conversations, letters, love poems. I probed way too much."

Frank wiped salsa from his chin. "Toward the end of his life this well-known elderly psychiatrist friend of mine concluded that every mentally ill person he'd ever worked with was basically lonely. He Insisted that loneliness activates physical and mental illnesses."

"Mental too?"

"Definitely some, 'though over-the-top ones are different. This psychiatrist ran his views by friends, and surprisingly most agreed, at least to the non-physiologically based illnesses."

"Such as?"

"He didn't say but I know he wasn't talking about autism or bipolar disorders. Maybe deep personality disorders like the one called borderline personality."

That got Bert's attention. "Tell me more."

"That problem usually starts in childhood. Something happening to take away a person's ability to relate. Because as you know, innocent children have no problem relating."

Bert nodded as Frank continued. "I'm guessing borderline people don't know, or can't allow, intimacy. Yet, being human, they must be still starved for communion...relationship with God, if they believe in God, and other humans."

Bert started to ask a question, then decided to let him finish. "Maybe that's why we've got such strong sexual drives. It's an instinct that demands relationship when it's healthy. When you lose or deny your sexuality you can become sick and toxic."

Bert said he had no trouble agreeing there.

"Did she ever talk about her childhood life or early relationships with men?"

Bert explained how her father made her do all the chores her mother wouldn't. He prevented her from going to college because then how could he survive? She was the unpaid, unloved mother in the house, not only taking care of all household chores, but watching over mom, dad, sister, brother. Then, when she finally got free, she jumped into marriage with a Canadian who had the old-world complex of all women being whores or saints. He turned her into a saint and saved his sexual favors for whores. "So yes, her early years definitely qualified her for some kind of personality disruption."

Frank smiled gently. "Could that answer your confusion about what went wrong?"

"Yeah, but then if she was so damaged, how could she have allowed herself to get so close to me to start with? We were that close for months," Bert said gesturing.

"Borderline personalities have no trouble getting close. They just can't stay close. When things get too intense, they have no alternative but to back away. Run away, fast."

"That's horrible."

"That's why it's called a personality disorder. One almost impossible to shake."

Frank paused, giving Bert time to gather his thoughts and reply. Frank's explanation made perfect sense to him, but when he tried to grasp it, he worried he was just looking to push blame on her.

Frank started to say something, but Bert stopped him. "It's true she did cut off the church healers, the massage healer, and even stopped going to church. Cut *me* off. Maybe she *was* shutting down."

Frank finally got a word in. "Seems like you've got your answer."

Bert tried to laugh. "Ok, so I'm playing psychologist to a psychologist."

"You said it, not me." Then Frank added, "Let me play the devil's advocate. Are you looking only from your eyes?"

"During our magic summer, we always looked from the same eyes. Then she stopped. That's an undeniable fact--not me saying it." Bert took a swig of beer. "The guys I read say God is the eternal flow of love we're meant to be in. I get that. So then isn't that what being in relationship is all about? Isn't God what makes relationship possible?"

"That sounds a lot better than the old description. But you sure you two were in a healthy relationship?"

"Isn't joy, laughter, and powerful sex a sure sign of health?"

Frank nodded and waited for Bert to get it all out. "But then the laughter stopped, the love dried up. Maybe she just didn't know she had to work at relationship. Maybe she thought the only important one was Jesus, the homeboy she kept in her back pocket. I couldn't convince her our human love was in fact helping her heal. She wouldn't accept that our human love was spiritual love. I think she was trying to convince herself she only needed the big guy's help–the one who frowns on sexual activity."

Frank heard Bert breathe deeply, recognized the intense hurt. "Berty Boy, you've dug a huge hole to jump into and can't get out. This obsessive need to answer what went wrong! Face it; you'll never know. Hell, most relationships fizzle out sooner or later. Why can't you just let go?"

"I've tried, Frank, I've tried hard. Yeah, it's driving me crazy, I know that. But how do I let go?"

"I'm a psychologist. My job is to tell you what you're doing wrong, not provide magic cures. Isn't that what religion is supposed to do? It looks to me like you've just invited God into that big hole of yours."

"But I keep thinking I failed her. Was I asking something of her that I just wanted for myself?"

"Stop blaming yourself, you can't heal everyone. You did your best. Just keep praying for her; she needs that.

She's on her own now. So are you, so move on. She's free to fly. You too. That's the best I can do, Buddy Boy."

Bert thanked his friend for the advice and they moved to other topics.

He hadn't heard from Brie for more than a week, waiting impatiently for that voice-message saying, "Come pick up your stuff. It's piled outside the garage door." And then he and Jim would pick things up and go to El Cancun for beer and tacos. Life repeating itself.

All he could do was wait and drive himself crazy asking why she'd done what she'd done. Ask how long it would take to get over her–as he now knew he must. Here's my fantasy, he told himself: I'll go away for a while—to some place where I can stop obsessing over her. Give her time to reconsider. And when I return after a month or so, we'll both have changed. I'll drive up Brook Road and she'll open her door, step onto the porch, and jump into my arms. We'll look into each other's eyes and what's always happened will happen: magic. We'll kiss and head for the bedroom. Our world of love will return.

Oh, why keep torturing myself? he thought. It's Saturday, and she's received my letter by now. I know she won't jump into my arms when I return from my trip; she'll give me a steady look and turn away. Then I'll say goodbye and walk from her porch.

On Sunday he knew the worst had come. He needed to forget the past and ignore the future.

Monday came with no letter or voice mail. He stayed at home playing backgammon with Jim and packing for the trip they'd agreed to take. Soon I'll be signing the new contract with the realtor, he told his friend. So much to do before then. It's impossible to clean and prepare the whole house and yard. But I trust you, God, he told himself, so do what needs be done, even if it means a clean break.

Having just said that, he needed to be more honest. Only yesterday on the way back from church he almost drove over to Brook Road. Knowing it was wrong but hoping....

Tuesday came, and with it the brief phone message. He went to pick up his belongings the second and last time. Vacillation had at last come to its final ending. His world had permanently changed.

CHAPTER TEN: WANDERING

THE MIDDLE OF APRIL CAME to western North Carolina, bringing melancholy and spring flowers.

Bert knew April to be the cruelest month not just because Eliot's *Wasteland* had told him, but because he'd permanently lost the two women of his life. He would move west, but first his house had to sell. After signing with a realtor, he accepted Jim's invitation to make a whirlwind northeastern trip, camping and playing backgammon. This would be the long trip not to let things settle back into the past but to let go of the present and move into the unknown future.

Brie knew it was the cruelest month because her healing had not improved, had in fact stalemated. She needed to have the metal rod removed that the dentist had inserted into the root canal, but she couldn't face the prospect. Her mother was into her eighth month of kidney dialysis and wouldn't last much longer. Her son in California was busy doing his music and tattoo thing and wouldn't come to drive her up to Connecticut, and that left her daughter, who hadn't jumped at the chance. And she doubted she could make it there herself, but certainly couldn't fly. She needed to see her mother. The future looked black for both of them.

Marsha knew it to be the cruelest month because her best friend Francine called saying her husband had tried to commit suicide. She knew he'd been unstable for some time. She needed to fly out to support Francine. Apparently, Max hadn't succeeded, but by the time she got there he could be dead. She didn't think Frank would come with her.

For Frank, April was a difficult month because he didn't have the foggiest idea of what was going on in his wife's head, didn't know how to help her, and certainly didn't relish flying with her to Montana to visit her friend's out-of-control husband. So he did the logical thing: he accepted the invitation from his colleagues at the University of Florida to fly back to his old university and take on some cases.

Jim didn't consider April the cruelest month because he was looking forward to a relaxing backgammon tour of the Midwest and Northeast. He and Bert would visit places they'd never been to and should. Only three were etched in stone for Jim: Niagara Falls, WestPoint, and Antietam. There were three for Bert: the Adirondacks, Hudson River Valley, and rural Pennsylvania. They'd camp as much as possible, spend as little money as possible, and argue or worry not at all. In short, a wide-open, relaxed pleasure trip that could last until August.

Bert decided their trip was to involve exploring, not cogitating or processing. He told Jim the only impulses whirling inside his head would be strategies for beating him at backgammon. Their trip would take them up the Atlantic seaboard to Canada, back down the New England states he'd never visited, and then west past the Great Lakes and Montana to the Northwest, which he'd also seen too little of. There Jim would leave for Viet Nam and Bert would venture on to join his high school buddy Edward, returning through northern California, Nevada, Utah, Colorado, and the greater Midwest—all of which both knew intimately, ending up in North Carolina, by which time Bert's house should have sold.

He looked forward to living cleanly and simply in the external world. If he, like Odysseus, had been ejected from battles won and lost, he'd venture forth not alone but with shipmates, leaving siege engines and swords behind. Knowing how difficult it is to abandon internal warfare, he purchased an expensive set of headphones to connect him to music located somewhere in the sky. That should help drown out internal chatter about life gone wrong and what might lie ahead.

Unlike his Greek hero of old, Bert wasn't headed home, but could pretend he was venturing toward a healthier set of obsessions. Maybe home for him meant getting back into God's grace and discovering a truer inner self that didn't think about women all the time. His shipmates, Jim and Edward, could help him leave the dangerous world of females behind. They would talk about books, politics, and memories from way back when. This would please Jim, who had long ago given up trying to live with a woman, as well as Edward, whose closeness to his wife might have come from spending five months of the year away from her while hiking and exploring the world. An all-male trip, Bert chuckled while packing the Element with essentials except golf clubs. It would even be good to suspend that addiction.

At the last minute, Jim rerouted their trip, heading north through Missouri and Illinois to Wisconsin, after his friend had put in an emergency phone call begging for assistance with his upcoming moving needs.

Before the two could venture forth, Jim had to pack his belongings. Only two months before, he'd lugged a dresser, small desk, and four suitcases into Bert's house to make his bedroom more comfortable, and now he had to repack them back into his three storage sheds. But he was happy things were starting to work out for his friend, and looked forward to their trip. He'd recently turned down an offer from his first ex-wife to move into her million-dollar Florida house because she'd refused to meet his requirements of losing 150 pounds and taking time to get to know her grandkids. "Screw her and all her money," he cackled at Bert, "I don't want anything to tie me down, least of all a grumpy 300-pound tub of lard."

They were now both footloose and fancy free, as Jim, who spoke in platitudes, said, adding, "Let's get it on." Bert knew Jim hadn't saved much from his carpentry days, so they struck a deal: Jim would pay for half of the campgrounds, and Bert for the other half—plus all the hotels and motels they'd stay in every five days or so. When camping they'd cook out—steaks plus potatoes, onions, and carrots wrapped in tinfoil. They'd have rolls and bagels, cheese and fruit for breakfast around the campfire when the coals were rekindled...after downing three cups of coffee. Lunch, they'd eat out, as with dinners while staying in hotels. Bert would buy them too. He calculated he could never spend out his retirement unless he lived to 120. "Or got married again," Jim reminded him. "Which you're not stupid enough to do."

Their first stop was Mammoth Cave in Kentucky, followed by the small Abe Lincoln museum and his early home site. Next, up to South Bend to visit Notre Dame, agreeing it was the prettiest campus they'd seen. "Chaming," Jim said, "just chaming, even if it is run by de pope." They loved the expensive west coast of Lake Michigan, with quaint New England tourist towns like Pentwater, then stopped only briefly in Muskegon so they'd arrive in time for their planned four-day stay with Jim's friend in the small town of Manistee. Walking along empty tree-lined streets, they found impressive stone churches with Tiffany art nouveau stained glass windows. One lady pastor told them their winter services had to be held in the basement since attendance wasn't large enough to afford heat for the big sanctuary.

They got to Traverse City in time for the cherry festival, but Bert couldn't stand the old-timer band and circus atmosphere that Jim said he took a shine to. Bert also had a hard time breathing at their ten by fifteen-foot tent camp site sandwiched between two huge RVs. He breathed much better at the state park at Tahquamenon Falls, a non-touristy place below Lake Superior.

Jim had always wanted to visit the famous Mackinac Island, which Bert hadn't, so they took the ferry there, and both got into the history of the fort, wishing they had an extra $600 to stay at the Grand Hotel. Rowdy freaked out when the militia fired their black powder muskets. He didn't quiet back down until they boarded the ferry for the ride back.

Bert enjoyed the quiet drive down to Detroit, there being one-fiftieth the houses and much emptier state parks on the western coast of Huron than on Lake Michigan. "The slogan 'Pure Michigan' finally speaks true here," Bert told Jim before going for a long walk on the dunes with Rowdy. "Right as rain," Jim said, "Let's keep on 'a trucking."

Most of the time they were able to get into a state park, even if it was a tiny spot sandwiched between RVs. All the camping areas with electricity and water were booked throughout Michigan far in advance, but tent sites could usually be found. Because it took almost an hour for them to erect Jim's huge tent, they usually stayed two nights. Most hotels and motels, like all the restaurants, wouldn't allow dogs, which meant they had to sneak Rowdy in, but in Ottawa the clerk said it was ok to leave him in their room all day. Otherwise, whenever they went to a museum or ate out, they had to find a shade tree to park under.

After telling Jim he wished he'd talked a vet into certifying him as a safety dog, Bert tried to convince the attendant at the Eastman Kodak museum that he'd lost Rowdy's safety vest. For fifteen minutes he walked with a limp, pretending to be disabled and in great need of Rowdy, then decided he couldn't keep faking it. The dog did better out in the car anyway.

Even before they reached Sheboygan, a town much smaller and attractive than they'd anticipated, the squabbling started. Jim had to spend two to three hours a day playing games on his iPad and wanted to stop at anything resembling a tourist attraction. Bert wanted to spend his time lying around camp, not driving aimlessly around a big city looking for tourist attractions. Jim slept while Bert drove, and Bert complained about Jim's failure to secure reliable driving directions and motel locations whenever they stopped at a McDonalds to connect to wi-fi—after attacking Jim for being too cheap to purchase wi-fi for his iPad. "Hey, dude, how about you 'bein too cheap to buy one 'a your own?" Jim countered. Bert lacked energy to tell him it wasn't the money but the prospect of getting addicted to it, like him.

They went around and around, tension immediately dissipating after they settled into a game of backgammon, where they could kill each other civilly.

In Lancing they toured the expansive Michigan State campus and spent all afternoon at the Oldsmobile Museum. The following day Bert played golf on one of the city's 22 golf courses. He had to rent clubs but they let him ride Rowdy on the cart. Away from noise and crowds, he relaxed into one of his better golfing days, mixing bogeys and pars, and purposely went slowly to pay back Jim for always being tardy.

They arrived late at Proud Lake Campground, had to set up camp far from the lake. Jim pretended to knock on wood for there being no rain, then went in search of someone to talk to. He brought back a friendly local who joined them for beer as they sat around the fire trading stories. Jim did most of the talking until the newcomer started bragging about all his female conquests. Bert listened for a while and then left for a walk around the lake.

The "Pure Michigan" slogan didn't hold true in Detroit, where everything was falling down or being rebuilt. They finally found the free art museum and spent most of the day at it, agreeing it was one of the best half-dozen in the country. Bert didn't mind coming out every two hours to water and check on Rowdy. It being Sunday, they'd found a parking space a block away. Jim took 83 pictures on his iPad and splurged $20 for the Diego Rivera special exhibit, which he had to wait almost two hours to get into. Bert didn't care for Diego Rivera so didn't join Jim but went wild over the medieval and renaissance rooms and limewood and bronze statuary, telling himself that once his life settled down, he'd have to get back into sculpting--not that he'd ever done much of it, but he could.

The following day Jim dragged his feet, spending too much time folding and re-packing his clothes at the washeteria, making Bert speed to reach the ferry for their island destination. By 5:35 they were still 30 minutes from Port Clinton, knowing they wouldn't make it. But they miraculously arrived at 6:08. Jim dashed to buy ferry tickets while Bert drove off to find a parking space, dump food from the cooler, run two blocks, and board the boat with exactly one minute to spare.

The next six days were spent with their church friends from back home, listening to Fred pontificate about

252

Middle Bass Island history, reading, lounging, and watching Lake Erie pound the back yard. Bert biked around the island's 750 acres, and they took ferries to other islands.

Neighbors from Toronto said they'd just left behind two million visitors for the Pan Am Games, so Bert vetoed that leg of their Canada itinerary, much to Jim's dismay. Fred consoled Jim, saying he'd heard the long empty drive from Toronto to Ottawa was called "Dead Boring." Then came time to take the ferry back to Ohio, and the two headed east, stopping at a pleasant grassy campground before reaching Cleveland, a city Jim wanted to spend at least four days touring, but Bert limited to two. Their GPS had broken, they had no Ohio maps, and Jim still hadn't purchased wi-fi for his iPad, so it took the better part of the day to find their way around the confusing city that was repairing roads for next year's Republican convention. Jim snoozed while Bert fumed.

As the sky turned black, they found a motel on the far edge of town. Bert collapsed. Jim was "raring to go" since he'd been sleeping while Bert maneuvered the endless road repairs. The next day they spent another two hours finding the museum. They liked it as well, or maybe better than the Detroit museum, particularly the Impressionist collection. Bert smiled every time he could identify a painting dredged back from his college art history class.

Jim begrudgingly let Bert talk him into leaving Cleveland and they headed toward Pennsylvania and New York. After a day's driving they found a motel 25 miles shy of Erie, but thought $185 too steep for a Day's Inn. An hour later they discovered their last chance, not named Last Chance, but Sunset Motel--one room left for only $65, and they'd arrived in time to watch the sunset. Trees, clouds, a huge field of grass with no people! Bert sat like a kid in the middle of the grass while Jim stayed inside glued to the tv.

The next stop was a campground on the shores of Erie, a lake much noisier than Michigan, Jim explained, because it was shallower. Bert collected a sack-full of smoothly polished rocks, thinking one day to glue these rocks, so different from the ones he was used to collecting around mountain lakes, onto a rustic board. Back at camp he and Jim decided to forgo grilled potatoes and hamburgers for a Mexican restaurant. Jim tried again to convince Bert they had to go to Toronto, but Bert again reminded him of the name of the highway between it and Ottawa. They scowled and debated whether to include Quebec or just settle for Montreal.

A day later two sub-teen girls and boys came to watch them play backgammon, to which they had to be properly introduced. After they left, Bert memorialized the occasion with some doggerel that one day he might call "Summer Fling":

> I love to say, *my love*
> even when no one's there.
> Today, Miranda, ten, became my love.
> While I played backgammon with Jim
> she and Emily joined our game,

plus Josh and Fred, all under age.
My Miranda cleverly helped me win;
smiling and laughing throughout the game.
I didn't kiss my love, just high-fived our win.
Then she and they ran off to other friends.

Bert dreaded driving through Buffalo, thought it would be another congested Cleveland, but was surprised to find it an easy drive with an interesting mix of new and old. They didn't stay but continued on to the Canadian side of the Falls, where they'd already booked a hotel, on the way speculating why the U.S. side had never been built up. The next three days they mostly went their own ways, Jim taking all the trams and boat tours, Bert content to explore by foot.

On his way past the casino's garish fountain, Bert was thrown back to a similar fountain somewhere in Mobile. He pushed back tears that rushed in for his lost Suzanne. The past kept intruding, despite his effort to outpace it. He walked faster, trying to stop asking her to forgive him for his precipitous affair with Brie, forgive him for looking forward to meeting a new woman in the southwest, forgive him for always needing a woman. He finally found a shady spot to relax in, read a book he'd bought for a friend back in North Carolina. He was thankful for having a summertime of enough confusion to keep him sane. And most of all, thankful for Rowdy.

After Niagara Falls, they drove to Niagara By the Lake, a well-groomed tourist spot where they went to see a Broadway production of Neil Simons' "Sweet

Charity." It was professionally done but boring. Then back into New York, a state Bert had always wanted to explore but would just be zipping through, stopping to visit the George Eastman museum in Rochester and having a fantastic breakfast in Syracuse at the type of neighborhood diner Jim had been looking for.

Before they reached the mouth of the St. Lawrence, they took a long boat ride around the Thousand Islands, then headed north. Back into Canada, they showed Rowdy's particular kind of passport, a letter from the vet certifying he was ok, and spent the day wandering around Ottawa. Jim wanted to explore the Parliament buildings but didn't get there in time since he'd dallied too long trying to talk to a young Chinese man who was busy protesting something in his native language. Instead he announced he'd tour the Canadian historical museum. Bert skipped it, seeing a notice that most was closed for repairs.

Bert roamed the wide streets admiring the architecture, especially the long flowing sculptural building with very little inside. He was able to find a comfortable chair on the third floor, falling asleep for much of the three hours he needed to kill waiting for Jim. They finally found each other and took the bus back to the hotel, where Rowdy had spent the time alone, no doubt barking and sleeping on the bed. Jim, exhausted from the long walk back and almost totally dehydrated, immediately fell asleep. Bert wandered down the street to find a cafe after taking the dog for his much-needed walk. He told Rowdy he should be very happy not being forced to come earlier; the sight-seeing was boring to a dog.

By the time they got to Montreal, their tempers flared again. Jim huffed and puffed, announced they should immediately pack it up and drive back to North Carolina. Bert stayed silent. They separated for the day and planned to meet for dinner at 6:00 sharp where they'd parked the car near the Old Port.

The whole time Bert was exploring Old Port, a trading post for French fur trappers that now pulled in over six million tourists a year, he kept turning around to look for Rowdy, forgetting he was back in the car with half-opened windows. That got him to wondering about parents he'd seen on tv who would leave their children in a locked car. They must have been improperly raised, he reasoned, or on drugs, or both. That set him to considering their punishment. If the child dies, it's obviously murder--but should the parents be locked away for life or put to death? What would that accomplish? It might achieve the public's momentary outcry for justice, but once they got out, there's no way they'd do a repeat performance. They were no threat to society. So, he concluded, they should be forced to perform menial, hard, very disgusting work once a week for twenty years...mucking out stables, cleaning sewers and zoo cages. He'd have to tell Jim this grand plan; it might help defuse the frustration and anger building between them. Jim, he knew, would agree but also find some way to disagree because he always had to have the last word.

Bert sat on a park bench at Old Port waiting for Jim to show up. He waited and waited and started boiling as 8:00 approached. When Jim finally did arrive, two-and-a-half hours late, Bert immediately started upbraiding him. Jim claimed innocence, saying he'd forgotten where they were supposed to meet. Bert knew he was lying. Around and around they went until Bert threw up his hands. "Let's shut up and find a good place to eat." Jim nodded, saying nothing. They roamed the streets, Jim finding something wrong with every restaurant. They finally agreed on an expensive French place and endured a silent meal. Bert picked up the tab and stomped out.

The walk back to the car was dark enough to send them in circles. They decided it was time to cut the trip short. Montana and points west would be out of the question; backgammon alone couldn't sustain their friendship. Also, Bert had just learned that his friend Edward was having second thoughts about joining him out west.

The next day Jim slept while Bert drove. Jim sullenly agreeing to the motel Bert found in West Virginia. Both tried to be civil at the fast food restaurant. Bert knew Jim would never come around, so when they got back to the motel, he offered the peace token. "We need to start over. Traveling together in tight quarters always causes discord. Let's just shake and stop quibbling. Let's end on a good note."

Jim looked hard into his eyes, started to reach out a hand, then laughed. "Yeah you're right, you know, but only 'cause I'm right." They both laughed and hit their beds.

The next day they drove quietly until they got to Tennessee. Jim slept as usual. Bert remained upset over the way their trip had petered out, concluding it had all been one big mistake. He was about to wake Jim up when the proverbial light went on inside. He *had* learned something—something very important that he probably wouldn't have if the continual travel hadn't cleared his head. He started singing. "So long, it's been good to know you. So long, it's been good to know you. So long, it's been good to...."

Jim snapped awake. "Shut up over there! Can't a body get some sleep! Cut the racket!"

What caused Bert to sing was a revelation sneaking into his mental network, possible answer to what had been bothering him since she threw him under the table. Not that he finally understood her motives; he'd never master them, needed to settle for simplifications like her religion or his alcohol. Answers that might stave off the beast of uncertainty.

But driving quietly along it hit him that he shouldn't have been looking toward her for answers; he should have been looking inside. His problem wasn't understanding what went wrong but needing resolution. While writing "The Mermaid" he'd been able to distance himself from his character (himself). Now he could no longer do that. He wanted the story to end either with explicit denial (not this half-truth, "It never was about love") or miraculous recovery ("Back into my arms, I need you"). Either ending would have been okay, but ambiguity wasn't. Unfortunately, ambiguity was what he got. His character's life had dead-ended in logical exhaustion. Had reached the state of infinite repetition. This or that would happen, but poor Bert-the-character would always remain trapped in the failure of not knowing what went wrong with something he believed had been ordained to last forever.

But that was Bert the character, not Bert sitting right here driving the car. This revelation cheered him considerably, set him to singing. Maybe Bert the character was fated to dribble out his life repeating, "what if, what if?" but not Bert the live one headed toward his own new future. He would just close that fictive door, say goodbye to what might have been-- had God or fate come to the rescue. Thus leaving open the real door for him that led toward anywhere unconnected to what went before. Such was life, he knew deep down: things happen and then we make up stories to explain why they did. Well, he was finished with that story.

Being a bad novelist, he reasoned, was one thing, but being stupid enough to let a story control his life, another. Once back home, he'd call Frank to tell him to stop trying to make sense of electromagnetic sensitivity. Tell him to get on with his own disconnected and perhaps pointless life, urge him to do what all good husbands do, humor Marsha before she too disappeared down the rabbit hole. He'd e-mail everyone he knew with the salient message: "So long, it's been good to know you" and keep singing it, though he couldn't get much farther than "and I've gotta' be movin' along." Chanting away, his smile got wider and wider, bringing him back fifty years to when he and the three other musketeers sang it on the ski train to Winter Park when they weren't mindlessly chanting, "99 bottles of beer on the wall...."

The two arrived back in North Carolina to find that Bert's house had just sold. Everything was speeded up. It had felt good singing his silly goodbye song to the former love of his life. But he knew the problem was bigger than Brie. While packing, it came clear he needed some resolution to deity's involvement in his failed love affair. Life would be so much easier, he told himself, if he–like Jim–could settle for pat answers to hard questions, or like Frank, could settle for no answers. He needed to know about God's role in their relationship.

That night he found himself talking to God. Not praying, just rattling on, the same way he rattled on inside his head all day, or when talking to a close friend after drinking too much.

I don't understand you. Yeah, I know I'm not supposed to, but even so, sometimes I think I have. Now I've lost you altogether. Used to be with Suzanne we'd throw everything important your way and wait. Even when we didn't like what appeared, we went with it. It usually eventually worked out in our favor.

So now she's gone and I've accepted her death, have to because I do know you were in it and who am I to question that. I bumbled along and told myself life for me wasn't over but living with a woman was. I never looked for one. Then along came that one and you know the rest. You let us love deeply, maybe even helped us.

Then I started wondering if I'd called her up, being on the rebound as Frank says, or if you were really in it. I told myself yes you were, but don't think she ever did. Anyway, I won't ramble on about that, it's all over. But I'd still like to know if you were behind her decision to throw me under the table. Well, maybe not behind it, but did you just *allow* it…for her or me, or both?

Why do I have such a hard time accepting what happened? If you were in it all along, then obviously it shouldn't be so hard. Of course, if she was *outside* your will, then I was right to step aside and stop worrying about you and me. Well, it took me a hell of a long time, but I did. Meanwhile, can you whisper lightly telling me you were or weren't in it at the very end? Then I can stop bothering you. I won't worry about the same thing happening again; I'll just accept everything, as Suzanne and I always did.

Here's another thing I'm telling myself: you're just having a hard time finding the right new woman for me—moving her into my sphere. Or I'm not quite ready. But it will happen—or not—and I'll know and accept. Also, keep believing love does conquer all. But I have one more question for you. How am I supposed to think about you—pray to you? This really bothers me, not knowing. Let me explain. I used to have that big garden back in North Carolina. Remember? Sure you do. I never worried about what would come up, anything would be fine. I didn't feel it necessary to pray to my garden. I didn't even think about it when I wasn't in it. I just watered and weeded it. And it usually did well by me.

I hear you replying, So what? Here's what: After a long time, I realized the garden would do what it's supposed to do without me using my head (or spirit) to help it along. This realization is profound! The only problem is that I don't know if the same applies to you. Do you want me to congratulate you? Thank you? Talk to you? Sometimes I think you couldn't care a whit; you're way too busy with billions and billions of more important things. Please tell me how to talk to you.

Bert smiled and finished his monologue. Before falling asleep, he decided he needed to talk to Rhonda one last time, have her confirm or reject what he thought to be truth. Maybe she'd speak for Him.

As usual, the two met for lunch at Matt's pizza on Hayesville's square–one of the few shops still open. Rhonda more than anyone had been responsible for widening and deepening Bert's thinking about God. They skipped small talk, even about his recent trip. He started by apologizing for dragging her once again into his personal battleground. She listened, said nothing, then they began.

"I'm in the middle of another spiritual quagmire."

"Suzanne."

"No. Yes. No...well, I've forgiven God for that...." Then he laughed. "You know...."

263

She smiled. "I do. So it's Brie."

"No, no, believe me, I've finally let go of her, as you and all the books insist. I actually think I have. But now I find she's not the only problem. It's bigger. It's my shallow understanding of God."

"Welcome to the group!"

The waitress came and they ordered the usual pizza.

"You know what happened. Brie and I thought we had a clear connection to God, then suddenly everything disconnected."

"You're wondering if it was Brie or God who pulled the plug?"

"It can't be God, yet I still have a hard time understanding how this woman who leans hard, and daily, on God, who apparently *does* trust God, could just shut off her flow of love for me if she knew God had put us together."

Rhonda smiled. "You know we can never jump inside her mind. But we don't have to, what's there doesn't really have to concern you...or your relation to God."

"It shouldn't...unless God *allowed* her healing to stop, which appears to be the case."

"Again, in your mind it's either God or Brie. You might not want it to be Brie, but it might be. You *don't* want it to be God, but it might be. Do you think God would give up on her?"

"Forgive me, Rhonda, but don't play psychologist with me. Of course, I don't. I don't pretend to know what God wants or would do, but fervently believe it wouldn't be anything to harm either her or me."

"That's a given. But to *surprise* you?"

Bert started to answer, then paused. "Maybe. I think God does interact with us, intercede with us for our own good. If I didn't believe this...."

"You wouldn't believe anything. Nor I."

"Maybe God would do it to surprise me, or push me off in another direction, but how about *her*? How could putting a stop to healing help her? She's too fragile. God wouldn't do that, couldn't, if God is love. Pure love can only promote and continue pure love."

"We're starting to curve this into a theological discussion. Let's get back to you."

"This *is* me; this *is* my problem! Believe me, I've always been thinking more of her than me, even though I know it's my problem." He stopped. "I guess I'm making no sense, so I'll just say again, I think I've fallen into the trap of doubting God."

"Not understanding and doubting are two very different things, Bert. Most people don't know that. We'll never understand God, and probably never stop doubting. Let's go back a minute. You said you finally got over your anger at God for what happened to Suzanne, right?"

"Yeah, but the situations are so different. Suzanne had a bona fide physical disease; Brie...."

"Go ahead, say it. EMS might be in her head. If so, it could also be that she's not the person she appears to be. Maybe you fell in love with your idea of her, not the real her."

"I guess you're telling me I made up my picture of Brie, and also my picture of God. Then fell in love with my pictures."

"We do that, don't we?"

"But if that's *all* we can do; if we can never reach the naked truth, then what we picture really doesn't matter; it's only the loving that matters."

"I'll go there with you."

"Ok, I'll go back over it one last time. I'm loving her; I'm loving God. She's loving me; she's loving God. We both think our loving is helping her healing. That God had put us together for that reason. Then she stops loving and I don't. Here's where I get confused. I've finally accepted that it's not my business to question her change. But how do I keep trusting and loving a God that allows her healing to stop?"

Rhonda reached across the table to take his hand. "Bert, I could give you answers. My answer, Richard Rohr's, Thich Nhat Hanh's, Meister Eckhart's, but you already know they're nothing but our feeble attempts to answer an unanswerable."

"Shit!" Bert almost shouted but instead nodded patiently. "I was hoping...."

"Your pastor would provide a good answer to an unsolvable question."

"Well, some answer. Any answer."

"I guess I'm finally learning this, intellectually. But...."

"You thought it would be easier."

"Well, I am trying to live with uncertainty," he said, knowing he may never reach ultimate closure but at the very least wanted to make closure for this conversation. He started again: "I guess I've accepted being in the dark about Brie. I'm having a hard time accepting being in the dark about God. Being in the dark about me. In the dark about how they all relate."

"As you know, Bert, this is the hardest part of your spiritual journey. You've come far, much farther than you know. You must learn to trust–not yourself, not even the masters, and certainly not the picture of the God you'd like to be in charge of your life."

"What then?"

"The good."

"The good? That sounds like California talk to me!"

"California talk?"

"You know, New Age philosophy. Everything is good. Surrender to the good in you. Look for the good in everybody. Find good everywhere. Good, good, good."

Rhonda laughed. "Well, believe it or not, I've never been to California. Maybe I should go."

Bert smiled. "I hope you do! Bob too, once I get settled. You can stop in Arizona on the way. It won't be long before I'll be there."

Their conversation came to an end. They sat smiling at each other. Rhonda reached for the check. "No! no," he said. "We're not splitting this time; it's on me."

Bert gave her a farewell kiss on the cheek and they exchanged a deep hug and left.

Two days later Bert said goodbye to Jim, Frank, and North Carolina and climbed into the van for the long trip west. A very long trip into the future, Rowdy seated quietly beside him.

PART TWO

CHAPTER ELEVEN: LOVING FRIENDS

MARSHA KNEW SHE NEEDED TO SEE BRIE; she'd been thinking of her ever since their boat trip on Lake Chatuge. There was no way she could help with her physical problem but she could show support. Brie needed that, and she needed to be there for her. Why had she waited so long?

When she got to Brie's, they hugged and cried. Marsha had come prepared to help unload her problems, but found herself jumping into her own troubles with Frank. "I don't know what's wrong, we don't connect any more. He's off hiding in his damn boat, and we never do anything together. We even talk about selling the house and moving to Rockport…."

Brie started to commiserate, but Marsha grabbed her arm. "Oh, Brie, forgive me! Here I am talking about me! How about you? How are you doing?"

"Well, my life's never exactly rosy," she said, trying to smile. "But I can't complain, I have the lake…and this wonderful porch."

Marsha asked about Bert; didn't she still have him? How *were* they doing? Brie shook her head, then smoothed her long hair. "It just didn't work. We're two very different people, maybe not made for each other."

"Oh, I'm surprised...and so sorry. I know how hard this must be for you."

"Yes and no. I'm relieved, actually. I know it's harder on him, he's going to keep ranting and raving for a long time. You should have seen this letter he sent. On and on about some kind of engram thing, sort of a personality chart. I mean he just rambled this way and that, got all tangled up."

"Not unusual for an intellectual. Frank leaves me behind too."

"Bert's really out there. But I did understand what he said about our personalities. And agreed. He's the classic romantic...always wanting what he doesn't have, head up in the sky. Thinks everything's spiritual, especially sex, and it all meets his needs...and mine."

"But you did once tell me that certain things he did *did* meet your needs," Marsha said, smiling knowingly.

"True, very true. And I'll have to admit he's very compassionate--when he's not moody and into himself."

"Ok, so what did he say about you?"

"He had me pegged. I'm the perfectionist, realistic, self-disciplined, orderly." She stopped, scowled a little, then went on. "But he also said inflexible and judgmental. A control freak! And I guess I am somewhat."

"Somewhat," Marsha said, thinking of what Brie couldn't control, the electromagnetic sensitivity.

"Yeah," Brie said, maybe reading her mind, "I can't control the wi-fi mess."

"No change there?"

"Not yet. I keep hoping and praying. Haven't given up yet."

Marsha remembered the article Frank had told her about, didn't know how to bring it up. "I remember someone telling me some EMS patients give up, can't see light at the end of the tunnel."

"Not uncommon, you keep battling the impossible, nothing changes. So yeah, the suicide rate's pretty high."

"No other options?"

"You can move into some EMS community way out in the desert miles from wi-fi towers and all. They live in these tiny bare houses without anything comfortable. Like living in prison, really."

"Is your house any better for you these days? I know you've fixed it up a lot."

"No, it's worse really. I don't know why, I fixed everything I could afford to fix. In the summer I can get out, go to the lake. Unless it's storming. Then in the winter I'm stuck inside. Have to sit on the porch, all bundled up, away from the heat going on and off, the electricity zooming around."

"What about that other opportunity you just mentioned--can't you find a better EMS community?"

Brie started to answer, then changed direction. "Well, for a while Bert tried to talk me into moving to the desert, said he could build a place away from wi-fi."

"And...?"

"I don't know. Guess I blew if off, maybe too fast. He has the money and know how. But whenever I think about it, my spirit says no."

"Why?"

"That's just it, I don't know. Am I afraid of relationship?"

"Even to him? He's a rare find."

"You think so?"

Marsha nodded. "Frank thinks the world of him. And you know, Frank doesn't like very many people."

Brie couldn't find words. "If I only knew...if I felt about him the way I know he feels about me...." She paused, then added, "But even if I did, would it be fair to him?"

"You mean being cooped up like you, not being able to get out...but isn't he pretty independent?"

Brie nodded. "It's just a mess. Sometimes I wish we'd never met. Other times I wish we'd hook up. But mostly my spirit says no."

Marsha shook her head. "I don't know what you mean there. Is your spirit different from your head--or heart?"

"That's hard to explain, especially to someone who doesn't know God."

"Know God?"

"Remember, we agreed not to argue about that."

"But Brie, I'm trying to understand, not argue. Your God speaks directly to your spirit, telling it something different from what your head or heart says?

"Here we go."

"Listen, this is important. I think you're not being fair. You are not trying to help me understand."

"My bible says..."

"Stop!" Marsha shouted. "Forget your bible. Let's talk about you. What's this spirit thing?"

"It's what connects us to God."

"So God talks to it instead of your head or heart?"

"This is so hard. Jesus died for us, and we have to..."

"Please stop, Brie. You're speaking words someone convinced you to speak. Talk to me like normal. Do you or do you not like Bert? And I mean with your heart, all of it."

Brie started to cry. "If I only knew."

Marsha put her arms around her. "I wish I could help, Brie. I think you are confused and afraid to trust yourself."

"I wish you could help also. Most of the time I feel so alone, don't know what to do...or feel."

"You said you might be afraid of relationship?"

"Yeah, that's scary. It's never worked for me."

"I don't know, Brie, I'm no counselor, most of the time am pretty confused myself."

"But you trust your heart?"

"I do. That's the one given for me. And there's one more: you have to *want* relationship. And then you have to work at it. Both of those are hard." She paused. "And I know what you're thinking now: "That's easy for you to say; you have a pretty normal life, and I don't'."

Brie wiped her tears and managed a small smile. "Gee, Marsha, I don't know what to say. You're so much wiser than me--even if you don't know God!' and she laughed. Then her voice changed: "Maybe I need to lighten up. Stop worrying and let go. Trust my gut, live a little."

They hugged and Marsha realized it was time to change the subject. "You don't get out at all? No more church?"

"I had to stop that, too many hits. Bert used to go shopping for me, but now the nice assistant minister at Ingles bags things up for me and hand delivers them. But I always have my lake to go to! And sometimes I go for a small drive somewhere. I'll get along." She found another smile, smoothed back her hair again.

"You should get a dog."

"Well, I have the neighbor's dog Klepto and the horses to look at. They're good." They looked across the fence below her land but found only two; the others had wandered into a far pasture.

They talked for another hour, then hugged and kissed a last time. Marsha cried all the way home.

Marsha not only worried about Brie, she worried about her sister. Francine's husband had been talking about suicide for a long time and had finally attempted it a second time, but again in such a way as to survive. Just another cry for help. Then one afternoon Francine

275

called saying things were looking worse. Would Marsha be able to visit if things didn't change? She knew she'd have to, but her own life needed tending. Frank and she had recently stopped enjoying intimacy. She hoped she wouldn't receive another phone call from Montana, would have time to somehow put their life back together.

Frank had been busy working up a consulting job back at the University of Florida shortly after Bert left on his extended camping tour of the northeast. He'd been thinking about it for months, excited to get back to important work and perhaps even bigger opportunities. Golf, walking the dog, and riding around in his boat didn't do much for the ego. Most importantly, he reasoned, the month or so he'd be away would do their marriage a world of good. They needed time-out.

On Thursday night he had a vivid and frightening dream. He was walking on his way somewhere when all of a sudden, a large truck came barreling down on him, forcing him to jump. The truck missed, but when he landed, he felt something pop down near his ankle. Frank wasn't one to pay attention to dreams, even though friends kept telling him he, the psychologist, was supposed to follow Jung's lead. When he got up the next morning and tried to tell Marsha, she ignored him completely, insisting he cancel his trip to the University of Florida. She'd just received very bad news. Francine had called again saying that Max had just attempted suicide again, and this time things looked very bad.

"That's terrible," Frank said. "You must go immediately." He hesitated, then added, "I guess you want me to go with you." She nodded.

Frank called the university to cancel his consulting plans. They didn't like it after all the preparation, but he wasn't on retainer, and told them something urgent had come up that he couldn't miss.

Their flight was uneventful. When they arrived, they learned Max was still in a coma. Marsha stayed much of the time with Francine, at the hospital in need of companionship. Frank found a spare bedroom to occupy, and watched television for two days. On the third he called Uber to take him to a good municipal golf course. He rented clubs and bundled up for a series of cold afternoons. Better cold than bored, he told himself. On the fourth day he returned from golf to learn that Max had just died without recovering from his coma. The kids arrived late that afternoon, and Frank told Marsha they should rent a motel for a day or two to let them process things.

When he and Marsha returned, they quickly sized up the situation. Having handled more than his share of family tragedies, Frank recognized that Rex and Irma had long ago distanced themselves from their father. When Frank gently probed, Rex went so far as to say it was probably better for everyone that Max finally accomplished what he tried to do before. Irma was non-committal, and Francine seemed relieved. "He'd always resisted my attempts to get him to a therapist," she told Marsha privately.

If Rex and Irma shed few tears for their father, they did for their mother. The three had always been close, especially after Max started his routine of disappearing on month-long hunting trips. Frank suggested he and Marsha remove themselves again for a few days, but Rex said they should stay to help with household arrangements. "We've agreed Mom needs to sell the house and move in with Irma," he said with authority. "I'm too busy right now to help make preparations for the move. If it's okay with you two to stay a while, I could give instructions on what needs to be done and then let you guys handle everything."

"Do you want to have a big garage sale?" Marsha asked.

Both Irma and Rex shook their heads, saying they didn't want strangers rummaging through the house. "I'd rather just give it away," Rex said. "Irma's married to a wealthy guy and couldn't fit anything else into their mansion. I maybe could, but don't want the stuff around to remind me of the bad days."

Frank pulled him aside and asked if their father had harmed them when younger. "Yes and no," Rex replied. "Not physically, just by totally ignoring us, treating us like we'd never be important to him."

The two men rejoined the women and Frank asked if they should contact an estate sale person.

"That's probably best," Francine said. Irma nodded and Rex said, "I guess first Irma and Marsha should go through the personal stuff. And I probably need to collect all of Dad's macho crap…it's worth a lot, and should be sold separately, maybe on consignment."

"Rifles, guns…?"

"You name it," Rex said. "Every rifle and automatic pistol imaginable. ATVs, motorcycles, boats, stuffed animal heads. You name it, Max shot it and bought it all home to prove himself a manly man." Rex shook his head and walked into the other room.

On his way to the kitchen Frank came up with a better way to help Rex. He joined Rex in the den and volunteered to go through his father's cell phone to locate some of his hunting and camping buddies. "They'd probably come up with a fair price, and everything would sell a lot quicker." Rex agreed, so long as he didn't have to be there when they came to get it all. They walked back and told the women their plans.

The next day Rex left and Frank went out to buy large packing boxes and start sorting things in the house. Francine told him where things went and he and Marsha began stuffing boxes. Into two bedrooms went everything destined for Francine and the kids plus the handful of things he and Marsha would take back to North Carolina. Although he never knew Max, and appreciated Rex's apprehensions, Frank couldn't bring himself to dump his collection of books, notebooks, and photographs of African animals. He put them aside, telling Irma to keep them safe somewhere out of her brother's sight. "Maybe after a few years he'll value them," he explained.

Into the garage went everything for Max's macho gear sale. The furniture and household items were left where they were for the estate sale manager to deal with, and leftovers for the dump or items for the Christian Love Ministries to pick up were piled on the covered back porch.

Two days before Frank and Marsha were scheduled to leave, they decided to change their itinerary. Rex pulled Frank aside, telling he'd finally found a way to thank him for all his help. Frank brushed it off, but Rex insisted. "Look at all that gear of his. Surely there's something there you could use. A rifle or motorcycle?"

Frank again said no, but Rex pulled him into the garage, pointing out choice items. Frank could see how much young Rex wanted him to take something, so he finally agreed on the kayak. "Perfect," Rex said, "that's the best choice. Do you have a lake back east to paddle in?"

Frank laughed. "Lots of them! And it will be good exercise for me. Thanks a lot, young man."

The same day Frank made arrangements for it to be shipped home and told Marsha to start packing. "No, I think I need to stay a while longer," she said. "Francine says I shouldn't, but I say I should. You can change the air flight tickets, can't you?"

Frank's plane trip home was uneventful. Driving from the airport, he did a little self-congratulating for helping Marsha's sister, and thought more about his upcoming consulting work. It would be good to pick Trouble up from the dog-sitter and relax, just the two of them alone.

They walked, played with the ball, and walked some more. Frank thought about golf, but couldn't work up the enthusiasm. Six days passed, and then a delivery man knocked on the door to present him with a kayak.

Don't ask why I paid to have the damn kayak sent across the country, he muttered and tipped the man. Water, yes, Motorboats, yes. Silly kayaks, no. He looked at it for another two days and finally decided to give it a try. Marsha's week-long extension had lengthened into two or three, and he was bored.

He drove to the boat dock where he stored his motorboat and bought two six-packs, bologna, cheese, and rolls. Then he lugged the kayak to the shore and tried to get in. It kept tipping until he stood next to it in the water rather than trying to get in without getting wet. Maybe that was how you did it. But how do you get the food in? Well, you get back out, dummy, and start again. Eventually he pushed off and tried to master the paddle. It wasn't like a canoe paddle, but turned out to be much easier. In fact, once he got used to things, the kayak was a whole lot faster and more interesting than a canoe. But not a motorboat.

Inside of an hour, he'd mastered the stroking and learned to handle waves from passing motorboats and ski-dos. He found himself smiling, pretending to be a water bug skimming along rather than some drunken sailor. Too bad he'd forgotten the sun cream.

The lake was noisier than he'd ever heard it. The loud ski-dos came swooping in too close, so he hugged the shore. Most of the people in motorboats and all of the ones in the tubs he disliked--pontoon boats--waved as they passed. He raised his paddle and jiggled it back and forth, hoping no one he knew would recognize him.

After a time, his back started hurting. Why doesn't the damn thing have a proper seat? He needed to find a comfortable shore for a beer and sandwich break. While he was eating, a fisherman motored slowly by and shouted for a beer. He shouted back, "It's yours! All you have to do is come get it. I'm damn well not going to toss it!" The fisherman laughed and motored by.

He took a short lunch break and then paddled twice as slowly for another hour, estimating he hadn't begun to cover a tenth of the lake—probably much less if he counted all the little coves and fingers. Something had been bothering him: it didn't look like the Chatuge he'd come to know, having motored over every inch of it many dozens of times. Then it hit him: he'd been looking up, from a fish's view, not down, from a bird's view. Everything felt different, and again, pretty good. He smiled most of the way back to the boat dock, paddling gently.

Instead of driving immediately back home, he decided to have a beer in the dock's clubhouse—such as it was, a bunch of metal picnic tables. The youthful bartender introduced himself and Frank brought two beers. "Well, Chuck," Frank said, handing the kid the beer, "is it always so busy around here?" Chuck chuckled, saying it was the easiest—and laziest—job in the area.

"Are you really old enough to serve alcohol?" Frank asked. Chuck said he was older than he looked, almost 20. Then he proceeded to answer Frank's next question about the island with the number 1 on a stick. "That one's Penland. Don't know if the islands are privately owned, but TVA owns the lake, ever since they flooded the farms way back when."

Even though he knew the answer, Frank wanted to hear the kid's spin, so he asked if people camped on it. Chuck said they did most every weekend in the summer, not so much weekdays. "You planning on it?" Frank nodded, even though he knew he wouldn't. "Then be sure to watch out for chiggers. They'll eat you alive."

"Are there any facilities—like toilets or water?"

Chuck shook his head. "You have to cart it all in and out. Plenty of people forget that last part. Every spring the TVA brings in a big barge for all the trash. It's not like public campgrounds. It's just first come, first serve—though some folks leave their tents up all week to sort of reserve it."

Frank knew that story, remembering Bert's talk about the monofilament line surrounding their ghost tent. He thanked Chuck for filling him in and left $6 for the beers. "Hope that's enough."

"More than. Have a good day and come back." Frank didn't feel it necessary to tell him he came all the time for his big boat--but rarely stopped in the clubhouse.

Two days later Frank decided to get an early start, immediately after his Trouble walk. Too bad he couldn't take him, the way he remembered Bert always took Rowdy. But Rowdy was a well-mannered dog, and a hell of a lot shorter and lighter. Driving back from the boat dock the other day, he'd searched for the road leading in to the Park and Rec, an ideal put-in place, not only because it had an official ramp that would allow him to get in without getting wet, but also because it was on the North Carolina side, a little wilder and prettier. This time he'd traded beer for water. Too much sun and beer before had given him a headache. He'd packed energy snacks in small plastic bags and, most important of all, a waterproof pillow that he'd figured out how to attach to the back of his seat. He was ready for action.

What he wasn't ready for was the woman who pulled up alongside him and waved. Brie! He'd only met her once before, on their boat trip when she had sat in back with Marsha while he played captain up front. If he had any doubts about who she was, her blue eyes more than reminded him. And her figure: tall, thin, and winsome. Was Bert the lucky one! She must be at least fifteen years younger than both of them, he calculated—something Bert never mentioned.

He jumped out of his truck and went to shake her hand. No, she was one of those women who had to give hugs, not hand-shakes. No problem there. Unlike so many women he knew who always backed their chest away, she pushed hers right into him. He didn't know what to do or say, so just held on.

"Like a hand with that kayak?" She said no she'd been doing it for months now and could handle things herself. He smiled and walked back to his truck to pull out his smaller and lighter kayak, looking over every now and then to make sure she was really still there. Which she was, all 5'7" of her, perilously close to his 5'8". Oh well.

"I presume you're going kayaking," she said, watching him fumble with his gear. "Maybe I should lead you around. You probably don't know the lake like I do."

He didn't say he probably knew it better; instead: "Good idea! This'll be my second time in a kayak, so don't get upset if I can't keep up, or do something wrong."

She immediately jumped in her kayak, then turned her head back toward him: "Mind if you go back and get my water bottles? I left them in the front seat. The door's unlocked."

He obliged, noting that quart plastic milk bottles were the perfect thing to stow in the front of the kayak. She had three. When he came back and handed them to her, he watched as she bent over to put them next to her knees.

She was ready to push off but he still had to apply his sun-block. "Want some?" he asked, knowing she'd already put hers on. She was a very organized Type A. How could she put up with Bert? He didn't need to answer himself, knowing that opposites attract. Also knowing he was another Type A.

Brie could wait no longer, pushed off. He was glad; that way she didn't have to watch him fumble around getting in or trying to paddle away. It took him twenty minutes to catch up. "You move right along," he said. She started to answer but he answered for her: "I do this all the time." She laughed an unlady-like guttural laugh, but the smile following it was very lady like. And sexy.

After a rest he thought too short they took off for the next cove. Then spent the next hour playing cat and mouse, she pushing off the minute he caught up with her. Eventually he shouted for her to stop at the dock for a coke. He was glad Freddy wasn't the one tending the bar. They walked away from the clubhouse with its wi-fi to a distant picnic table. She asked how he was doing and he asked if she always paddled so fast and furiously.

"I do it all the time."

They got back in the water as the afternoon breeze started whipping the lake. "We're going straight back," she shouted over her shoulder. "Don't want to fight the waves. If they get too big, head straight into them, don't let them catch you sideways."

They had to paddle hard against the wind. His arms and back ached. Half-way across, three waves tried to swamp him. He lost sight of her, concentrated on keeping his kayak straight. When he arrived at the Park and Rec ramp, she'd already unloaded her kayak and carried it up to her car. Looking at the sky and wondering if it would rain, they decided to hurry home. Had Brie been anyone other than Brie, he would have insisted she accompany him to dinner at the Fieldstone Inn. And then, of course....But Brie was a woman who couldn't go out for dinner and he was a guy with a close friend desperately in love with the woman. He thanked her for the day's adventure and asked if she'd like to do it again. She nodded and told him to come by her house the following day for coffee. "Bert's probably told you where it is, a short way up Brook Road. I'll be sitting on the porch around 7:30. Bring your dog."

That night Frank told himself two things. He hadn't cheated on his wife in 24 years. Secondly, Brie wasn't flirting, she was just lonely now that Bert was gone on his trip. The woman's smile was made to arouse, but that wasn't her fault. Well, she might be a little coquettish, must know very well what her looks do to men. But she wasn't going to do anything to this man right here who hadn't cheated on his wife in 24 years.

Then he proceeded to fantasize about climbing in bed with her.

He found her sitting on her porch, just as she said. Later he learned she spent most of her time there because the house still hurt her. She went inside for coffee while he studied the horses in the far pasture. They talked about her place and then his house perched up on the mountain with a great view of the lake. They talked about Trouble and Rowdy, not about Marsha or Bert. After they were running out of things to talk about, he asked her if she'd like to go on another lake adventure in a couple of days.

"How about *for* a couple of days," she replied. "I was planning on an overnight. Care to join me?"

"Do I!" he didn't shout. Instead he pretended to mull over the prospect, said he could rearrange his schedule a bit. Then added, "What about Trouble?"

"Bring him along," she said with a smile, "but you need to get him a dog life vest. You can get them at the sporting store in Murphy." Then she stood up and pointed toward the far corner. "Come see my chapel over there."

He followed her, noting the beginning of a small garden on the sloped place between her house and the fence that separated her yard from the pasture. The pasture belonged to people who kept sixteen large and semi-wild horses for rodeo shows. The two followed the fence until it intersected another one leading to the road. Next to the intersection was her outdoor chapel-- six low wooden seats made from 2x6s nailed to oak stumps in front of a tall cross of hickory limbs that had been tied together with leather strapping. "Bert helped me with all this," she said, then added wistfully, "he helped me with a lot of things."

Why the past tense and nostalgic tone? Frank wanted to ask. Bert hadn't said anything about a break-up before leaving for his trip. Then he decided he was making something out of nothing. They sat quietly on the planks until she got up and guided him back to the firepit where outdoor meals were cooked. "Maybe I could come back later this afternoon with a steak," he said. She shook her head. "No, I've got the knitting ladies coming over. But thanks anyway." They went back to the porch and talked until he felt it was time to leave.

"What time should we be going to Penland?" he asked. "That's in two days, right?"

She nodded, saying to meet at the Park and Rec at 8:00 and telling him to bring enough water for two days, and matches. "I've got the cooking gear," she added. He said he'd bring steak and corn on the cob for dinner and eggs and potatoes for breakfast, plus coffee and bread.

"No bread for me," she said. "I can't stand gluten free; tastes like cardboard. But I can't eat wheat, have to eat corn chips and rice cakes."

He smiled. "Then I'll add corn chips and rice cakes to the shopping list. Anything else?" She shook her head and extended her hand for goodbye. No hugs this time, he noticed. A woman of conflicting signals.

The following day dragged by slowly. Frank focused on practical matters of buying and finding what he needed for the trip. He located a good canine life vest at the sporting goods, but on the way to the checkout, pictures flooded his head of the dog galivanting over the island, his thick fur getting infested with ticks and chiggers. He told the checkout lady he'd changed his mind, went outside to the car, but then came back in to find waterproofed bags for his clothing. At home he studied the internet for the proper way to stroke a kayak paddle, then walked Trouble around the yard. An hour later he realized he'd forgotten to buy a bottle of carbonated grape juice, so made another trip back. If not champagne, then pseudo-champagne.

Back home again, he started packing his clothes. The swimming suit was too small, but he'd be damned if he'd drive back to the store another time. He found a pair of scissors and cut the legs off a pair of jeans, then sat on the couch congratulating himself for remembering waterproof sacks at the sporting goods. Then he jumped up, congratulating himself again for thinking to trade his usual baseball hat for the wide-brimmed one with leather straps to fasten around his neck. He was ready to go. Oh yes, he forgot to drop Trouble off at Doggy Do! There was just enough time to get there before closing.

When Wednesday came, he was up at 5:30. He straightened the house and cooked his favorite breakfast of three eggs, bacon, potatoes, and rye toast, then loaded the truck. He arrived at the Park and Rec at 7:30 to see her sitting in her kayak next to the ramp. In a half-hour they were in the water paddling for Penland.

Once again Brie paddled ahead, but slowly. The lake was smooth, as usual in the early morning. When they reached the island and hauled the kayaks up, he volunteered to unpack them so she could swim. She showed him where the different piles would go, everything on the ground except for cooking equipment and food, which went on top of two sets of eight-by-ten-inch planks nailed between trees. Then she showed him where she usually strung her hammock, plus tent just past it, and said he should maybe start gathering wood. He congratulated himself again for remembering the bug spray, and soaked his legs and arms. It didn't take long to complete his tasks. He ambled out to the lake, watched two green flippers flap in the air and disappear, replaced by a head breaking the surface. He waved at her and shouted that he was going to try the hammock. "Wake me if you have to."

Brie returned in time for lunch--sandwiches prepared earlier plus corn chips. He'd also brought along powder to make lemonade. Then she said she was ready for a nap—after erecting her tent. While she was spreading hers, he took his old one from the kayak to lay out on the far side of the firepit. "Oh," she shouted before he started to put it up, "That's too close to the fire over there. Why don't you put yours over here, next to mine?" He studied her face to see what was up and saw her studying him, smiling innocently.

Later in the afternoon she returned to the lake while he walked the shore to examine rocks and driftwood. The breeze had picked up on the lake, which was good because it blew the mosquitoes away. Come late afternoon, Frank missed happy hour. He was also starting to get a little bored, so took his time building up a fire large enough to produce good cooking embers. Eventually she returned from the lake and climbed into her tent to change clothes. She came out with a pack of cards. "Play gin rummy?" He nodded and they found two flat rocks to sit on, pulling the ice chest close for a table.

While tending the steaks he couldn't help thinking that for Brie, the trip had already produced what she'd come for—detoxing in the lake. For him, it might produce what he'd been thinking about, although he wouldn't take bets on that possibility. They small-talked while he cooked and served, after which she asked him to give grace. Not knowing how to do that, he said it would be more meaningful coming from her. Her words came easily and naturally. They toasted with their pretend champagne and ate while watching the sun start its descent. The boats had quieted down; birds wouldn't begin their small talk for another hour or two. Despite the awkwardness of eating from lap-top plastic plates while trying to stay balanced on stones, not chairs, the meal was enjoyable.

Half-way through dinner she asked if he missed being a psychiatrist. "Not a psychiatrist, a clinical psychologist—big difference. Diagnosing, not counseling. Yes, I miss it, in fact might soon be returning to the University of Florida for some consulting. After Marsha gets back."

Brie's eyebrows went up. "Where did she go?" He told her about Marsha's sister's family, keeping it short, and then after a few minutes asked if she wanted to talk about her former life. "Hey, I'm a shrink, remember, I'm used to listening to secrets." She smiled but said she didn't want to discuss her past life.

As it grew darker Frank could see she was tired. Maybe back home she went to bed at sundown, whereas he stayed up until midnight. When she saw him starting to get into his tent, she said, "Wait. I'll change into my pjs and then we can play another game of cards. See, I've brought my trusty battery lamp."

He waited until she called from inside, then removed his shoes and hat and crawled in. Or tried to crawl; the zipper stuck. She laughed and unzipped it. When his eyes adjusted, he saw her sitting on top of her sleeping bag, the lamp hanging beside her casting shadows on the wall. It also illuminated the beautiful silver-blond hair which she'd brushed until it glowed. He stifled a gasp and tried to sit down in front of her gracefully. They said nothing, and then she opened the cards and shuffled. This is like some kind of mysterious ritual, he thought.

They played the game silently except for occasional comments on the cards. He couldn't concentrate on the silly game, his mind being focused elsewhere. He guessed she knew it also.

The awkward moment came when he said it must be time for him to hit the hay. She asked if he could first give her a brief shoulder massage; the kayaking had taken its toll. She rolled over on her stomach and he straddled her legs to gently massage her shoulders. After several minutes he found himself pulling up her pajama top for a smoother massage. She remained silent and relaxed.

The massage was anything but brief; it worked its way lower and lower until he started pressing firmly against her buttocks. It came as a surprise to both of them when she rolled over and let him continue with a frontal massage.

Outside, the whippoorwills started their mournful calling. The moon rose slowly, casting dim light inside the tent, which had gone dark after the lamp was turned off.

Sitting on their rocks around the campfire, the two enjoyed Thursday's light breakfast. "If this is light, I'm an elephant," she said. "But your cowboy coffee beats my cowgirl coffee."

She insisted on doing the dishes—using heated lake water—while he went for more wood. He'd discovered a narrow trail to the middle of the island that kept him from brushing against too many trees and bushes. He held his breath, hoping not to find rashes on his legs and back, and always bathed in the lake after returning with armloads of dead branches. His goal was to keep the fire burning all morning even if they didn't need its heat.

Brie fastened her flippers and waddled toward the lake. He'd brought along a novel, but after an hour of getting in and out of the hammock to stoke the fire, he got restless and rearranged things in his tent, now used for storage. He checked all their food and water supplies and found they had more than enough to stay another night. Could he convince her?

Back outside, he scanned the lake for green flippers sticking up in the air, followed by a smiling lady bobbing up. It still being early, the boats hadn't started their daily rounds. But the ski-dos had, and when one came in too close—which wasn't often since their cove was narrow and fairly shallow--she'd clap her hands over her ears and shake her head. Later she explained that loud noises like those made by ambulances or police cars with sirens and bright flashing lights produced the same effect as wi-fi and big electricity sub-stations. "Out here I'm a lot safer than at home, even though I carefully chose that place as far from wi-fi towers as possible."

When she came out for a late morning break, he handed her a beach towel, then led her to the hammock and went back to his book, sitting on the rock made more comfortable with the pillow from his kayak.

While she slept, he mulled over the three things he missed: comfortable chairs and a table; music; and Trouble. Well, maybe golf too; you can read, stoke the fire, and walk the beach for only so long. Maybe he wasn't cut out to be a camper.

She slept for an hour and asked for coffee, please, you're closer than me. He brought it and told her he'd found enough food and water for another day. "Interested?" She nodded. "Maybe. Let's see what the weather's going to do."

The rest of the day went as before, except slices of ham and corn chips replaced steak and potatoes. And the night went as before, except more intensely.

On Friday morning they slept in. There were no more eggs, just corn chips with coffee. She asked him why he didn't like to swim in the lake, and he didn't have a good answer, so he jumped in and swam around for a few minutes, then dried off with her towel and said he'd walk the beach while she continued swimming.

The beach was not really a beach, just a lot of rocks and washed-up trees and branches. It gave him something to do. While he walked and stumbled, his mind wandered: should he be feeling any guilt? No, his vocation taught him to observe hidden motivation, and hers wasn't too hidden. She was obviously enjoying herself as much as he. She was the one who called the shots. Besides, they hadn't planned it; it just happened.

Back at the campsite, he decided he didn't need to gather more wood; they'd be leaving pretty soon. In fact, as he was thinking that, Brie came running up, pointing at the clouds. "It's going to rain, maybe storm. We've got to hurry!"

Black clouds formed the minute they shoved off, and then the wind picked up. Paddling was difficult. They both had a hard time keeping their kayaks pointed into the waves because the waves kept shifting direction. We'll make it, Frank told himself; it's less than a mile across. As they got closer to the Park and Rec, the waves subsided, and when the rain came, it was too late to do them any harm. They pulled their kayaks out and threw everything into his truck as fast as they could, laughing.

The rain returned on the drive home—this time pounding down. "We made it just in time," she said; "I hate to think what would have happened if this caught us half-way across the lake."

When they got to her house it was still raining, so they dashed inside to wait it out before unpacking. While she puttered around in the kitchen fixing tea and popcorn, he automatically looked for the tv; it was time for the news. Then laughed; the news never came here. But the couch was a real couch, not a rock, so he stretched out and awaited tea and popcorn. They talked for an hour, then she asked if it wasn't probably time to feed Trouble. Before he responded, she told him she had to detox in her sauna and then suck oxygen for an hour. They both went outside to the covered porch, where he kissed her before pulling her kayak and packs into the garage. "I'll come back tomorrow or the next day if I've left anything behind," he shouted to her, then waved and watched her disappear inside.

I might have been playing Bert, he told himself on the way home, then texted him after arriving. Not much news here, weather good except for afternoon thundershowers. No golf, just life as usual. Text me what's up with you two—that strange friend of yours who talks like a teenager. I look forward to hearing all about your sights and sounds…in what, three weeks? So long for now.

The following day when Frank went over to pick up his stuff, he found it piled up on the porch with a short note:

This was enjoyable but had to end. It should always remain a dark secret between us.

Brie

Later that night while trying to fall asleep, he mentally composed a farewell speech to Brie. They had to be thankful for what it was, and yes, it couldn't last. He enjoyed kayaking, but would probably sell his because it would be hard bumping into her without being able to get together. She was a fine person, and a very lovely one. He'd always cherish their time together, keeping it a dark secret, of course. He hoped she'd recover soon, and would keep looking on the internet for new developments on EMS. If he found any, he'd print them out and put them in the mailbox he noticed at the front of her property.

The following day when he went to get the pack that he'd forgotten, he had his chance to deliver his farewell speech. He hadn't gotten very far into it when she stopped him, putting her hand on his arm and looking directly into his eyes. "Say no more, Frank. I've known all along. But isn't it good to have some dark secrets?"

CHAPTER TWELVE: KISSING THE HAG

BERT GOT A LATE AFTERNOON START after loading up his van and leaving western North Carolina. He'd paid no attention to the fact that he was about to drive through the entire south in the heat of the summer, needed to stop early to conserve his energy. After grabbing a bite at a fast food place, he found a motel outside of Atlanta and settled in, trying to locate something on the television. Nothing there, so he opened his laptop. Checked the news, played a game of poker, and then wondered if he should open the computer file he'd closed around a year ago. He decided it might be ok to reopen the *Mermaid* file to see if he'd spent too much time blaming her. To see if he could live with what he'd said about God's role in their love. He wanted the words not just to *sound* true but *be* true. Not petty or selfish. He would read them from the perspective of someone who knew nothing about this Bert guy. A challenge.

Imagine that, he told himself while searching his disorganized computer files, I think I've finally distanced myself enough to be able to objectively examine what's happened. Getting nowhere, he finally concluded he'd deleted the file after all, then half-remembered burning a CD and throwing it in one of a dozen cardboard boxes of books he'd taken to the storage shed or given to the library. No matter. Some might call it good luck, others, providence. He called losing the work just a felicitous happening. It had served its purpose.

Somewhere he'd read that memoirs—for that's what it was, sort of—either celebrate the good or analyze the bad. Had he analyzed things honestly? Learned anything? Not about *her* motives, but maybe about his responses? Back then he was too close to feel anything other than confusion and betrayal, but maybe the book he'd picked up last week at the Atlanta bookstore would shed some insight on what he'd been through.

Women Who Run with the Wolves, written by a credible Jungian psychiatrist, wasn't the kind of book he'd normally read, but there it had appeared, literally falling off the shelf onto his foot when he reached for a book on local history. "Ok, another blasted sign," he'd told himself, fed up with synchronicities and improbabilities. After shutting off the computer, he picked it up and started reading.

The next morning before going out for breakfast, he knew it was time to call Frank. He had left without getting to see him, and the brief e-mail he'd received sounded distant and guarded, unlike the Frank he knew. But calling would take too long to explain on the phone, so he turned on the laptop and started a long e-mail.

"Lo Frank, 'yer long-lost friend out here, bored and lonely in some stupid Texas motel. As you've gathered by now, I packed and left; sorry to miss saying goodbye, but we will stay in touch. In fact, right now! So buckle up; here goes.

I'm in the middle of a challenging book you need to read, *Women Who Run with the Wolves* by a famous female psychiatrist. Yeah, I know you never did take to Jung, think you know it all, but give this book a try. Well, I know you won't do that, so I'll help you out here by summarizing a tale that spoke to me, Skeleton Woman. In my next e-mail I'll try to apply it to my life. Don't worry, I won't try to apply it to yours—that's way too complex.

An Inuit story about love. Not our culture's kind, romantic, but almost the opposite. Teaches us men we need to sleep with the ugly hag.

Some previous lover has thrown her over the cliff. She's down at the bottom, bones collecting barnacles. Fisherman paddles up, throws in his line hoping to catch the big one—big enough to feed his family for weeks. Ah ha! He's hooked it, hauls it into his kayak. Oh no! It's no fish but some pile of ugly old bones! Throw it away...but he can't. It's all tangled up in his line! He paddles like mad for shore, but bones stay tangled in line and get pulled right behind. He can't get away!

He jumps out, runs like the wind for the igloo. But there she is, bumpety-bumping along behind. He jumps in, fastens the flap. Safe at last! Starts to bundle up for sleep but turns around to see Skeleton Woman staring right at him! On the way back she'd gathered strength, but her bones are still all twisted around. He's terribly frightened of course, but eventually calms down enough to feel some compassion for this ugly thing. Reaches over, untangles the fishing line, straightens out her bones. Eventually crawls under the robe to fall asleep.

As he sleeps, a tear forms in his eye. Skeleton Woman, now reviving and putting on flesh, crawls over and drinks his tear…for an hour, in the process creating a whole body with all woman parts, breasts and the rest. Then she crawls under his robe, embraces him, and pulls out his heart. It's a drum, which she beats. Then she puts it back in and snuggles up to him. Later, when he wakes, they make love and become one for life.

Ok, you say, just another silly tale Eskimos made up to while away a long winter night. But like all aboriginal stories and our own folk tales, packed with meaning for those who hear with the other part of their brain…in your case, the undeveloped part. Well, maybe not totally; I do recall that you liked Chaucer and even Joyce. There's hope. Now just listen to the famous psychiatrist's interpretation. (By the way, I've condensed and probably distorted both the story and her explanations, but that's my prerogative.)

The story describes love not as a romantic tryst—a flirtation or pursuit for simple ego pleasure—but as full union… 'when the combined strength of male and female enables both to enter into communication with the soul world and participate in fate as a dance with life and death. Not life-then-death, but life-death-life.' Death for the Inuit, apparently, isn't something bad—to be feared the way it is for us. It's not the end; a dreaded event to be avoided as long as possible, but something to be embraced. It's always followed by life, like spring follows winter. But the hunter has to kiss the hag!

The story says we're *supposed* to catch, then run, then get entangled and become horribly frightened...but then shed a tear of compassion that allows transformation to happen—produces a different, less ego-oriented love. There are two transformations in it, both the hunter's and the skeleton woman's.

That's part one. I'll write again later, trying to apply the tale to my life. Hit those balls straight! Bert

Bert took his suitcase to the car and headed west toward Dallas. When he got halfway there, he told himself it was too hot and boring to continue driving, so stopped at another motel in the middle of the afternoon. Flopped out on the bed, he decided to reread the Skeleton Lady story. Then started another e-mail.

Hello again, Frankie Boy. By now you've digested the folk tale. Needless to say, it's just my simplification of something much deeper. No doubt you've improved on mine and her interpretation. Hey, you're starting to think Jungian analysis might be ok after all! So here's part two, my application.

Catching: First, I caught Brie, in the sense that I initiated our friendship. She might have worn that ugly hat and scarf but was certainly no hag. We moved toward love slowly, but eventually fell into our la-la land on the magic Penland island. Was our romantic love blind and self-absorbed? Probably; I couldn't face any imperfections in my dream lady, nor she in her dream lover (she even insisted on my acting out elaborate fantasies during our nighttime sexual activity—something I eventually put a stop to).

Death: We couldn't let our illusions and expectations die. We carefully skirted the deeper issues that could lead to their death, told ourselves our love would never stop. I never did figure out what her expectations were, but mine involved marriage and living happily ever after, despite this disorder of hers that would keep me from doing just about everything I love.

Running: As a psychologist, you might say she ran away because she suffered from fear of intimacy. That's what I thought, clinging to your borderline personality explanation. But this psychiatrist who interprets the story would say the deeper issue was mistrust. She couldn't see we'd both have to embrace Lady Death...not dying literally, but killing off our fears and illusions.

Passion and *Compassion*: We had passion—superabundance of that—but maybe not enough real compassion. I thought I did, providing comfort and faith that she could beat EMS, but I could have been running errands and helping out just to make me feel better...and keep alive that fantastic sex. I was convinced our love was not just physical, but also spiritual, hence couldn't help but provide the healing she needed. I could talk God into healing her. I still think that's some form of compassion, even if it's got some fantasy to it.

Fear and *mistrust*: She didn't believe our love was promoting healing, no matter how many times I told her. Couldn't let go of her fears: that I'd become an alcoholic, that her daddy God would punish her for all that sex, so wouldn't heal her EMS. More than once she insisted she could handle only one thing at a time, meaning her healing, as if she were the only one doing it. But many others were also trying to help her heal, and she pushed all of us away. Stopped attending our Presbyterian church, stopped going to the Episcopal healers plus her massage healer down in Blairsville, and eventually stopped letting me help. I think it all came from fear and mistrust.

Ok, I hear your grumbling. Here I am, playing psychologist and spiritual guru at the same time. Pretending to understand Jung and the human psyche. Hey, at least I spared you the interpreter's comment about the hunter-fisherman casting his line into the deep unconscious where Death and Life are one. Anyway, I'm having fun, and am almost finished. Now I'll try to examine what went wrong with our relationship from a different perspective, one you probably dislike as much--the new spirituality that's sweeping the country.

Again, running away. *She* ran from me, as I just explained. But after she ran from me, *I* also started running from me—went into the hiding that could be what caused that terrible winter congestion and fever. I didn't stop to listen to what was happening inside, kept getting sicker and sicker, almost dying of fear, worry, and anger. Stressed out beyond stress. The Black Hole kept sucking both of us in, deeper and deeper. I fought, but she gave up, too tired from fighting EMS and too worried about God's disapproval.

We lost the love, joy, harmony, and bliss that we'd said would last forever. Winter killed us. But then Spring did come, bringing a tame and short-lived recovered. I guess I never kept you posted on our daily ups and downs, but sometime in April she invited me back. Like a fool, I went running back, and we reconnected briefly. But it couldn't last because we couldn't let love flow naturally (hell, *she* couldn't).

Well, Frank, now I'm blushing after rereading these two letters. So predictable: "two people fall in and out of love." What's new? But I still think "love" for most people these days is basically narcissistic romantic love--what all our movies, magazines, novels, and songs celebrate. Isn't there a deeper, more mature type of love like this psychiatrist talks about--one that doesn't just accept Death, Loss, and Disaster, but embraces it and therefore moves into a higher level?

I hope so, am still trying to learn what love is all about. I guess you told me once that's my obsession. Perhaps I'm starting to change my expectations. Needless to say, I'm still looking for that ideal soul mate, insisting she be good looking, tall, thin, smart, and sexy as hell...or at least turn into that after I kiss the hag. But I'm not going to cast out my line and reel in just anything. And when I do catch something, of course I'll run toward my igloo, but hopefully remember to shed a tear of compassion.

Bear with your friend, Frank, and keep hitting it straight."

Bert drove without incident the rest of the way to Dallas for a prolong stay with his daughter Lynn and Freddy. A few days after he'd arrived, Frank e-mailed his reply.

Howdy Bert Boy. Got your tomes. I see you're still trying to figure it out, though I thought you'd said you'd left her far behind. Well, we all try to figure difficult things out, and from what you've said, plus from what little I know, Brie is a very mysterious woman--complex and contradictory. Believe it or not, I did enjoy your Jungian trip. And it made sense, even though I prefer simpler answers. A behaviorist might explain what happened another way: maybe because of her current physical condition, maybe because of her childhood background, or maybe because of previous male relationships--who knows—she was predisposed to throw up fences whenever she encountered confusion and doubt. I'm sure you weren't the only recipient there.

Your disposition being so different, your reaction was to advance instead of retreat. Even if you two could have talked things out, perhaps with the aid of a counselor, you may never have been able to overcome your differences. There's also the matter of the opposite way you saw God participating in your relationship. You two might have thought you believed in the same God, but obviously had quite different pictures of how that God works in a person's life. Yours saw God rewarding love with healing; hers saw God disapproving and withholding healing until she proved herself worthy. This difference would prove irreconcilable—since you two kept holding tight to your pictures.

There was also another thing causing conflict. She made it clear she wasn't ready to look into the future, whereas you kept trying to get her to walk down your road. But you had to know that would be a very rocky road. She did, and maybe stopped you short for your own safety.

I think you know all this, appear to have distanced yourself enough to start settling down. But here's something you still can't get through your thick noggin. We aren't all the same! Everyone's different. You know that but can't live with it.

You tried to remake her into your perfect lover. You couldn't do that, so kept beating your head against the wall for some explanation that would let you off the hook. Wouldn't it have been easier to just accept that we're all radically different? Most guys in your situation would probably just hit the bottle for a while and whistle *c'est la vie*, but you're a romantic, and also had worked God so thickly into your love nest that the uncertainty drove you nuts.

But you've come up with a workable answer, so stick with it and carry on. Especially keep hitting those golf balls; exercise is always the best remedy. Loving golf is a hell of a lot easier than loving a woman. Sometime tell me about your pickleball; I might want to take it up.

This wise counselor is done pontificating. You'll notice he hasn't said anything about his own love life. Maybe one day he'll get around to examining it. If I do, I'll tell you what's happening here. But I'll give a hint: all's well. So long for now. Your buddy, Frank

CHAPTER THIRTEEN: DRIFTING and DREAMING

–THOUGHT YOU DIDN'T LIKE POOLS. Lynn, speaking from inside.

–Don't use them to swim in, just lounge in. Bert, from outside.

August, the hot month like all the rest in Texas in summer, was a little hotter than usual. The whole country was messed up, especially Dallas.

–Can't join you right now. Have a meeting. I'll try to get back before you fry.

–No hurry, no worry. I might be here all day. Won't fry, might wrinkle.

She closed the patio door and disappeared into the garage. He threw the ball, trying to hit the edge of the pool to make Rowdy jump in. One time in ten he'd make it. Unlike Bert, Rowdy did like to swim, but only when forced. Then he'd paddle aimlessly, yellow tennis ball in mouth until he was forced to relinquish his treasure for another throw.

–You and I could do this for months, Bert decided to tell his best friend.

–Please do, Rowdy answered.

Bert had arrived only yesterday after an uneventful drive through the country he disliked, Louisiana and East Texas. But he could handle another month in the pool, kill time before pushing on to Arizona, which he guessed might be even hotter.

Most of his life he'd been afraid of water. Never learned to swim as a kid because Denver's polio scare had shut down the public pools–all four of them. Years later Tom forced him to put on flippers and join him in the Pacific kelp beds. Tom, who'd grown up in Pasadena, snorkeled like a porpoise. Before he disappeared, he shouted back, "Oh, I forgot to tell you, you'll want to remember the spot where you dive below, 'cause that place might be the only hole in the kelp beds. I have my knife but forgot to give you one. Good luck." Bert didn't need luck or a knife because he'd already determined not to dive. The green ropes were tugging at his heels. His big problem was just making it back to shore. On the way back he told himself he'd never go swimming in the ocean again. Maybe not even a swimming pool.

The memory snuck in and he immediately banished it. Threw the ball again, counted to fifteen. What would I do without him, he asked himself again. The dog he'd reluctantly got for Suzanne, who mysteriously asked for a lap dog after all their big ones, including Jonah at 165 pounds. Rowdy had done his job by her, and now by him. Maybe he'd have to write a book about him, or another poem.

–I'm back, Lynn shouted from the back gate.

–Welcome back!

–You didn't bake, or was it fry? Simmer?

She disappeared into the house and returned with two gin and tonics.

–No bathing suit? You don't swim?

–Not much. Not like your boys, and of course Nemash, before he went to dog heaven.

They talked about her favorite dog Nemash, her job, his trip, and Freddy's recent operation. Eventually Freddy got home from work and they all went out for a Mexican dinner. She didn't ask what happened to his strange girlfriend and he didn't volunteer, already having begun the process of forgetting her.

Since he'd made it successfully through Georgia, Louisiana, Alabama, and east Texas, he told himself he could tough it through west Texas if he just closed his mind and squinted his eyes. Eventually he got to New Mexico and Arizona. He'd been there before, in fact had lived with Suzanne up north in Payson, but I-10 took him south. If he was going to go to the desert, he might as well go all the way. Before getting there, he drove through Benson, told himself he had to come back to the Dragoons sometime. Why hadn't he opted for Utah, with all those wonderful red rocks? Oh yeah, Utah's cold, Arizona's warm.

Tucson came sooner than he thought, so he stopped for two days to see what it was all about. A big town on the move, no doubt destined to be another Austin or Asheville. He liked what he saw, especially the downtown area, but it was still too big. He got up early on the third morning and headed south on I-19. Fifty or sixty miles to Mexico, past lots of opportunities. First, Green Valley, the retirement destination for old-timers. On his last brief visit he'd considered moving there. He was the right age for all the activity centers that came attached to house purchases but didn't like to be reminded of his age, didn't want to turn wooden bowls, throw pots, or swim with overweight people. He kept driving south.

On his left, a big sign said Tubac, "the town where art and history meet." Ralph and Hamilton had finally bought their home and invited him to stay in it for a month while they were down in their summer place somewhere in South America. He'd drive to their place, but first more exploration. Back on I-19, he found Rio-Rico, a sleepy Mexican community. Maybe too sleepy but home of the Robert Trent Jones Golf Course, which he'd liked before. Still, no energy in the place. He couldn't even find the town, assumed there were just houses lost up in the hills and that famous golf course—which he didn't have time to play.

Twenty more miles to Nogales. First Nogales USA; next, Nogales Sonora. The first, too big, the second, hidden beyond the tall metal fence with dozens of billboards announcing cheap dentists. No doubt a good place to find Mexican food and get cheap crowns. His passport was stuffed away in some suitcase so he

314

couldn't check it out anyway, so he turned back north. By now it was starting to get dark.

Again, the artist community called Tubac that boasted of being the first town in Southern Arizona. He dug out his wallet for Ralph's address: "2322 Tumacacori, in the Barrio." The Barrio; no doubt a hovel. But when he got there, he found it was the expensive part of town and 2322 was small but lovely. Thank you, Ralph and Hamilton. He'd wait until tomorrow to unload the van; now just find the hidden key and eat a sandwich on the back porch. Relax. He'd made it.

The next day after unpacking he found the Resort he'd played twice before with Jed and Freddy. He played it again, and then ordered a carne asada and Dos Equis on its outside patio. There was an interesting aroma in the air, no doubt from all the pot plants. Golfers sat talking and sipping drinks. Beyond, a few lazy cows tried to reach fairway grass through the fence.

The following day he and Rowdy found a dog park and discovered the Anza Trail next to it on the Santa Cruz river, a small stream that flowed north, not south, from Mexico and went underground on its way past Tubac to Tucson. He looked up to see tall cottonwoods lining the banks. His favorite tree, next to the quaking aspens back in Colorado and North Carolina tulip trees. Lush grass on the path that no one seemed to be using! The Santa Cruz clean enough for Rowdy. Bert smiled. Huge trees here in Arizona!

He soon discovered that the trees hugged the stream but didn't venture far beyond. The place was still desert, if not saguaro desert, which didn't start until lower down, near Tucson. It was called grasslands desert, as he later learned in the famous Desert Museum outside of Tucson. The prickly pear, ocotillo and cholla, not to mention snakes, scorpions, and other stinging things, favored both climates. Like Rowdy, he learned to step carefully. And spent a lot of time removing burrs from Rowdy's paws.

At first, he'd scoured his new area for a house to buy, but then remembered his father's advice from long ago: "Settle into a new venture before taking risks." He decided to rent for the first year, and almost immediately found a wonderful bachelor pad. He liked it mainly because it was in the very center of historic Old Town. Gerald, the former renter in the process of moving out, convinced him it was a good deal, despite the broken dishwasher and obsolete fridge. They were easy to replace; he'd buy them himself instead of hassling the landlady, who appeared to be very friendly but short of cash.

Gerald had his photos tacked up on every inch of the living room walls: mostly closeups of local flowers, all in black and white, plus an occasional hummingbird or scarlet flycatcher, also in black in white. Bert couldn't help asking if he took black and white photos of the famous Arizona sunsets, and Gerald shot back a hostile look. Bert immediately said he'd always been a fan of Ansel Adams and knew how much harder shooting in black and white was, especially these days when all digital cameras take spectacular color shots.

Gerald took three days to finish packing framed photos and clothing, which Bert helped him cram into the van. Afterward they went for margaritas at the local pub. Gerald turned out to be not only a professional photographer, but a semi-professional gabber, having the kind of memory that allowed him to marshal limitless facts to support his favorite topics--some of which seemed to border on conspiracy theory.

Bert listened passively until Gerald brought up the subject of electromagnetic sensitivity. Bert smiled, said he happened to know a lot about that subject. Gerald told him that earlier that morning he'd run across a web site insisting the U.S. medical community was being hoodwinked; in Europe, especially the Scandinavian countries, researchers confirmed a link between intensive exposure to wi-fi and brain cancer.

"You might be the first person I've talked to who believes it's real," Bert said.

"People believe what the world teaches them to believe," Gerald replied, scratching his arm. "Most of our research says only a handful of physicians here admit it's real. They claim only 3 to 4 percent of the people are affected but offer no solid statistical backup."

"Do you know what's behind EMS?" Bert asked.

"I'm guessing these strange neurological conditions could be tied into auto-immune disfunction or failure. They might go back to childhood trauma or have some environmental cause. We need to find out, not keep saying it can't exist because we all need our cell phones."

Bert was amazed Gerald knew so much about the rare disease. He listened to him talk for fifteen minutes, toward the end quietly shaking his head. When he was younger, he would have given anything to be able to marshal facts like Gerald, who never doubted and always knew. But now Bert felt himself doubting, not knowing. He decided not to open the long story about his former love. Instead, he thanked Gerald enthusiastically for his enlightening information and told him he'd look him up down in Mexico if he ever went there. He shook Gerald's hand, saying, "Have a safe trip to the Gulf of Cortez. Swim with a few dolphins for me. Oh yes, I forgot to thank you for your fine adobe. I'm sure I'll love it."

Bert settled into his new place. It was small but historic–the original two room structure having been built by Spanish soldiers at the nearby Presidio fortress around 1774. The best thing was its front west-facing porch and yard--private and shaded by old mesquite trees, yet across from enough civilization to provide low grade stimulation...especially for Rowdy, whose most important job after chasing yellow tennis balls was guarding the adobe from threatening cars or people.

On September 5 Bert wrote in his day-planner: "I've moved into my new house and out of my old mind."

On September 6 he decided it was time to learn more about this new place he still couldn't call home. Time to find the cultural center of the town "where art and history meet." He attended five different talks during the next week, three of which were free.

The first was at the Presidio across the street from his rental. Mexican soldiers had built the original fort back in the mid-eighteenth century. This one was a reconstruction, and now housed a very informative museum. Arizona State Parks ran it with one paid director and local volunteers. Bert spent most of the afternoon trying to memorize all the time lines and Spanish, Native, and White leaders on the storyboards. This was something he needed to learn more about, especially given the house he was now living in.

The second event was an opening for one of the area's more famous painters. Since the subject was uninspiring cowboy art and landscape oils, he left after two glasses of wine and a handful of snacks.

The third involved another artist's opening, but better because her large acrylic paintings were whimsical and playful, not pandering to what Bert was rapidly discovering constituted the predictable tastes of buyers from Tucson and Phoenix.

The fourth event he stumbled into as he left the library housed in the community center. A friendly man who called himself Watson invited him to their quantum consciousness gathering, something he'd heard about but never understood. Watson introduced the half-dozen men seated randomly in the small room with dim lighting, encouraging him to share his story. Bert limited it to the essentials--where he'd come from and when. Group talk resumed for fifteen minutes, followed by a video by a famous quantum consciousness professor back east. It lasted almost an hour. Bert paid good attention for half an hour, then found himself falling asleep. He wanted to leave, but had to wait until the end, thanking them and politely excusing himself.

The last event involved an all-female group called "Women Spirit Leaders," led by a rather large Spirit Woman who introduced herself as Duwassa of the Desert. Everyone knew her; she'd apparently lived in the area for twenty years. Before reading from her fourth self-published book, *Souls in the Sand*, she explained the book's genesis, describing the animals who had inspired her and in fact helped with the writing.

The first spirit helper was a badger. Bert assumed she was talking metaphorically but soon learned he was the real, furry kind. He told her to use a pencil, not pen, because ink wasn't natural. Bert wanted to ask if she ever used a computer, but this was not an interactive kind of gathering.

Duwassa's second spirit helper was a bird. From her brief description, it sounded like one of the pretty vermillion flycatchers he'd seen flitting around town, but could have been something else. The bird told her she needed to write between 9:00 and noon, not before and certainly not after.

Her fourth spirit friend, a wise coyote, was the one she talked most about. He had dictated the bulk of the book's content. He also informed her she should be proud of her lineage, which included several creative humans from different time periods and cultures. There was Cynthia back in the thirteenth century, wife to one of Edward Longshank's nobles. Next, an unnamed servant girl of the fifteenth century who'd converted to a new Protestant sect. The new religion frowned on the woman's past, but she secretly remained a woman of the earth, savant and healer who used herbs to cure ailments like the gout.

Bert listened attentively. The talk kept his attention more than the confusing mix of science, religion, and philosophy of the all-male group. He didn't believe a word of it, but all twelve of the women did. Half-way through he concluded that Duwassa probably was sane, and really did believe everything she said. No doubt she didn't go so far as to think the animals talked to her in human speech but used telepathy. He'd always had a hard time with shamanism and especially things like shapeshifting, but he liked to keep an open mind.

Later in that afternoon, while walking the Anza trail and still mulling over the woman's words, he couldn't shake something she'd said. Her second husband, who died when she was 39, had reappeared at a critical time in the book's writing. He'd come back to encourage her, not with words of approval but harsh words of correction. His job was to keep her honest, and he wasn't polite about it. That part Bert figured she might not have fantasized.

Bert was never to see the lady again; she returned soon after to her home base of Sedona. He liked her, even though he could never figure out why she'd called Apaches well-meaning natives who were just trying to hold onto their land. True, he thought, but there are better and worse ways of doing that. Or were there? He thought back on the inhumane treatment of the cooperative Cherokees of western North Carolina; maybe he too would have gone on the rampage. He knew he'd always carried a huge guilt for the way his white ancestors had systematically decimated not only natives, but everything they came into contact with— wolves, buffalo, birds, trees...and now the oceans, weather, and everything they should know they need to stay alive. But back then they didn't tie young women spread-eagled to fence posts and...well, he didn't care to reenact those grizzly Apache scenes from all the books he'd read.

Anyway, Duwassa must have needed to believe people were good. Bert doubted she could allow the truth of Apache sadism to enter her consciousness. He waved an optimistic farewell to her and kept walking east on the trail.

Half-way down the Anza, however, past the Barrio with its expensive houses, his dreaming mind came back to her. He wondered if Duwassa had been right about dead people keeping in touch with people they'd loved. Had Suzanne been trying to contact him? Maybe he hadn't been receptive. Maybe she, like God, knew everything he was thinking, feeling, and doing. Maybe she was floating around somewhere trying to influence him this way or that, and it was time he learned how to listen. What if he could enlist her aid in things she approved of? Would she know what new woman might be right for him? Should he track Duwassa down and learn how to contact Suzanne? He looked at Rowdy faithfully following behind and decided it might be safer to ask him.

Bert was sitting on his porch reading another historical novel one afternoon in late September when it happened. Rowdy growled and dashed into to the street. Bert didn't mind the dog always rushing to tell the world not to enter his domain, but this one about to enter wasn't a tall human but a small monster. Maybe three feet long and two-and-a-half tall, it had to outweigh a lot of big dogs, and certainly made Rowdy look like a rodent. Its hide of silver-grey nails bristled like a porcupine but spoke of death instead of punishment. It looked ready to shed machine gun bullets or flame-throwers. The monster moved slowly, pushing her four small ones ahead, afraid of nothing, knowing nothing would dare approach. "Come meet my razor teeth," she snorted, ripping up grass and prickly pear cactus on the side of the road in search of anything worth eating.

Rowdy had never read about javelinas, didn't know they weren't pigs but peccary, didn't see its sharp teeth made for ripping out intestines. He knew only what his ancestors had known, that anything that moves is fair

323

game for a brave cocker spaniel. And the damned monster was invading his territory!

Bert held tight but the rope didn't. Rowdy ignored the four piglets following momma and ran directly for her. Before Bert could get halfway there, shouting as loud as he could, the howling dog was racing back toward the safety of his house. To hell with defending the house, just make it back.

Bert dashed to examine the damage, bad yet hopefully not fatal. Rowdy, like an obedient dog now, let him probe the four wounds. Two deep ones on his side, and another had missed his genitals by an inch. The last had barely failed to penetrate intestines. Maybe he would make it.

Bert had to find a vet but knew his own new one didn't keep Saturday hours. He tried to find one in the small Yellowbook that listed only businesses that paid. Nothing there, so he started calling his two new friends. One said try Rio Rico, halfway to Nogales. An hour later he found Dr. Marlin and rushed up to shake the vet's hand, thanking him for being open.

The doctor examined Rowdy and came back with the verdict. Yes, he could help, and it would cost only $875. Bert asked if all that was necessary. Dr. Marlin, who turned out to be one of the more expensive vets in all of Southern Arizona, yet paradoxically located in a poor area, consulted with himself again in a closed room and reappeared with a second estimate: $176. "Done deal," said Bert, and Rowdy was saved for another day.

Southern Arizona's monsoons he'd heard so much about turned out to be something of an anticlimax--just afternoon rain but no huge winds or floods. The monsoons did cool things below ninety-five degrees. Tubac's 3,200 feet elevation brought the temperature down at night. He slept with the doors and windows open and closed them in the morning, as everyone advised. And started sleeping afternoons since it was too hot or wet to go outside where he belonged. It was hard a routine to get used to.

He'd rarely slept in the daytime before, and now discovered that he dreamt even then. His afternoon dreams were as unpredictable and frustrating as the ones at night. Probably unusual enough to qualify for Reuben's dream study group, which was already full, and Reuben would never invite the newcomer anyway. He wished he'd kept to his habit forty years ago of recording all his important dreams, but if he'd been too lazy to keep a log of books read, no wonder he'd overlooked dream control.

Some of them recurred intermittently, like Nazis grabbing him for horrible operations on his body and brain; forgetting the combination of his high school locker; having to jump from a tall building and fly like Superman, arms outstretched, to get away; not remembering where or when his English class was supposed to meet; being late to the cafeteria and having to pay $5 for coffee, which was cold and came in an unwashed cup; having to pee or poop but never finding a restroom.

Or the prophetic dreams, always the ragged hippy group. Sometimes making everyday hippies look regulation, these street people. Meeting in some kind of half-demolished church or just lying around half naked on the beach. He would join them, try to convince them he was one of them. Or were they really just drop-outs, not spiritually advanced humans? By the time he'd wake, he'd remember none of the important talk, just the feeling that they might be the real group he needed to join.

Bert was used to having strange dreams and remembering the ones that struck him as important. Back in college, his Individual Psychology course was devoted mostly to dreams. The teacher insisted they are a good index of personality since they shadow forth known and unknown personal issues...plus sometimes larger ones emanating from the collective unconscious. In class they read Jung and drew pictures of their dreams, replaying them together in small groups.

At the end of the semester they were surprised to learn Dr. Bach was a famous Los Angeles psychologist come slumming that year to their college. It was rumored he counseled his divorce cases by having them battle it out with boxing gloves while waltzing around the rink on skates. Bach's course remained one of Bert's favorite classes, and for years he kept a notebook next to the bed to write them down as soon as he woke. Dr. Bach had warned them against purchasing dream interpretation books, saying they were all worthless.

Having nothing better to do than nap, and unable to step outside for more than a minute, Bert started rummaging inside boxes he'd piled in a corner of his den, looking for old dream notebooks. He finally found one that included what he'd always considered his most meaningful dream...not that he'd ever understood it. It was titled simply, "Prophetic Dream, May 19, 2008"—back when Suzanne was still alive and mostly healthy and they were living in their newly-constructed house.

A Strenuous hike up Siler Bald, from 2,000 feet to the 5,200-foot summit and back. Beer and a glass of wine plus a light supper of frozen Colonel Tso Chinese, and to bed early, exhausted. Two hours later I wake with this dream, recognizing it to be one of the kind I call prophetic.

Suzanne and I are inside our new house, probably in Colorado not North Carolina. Charlie Gibson is on the television announcing they've just found some object. From his description I immediately know it's from another planet. I talk to Charlie on the tv, saying, "Don't you realize this is 100% proof that aliens do exist?" He answers to his television audience, not me, "This discovery is absolute proof that life from somewhere else does exist and has reached our planet."

Suzanne and I are struck by the strange weather. Perhaps tornadoes or a bad storm. An eerie greenish light covers the evening sky. We ask each other if the end of the world is near. Then the thunderclouds clear, leaving just rain, and then the rain stops. We open the windows, breath in the pure, crisp air.

We walk around the house, look out all the open windows, and decide to go sit on the back porch. As we look up at the sparkling trees, a flock of birds swoop down to settle on the closest ones. They're just ordinary blue jays. Next, a most unusual flock that I recognize to be the same kind of bird I saw up on Siler Bald--the beautiful something or other grosbeak. These are followed by another flock of unusual ones that I don't recognize. Maybe they're small parrots, very colorful. And finally, twenty to thirty small white owls.

The owls flutter all around the porch, circling it repeatedly, and land in nearby trees. One swoops down directly toward me. I don't know if it's threatening me or not, but something tells me he's just curious...maybe even laughing as he nears me. I recognize him to be the young male cock-of-the-walk. I duck and he veers off. Then a female white owl gradually flies down and settles on the porch railing three feet away. I slowly reach out to touch her, petting gently. She doesn't move.

I look for something sweet and moist to feed her, but find nothing. She remains quite still, and I look over at Suzanne in disbelief, all the time continuing to gently pet the owl's white fluffy feathers. Then all of a sudden, a beautiful young woman dressed in ordinary—but all white—clothing is there. It appears the owl has turned into her. I'm speechless.

I finally stammer, "Are you..." but can't continue with my question asking if she's an alien from another planet, as this might be rude. She stays perfectly quiet, saying nothing. I guess she probably doesn't speak our language. But it turns out she does, and we begin to converse. Unfortunately, this is when I wake up.

The second dream that Bert found in the notebook also involved storms and possible danger.

Dark grey clouds swirl angrily above as we lay outside on a blanket. We might be at some kind of concert but I can't make out who the other people are. Suddenly, the sky begins to turn darker and darker...and falls completely black. So black we can't see a finger in front of our eyes. Deathly silent, and deathly black. We speak not a word, just lie still, confused and afraid.

After several minutes a white moon-sized orb appears on the horizon. It doesn't move, and soon vanishes. I turn around to see the same pure white orb on the opposite horizon, which also vanishes. Then directly above, another much bigger white orb the size of a football field which again goes rapidly away, leaving us in pitch black.

For some reason, I'm not afraid like my friend. I know daylight will return, as it does. This was no solar eclipse, I tell myself, they don't produce total blackout. I know it to be an omen, a forewarning. My friend gets up and wanders off. Something pulls me toward the tent that's always been there. Inside are five or six older women calmly seated. I know them to be holy women, despite the fact that their faces are orange.

329

I ask them what's happening. "You know," one says, and I nod. The end of the world. "Yes." What am I supposed to do?" "You know." I stop nodding. "Just go outside and tell them." "Why me?" No answer.

"Tell them what?" "That all is well, all will be well. Not to fear, just accept. Tell them they must not turn aside, must go forward." I hesitate, shaking my head. The women remained silent, calm, and self-possessed.

After a time, I speak. "If I do this, you must promise me one thing. Do not let me say the wrong thing. Is that a promise?" They nod and I go outside.

People walk side by side toward the tent. The moment is very solemn.

I speak the words I was told, adding some of my own that aren't really my own. No one protests; no one even speaks.

The first wave moves slowly away, making room for the next. And the next, for hours and maybe days. My words are always the same, and I know them to be the right ones. Not all the people obey; some turn away and disappear to the left, not the right. But most come calmly forward.

This is when I wake.

That apocalyptic dream had been in black and white except for the orange faces. It didn't frighten Bert, and he remembered how vivid it remained while he replayed it three times in his conscious mind before writing it down detail by detail.

He flipped through more dreams, none as interesting, and then found a small spiral notebook he vaguely remembered putting in the box more recently. The opening dream had been titled "November 15, Three years and two days after my Suzanne's Death."

At first, she and I are walking a city street, then passionately kissing inside a public building. People stare. Maybe it's an airport lobby because next I'm a mile up inside the plane looking out the window. There she is far below, waving, maybe smiling, and climbing into our silver Element. Driving away. The plane lurches and she vanishes.

Many of his crazy dreams remained inscrutable, but this one was too obvious. Obvious and disturbing. All those long-suffering years. Friends had told him he had to move on, but he knew he could only move away, not on. He'd sold or given away most everything, reduced the price of his house by thirty thousand, and headed west thinking somewhere else the tears could stop.

The tears obviously hadn't. He kept picturing her alive back in North Carolina, couldn't stop seeing her, wanting her. Something as small as their daily walk--at first, a mile down to the Hiawassee River and back, then a half mile to the new courthouse complex outside of town, then a block around the old courthouse in the Hayesville town square. Every morning, even with the temperature hovering near freezing, bundled in sweaters and coats, scarfs and gloves, brushing off the snow. At first hand in hand, then arm in arm, then his hand tight around her waist to keep her from falling.

Then steading her as she tried to master her new walker.

When she had to go to the nursing home, he'd wheel her around outside in good weather or lift her into the car, noticing she'd dropped from 130 pounds to around 100. They'd go for long country drives and park to let Rowdy sniff at the trees. She'd often fall asleep.

Together for 34 years. Only one argument the whole time, sleeping at far sides of the bed without making up, but regretting it the next morning and vowing it would never happen again, which it didn't. Seeing everything from the same eyes, two bodies become one soul, one complete whole.

At the end, when he knew the time had come and could deny it no more, he clutched the frail body wrapped next to him in the narrow hospital bed they'd installed in the living room. He whispered in her ear, "It's ok, my love, my always precious love, you can let go now. I'll be ok. You'll be ok. You'll be in a better place. Just let go."

Which she did, without smiling or talking since she was long past both, the morphine having settled in the week before. Then he wept daily for two years.

Now he was in this new place, this desert place, still trying to put her out of mind when she showed up again. He was trying to move on, not turn away. To be honest, he was also looking for someone else, as he was pretty sure she wanted him to. She'd told him something like that back when she was still able to talk, but he never wanted to.

He'd never wanted to, but in fact had. Had fallen in love with Brie, no doubt thinking he could help her with her own neurological disorder. Frank probably was right; it was just rebound, shouldn't have happened. Even so, hadn't their summer of love taught him it was possible to give his heart to another, as Suzanne wanted him to? It could happen. Maybe years from now, his new soul-mate and he could open boxes of photos and letters and replay the good times together with the real love of his life. He could allow someone else into that private place. It could happen. But would it?

One Friday in early December Bert played golf on the course that allowed Rowdy to ride in the cart. The clouds drifted lazily from east to west, and the faint smell of something decaying near the pond told him it was still summer instead of winter. Somehow the seasons never behaved properly in this strange place.

The course being crowded, on the seventh hole he joined up with another golfer waiting for the foursome ahead. She turned out to be a pretty woman named Chloe, and they immediately started talking like they'd known each other forever. They talked mainly about how wonderful it was playing golf on such a beautiful day.

Part of the glow came from both hitting the ball so soundly. He picked up five pars on the back nine and a birdie on the front, for a score of 81, one of his lowest ever. She was equally pleased with her 105, the 50 on the front nine being her second-best score ever. She even hit two 170-yard drives. He marveled at her natural swing, especially since she said she'd been playing only a handful of years.

By the time they reached the fifteenth hole, the Arizona sunset had turned skies red and they concluded they wouldn't have light enough to finish. They launched their drives on the eighteenth into the dark, but the balls magically showed up in the middle of the fairway. They reached the green, settling for two putts since they couldn't see the hole.

They laughed all the way back to the clubhouse. Rowdy reluctantly agreed to stay and guard the car while the two went inside to share a taco plate. They recounted their game and agreed to play again. He got her phone number and walked her back to her car, where they talked for another fifteen minutes before driving back to their houses.

He went to bed at 8:00, slept for three hours, and woke to read four brutal short stories about the Iraq war. The soldiers insisted all they wanted was sex, but Bert suspected some might have wanted intimacy. Then he realized he'd just experienced great intimacy not focused on sex. Strangest of all, he'd experienced it with a virtual stranger. He kept replaying the new realization for half an hour, and finally fell asleep thinking about her blond hair and long legs. Maybe that innocent intimacy had something to do with sex.

He awoke again four hours later and couldn't get back asleep, so took to praying for the people in his Hayesville church, including Brie, as he sometimes did late at night. He prayed by mentally going up and down the two church aisles, visualizing and wishing good things for each of the thirty-five regular attendees. For almost the first time, praying for all these people he'd come to care for back in North Carolina came easily, naturally, and, strangely, intimately. He'd been having a hard time praying to a God he believed existed but couldn't visualize or know. But this night he was able to do it, as easily and naturally as hitting the ball had been all day--or talking to Chloe at dinner.

CHAPTER FOURTEEN: SETTLING IN

HE FOUND ARIZONA WINTERS strange but delightful. Cold at night but, as expected, sunny all day. All winter he wondered and wandered. Wondered what was next; wandered the city and desert by car, still too worried about those rattlers or drug lords crossing over from Sonora to go on foot. He visited the nearby Equine Ranch that rescued horses that drug runners had whipped, beaten, or shot as payment for carrying hundreds of pounds of drugs north through the sweltering desert. One seventeen-hand tall stallion cowered abjectly at the far side of his private corral, going berserk the second anyone tried to get close. A spindly donkey tried to walk, her back legs rigidly crossed and permanently crippled...so pathetic that a visiting couple from Michigan took pity and paid to have her shipped home to be pastured. Several at the sanctuary, which operated on private, not government, funding, were Premarin mares who'd been tightly penned like turkeys and kept continually pregnant so their urine could be drawn and used for estrogen. It's totally outrageous, Bert thought, then reminded himself that good people were doing something about bad people, not just ignoring or complaining. On the way out of the office he left $50 in the donation dish.

He drove over the border to Sonoran Nogales, not for cheap dental work, but to help volunteers from the

Tubac church distribute food and clothing at the commodore they ran for poor kids. He'd have to learn Spanish; no more dragging his feet there. He bought an internet program, plus headphones, but suspected he'd have a hard time keeping it up. The problem wasn't lack of time; there was too much of that. Just lack of motivation...or, perish the thought, apathy. If he could learn just a handful of sentences, he might be able to do a small amount of good handing out dollar bills to Mexican kids badly in need of them.

A few months later his landlord brought over a medium-sized flat-screen tv and proudly installed it in a middle shelf of the bookcase facing his den couch. Bert didn't have the heart to tell her he'd deliberately left his expensive tv back in North Carolina but he did make a mild complaint about paying for services that he didn't really want. "No, that's what this is for," she said, producing a rooftop antenna. After he got it hooked up, he found he had almost two dozen stations, half in Spanish, but all the ones he needed for sports and public broadcasting. Maybe this is the universe telling me how to learn Spanish, he thought.

One Sunday night he fell asleep half-way through a soccer game and woke to some kind of talk show. Reaching for the remote, he heard the announcer's topic: "What does America think about sex and love? Does it have to be love?" Maybe I'll listen for five minutes, he told himself, but only five. Predictably, the four women, all in their thirties or forties, argued for love. The fifth said she'd given up on finding that, would settle for good sex. Audience laughter. Two minutes of his five left--all taken up by ads, so he had to wait a little longer to hear what the men had to say. Mainly young, four said they'd take either sex or love, didn't matter. The fifth, a good-looking older guy who refused to smile like the rest, said he'd no longer make love to a woman he didn't love. Camera to the women eagerly listening, followed by pan-out to the female audience applauding.

Bert changed the channel but found nothing, so went to bed mulling over what America watched.

In late spring Tubac was too hot for golf, unless he was fortunate enough to secure a 7:00 tee time. He stayed busy reading, walking the streets and Anza Trail, and relaxing on the front porch. Mainly passing time. He met new people every week and convinced himself he was starting to feel at home, but most of the time he just hibernated.

It had been a long time since talking to Frank. He called to fill him in on his move to Arizona, then was surprised to learn Frank had also moved--east to Southport on the Atlantic. "Why?" he asked.

It took Frank almost a minute to answer. "Sorry there; had a frog in my throat. Why did we leave? Good golf courses, off-shore breezes, and of course, splendid fishing. I knew Marsha was ready for a change, and western North Carolina no longer spoke to me. While you were gone, I encountered some strange happenings that we don't need to go into here, except to say they almost drove a wedge between Marsha and me.

Anyway, it didn't take long for our house to sell--plus the boat—and we found a nice place here the same week we arrived."

They small-talked some more. Bert wondered if something was bothering his friend. "You sound so different, not the feisty old guy I know," he said chuckling.

Frank tried to think of appropriate answer but couldn't. Instead he said Trouble was scratching at the door; he'd call him back in two or three days.

Later the same day, Bert's high school friend Edward called after returning from another South American trip. He asked if Bert had received all the photos he'd e-mailed. Bert apologized for being such a poor correspondent; Edward's trip had caught him at a bad time. Well, this is just a lame excuse, he told himself; I was just too damn lazy to support my friend. Then he told him how much he enjoyed hearing about all of his interactions with the people, even those who didn't speak English. Back in high school Edward, like him, was the shy one always standing behind others. Maybe his world travels had opened his mind and spirit.

Bert related his struggles keeping Rowdy away from javelinas, coyotes, snakes, and poisonous toads in the desert, and then his friend suggested they reconnect up in the cool mountains of their home state. Bert agreed; it was past time to get together. Edward had excess frequent flyer miles, and Bert could drive up, so they'd have a car. They'd meet in Denver and maybe visit old haunts--East High; the country club where they used to sneak down the creek shooting their bows and arrows at distant squirrels; Larimer Street, the skid row haven of interesting army surplus stores and pawn shops, now replaced by expensive shops catering only to the wealthy. They'd stay with Tom or Wolf a few days before heading to the mountains.

"We need to take old Highway 6, not I-70," Edward said. "Someone told me Clear Creek Canyon's gone bananas with zip lines, rental kayaks, float boats. We need to see that."

"Yeah," Bert added, "They've even paved the O-My-God road up to Central City. Tamed it the way they felt they had to channelize rivers."

Their plan was to tour for one or two weeks, camping out when they could and ending up at Bert's son's place in the northwest corner, Steamboat Springs. They'd go in early July.

Driving up to meet Edward, who didn't play golf and never would, Bert made several stops for his monthly quota. First Phoenix, of course, but only for nine holes because it was too damn hot in July. Then another nine in Prescott, where he'd almost settled instead of Tubac. It was cooler, but not cool enough. Then eighteen holes up in much cooler Payson. He was surprised to find this small mountain town where he'd lived with Suzanne for three years back in the 80s had suddenly jumped into the modern world--fast-food and big-box stores, unbelievable traffic. It took him an hour to find the house where they'd lived in at the edge of town. There, at least, everything looked the same, including the stupid shop he'd built in his back yard. He decided not to visit the place where she'd operated her antique store for two years; memories had already caused enough punishment.

Next he drove to the Four Corners area, one of his favorites, stopping at the town he'd always liked, Cortez, even though it was dead like all small underdeveloped Colorado towns. He was again surprised to find something had brought the town to life. Couples and older people lounged around the unusually shaped manmade lake while kids tossed frisbees back and forth. This is the good result of Colorado's prosperity, he told himself; not everything had changed for the worse. The golf course was also new, and interesting if not overly challenging, so he played it for two days.

The next stop was Grand Junction, another town he'd once considered moving to with Suzanne thirty years ago. It looked to be turning into another boom town like Boulder, Fort Collins, or Durango, not to mention Breckinridge and all the ski towns. He drove around the inner city for a while and then headed east on I-70 to Denver to pick up his friend at the airport.

Edward and Bert toured the middle parts of Colorado, alarmed at finding young people dressed in Spandex and expensive boots swarming the roads and trails. Edward couldn't stop talking about the good old days when a person could hike for days without running into anyone. Could drink from a fast-flowing mountain creek. Could, blush, bury a can instead of having to pack everything out.

"You remember that guy we ran into up near Camp Hale?"

Bert shook his head, no. "Yes, you do! It was September or October, cold as a witch's tit. Up walks this guy dressed in a light Levi jacket, carrying a horrendous pack full of pots, pans, and a ragged Indian blanket. Looks like a real mountain man, though he couldn't have been more than thirty. Is it coming back now?"

Bert smiled, nodding that he did remember. Edward continued. "There we were, Tom, you, Wolf and I all huddled around the campfire when out of a pitch-black night, in saunters this stranger asking if the coffee's on. Was that, or was that not something!"

They replayed the camping trip until Edward launched another monologue about his beloved home state going to the dogs. "Everyone's super-rich, under forty, and dressed like ads for outfitting stores. They're everywhere--hiking, biking, hang-gliding, board-surfing the river, running, kayaking. The state's gone nuts!"

He kept complaining while Bert drove northwest toward Steamboat Springs, perhaps the only place in the state that had survived its boom by retaining its unique home town atmosphere. Edward and Bert stayed in one of Jed's empty cabins and helped him with building projects. They wandered the downtown streets. They unsuccessfully fly-fished the Yampa. They drank happy hour beer and ate at three of the seventy restaurants. One day they realized what they'd come for: to reenact the river trip they'd taken after graduating from high school...one last outing before heading off to their separate colleges.

On that trip they had borrowed a canoe and spent lazy days floating down the quiet Yampa, jumping out time after time to drag the boat over shallow riffles. They forgot to bring a map, and worried about floating all the way into Devil's Canyon. After three or four days, they made it only as far as Craig, forty miles short of the Devil. They talked about stashing the canoe and hiking into Craig for a sit-down dinner, but were too tired. Instead, they made camp early and sat nursing cups of black coffee.

On the following day while idly paddling, they craned their necks upward toward three vultures perched on top of a cottonwood. Suddenly the river took a sharp left turn, exposing a partially-submerged cottonwood on the far bank. "Watch out!" Edward shouted, "Big trouble!" Before they could agree on which way to push or pull, the current propelled them directly into the low-hanging tree. Shouting and gesturing wildly, they hit it and immediately overturned. After what felt like hours but was only minutes, they found stable footing on the river bottom and were able to stand safely. Then, after three hours of hard work, they pulled the boat out.

The next day, when it was time to head back to Steamboat, they beached the canoe and walked three miles to the nearest ranch house. The rancher's wife graciously feed them slices of her freshly cooked peach pie. Then they piled into her four-wheel truck, picked up the canoe, and headed back to Steamboat. Kids.

On this second river trip they were almost fifty years older and no wiser about running rivers. After losing control several times on the first day, they joked about encountering a repeat performance of the capsizing. Had they known the Yampa better, they might have guessed that likelihood was pretty good, because now it was early July, not late August. The river was twice as high and three times more dangerous. Had they been reading the town's daily newspaper, they might have learned about the teenage boy taken out in a body bag after his canoe capsized.

Despite their casual attitude, they made it without effort to the campground that had recently been built alongside the river to accommodate the influx of youthful kayakers and canoeists. Early in the morning they had driven down from Steamboat to stash their tent and food in the campground, and then driven both cars past it to the ending point near Craig. Then back again in one car to the put-in near the old coal mining town of Mt. Harris. Children no longer romped in the playground next to its railroad tracks the way they did before the start of World War I. The town flourished until being liquidated a few years before Edward and Bert took their first river trip, and the houses that employees had rented for $8 to $35 were sold and moved downstream to Hayden.

Before reaching Hayden this time, the much older river rats would be able to look up from their canoe to see smoke billowing from the coal-fired electricity plant, and past it, coal pits that feed it as well as other plants north of Denver. While setting up camp, Bert said his son had told him that for twenty years after moving to his place west of Steamboat he'd been kept awake by the sound of forty to seventy rail cars rumbling by ten to fifteen times a day. "Now they make only one trip a day," Jed said with a smile. He told him most of the younger liberal residents of Steamboat were glad to learn the plant would close in 2022, but its No. 1 ranking in carbon polluting never bothered old-time ranchers and plant employees. He said he'd also be happy to see it go, but admitted to being selfishly worried about what would happen to Craig's golf course after the plant's closure decimated Craig.

The subject caused Bert and Edward to rehash their shared views on environmentalism, Bert pointing out that Jed had explained how the local ranchers—most of whom he knows and likes—have a long-standing anti-environmental stance not just because of their dislike of governmental regulations but because their livelihood depends on extracting natural resources. Because they own the land, they theoretically manage its resources, but for the majority of ranchers who can't make an income raising beef, managing means extracting everything they can—coal, timber, water, gravel.

"In addition," Jed said, "they sell hunting rights to the deer, elk. bear and birds they don't own, plus fishing rights to the trout they think they own, as well as travel

345

rights for the winter dogsled teams that need to use the land for their tourist trade." Bert had squirmed when his son went on to say he hoped the hunters wouldn't discover the osprey's nest on the river's edge below his own place. He and his kids had come to love the big bird and its baby-sitting mate. "It was bad enough when the train hit Bogey," he added, "our Lab's death at seven totally demoralized my boys."

Since both Bert and Edward were on the same side of the issue, they eventually moved to other topics, including what they'd do if and when they survived their river jaunt. After camp was established, they cooked steak and vegetables wrapped in tinfoil and went for a short exploratory walk before retiring early.

The opening stretch of the river being shallow but with enough water to prevent their having to continually pull it off the riffles, the next day they took it easy. At lunch time they beached the canoe and walked toward the only tree in sight. They saw two vultures sitting on its low-lying limb and Edward asked, "Could this be the same tree and the same vultures?" After eating, Bert stretched out to nap while his friend went exploring.

Two hours later while they were floating lazily along, the river suddenly took a sharp left turn and the current swept them toward the right-hand bank. Edward kept shouting, "Hard left! Hard left, damn it! Dig in!" Bert tried to reply but wasn't able to finish his sentence while concentrating on keeping a grip on his oar.

The minute they hit the closest limb Edward flipped out the right side of the canoe and Bert disappeared out the left after Rowdy. He made a desperate grab for the closest limb but couldn't reach it. The current swept him under the half-submerged tree with its thick limbs. He had just enough time to fill his lungs with air, but not enough to reach for his life vest to see if he'd remembered to button it. After that, time stopped. No time to say or think anything. Dark and furious.

What was happening? Time slowly came back when he realized he might have buttoned his life vest at the bottom; it didn't seem to be pulling away from his chest. He guessed he could survive if only the current would carry him past all the snags. What was left of his jacket would eventually bring him up. But if it snagged on an underwater limb, he was a goner.

"My life is supposed to flash before me," he thought for a brief second, trying not to swallow. He felt himself getting tumbled around in a confusion of boiling water. Couldn't hold his breath much longer.

The current kept pressing him under the submerged tree. He couldn't see anything. Water tumbled him deeper and deeper past the submerged tree branches. He kept picturing a limb snagging his vest—which he somehow knew must be flapping away from his body.

Almost out of air, he tried opening his eyes to see if he'd made it past the submerged tree. He had; suddenly he bobbed up. Water poured from his mouth and air filled his lungs.

Now, would the current push him close enough to the bank to grab for low branches and roots? But even if he could grab on, it wouldn't help; the bank was too steep to scramble up. He didn't know how he knew this, because waves kept him from seeing clearly, kept tossing him up and down...but he had enough clarity to realize the worst was over. He figured he might survive, eventually find a purchase somewhere to scramble up the bank.

The current subsided. For a moment he thought he heard angelic voices in the distance, peacefully singing above the raging water. He twisted his neck around to look upstream but couldn't see the canoe or Edward. He tried yelling but the river drowned out his call. Then the current picked up strength, sweeping him farther and farther downstream. He prayed it keep him still facing the bank ten feet away, and that his life vest still buoy him up. There was a chance he'd survive.

The second he stopped fearing for his life his rational mind took over, telling him the Yampa would have to settle down in another few hundred yards. He'd make it out...but Edward probably hadn't.

Just as he was beginning to relax, the current turned sharp left on an outward course and propelled him toward the middle of the river. Then, just as fast, it reversed again and pushed him back toward the bank. Bumping into it, he reached up to grab a thick root poking out from the mud. He pulled and pulled, but the slimy root kept slipping from his fingers—fingers numb from the cold. Even if he could keep his grip, the root was three feet above the water--too far up for him to be able to climb the bank.

He felt his feet stand firm against the current but doubted he'd be able to walk downstream. On his first step he immediately slipped on a rock and lost balance. Fortunately, the current kept pushing him toward the bank.

He didn't stop reaching for roots, pulling and slipping, and finally caught a firm one. He wanted to push his feet off the bottom but his toes barely reached it. The water roared in his ears. He lost hold of the root and continued slipping downstream. His arms ached and fingers felt dead. Only seconds ago, hope stayed alive, but now he was ready to give up and let the river do what it wanted to him.

He shook his head and reached one last time for a thicker branch, pushing his toes hard off the rocks and sand. It worked; he let go of the branch with his left hand and stretched out for thick grass on the bank with his right. The bundle of grass held.

He lunged hard and managed to scramble up to level ground above.

He lay still for minutes, then rose and began shouting for his friend. No answer. He shouted for Rowdy, knowing there was no way the dog could have survived. He would have been swept to his death downstream—one small dog with no floatation device against a raging river.

He continued shouting for Edward, knowing in his gut he'd died. By now he would have heard him shouting...and would be standing somewhere on the bank above the submerged tree. But no one was there.

What would he tell his best friend's son? That his father had managed to survive enemy fire for two years in a country across the ocean but died trying to fight the current? Worst of all, he knew it was his fault; Edward had told him to steer hard for the middle, but he couldn't bring the stern around in time.

Still, he didn't give up shouting while trudging upstream...too exhausted to run. He kept scanning upstream and down, hoping against hope. And after three or four minutes he finally heard a voice. "Are you alive?" Edward yelled, running toward him and collapsing in Bert's arms. Less than five minutes later Rowdy came bounding back. They had all survived. But how? they asked each other.

"What happened to you? Why didn't you get swept under the tree like me?" Bert asked.

"I got trapped under the canoe," Edward answered. "It had some kind of suction pressing it down. Maybe it was caught in a quiet place of the river, I don't know. All I know is that push as hard as I could, it wouldn't go up. I was standing in five feet of water, couldn't get traction to raise the canoe."

"What did you do?"

"I kept trying, then gave up and pulled it behind me. No way I could push it out toward the current, and to my left side was the tree. I backed up and luckily the river bottom got higher. I was able to push hard enough to break the suction."

"Then you were able to make it to the bank?"

"Yeah, I kept creeping toward it, holding onto limbs and pulling myself straight ahead. Once I got there, I found enough roots to scramble up." Edward scratched his head. "So what happened to you?"

Bert replayed what he could remember, saying it felt like it lasted forever but probably took only a handful of minutes.

For the rest of the day they tried unsuccessfully to pull the canoe from its stranglehold under thick submerged limbs. Eventually they gave up and started the long walk a mile downstream for help. The following day they talked a carpenter with a chain saw into standing chest deep in water to cut the canoe away. It took three hours and damaged two seats, but the craft finally bobbed loose.

A week later while fishing on a much quieter stretch of the Yampa below Steamboat, Edward joked about being baptized in the river. Bert said they were a little old to get reborn. Three days later they had their second baptism, this time in the Strawberry Creek hot springs pool. This one was a little quieter; they just dog-paddled around the pool surrounded by a dozen high school girls in bikinis.

A month after he got back to Tubac, Bert called Edward to wish him a safe trip to the orient. Then he settled down on the leather couch and opened a novel. Suddenly the cell phone he'd just put down started ringing.

He and Frank talked so long somebody's phone suddenly went dead. He plugged his in and took Rowdy for a long walk–no doubt exactly what Frank did, since both knew they weren't finished talking. Frank, the scientist with a passion for detail and exactitude, had insisted they talk every fourth Tuesday of the month, usually around 2:00 in the afternoon to accommodate the three-hour time difference. They'd covered all the small stuff–golf scores and altered swing thoughts, weather improbabilities, why Frank needed another boat, and how Bert managed to survive without sex–and were about to launch into something bigger when a buzz announced Frank had an incoming call.

"Hey, Buddy Boy, I almost forgot," Frank said on the re-dial a few minutes later. "I might have a girl for you. Do you remember my telling you about my ex-girlfriend's sister who had a bad case of EMS so similar to Brie's?"

Bert said he did, and Frank went on to explain he'd written his ex-girlfriend asking how Becky was doing. She wrote back saying Becky had left Florida, decided to move out west, maybe Sedona. He thought that was where her father was, at any rate. And miracle of miracles, she'd lost almost all symptoms.

"I have no clue whether she's hitched up to somebody new," Frank said, "probably has, if she's as foxy as her older sister. But it's worth a try."

Bert said he'd been wanting to visit Sedona for some time and would try to look her up. But he wanted to know what Frank meant by 'hitching up to somebody new.'

"She was married to this guy with a cow name. "Angus. No, Holstein, that's it, Holstein. Then got divorced. Maybe she still goes by Holstein."

"And if she's reverted to her birth name, what's it?"

"Chase. Good luck, buddy. Let me know how it goes."

They talked more about novels they'd been reading, America's political situation, and Frank's problem finding the right boat. Before closing, Bert asked about Marsha, adding, "I can't tell you how glad I was you two got things settled. We need more happy couples in our country these days."

Two weeks later Bert was driving north, had just left Phoenix on his way to Sedona. The cell phone rang, Frank again. "You been to Prescott yet?"

"Sedona. I'm on my way right now. Be there in a couple hours."

"Prescott, it's Prescott, not that other place."

"Ok, Mr. Bird Brain, good thing Prescott's not Show Lo way up north! I'm almost to Prescott now. You hear anything new about where she hangs out?"

"No, but you might try the American Legion. I think her father might be somebody big there."

"Thanks. But before you hang up, do you have any clues about her looks? Tall, short? Blonde? You know."

"Sorry. I don't remember meeting her. But her sister, the one I dated with the fantastic figure, was tall. Taller than me."

"All of five-foot five?"

"Lay it on thick."

"Ok, maybe seven. No other clues? How old would she be?"

"She was eight or ten years younger than her sister I dated. I must have been around 30 then. Now I'm almost 65. That makes her...."

"I can do math. Thanks, and good luck finding that boat you're looking for."

Bert was glad it was Prescott—closer and not so New Age crazy. It would probably take him three or four days to track her down. Prescott was one town he'd thought about relocating in, never the overpriced mecca. He whistled a happy tune until finding a decent motel.

Nobody had ever heard of a Chase at the American Legion. "Maybe try the Masonic Lodge? Elks?" somebody said, but he didn't want to try them.

He went for a long drive and enjoyed getting to know Prescott. The downtown had some history and decent restaurants. It was time to give the golf course a try. He finished 18 and stopped for beer at the grill. After his third, he opened up to the guy sitting next to him at the bar, out of the blue asking him if he had any ideas about finding some guy named Chase or his daughter named Holstein.

"Chase? You couldn't mean Walter, could you?"

Bert almost gasped. "Maybe, how old?"

"Around 80, give or take a few. Pretty decent golfer, favors a hook."

"You play with him?"

"Once, couple years ago. He's pretty much a loner, doesn't join."

"Any idea where he lives?"

"Yeah, not that far from me, just past the base of the Thumb."

They talked some more and Bert's new acquaintance told him to follow him home. The Thumb Butte area was located a few miles west of town. They stopped at a gravel drive with a locked wooden fence.

"Well, this is it. Looks like he ain't home."

Bert thanked him and reminded him he owed him a few beers. Then he continued up the road, killing time until 5:00. Near the top, the tall pine trees told him he was back in Colorado.

He returned at 5:30, found the gate open, and held his breath driving in. What could he say? That he wanted to ask his daughter, whom he'd never seen, for a date? The guy could be a criminal for all he knew, though from the look of the house in the distance, that wasn't likely. He had no idea how to get started. He backed out of the driveway and headed down to his motel. Maybe if he thought about it for a day or so he'd come up with a plan. He stopped for a six pack and half way though phoned Frank, who told him to be a man and go back.

Tomorrow came, a new day. He'd come this far, might as well give it a try. He went early enough to catch the guy before he went off to play golf or do whatever he does. If he went too early, he'd still be asleep, so he picked 8:30.

The sun was shining and the yard was grass instead of the usual southwestern pebbles. It didn't feel like late summer; not hot enough. The fence to the house had again been left open. He parked and this time went all the way to the house and knocked.

She, not her father, opened the door. At least that's who Bert figured it was. She was fairly tall with the same figure Frank had told him her sister had. He tried to remember the speech he'd prepared for her father, but couldn't find the words.

"Hmm. I was prepared to find a Mr. Holstein here. No, I mean Chase. Does he live here? Oh, I'm sorry, I'm not a salesman. My name is Bert, Bert Brightson. I, uh, well, it's a long story. But I guess I just need to know if I have the right house. And I'm sorry to be bothering you."

"I'm his daughter. One of them. He's left for golf. Can I help you?"

All the novels he'd read, movies he'd seen about chance meetings like this, and he still had nothing intelligent to say. But had to start somewhere. "You don't know me. But I know about you through my best friend, Frank."

"Yes, Bert ???"

"Frank and I play golf all the time down in Hayesville. No, I mean over in Hayesville, way back in North Carolina. Now I live down in Tubac, south of here. He told me he used to know your sister back in med school. Oh hell, I don't know how to say all this. My wife died a couple of years ago, and Frank said...." He stopped, having no idea where he was headed.

She intervened: "You're lonely. Frank told you to look me up because he always wanted to date me and couldn't, so maybe you could. Right?"

How to answer? "Well, sort of. He did date your big sister but I don't think he ever knew you. Then later he got married. But yes, not very long ago he did tell me to look you up. And...."

"And he told you to look me up. But how in the world did you find me?"

"He said your name was Becky Holstein. That right?"

"Used to be, sort of still is. Go on."

"Well, I don't really know where to go. I'm sorry to be bothering you so early. I mean you've probably got to get off to work, so I should be...."

"Not so fast. I can see you're real practiced at this sort of thing, trying to pick up a woman."

"Not really. This is actually the first time since maybe thirty years, back before I got married."

"I know, to the woman who recently died. Tell me about it. You obviously loved her."

Bert didn't want tears to rush in, turned to hide. "I'm sorry, this is, I mean I...."

She understood, changed the subject. "Frank who, by the way?"

"Oh yeah, Frank Arruda. He met your sister in Gainesville maybe fifteen, twenty years ago. I think she was studying to become a nurse."

"I might have met the guy once when he came to see her. I was staying with her. He's short, muscular, articulate, if I remember right. Pretty decent looking. Probably went on to become some kind of doctor or dentist."

"Shrink, actually. We were buddies back in college. Then met again after we'd both moved to North Carolina."

"After your wife died."

"No, not after, but not too long before."

'What did she die of?"

Bert didn't feel like going there, changed the subject. "Actually I..." Then Rowdy saved him by jumping out the car window and rushing up. "Rowdy, don't jump," he said. She smiled, reached down to pet the dog. "Ok, Mr. Bert and Mr. Rowdy, come on in for coffee. And maybe a dog biscuit or two. I'm not going to be working today."

They sat at the kitchen table for almost two hours having coffee and stale donuts, Bert thinking Frank had been right; she was still semi-gorgeous. He was particularly attracted to her large brown eyes which looked so innocent and child-like. He finally relaxed enough to relate his whole story, starting with her older sister and Frank, then telling how Frank learned her

EMS was so similar to Brie's. This part caused her eyebrows to raise.

"So you want to know if I've gotten better?"

"Yeah, that and if you're single." Might as well go all the way, he'd come this far.

"My, my, aren't you the shy one."

"Well, as I said, I haven't asked woman for a date in years. It's all Frank's fault." He tried to laugh. Then explained that Frank had told him he'd learned her symptoms had all but vanished.

"A miracle, yes. But what about this Brie woman. How's she, and where?"

He explained they had to part; she was back in North Carolina and hadn't gotten better.

"I'm sorry to hear that. I was just the lucky one." They went on to talk more about EMS and other unusual health situations, then where they used to live. He told her how difficult it was to leave mountains, lakes, and tall trees for this new environment. She knew what he was talking about, having lived in Washington for some time, then Idaho. They avoided talking about their personal pasts, mostly small-talked.

After he learned she'd never been south of Phoenix, he suggested she'd consider taking a trip down to Tubac. "There's this great little casita down the street, not expensive, where you can stay. They owe me something, might rent it to you for half-price. You'll like walking around all the shops and studios."

She said she might be able to arrange it. Wasn't big on shopping but liked to explore new places.

"Do you have any dogs, cats, or horses you have to worry about? Chickens?"

No, she just had herself. And would e-mail him after she checked her work schedule.

They shook hands and he left. But after reaching the gate, he glanced in the rear-view mirror to see Rowdy running as fast as he could to catch up.

Becky Holstein, it turned out, wasn't entirely pleased being a cow. She'd stopped using the last name some time ago, then thought her new married name wasn't much better, Bennett. Too English, said it always reminded her of the prig she'd married.

"So, after Bennett, what's next?"

"What do you think goes well with Chase, Mr. B?" They were sitting outside on his metal patio furniture, watching small birds attack the feeder. "I guess you know that's my family name." She paused, then added, "Sort of, I was adopted by him."

"Becky Chase or Chase Somebody?"

She laughed. "You know, I've never liked *Becky* either. If I'm going to change, might as well make it a big change. Maybe Hillary Chase. No, I don't like that. Carmilla Chase. Like that?"

He smiled. "I like the sound of it but think it's the name of some vampire hero."

"You're quick. So how about *Charlene*. I like the sound of that."

"That's a lot better. I'm pretty sure there's a pop singer with that name. Yeah, I remember her song, 'I've Never Been to Me'."

She smiled. "I'd forgotten, but yeah, the song fits my life," then hummed a few lines. "Ok, then, that's it, Charlene Chase. Are you absolutely sure you like it, Mr. B?"

"Absolutely. There's another thing about this Charlene name. The singer, she's also very pretty." He waited for her reaction, another smile. "But now might be the time to tell you I'm not overly attracted to *Mr. B*. I prefer *Bert*."

"Sorry, I guess I was trying too hard to be cute."

He took Charlene to all the places he liked, including the Resort, not for golf, but for carne asada. Since it was Saturday, he asked her if she liked to dance. One of the local restaurants featured Saturday night bands on the big patio–during the winter season, not summer, when not much happened at all. She loved to fast dance, and it quickly returned for him. "I haven't done that for years," he confessed while sipping a beer during break.

She said she used to dance all the time but hadn't done much these last several years. This might be the time to learn more, he thought, and asked whether her breakup had been hard. She said Bennett never beat her, but verbally abused her. "No, that's not quite right either. Mainly he just ignored me. He was always too busy working."

Then she asked him whether he wanted to talk about caregiving for his second wife, and he did...but it was a very long story and a very sad story. This was not the right occasion for it. Besides the band was back. They danced continually for the next hour, mostly fast, sometimes slow. He liked the way the guys leaving the inside of the restaurant always stopped to watch the dancers–keeping their eyes on her. It reminded him exactly of what used to happen with Suzanne.

Charlene stayed almost a week, then gave him an enthusiastic hug before leaving for home. A day later he found himself missing her, wondered if it was too soon to write her. They hadn't done anything more than talk, dance, walk, and kiss twice. The only way he'd find out if she was returning to Prescott for good was to write. So why wait?

Dear Charlene,

I do like your new name. Are you going to go to the agency somewhere and have it officially changed? Maybe you don't have to; it's always been your family name, and lots of people change their first name. Anyway, I like it. And I guess I'm trying to be bold enough to say I like the person behind it. Today I find myself missing that person...and we've barely met. Is there a chance we'll meet again? By the way, I'm putting my phone number below.

Yours, Bert

Charlene called back a few days later after receiving the note. She said she had a fine time and would love to see him again. Would he like to come back up to Prescott? There were many things he hadn't seen, and of course her father would love to play golf with him. He always told her what a great course it was, had kept trying to get her to play, though she hadn't since he'd taught her as a teenager.

A few days later when he arrived at her place in Prescott, he was surprised no one answered the knock. He checked his cell phone; it was the right date, and more or less the right time. What to do? Had she been leading him on some wild goose chase?

Before getting back in his car he walked around the house, found a doublewide parked behind a row of bushes. It was a fine April day, brisk but not cold. The sky was blue and there was a gentle breeze. He went and knocked, and she jumped out, apologizing for not being ready. He told her it was fortunate she'd been in her father's house when he got there the time before. She agreed, saying she cleaned the place every week as payment for free rent. They stood looking at each other for a while, then he opened his arms and she fell into them. They kissed. He told her how glad he was she'd asked him back.

After sitting outside at her wooden picnic table with coffee but no stale donuts, they went for a drive up to the top of the Thumb Butte. Later that afternoon he met her father. Walter was pretty much the man he'd expected to meet. Bert understood why he and his daughter didn't spend much time together. Not that he was drunk or dressed like a hick; quite the contrary. He looked like a lawyer, not amazingly enough, because all he could talk about was his practice or state or federal law. Law, law, law. He was obviously bored to death, should never have given up his practice. He was cordial enough, but Bert wondered if he'd be able to stand the legal onslaught.

Fortunately, talk switched to golf once they got on the course. Walter played five days a week, and the man who'd told Bert about Walter was right, he favored a hook. Called it a draw, but Bert knew it better as a hook. Bert knew how to correct the problem, but also knew Walter didn't want to change. He'd learned to live with it, like so many more golfers live with their slice by aiming to the left side of the fairway, sometimes all the way to the adjoining fairway.

After the front nine Walter asked if he wanted to stop for something to eat. Bert never liked to interrupt the flow but concluded his new friend did. They went in for a hamburger and talked about what Bert used to do and why he moved to Arizona. Bert left out the part about his wife dying, concentrated on weather and golf. Before returning for the back nine, Walter asked how he'd met his daughter, and Bert launched into the story, concentrating on the EMS part. He was surprised Walter didn't know much about her episode; apparently, she'd been living off in the northwest, and they'd lost touch. She'd recovered before coming back to Prescott and didn't like talking about it.

"When did she come back here?" Bert asked.

"Less than a year ago. It surprised me no end. I bought her this doublewide, but don't think she'll stay. She's moody, probably wants to get on with her life somewhere else." Walter gave Bert a meaningful look, but Bert said nothing. They climbed in the cart and finished before dark. Bert shot a 46, not great, but was happy for once to get beat by four. They both had shot 42 on the front nine.

That night Walter took them both out to a fancy restaurant and ordered top steak for everyone and an expensive merlot. They had pleasant small talk, avoiding politics because Walter was conservative and Bert and Charlene were liberal. On the way back, Bert asked Walter if he wouldn't mind swinging by his old motel; he'd forgotten to see if they had openings. Walter insisted he stay at his house; three bedrooms were two too many for him. Bert accepted, staying for the next three days and playing golf with Walter for two.

Despite the law talk and political difference, the two of them hit it off. Bert wasn't surprised when Walter said he was glad to see his daughter dating such a good golfer. She'd been lonely too long, needed a good man.

Bert smiled; he guessed he *was* dating her. And her father should know whether she liked him or not.

Before he was to leave for Tubac, Bert gambled talking about the future. He asked her how long she was going to stay with her dad, and she said it was time to move. He asked her if she liked Tubac, and she said yes. He asked her if she'd consider moving somewhere close to him, and she said yes.

Then she took his arm, led him inside the doublewide. "See all this stuff?" she said. "All this valuable stuff? Most of it is Dad's. Nothing much to look at; I could leave it all right now. So yeah, let's go to Tubac. I'm ready for a change."

Bert felt something jump inside. "Boy, I'm ready too...But do you mean right now? Today?"

She laughed, "Why not?" Then told him he could help her pack. She didn't have much, it could all fit into one small trailer.

"Tell me how to help you pack. Then I'll go get a U-Haul-It."

"Smallest one possible. You go get it now while I throw everything together. I don't have much, just things like that mannequin over there."

"Mannequin?"

"I sew. It's a good living and I'm my own boss."

Bert resisted telling her about the other woman he knew who used a mannequin—the mannequin he'd bought for her to sew costumes. Instead, he said, "So am I my own boss. As you know, I'm retired. But I piddle around with this and that. Wouldn't mind getting back into sculpting. I love wood."

"So do I! We'll have to take my table over there. I made it myself! But it has to be disassembled first; it's too heavy. You can put it back together the right way, not with those stupid sheetrock screws."

The wood was attractive, probably mesquite. The legs didn't look right; they were too thin to hold up such a slab. He'd talk to her about that. He smiled and let his mind wander. Back in Tubac they might find a house outside of town with a shop in back, one side open to the elements. And a sewing room for her. There could be a future after all.

A few days later on their way south, pulling the trailer filled with tables, sewing machines, books, cooking supplies, mannequin, and boxes of fabric, feathers, leather, hats, and boots, they talked about the changes that life delivers. He decided it was time to press her about her bout with EMS but didn't know how to begin. He finally just asked abruptly if she'd totally recovered.

"I think so," she replied hesitantly. "It kept going on and on, and I thought would never end. But one day I woke up feeling almost normal...."

"And then?"

"Then I just slowly came back to myself. Never did figure out why." She shook her head and smiled. He could tell she didn't want to talk more about it.

At lunch Bert asked what Walter had said when she told him she was leaving. She said he was pleased, knew it was coming. Would be ok by himself; "He's such an independent guy. And his golf keeps him busy."

Bert told her how much he'd gotten to like him, and how they'd actually discussed the possibility of Bert and her getting together. If that happened, Walter had promised to visit every now and then; he would stay at the Resort.

"It's not too fast, this new adventure?" she asked.

"Not for me. I was bored to death. And maybe you were right when we met so long ago–how long? Months? Anyway, I guess you were right, I was lonely."

"I could tell right away that first day we met. Saw it in your eyes."

"You're psychic too?"

"I've been told that. But I don't give readings."

"How about predicting the next place we're going to stop for lunch?"

She laughed. He laughed. Rowdy stopped trying to look out the window and settled into her lap.

CHAPTER FIFTEEN: CROSSING BORDERS

HEY BUDDY, I JUST LEARNED how to do this text thing, you don't even have to spellcheck or have perfect grammar. I'ts fun to screw up. So here goes. thanks for the lead, it worked. Met Becky whos now Charlene and now lives here in tubac not with me but nearby, in a rental Caseeta. We do lots of things together not all things yet unfortunately but things we like like walking Rowdy, cooking, reading and playing bored games. We talked a little about her e m s and shes one who survived, made it out the other side. I went on line again and found another video about this woman jusst like her who had to move to westvirginia searching for a golden cage which she finally found in the middle of nowhere and lived in fortwo years. Same story as hers and you know who's. The video said doctors are starting to grant it might be a real condition but still say very few people are affected. A friend I met the other day said maybe four %. Same numbers as my Suzannes psp you mite recall. If thats true then our talk a year or so ago was probably just alarmest. Three or four percent is a lot maybe thousands or a couple hundred thousand but not enough to cause things to change. They'll just have to learn to cope—mainly by changing their living situations. Anyway my new girlfriend has changed hers to near my place, I'm happy to say. Very happy to say. Her story makes me wonder if Brie's condition mite have been more mental and emotional than physical. I guess I'll never know, having banished her from my mind. Well thats all for now, say hello to Marsha and give Trouble a bone for me o yeah, I'm thinkin of tryin to learn to tango. Golfs easier which by the way has actually improved. Now I'm driving straight and long sometimes almost 230 and most irons are solid contact. Putting still soso. So there. Tell me if you ever shoot your age I haven't yet but do hit low 80s ever now and then. Hope you can read this. I'll try to learn to do this texing better. Bert

Back in western North Carolina Bert had worried about trading mountains for flat land, green for brown, cold for hot, wet for dry, known for unknown, friends for strangers. But once he made the move, he didn't question whether he'd done wrong to leave North Carolina; something inside told him it was right, was meant to be, even if he still had trouble with destiny talk.

His discovery of the Anza Trail helped him acclimatize. Today, walking down the road toward it, he found himself silently praising the beauty and peace all around him. Then his inner motor started spinning harder than usual. It started with processing his morning phone call to Charlene. He'd asked her to spend Valentine's Day with him, ending up with dinner somewhere, but she'd already made plans. On Valentine's Day! What was up? He walked and fumed, trying to banish the jealousy. After all, he should claim his kiss; every man who sees his woman twice the week before gets that privilege. Was that something he'd heard or just made up? Yet, to be truthful, they hadn't been doing much kissing since her move...her move to be closer to him.

Remembering Frank's advice about letting people be who they are, he told himself not to appear too eager, to proceed slowly.

Suddenly he shouted to Rowdy to watch out for the car. The dog immediately came back, wagging his tail saying he'd just been testing Master to see if he was paying attention. Bert slowly went back into his head, this time pondering if what he desired, yearned for, longed for, was not just another woman to love but to love a woman in a new and better way. What was the meaning of that biblical phrase, loving a person as yourself? Did it mean allowing God to love through you? Hadn't he done that with Brie? He knew he had with Suzanne. Hadn't he?

Why couldn't he just experience his purpose in life instead of always having to think endlessly about it? Sages say life's purpose is to become kindness incarnate. But that seems to be about being nice, not loving, and certainly not loving a specific woman-- flesh and blood woman--in the concrete. Someone like Charlene. Would he be able to love her without hurting her or getting hurt? Yes, he was ready to face and embrace uncertainty. He'd ask nothing of her, expect nothing. Well, that was the theory. He'd learn to give love without wanting anything back. No reassurances. He'd risk it all.

At my age, he thought, to be so focused on another woman, always thinking about climbing into bed. His loving should be directed toward a desert landscape, *this* desert landscape. Much safer. The book he'd been reading about the solace of wild and fierce desert and mountain landscapes told him he should spend days or weeks camping alone in a particular place, paying close attention to every detail. Listening not to what he thought was in the landscape, but what wasn't. If he did that, the sheer nothingness of the desert would draw him into its emptiness and indifference.

Yeah, yeah, talk, talk. How could a desert strip him bare, teach him to embrace his uselessness? The desert is just desert. Trying to live more closely to the bone pulling him out of his self-absorption? Breaking him and putting him on the road to wholeness?

That's the theory, but Bert knew he'd always been close to nature. He'd always hated being cooped inside, gone outside whenever possible. He'd read dozens of books about aboriginals--held them up as models, except for their inexplicable violent side. Had retired early and left the world for an empty mountain top. Built a wilderness cabin, off the grid, and roamed the hills. But he had to admit, always with a woman. Always a woman alongside him. He'd never taken to the hills by himself. Never a John Muir, sleeping alone week after week in the wilderness with his twin gods, Yosemite and Jesus. His friend Edward was also able to go it alone--walked the whole Appalachian Trail by himself and travelled to one strange country after another alone. Why couldn't he?

Maybe he was too hard on himself. He *had* listened to silence up on the mountain, melted into it. He'd let the vast silence slowly grow inside. It never left off growing; Colorado's ski slopes and alpine lakes still lived inside him. Nature *had* healed him, taught him to listen and observe. All his life he'd silently given thanks. Even when he was a young atheist, he'd thanked the universe for its beauty. On top of Bradley's Bash at Winter Park, before pushing off for the downhill run, he'd scan the distant mountains, smile, and silently applaud.

Maybe his closeness to nature had taught him something about loving. He might be ready to love a woman, his last woman, not just any woman, but his final soul-mate. It was, after all, February 14, the day of love...the second time he'd be spending it alone. Two years after the Valentine's day he'd missed with Brie because of winter congestion.

Next week Bert received a package containing a book from Frank. Inside, a letter encouraging him to use his cell microphone to send text messages, not type them out, dummy. The letter continued to its real subject: "I have something that might interest you. I'd been rummaging through my old notebooks, looking for some wisdom on guilt and depression. Then I found this on overcoming grief and thought about you. Yeah, I know you think you've come to terms with your grief over Suzanne, but how about Brie? Read the last chapter of this book on how to overcome grief."

The chapter gave detailed instruction for writing the Grief Resolution Letter--saying good-bye not to fond memories but three things: 1. Pain, loneliness, confusion; 2. Physical closeness that's no more; 3. Emotional incompleteness.

A year ago, the advice would have spoken to Bert but now it left him cold. Happily cold; it told him he'd actually said good-bye to all three numbers. The fact that he'd allowed Charlene to enter his sphere, even if she still hadn't moved very far inside, proved he didn't need to read the rest of the book. He took it to the library's "Free Books" shelf and found a comfortable place outside to phone Frank.

"Hi Frank, just calling to thank you for thinking about my grief problem. Hey, it's finally getting better."

"You sure you're not dying of loneliness out there all by yourself?"

"Well, I'm not all alone, at least during the days. Like I texted you not too long ago, your friend's sister is keeping me occupied."

"I'm glad that's working out."

"For the time being, yes. Anyway, it does still get very lonely in the middle of the night.'

"I might have told you that back in the days when I was practicing, a very reputable psychologist claimed most emotional problems stem directly from not being able to meaningfully connect with another. I think we've all experienced that."

"That's amazing...so simple! Unlike most of you shrinks, who feel so compelled to make things difficult," Bert snorted. "That's necessary of course to make piles of money!" He heard Frank laugh, then added, "I hope you're still connected tightly to Marsha."

"Well, it got rocky there about the time you left for the desert, but we managed to patch it together. Now I'd say it's good, but not like it used to be. I guess things always diminish. Anyway, in another recent study I just read that loneliness is a public health threat second only to obesity, smoking, and drinking."

"Seems to me they're comparing apples and oranges. Those three could be what *cause* loneliness. Aren't they the cause of a lot of breakups?"

"Maybe," Frank answered. "Anyway, the same article quoted an older study—maybe 2010—that claimed loneliness affects the mortality rate as much as three-fourths of a pack of cigarettes a day."

"Well, I don't believe everything I read; I distrust most of these so-called scientific reports. Aren't they usually correlation studies that can prove anything?"

"Yeah, you might just be a tiny bit more informed than I've given you credit for. Anyway, *I'm* not going to die of loneliness. *You're* not going to die of loneliness. *We're* going to stay alive for golf."

"I'm doing my best out here to stay connected to bunches of people. Most every evening I'm doing something with somebody. And of course, I have this happy dog to sleep with."

"Speaking of…there's Trouble scratching at the door. Better hang up. Good talking to you, and give Rowdy a big bone for me."

"You too, give Trouble a bigger one. He's bigger. See you, Frank."

Bert, Charlene, and Rowdy were walking the Anza trail when a horse came trotting up. "Good thing that's not a javelina," Bert laughed. The horse stopped while the rider introduced herself, said she'd just moved from Minnesota and found a fantastic ranch across the Santa Cruz for boarding her horse. They talked about different reasons people give for moving to the southwest.

When they got to discussing Tubac galleries, Bert was so impressed with the woman's enthusiasm over a horse painting at the Stone Gallery that he went that afternoon to see it. It was just a simple portrayal of an Indian pony; what made it special was the way the artist had captured the animal's stance, its weight balanced on three feet. Or maybe it was the sepia tones, reminiscent of Curtis' Indian photographs.

He wasn't in the habit of buying art work but knew he needed this one, and also needed to meet the artist. The price was $280, so he offered $325 with the proviso that the artist would get $200 instead of the standard

50/50 split. The gallery owner agreed and gave him the artist's e-mail address. Later that afternoon he texted Jorge Rodriguez, saying he had just bought the pony picture and would like to come to Mexico to meet its artist. Jorge surprised him by responding they could meet the following morning at the deli in town.

Jorge turned out to be a middle-aged Mexican from San Carlos in Sonoran Mexico. He'd lived his early life in Guaymas and later in Tucson after graduating from the University of Arizona and working part time at a Tucson art gallery. When he was 38, he decided it was time to commit, and the Mexican in him won out. He married Sophia, his high school sweetheart, and opened an art supply store in San Carlos...mainly because she loved the water. It came to suit him fine after he was able to purchase a small studio apartment with a partial sea view and more importantly a well-drained patch of land for a vegetable garden. It took the better part of two years to prepare the soil and build raised beds. By this time, they had a daughter and another child on the way.

Jorge had come to Tubac to exhibit at the weekend spring art festival. Like a hundred or more other artists and craftsmen, he'd pitched his 10 x 10 tent and hoped for the best. Jorge's wife had stayed behind with the kids, leaving the artist with nothing much to do except sit and greet. Bert took him to a restaurant known for its marguerites and tacos. After an hour of talking and drinking Bert decided it was time to call Charlene, invite her to meet his new friend. She joined them and they continued talking into the night.

After Jorge returned to San Carlos, he and Bert continued their friendship using a special phone connection Bert had found. Their talk started out polite and guarded, but on the third or fourth call they opened up. Jorge said he was having a hard time putting into words what had been bothering him. "Me, I'm just another half breed," he said. "Back in Tucson I used to think like you guys, now I think more like me, a Mexican. I understand the political mess you people are in, and how so many can be against us. Nothing new there, I get that. But what I still don't is why your country needs to wall us off from you."

Bert didn't want to launch into a long talk about the president he disliked so much who'd stirred up a hornet's nest, so he paused before answering. "Last week at our men's group, once again we got into talking about how we'd always felt God in nature. You know, sunsets, trees, animals. When we talk like that, we always stop short, automatically assuming everyone agrees. Who *doesn't* feel the divine presence in a lovely landscape?"

Jorge didn't know whether it was a question or not, so simply said, "Sure, who doesn't?"

"But not everyone in our group did. There's this one close friend who's intelligent and spiritually alive. Both he and his wife wake up to an hour of meditation every day. They claim to be Buddhists. But he said he never feels anything special outside. 'Just trees and sky--so what?'"

Bert paused, then concluded: "It flabbergasted me, blew me away, his indifference to beauty."

Jorge didn't know how to answer. "I understand, my friend. But how does this relate to my question?"

Bert laughed. "Sorry there. I was making a leap. I was trying to figure out how people we like can think so differently from us–especially about important things, not small stuff. We assume they think like us when they obviously don't. Maybe they're the same ones who watch dancing with stars shows, Oscar awards, trash movies, and read Hollywood tabloids. Hell, they probably throw their money away on the lottery, and eat too much. Even good people who should know better do all that."

He paused, then told Jorge to hold on for the conclusion. "These same people are probably the ones who think they're better than others. They might be in the majority. I hope not; I hope we'll go back to being a country that welcomes others."

Jorge nodded into the phone. "That helps but doesn't really explain why your people want to wall us off. I mean, yeah, there's racism and all, but I didn't encounter much prejudice back in Arizona at the university...."

"That was a while ago, and at a university. We've still got our centers of sanity but now hate and anger seem to have taken over... all kinds of white supremacists, neo-Nazis, skinheads."

"Aren't they just crazy fringe groups?"

"Yes and no. They don't go around shouting 'Heil Hitler.' They keep a low profile but are more powerful than people think. They have well-placed leaders influencing legislation, and prominent social media platforms. Don't think they didn't help elect Trump and keep his followers stirred up."

"Is it that bad?"

"Well, I don't know. The other day I was checking out magazines in a supermarket and counted fifteen different ones on weapons—assault rifles, automatic pistols, knives. Who knows, probably flame throwers and tanks. Fifteen! And only one on golf!"

"Ok, I see that. But you people have the longest democracy ever, and truly love your freedom. And how many buy weapons of mass destruction?"

"We've always loved our freedom, but the world's getting so dangerous that many just pay lip service to freedom. All they want is to be safe. Maybe that's what's behind all the hate and anger."

"Scary. Do you think it'll get worse and worse?"

"Maybe not. The pendulum always swings. I hope what's been happening is just backlash."

Jorge said it was probably time to hang up, but he had one more question. "Bert–if I may freely call you Bert now, not just Mr. Brightson. What you say helps. And what you said earlier about tv reminds me of another thing. Something not as bad, but still a problem, at least for me. Sophia and I both watch too much tv because there's not much to do here." He paused to clear his throat. "Most of our shows come from the U.S. But what comes in from Mexico City isn't any different. Hollywood is everywhere. The whole world is Hollywood. Someone told me that in India they call their movies Bollywood. I guess it's just a fact of life...but I can't relate to it in my sleepy town here."

Bert didn't know where Jorge was going but was in the mood to talk. He said he understood, he too had a hard time relating to Hollywood. "I wonder about the sex life of all those stars. You can't help thinking about it, they parade it everywhere. Twenty years ago, I'd have given an arm and leg to be able to snap my fingers and have another beautiful woman smother me with kisses and take me to bed. But wouldn't it change a person?"

"How so?"

"Wouldn't it become a habit? Unlimited free sex could be very addictive, but it's just sex."

"You are suggesting sex is not healthy? Maybe too much sex?"

"No, not that at all. Sex with love is always healthy. But isn't sex without love just lust? I guess I'm a bit of a prude, but how can you love a new person every day?"

"I see your point. Sex without love...."

"It seems to me you could reach a point where you wouldn't know what meaningful love is." Bert threw up his arms. "Sorry, I guess I'm just being old-fashioned."

Jorge said he understood and it helped answer what had been bothering him. "Thank you, friend, you have helped me feel not so much I'm missing out on life down here. Down here in my backward place."

Bert got ready to end the phone conversation when Jorge said, "One thing more, please. This about my Sophia."

"Shoot."

"No shoot!" They both laughed. "I don't know how to say this. It's about the tv again. She worries about—well, some of her body being too small. Says for me not to look at all the women on the tv. 'I can't be them,' she says, crying."

Bert encouraged him to continue.

"I say to her, 'No matter, I look at you, not them.' But sometimes she does not believe. You think we've been tricked by the pretty Hollywood women?"

"I do. What we're taught to want always influences us. And our world tells us what to want. Now what matters, just what looks good and everyone is supposed to have."

"Big you know whats!"

"Not just that. We expect our mate to tell small lies to make us feel better. We do the same. We don't really know what we want. The world puts wants into us and convinces us they're our own."

"And that's what's causing my Sophia to feel bad?"

They talked some more, then Bert said he'd like to drive down for a visit. Jorge told him anytime, said it was a good quiet place to relax. "We'll leave off the stupid tv."

"Be happy there, Jorge. And give Sophia a hug for me–a real hug. I'll try to visit you in a month or so, maybe with my new girlfriend. We'd better stop now, my cell phone's almost out of juice. When we come down you can show us how authentic people live. And let me ride your pony, too."

Bert was tired of stepping around boxes of books he'd stacked in the corner awaiting shelving he'd delayed buying because his rental didn't have room for anything more. It was time to ditch the books he'd never reread. He opened the closest box and dumped all the books out. The first two he examined made him wish he'd never started.

The enneagram book hurled him back to his long letter to Brie contrasting their different personality types— hers the perfectionist and his the romantic. Because synchronicity seemed to be the rule in his new place of abode, he guessed the second book would undoubtedly tell him whether he was or wasn't a hopeless romantic. It did. Alan Bloom's *Love and Friendship*, unlike his famous *Closing of the American Mind*, approached the subject from his classicist background. The Greeks were fascinated by *eros,* if not *agape*—which St. Paul had told them they knew nothing about, had just invented a word for and were still waiting for it to be filled with meaning.

Eros, Bloom argued, was similar to what Bert did know something about—romantic love. Everything he read spoke personally to him. Beauty, the prime mover, brings joy, and joy brings everything else good that feeds the soul, including intimate sex. Beauty flowing from the eyes of the beloved creates romantic love.

Bert closed the book with his finger in it and wondered how many people had, like he, grown up experiencing wave after wave of precious romantic love. Somewhere he'd heard few actually do. He *did* know that most people have a hard time taking it seriously when they get older. They call it puppy love and can't believe it comes from the soul.

That seemed to be the message of the silly movie he'd seen a few weeks ago at a party built around a cult movie he'd never heard of, let alone seen. "Love, Actually" was hilarious and at times funny, but a far cry from "Love Story," let alone Zeffirelli's "Romeo and Juliet" or even Hemingway's *Farewell to Arms.* Hmm. True romantic love pits two loners against the sordid world that can't understand their love so works to destroy it. But now, Bert reasoned, if "Love,

Actually" is the authoritative work that everyone at the party took it to be--some having viewed it four or five times—then romantic love now is us *and* them...a playful game of hide and seek, not a private matter of us *versus* them—ending up in a suicide pact when *they* win. It's no longer dangerous love, just harmless horseplay.

Bert told himself he was creating a red herring; the movie didn't really pretend to speak seriously about love. It was just a fun comedy. But he couldn't curb his mental tirade. What happens when love becomes a public game of finding the mate--and parading her before others just to prove you have it all together? Hmm. Could he have been guilty of that with Charlene?

Then Bert's mind went back to his junior class on Nineteenth Century British Literature. In Byron's *Don Juan*, the lovers were fed, not threatened, by public disapproval. That sounded just right to him and the rest of the eighteen-year-olds in his class. Byron—the consummate libertine--had hinted that most romantic love thrived on its being illicit. But none of the couples in the 2003 movie had grown up being taught that sex outside of marriage was wrong. That removed the thrill of it being illicit.

The sexual revolution, Bert would definitely remember to tell Jorge during their next conversation, promised to free people from guilt but in fact managed to diminish their full experiencing of romantic love. Maybe even killed it off. What's romantic about unearned, freely available sex? He looked forward to hearing what his traditional Mexican friend would say about this new turn of events.

He went back to Bloom, read about the kind of love that lies dormant until awakened. The sudden, intense contact forces lovers to get carried away by passionate feelings beyond their control. They want only one thing: to be now and forever with the other. Even if it means making that suicide compact.

Bert smiled and put down the book. All this was exactly what he'd thought; it felt good to be verified. Did it have anything to do with him personally? Hmm. If the pain that romantic love produces is linked to the most ecstatic of pleasures then Bloom could be right-- love is a self-forgetting that makes man self-aware. We can choose to call it illusory but its effects are not illusory. Bert knew it was love that drove him on, pulled him upward in his quest for perfection. He needed a beloved to help him.

Would he find his beloved in the few years left to him? he kept pondering while going to the kitchen for a beer. Could he find a woman capable of love, not just sex, comfort, or attraction? Who would willingly take on the risk and pain? He doubted Charlene fit that picture. Would he continue to search? Yes, because he could not live alone. Not because he was lonely; he'd outgrown that. Not because he needed sexual release; he could handle that. Not because he was bored; there was always golf, pickleball, casual friends. But because he was incomplete.

He could find beauty and joy walking the Anza, breathing the crisp desert air, smelling the cottonwoods. But his heart ached for the beauty of a woman's eyes. The beauty of her soul. The beauty of her body. The beauty of her feel and taste. The beauty of feeling and tasting her beautiful body. Aggh!

He tried to tell himself he could settle for the less intense love of friendship. Friends look with the same eyes toward the same things; they risk less. Lovers look into each other's eyes and get lost. Sometimes hurt each other. He should probably settle for friendship. Hell, he didn't know.

Bert didn't want to wait another month for his big trip to San Carlos. He invited Charlene, but she wasn't interested. No problem, he'd go alone. April, he knew to be an excellent time to visit; if he waited two months, he'd be facing heat worse than where he lived.

After a long six-hour drive, it took him another half-hour to find the house. It turned out to be larger than most in the poor neighborhood, facing the sea a half-mile away. Jorge greeted Bert with a hug, and lugged his suitcase into the small den with a pull-out bed.

Before Sophia returned from shopping, the two men walked down to the Sea of Cortez, Jorge talking excitedly about going scuba diving to see the exotic fish the sea was so famous for. While he explained his arrangements to borrow a friend's gear, Bert smiled but inwardly frowned, not having enough nerve to reveal his fear of water. Maybe he could fake a cold the day before they were to go.

They sat on a pier watching the gulls when two youngsters bounded up. Ramon was nine, Carla, ten. He was taller than his sister and looked much older; could easily pass for a teenager. Barefoot and dressed in shorts and t-shirts typical of Stateside teenagers, both immediately greeted their father's new friend in English, chattering excitedly with none of the reserve Bert would soon find in Jorge's adult friends.

He's taught them excellent manners, Bert thought, noting they addressed their talk as much to him as their father and carried on like they'd known him for years. He was even more impressed when he discovered they hadn't brought the ever-present cell phones. They stayed for a few polite minutes of chit-chat and then bounded off in search of sea-shells, waving goodbye over their shoulders.

Jorge talked about their upcoming dive. "I usually use a mask and fins; they're good enough for me," he said, gesturing toward the incoming waves. "But when I told him you were coming, my good friend Carlos insisted we use his scuba gear. And of course, he'll take us out in his fancy new boat. He's a show-off, but a nice guy; you'll like him."

Bert grimaced. "Take us out—um--how far?"

"Well, not too far," Jorge said, smiling. "But when we go out beyond the shore area, we need scuba gear. Way out there we'll be able to go deep enough to see the really good fishes."

Bert finally worked up his nerve to respond honestly. "How about a pony ride instead? I-- er--well, I'm not overly fond of water. To be honest, I'm a little afraid of it. Don't know why, maybe a bad childhood experience."

Jorge chuckled and said they could settle for a boat ride. Then asked why his new girlfriend hadn't come. Bert didn't know how to respond but mumbled something about her being too busy moving into her new place. One worry after another, he thought— water, women.

On the third day of his visit Bert asked about the backyard shrine containing pictures of a family group. Jorge immediately turned his head, and Bert heard him weep. Several minutes later he began the long story.

His father had been a wealthy banker in Guaymas, an honest man admired by all for helping the poor and sponsoring community programs. One day many years ago, while Jorge was away attending high school in Tucson, a powerful drug lord from near Mexico City came north exploiting towns along the way-- always leaving tragedy in the wake. In Guaymas he learned of Jorge's father's position in the historic old bank of Sonora. He abducted him as he left, demanding he use his bank connection to launder $200,000 a year--

"nothing much for a man of your means, so easily done."

Jorge's father was no idealist; he knew he'd probably escape jail for obeying the command. It was what people in his position had always done to survive. But for him honor had never been just a word; he had his name to live with. He worried how the tarnished name might scar his oldest son. But he also knew what could happen to him, his wife, and two youngest. The drug lord had given him an hour to seal his fate, the longest hour of his life.

Guaymas was no sleepy village; among other things it had a large police force. They should offer protection; it was after all one of their jobs. He called them and explained the situation. But then Senor Rodriguez unwisely decided to ignore the drug lord's command, and police protection never came. He was immediately bound and taken to an empty warehouse. His refusal to cooperate surprised and greatly angered the drug lord, who issued harsher treatment than usual.

They beat him and his wife almost to death, then gave an ultimatum that he come up with $300,000 inside of a week or they would kill the two young sons his thugs had gone to kidnap. But his father had been so severely beaten he couldn't get up, let alone walk, and his mother died inside of a few hours. The sons were left to their slow death after being thrown into a well-guarded swamp. That happened three days after Senor Rodriguez's own death.

Up in Tucson Jorge learned of the tragedy only by accident, coming across it in the middle pages of a week-old newspaper. By the time he got to Guaymas, the Catholic church had arranged a proper burial for all four. The word they'd sent to Tucson had arrived late, so hearing nothing, they had to assume he wouldn't be present. Although he missed the services, he returned to a town supportive in every way, people attending to him hourly with food, prayers, and endless condolences.

Bank officials, who'd known Jorge since a boy, gave him living expense money for his time there and wired his father's bank account, which the drug lord had not been able to get his hands on, to his Tucson bank. Jorge stayed a week pondering what to do and finally decided it was best to complete his education. That decision was prompted mostly by the sight of his home, burned to the ground after being stripped of valuables. Four faded photos were the only thing left of his past, and as much as he appreciated the community support, he knew if he ever did return to Mexico, it would have to be to a new place. He would use his father's money to complete his education and start up a new business in some new town–or simply stay in the States.

When Bert asked him if he feared for his own life after returning to Mexico, Jorge said no, he figured the drug lord was too busy raiding elsewhere and had already enacted his full reprisal. Jorge had spent months plotting strategies of revenge, all of which he knew to be impossible. Meanwhile, the padre of his small church in Tucson convinced him his best revenge would be returning good for evil– following his father's lead by becoming a powerful force for good in his new community. After graduating from college, he had come back to the country that had failed him, like so many, because it always allowed corruption to go unchecked. But it was still his country.

Bert was horrified by his friend's story, yet not surprised. He'd heard it hundreds of times in novels, history books, movies, and newspapers. Humans brutalizing humans. The news devastated him just the same, knowing how it had to leave his new friend emotionally scarred for life. His only response to the story was weeping with him.

The following day Jorge had to work in his paint store, so Bert walked down to the beach, trying to shake his friend's tragedy. He scanned the water for whales or dolphins to lift his spirit. But he saw only birds flying high above the water.

Jorge returned an hour before supper, and they sat together under a mesquite tree back of the house. Talk came slowly. Bert started to congratulate his friend on surviving his harrowing experience without getting trapped in anger and pessimism, but Jorge cut him short. "Something like that obviously takes the staying power out of the strongest person," he said, "but if anyone had been raised to get through, it was me."

Bert quietly asked him to continue.

"My family.... You might not know how stable and supporting the Mexican family can be. At least the ones like ours that are financially secure. We had no crippled kids to raise or bad neighbors to fight. All we did—what you guys call our extended family—was eat and play together. Twenty or thirty of us sitting around strumming guitars, singing, talking. I grew up strong, very strong. Even when I was the new Mexican at your university, I immediately fit in, never thought of myself as an outsider."

Bert smiled, relieved the topic was starting to move away from the horrible scene that kept playing through his mind. "It's good to hear that. It was true for me; I guess we were the lucky ones. So many people these days never had that solid base to grow from."

"I guess that's become your country's biggest problem—disappearing families and isolated communities?"

"You're telling me the same isn't true of Mexico?"

"You'd think so. Our government's always been corrupt; our people always poor; and everything's always looked bad on the outside."

"But….?"

"On the inside there's still glue holding things together. You know, the church still teaches morality and instills confidence. The families build trust and self-respect." Jorge stopped to clear his throat. "A Greek friend of mine back at the U of A told me the same thing was true of his country. Outside, nothing but problems, but inside, ok. He said you never see poor beggars begrudging wealthy Germans, Japanese, Americans for arrogantly tossing money around. They're happy. Your poor aren't."

"Strange isn't it? But I guess true." Bert reached in his pocket for a nickel to toss up in the air. "Heads it's mine. Tails, yours." He held it up. "There you go, tails."

"And...."

"That means you have to let me buy lunch. We need to go to your favorite place, sit down and have a beer or two and some of that good Mexican food."

"I know just the place."

Half-way through their meal the conversation drifted back to family and community.

"Strong families," Bert ventured, "breed not just children but compassion and love."

"Very true. And the same is true of strong communities."

"Unfortunately," Bert continued, "the reverse is true of so many rogue countries these days—Libya, Syria, Nigeria, the Congo. They bomb the people and countryside and sow the dead land with seeds of hate."

Bert scratched his head. "As long as we're sitting here being so wise, I should throw in something my own country has started teaching. Morality has been replaced by situational ethics."

"I found that at the U of A," Jorge agreed. "But I continue to think that deep down people are still hard-wired to look for good over evil, right over wrong. They can't think it's right to do whatever a situation allows."

"I hope that's still true," Bert said. "I do know people risk their lives to pull a stranger out of a raging river. They help victims of hurricanes and forest fires. I remember my dad saying long ago that you can't change human nature. I've never known whether to agree with him or not."

The waiter brought the check and it was time to call it a day.

The following day Bert said he had to get home. Driving back, he couldn't stop replaying Jorge's tragedy. Eventually he shook his head and consciously took to remembering his friend's obvious love for Sophia, Carla, and Ramon. All that cemented their bond. Bert knew they'd be close for life, knew he'd be coming down to visit once or twice a year, always bringing something special. His first present would be a new refrigerator, which he'd have secretly installed while they were away. Plus a suitcase of comic books for Ramon and several new outfits for Carla. Maybe he could make up crazy stories for the kids at night like he used to do with his own.

PART THREE

CHAPTER SIXTEEN: LETTING GO

BERT'S OLD FRIEND LYLE in Oregon called to catch up after not talking for three or more years. Bert hadn't kept up with the one who always sounded like a broken record, replaying stale jokes and personal exploits--forever stuck in the past and refusing to grow. Bert had lost patience with Lyle's endless patter, especially about the benefits of living in an old hippie commune where he could keep up with his habits.

Lyle told him his Roz had moved on, saying she had demons to contend with. Bert said nothing, knowing him to exaggerate and push blame on others. He'd been unsuccessful with at least six different women since their school days. Then they talked about how hard it is to connect with a woman. Lyle talked while Bert listened.

He listened absently, noting not what Lyle said but how much the language he used sounded just like Jim's. It was bad enough having another friend who talked like a perpetual teenager, but at least Jim didn't rant about sexual conquests and famous sports figures he'd bumped into.

"Tell me about your latest love," Lyle eventually asked. "Describe her down to her most luscious detail."

Bert refused. He didn't know where he stood with her and wouldn't share it if he did, so he tried to change the subject.

Lyle wouldn't let him; he had women on his mind. "Come on now, just tell me what she looks like."

Bert obliged a little by describing her eyes and hair.

"Sounds like Roz," Lyle replied, going on to describe her anatomical features in detail.

Bert listened for a minute, then said he had to go somewhere soon. Lyle didn't take the hint but recounted the time he'd been drinking with John Elway.

Bert groaned, then came up with a way to get him off the phone. "Lyle, you just asked me to describe Charlene. Well, I forgot to mention her complexion. It's fantastic."

"Complexion?"

"Yeah, the prettiest ebony you've ever seen." Bert paused for emphasis. "She's black, Lyle, a foxy black lady!"

Silence. "Black?"

"Yeah, Lyle, I'm dating a black woman. Something you've probably never considered."

Silence. "Oh yeah, well, hey, I've got nothing against them kind."

"Don't try so hard, Lyle. I understand. But now I've got to run; something just came up."

"Yeah, man, I well… call again man. I, uh…."

Bert stifled a laugh "So long, Lyle." Then he hung up and deleted Lyle from his phone contact.

Bert pushed his feet up on the couch, thinking about how striking Charlene was. He was proud of going out with her. But had he'd noticed a change? Back in Prescott when she surprised him with her sudden decision to move to Tubac, he'd automatically assumed the best. But now feared the worst. She'd been living in a small casita a few blocks north, and they usually connected only a couple of days a week, sometimes for golf, though she didn't like to play more than nine holes. Sometimes they went to dance at Mike's. He liked being with her, not just looking at her and dreaming about what could be, but talking to her. She was intelligent, sensitive, and very independent.

But now…hmm. Was she distancing herself? He asked himself what he must have done wrong, then changed it to what she had done wrong, then left it alone. He'd give her one last chance, called to invite her to dance. It was Saturday and Mike's had a good band, Bad News Blues out of Tucson.

Her phone went to voice mail. He recorded and waited an hour but she didn't call back. He went alone, not liking the idea of dancing alone like some of the women or the fat cowboy who was always drunk. But he could enjoy sipping a glass of wine and listening to Bad News Blues.

Mike's was crowded as usual. He arrived late; the only place to sit was in the corner away from the dance floor. He scanned the area and saw Charlene dancing with a guy who had to be ten years younger than he, a lot thinner, and certainly a better dancer. Kissing him in-between dances!

Maybe Bert didn't need a glass of wine. Before the waiter came, he rose to leave.

It was time for Bert's third visit to San Carlos; hopefully May wouldn't be too hot. He didn't know what was attracting him so much to Mexico—probably just his newly found friends. Not speaking the language bothered him, but he'd gotten through customs successfully before and made the drive without incident.

Carla met him at the door, smiling as usual and leading him into the living room, where she quickly parked herself in a floppy chair with her favorite doll, a cuddly pink horse. While waiting for Jorge, he tried unsuccessfully to engage her in a conversation about school, then switched to which of her dad's paintings she liked best. "That's easy! All the ones with horses," she said, pointing toward two on the far wall. "Daddy promised to get me my very own pony pretty soon!"

The next night Jorge took Bert and Sophia to a new Greek food shack, insisting that he pick up the tab for a change. It was a small hole-in-the-wall at the far end of a deserted shopping mall. Bert looked around, mentally replacing cheap metal tables with sturdy wooden ones, hanging pictures and plants on the walls, installing inobtrusive lighting, doing something about the stained concrete floor. But the lack of atmosphere hadn't stopped people from coming; the three had to wait almost an hour to get seating.

Bert was not surprised to find the food excellent. They were finishing their desert when a woman walked up to say hello to Jorge and Sophia. He introduced Bert and invited her to join them for coffee. She'd come alone, so sat down with them in the empty chair next to Bert.

Leticia was anything but shy; she immediately took charge of the conversation, asking Bert to explain where he'd met Jorge, and then detailing her recent divorce. While she was elaborating, he studied her face. Not pretty, but very expressive. Her facial coloring, neither light nor dark, showed an equal mix of Indian and Spanish blood, and she was also taller than average.

Looks had always been important to Bert. His first wife, at 19, had that delightful demeanor of a teenage girl trying hard to look like a woman, and his second, at 30, was a woman who looks like every female wants to look. He'd always considered her the most beautiful women he'd seen, right up until her end thirty years later—when everyone at the nursing home said she looked twenty years younger than she was. She'd spoiled him into liking women who look naturally rather than artificially beautiful. She rarely used lipstick; cut her own hair, which was straight but somehow perfect; and spent less than $200 a year on cosmetics and clothes. Este Lauder Gold, the only extravagance he could talk her into.

Leticia obviously spent time making herself as attractive as possible, yet in a way that remained natural and helped disguise the fact that she was a bit overweight. She wore a large red flower on the right side of her head that matched the color of her lipstick. Her hair, dark brown and probably not dyed, cascaded down the right side of her face in lush curls. It was just as curly on the left side but swept back. One strand had sprung loose from that side—maybe with the help of a comb—hugging her left eye and cheek and flirting with her lips.

Her eyebrows were full, not tightly shaped and tamed like so many movie stars', and her eyes were matching brown. Although she'd put on artificial eyelashes, her cheeks didn't appear to have makeup, though no doubt they did. Her lips didn't pucker into a fake female look but remained slightly open—maybe because she spent so much time talking.

Bert was sitting too close to make obvious visual downward detours toward what he saw bulging from her colorful blouse, but he was able to glance that way every now and again by scratching his eyebrow and casually lowering his head. A tasteful gold pendant hung poised between them.

The longer he listened to her talk—inconsequential but still engaging—and studied her face, the prettier she got. He was not disappointed when Jorge insisted they all go to a cantina to dance.

The two of them fast-danced while Jorge and Sophia sat sipping margaritas. After an hour, they left and Bert walked Leticia back to her car. He held the door open for her and asked if they could get together the following day. She agreed to a lunch date—without Jorge and Sophia.

Bert had consulted with Jorge where to take Leticia and they ended up at one of the more expensive places, the Sunset on the beach. Leticia ordered a shrimp plate, which he seconded. They made small talk, and after dinner she dropped a bomb. "Mr. Bert, you could sell your house up in the States and move down here. Stay in my house, play your golf all afternoon while I paint, come home to maid Alecia's good food. Then make passionate love all night."

Mr. Bert almost pinched himself, decided not to say she'd stolen the thoughts from his mind. Instead, he smiled at the woman seated across the table and hemmed and hawed. Finally, he came up with a moderately decent reply: "Leticia, your words are as gracious as your face is beautiful. I honestly don't know what to say. Nothing would please me more. But this hits me so fast, I'll have to ask myself if I could handle all of it."

"What's to handle, I think you Texans would say."

He could correct her about Texas later. Meanwhile, what would he say? He studied her face again, having already studied her body. What was she, probably fifty-five, maybe pushing sixty? Hard to tell with all the makeup--his only real objection. What would she look like after a morning shower? He already knew what she'd look like in bed, having explored those thoughts, but deciding to postpone them for as long as he could.

Her eyes always asked what he was thinking or doing. When they'd tried to tango--when *he'd* tried to tango-- her eyes kept telling him to move slightly this way or that. But encouraging him, not finding fault, as he did himself with his awkward moves. She never tried to lead.

"Nothing to handle," he finally replied. "I can't think of anything I'd rather do. I'd never thought about moving here...but then, I'd never met you." So far, so good. "Here's the deal: we'll have dinner again tomorrow night and I'll give you my answer. Promise you won't make the offer to another guy?"

She laughed. They sipped their drinks and went back to small talk. After another margarita, Bert found himself dancing like a drunk cowboy. It felt good, and he noticed that she approved.

A few days later Bert and Jorge sat in Jorge's small back yard discussing differences in Mexican and North American Catholicism. Jorge confessed to having fallen away during his Arizona college years.

"In Tucson I stopped attending church," he said, "and when I came back to San Carlos, I found everything too controlling. I had hard time believing—mainly in church, not God."

Bert smiled. "Like almost everyone I know."

"I don't want to be like everyone else. I want to believe. I *do* believe in God. Well, should I tell you my solution?"

"Go ahead."

"I bought these small things that fit into my ear. They play music. I sit very politely and listen…to the music, not the priest."

"Good solution!" Bert laughed loudly, then paused to collect his thoughts. "What you've been telling me, Jorge, opens a conversation I'm not prepared to have because I haven't worked it all out in my head, but I'd like to try with you. Is that ok?"

"I like it, please continue."

"It's about the big difference between our religious traditions. Your Catholicism is safer in that it doesn't ask you to try to understand God. You don't form pictures of God in your head, you just do what the church tells you to do and hope for the best...in your case, with music playing in your ears."

Jorge laughed. "True, so true."

"My Protestantism tells me we're supposed to have a personal relationship, not some impersonal form of worship. Unfortunately, that *makes* us form God pictures in our head. Then the pictures come between us and God instead of drawing us closer. I learned this the hard way."

Jorge nodded and Bert decided he needed to tell his friend about his failed relationship with Brie. He talked for an hour, leaving out nothing, and ended up stressing how she'd tried to control God...and next admitting that he had also. "We both used God to cement our human love. I know this sounds weird, and to explain it would take forever because it's taken me months to process, but the point is I've finally learned the hard way that love never controls, never even understands, always lets things be. And that goes for love of God even more than love of another human. Maybe love is always born out of suffering and not knowing."

Jorge kept nodding politely, then asked how Bert could worship a God he could never know.

"That, my good friend, I cannot answer. My beliefs have changed, continue to almost daily, but that doesn't mean I understand them any better. Maybe it'd be best if I could just get rid of all beliefs-- give up trying to know or understand the mysteries. As I said before, I'm still trying to work things out."

The following afternoon Jorge took Bert to the stable to help him groom his horse. While they were busy brushing, Carla came rushing out saying that Marcos called on the phone and was on his way over.

"You'll like him," Jorge said. He's a bit odd, but very, very smart. He loves to argue, especially about God-- who he doesn't believe in. He studies bugs: scorpions, jejenes, stinkbugs, seedbugs. Bert asked him what a jejene could be, but Jorge didn't have time to answer because Marcos came walking up.

Short and thick-muscled, he looked more like a wrestler than academic entomologist. His unkempt hair and ill-fitting clothing reinforced Bert's initial impression—until the man smiled. Immediately before starting to talk, Marcos had a nervous habit of shaking his head back and forth, giving the impression he was trying to push his words out. The nervous tic lasted but a few seconds, though sometimes he'd get stuck and have to rub his chin to break the spell. Bert was reminded of a singer he'd heard many years before who stuttered uncontrollably until he opened his mouth and mellifluous lyrics tumbled out.

Marcos didn't want to talk about bugs. "Let's have an old-fashioned, knock-down, drag-out battle over the existence of God."

Jorge looked over to Bert, who was slowly shaking his head. "That's no longer my cup of tea, Marcos. I've spent too much time attacking and defending, going around in circles. It bores me now. If I were to say anything, it would be to quote Meister Eckhart's famous words about God being an underground river of wisdom fed by different wells too deep to see. But I can't honestly say I understand those words, and guess you don't want to hear them anyway."

Marcos nodded. "Guess not. Well, we could talk about my bugs. Maybe you'll be glad to hear that the jejenes—the little guys who can wiggle through tiny mosquito netting and whose horrible stings last all day aren't found here in San Carlos but prefer marshy areas farther south."

Both Bert and Jorge smiled, happy to listen to Marcos' fascinating tales of insects. After an hour Marcos threw up his hands: "Well, just listen to me go on and on! Don't you think it's time we visit the cantina for a margarita?" Which they did.

Two days later Jorge and Bert walked the horse around the stable, discussing Marcos' sense of humor. "I 'kinda wished you'd taken him up on his religious talk," Jorge volunteered.

Bert shook his head. "Nope, I really meant it that it's one subject I've given up talking about. I guess my friend Frank the psychologist finally convinced me I didn't know what the hell I was talking about."

"I doubt that. Anyway, you *have* helped me see the good and bad side of my own religion." Jorge started to continue, but stopped to straighten his thoughts.

"Well, if you don't mind, I still have one big question. It's not about whether God exists—you know, I'm a believer—but if I can ever know anything for sure about this unknown invisible power."

Bert's answer was quick and short. "I have my own answer for that—you won't know by using your brain or especially your emotions but what people for a long time have called your soul—or spirit."

"Now you're probably going to-confuse me even more."

Bert laughed. "No, I'll just remind you of the old-fashioned answer that something deep inside tells us we haven't been created to *get into* union by going to church and doing all the right things. No, the sages say we're already *in* union. We know it whenever we look at a flower, listen to a concert, paint a picture of a horse, pray, laugh, make love—do all the things that make us feel whole inside."

Jorge smiled. "So I guess I believe in God my way, not just the church's way."

"Exactly. You already feel united to God, don't need the church to connect you." Bert paused. "And no matter what Marcos or I say, you will always know in your heart what you already know and are not afraid to admit."

Jorge reached out to shake Bert's hand. "Thank you, my friend, you are very wise."

Bert laughed. "No, this is something I think we all know but just have difficulty admitting to ourselves. Anyway, that's all you'll hear from me on the subject!"

The following day before Bert made his farewells to the Sanchez family, Jorge pulled him aside to ask about Leticia.

"Oh boy," Bert replied. "She's one hell of a woman! How could I refuse her offer to join her down here? I've been asking myself that for days!"

"Yeah, how could you?"

"I just don't know. I really like the woman, and I'd like being nearer you also. But it's hard for me to think about leaving my country--even though it's a country that's driving me crazy these days." He paused, tried to smile. "Well, there might be two more reasons. I'm afraid I'd never learn Spanish, and I guess most important of all is the fact I haven't given my new home enough of a go to see if I belong there. I'm starting to really like the place."

"Did you leave the door open in case you change your mind?"

"I hope so."

Bert gave Sophia a hug and Jorge followed him out to his car, where Bert pulled chocolates and balloons out of his duffle bag for the kids and a bright red scarf for Sophia. "Sorry, I guess you don't count," he said to Jorge, smiling and shaking his hand soundly. When he turned to leave, Jorge found a thousand-dollar peso bill in his hand and smiled, shaking his head on the way back to his house.

Back in Arizona, Bert took Rowdy with him to the Rio Rico golf course, the only one to allow dogs. Rowdy was always well behaved; wouldn't poop on the grass and knew not to walk on the greens or dig in the bunkers. Loved to chase ducks in the pond, which Bert guessed had too many chemicals, but if the ducks could survive, so could a dog.

On the third hole he drove the cart past the restroom and suddenly pulled up to an occupied tee-off area. He'd been so busy attending to his own game and watching Rowdy that he hadn't noticed someone playing in front. There she was, the attractive girl he'd played with once a couple of months ago. What was her name? Clarise? No, Chloe. She was alone, about to hit. Since he'd unknowingly driven his cart right up, he couldn't back off, but there he was invading her territory just before she was about to swing. What to do?

He did nothing, tried to be invisible while she backed away from her ball and glanced over. Then she smiled and invited him to come up. "Hello again. Come play with me, watch to see if I keep that left arm straight."

He smiled, offered to shake her hand. "In golf we always shake hands. I don't know why, do you?" She laughed.

"Go ahead and hit," he said. "I seem to remember Chloe smashing drives out there 170 yards." He didn't say he also remembered how beautiful she was.

"Now you're going to remind me to not let the driver flop back over my neck," she giggled.

"Right," he agreed. "And one more thing: never, never, never sway." He paused, then corrected himself: "Come to think about it, you *don't* sway! I'm the one with that problem!" They both laughed again.

Like Bert, Chloe liked to play different courses, and they started playing together twice a week. There were eight from Nogales to Tucson, and a dozen or more up there. She always let him book the tee times, not worrying about cost since her divorce five years ago had left her comfortably positioned. Bert also had enough funds to afford the $150 to $200 prices found in North Tucson, but refused on principle paying more than $75. He used one of the internet booking sites to make that possible, which meant they could play any time they wanted.

She'd never played pickleball but was willing to try. His pickleball friends, mostly guys, tried not to stare at the beautiful blonde Bert brought one morning to the court behind the convention center. She quickly learned the rules and how to swing, and they started playing pickleball or golf together four times a week. They often came back home to pick up their dogs and bring them to the Cowgirl bar that allowed dogs. They'd have a beer and usually split a pizza or pasta dish for dinner.

Chloe turned out to be more of a kindred spirit than Bert had figured. She too had jumped into local history, knew a lot about Kino and de Anza, and had even joined the Friends of the Anza group. She said she had in fact been one of the helpers removing trash from the Santa Cruz on the same work day as he, back in the October after his arrival.

They traded bread recipes and he gave her some of the sourdough starter he'd inherited from his landlady. Eventually they began cooking together—at her place since the kitchen in his small adobe was too cramped. One thing led to another, and after they'd been cooking and playing golf and pickleball for a month, he found himself falling in love. "Oh no," he muttered but silently approved. What would be, would be; he hadn't brought it on.

June having arrived, it was time to leave the hot desert. Chloe would be going to her second home back east for the next six months, and he needed to get back to cool Colorado. He called his son Jed to schedule a stay in Steamboat Springs, driving up in one long day without stopping for golf. The two of them played golf and countless outdoor games with the kids. Toss the washer into the box. Shoot the bb gun. Swim the Yampa. Throw the frisbee for the dog. Splash around in the kiddie pool. After a couple of weeks, Bert wondered if he was missing somebody.

He'd been lying in bed late at night reading Anne Sexton again, needed to start a poem of his own.

Maybe use it to figure out what he liked about Chloe. The way she giggled when whiffing the golf ball and looking down to see it still perched on the tee. The way she jumped up and down when it went where she wanted. The way she danced wearing all the gaudy cowgirl getup. The way she smiled at him, cocking her head and arching her eyebrows. But not yet the way she kissed, because she only allowed hugs and small pecks. He had a difficult time trying to composing something:

The little girl inside you likes to giggle
But I've never heard her cry....

Bert stopped; nowhere to go with that...too close to the old song, "She makes love just like a woman...and she breaks just like a little girl." That song didn't fit her; in fact, he couldn't find a little girl inside and she was too tough to cry about anything. She was also probably too used to controlling to commit. The way things were going, he'd never find out; after walking back to her house from the Cowgirl, she would give him a peck but wouldn't invite him inside. He wanted to get past her glamorous outside. All they talked about was golf or upcoming city events. She refused to venture into private spaces. And of course, he'd known her for only a few months.

He knew she wouldn't want to hear his ramblings about important things like destiny or death. Would definitely freak out if his eyes got misty over a stray memory of Suzanne--whom she'd never asked about. Whenever they got together with another couple for dinner or drinks, which she always wanted to do, they all stayed focused on predictable things retired people talk about—politics, cruises, the fabulous places they'd visited. He'd sit listening, bored. It wasn't part of his world, not even a world he was jealous of, because he knew he could have joined it--he had enough money and savvy to play the game but it never interested him.

What would happen if they ever did really connect? Would the intimacy he wanted be possible, or would she always keep her distance? He wasn't even sure any more if the intimacy he wanted had to be that sexual kind. He decided to leave it at golf, pickleball, pizza, and dancing, doubting he could cut enough ribbons to find something inside. Anyway, her giggling was fun; it helped him relax and hit his golf balls with loose wrists. Playing with Frank back in North Carolina was always enjoyable, but usually threatened to ruin his soft swing.

Bert knew it would be too long before he'd see her again. By the time he'd get back home she'd still be at her house back east, wouldn't return to Arizona for another four months. He needed to push her out of his mind, return to throwing washers in the box with the kids.

After Bert's second week with his son in Steamboat Springs, Edward called to say he was returning to Colorado for a month. He said he didn't relish repeating the river plunge but insisted Bert stay at his summer cabin. An excellent arrangement for Bert, since he liked the old cabin and didn't want to impose on his son any longer.

The cabin was located fifty miles southwest of Denver, near Pine. Eighty acres alongside Deer Creek had been purchased and developed back in 1900 by a handful of wealthy Denver businessmen. All the rustic cabins faced the river—more of a creek, but one that ran year-round and bubbled and tumbled like mountain creeks are supposed to. One ugly modern cabin past the small lake and lodge toward the highway housed Clyde and his wife. They weren't part of the original founding group but were considered family since they'd lived in it every summer for forty years, doing minor maintenance and mainly just watching out for poachers or trespassers.

The Deercreek Association had strict rules: only family members and their close friends could stay in the cabins, which were owned by them but not the land they sat upon. The cabins couldn't be sold, only handed down to immediate family members. Everyone was required to take four or five meals a week in the lodge's dining room. No firearms, four-wheel run-abouts, loud noises after 10:00 p.m. Everyone abided because Clyde made sure they did. Needless to say, the place stayed open only during summer months, and even though all of the founding families kept expanding, everyone knew everyone. Meal-time brought prolonged socializing, and occasionally adults orchestrated a group sing-out or youngsters threw together a skit.

This summer's cook was Mitch, a young Navaho from Arizona whose grandmother kicked him off the reservation when he was seventeen, telling him it was time for him to make his way in the world. Before throwing him out, she changed his name from Ahiga, Boy Who Fights, to Mitch. Needless to say, when women on the 'rez learned about both unholy things she'd done, they shunned her for months. But she knew what would have become of him had he stayed there.

Mitch learned to cook in Southern California and then settled in a Denver suburb. He was overjoyed when the Association invited him to cook, housing him in a small cabin near the lake and paying him good wages. He enjoyed taking to people between duties, and they raved about his food. Bert came to favor the eggs benedict breakfast, telling Mitch it was the best béarnaise sauce he'd tasted. The cook offered to give him his special recipe, but Bert declined, saying he liked to bake bread and make soup, but that's where his culinary interests stopped.

Bert approved of the new lodge built fifteen years ago after the former building burnt down. The fairly modern looking log structure was designed by an Association member who was a famous architect in Colorado Springs. Bert much preferred the old cabins, including Edward's, with its unlevel steps and mismatched windows. It reminded him of all the others he'd visited years before. All smelled the way old mountain cabins are supposed to smell—a smell Bert couldn't put into words but was the same for each in his Colorado memory bank: the small log cabin Tom's mother had built near Ward back in the thirties; his mother's aunt's cabin near Manitou Springs that they'd visited back in the late fifties; the tiny cabin his family had rented a few months after arriving in Colorado from Minnesota--that cabin about to fall into a tiny stream outside of Tiny Town, a decrepit tourist spot featuring tiny houses, a tiny railroad, and tiny signs telling of tiny but very important happenings.

Most of all, the smell of Edward's Deercreek cabin brought back memories of staying in his distant cousin Farrington Carpenter's ranch twenty miles west of Steamboat Springs. He and his sister had been fortunate enough to spend two weeks every summer there, from the time he was seven to twelve. They rode horses all day long, ate breakfast with the cowhands on the porch's long table, and slept upstairs in the small bedroom with that musty smell.

Into their second week at Edward's cabin his cousins from Wyoming came to visit, so the two of them took off to explore the area around Camp Hale where they'd camped two summers back in the late 60s.

"Too bad we didn't invite Jim, Wolf, or Tom," Edward said on their first night camping. "Too bad we didn't bring cots," Bert replied. Then they proceeded to reminisce about ski trips the Four Musketeers had taken almost every weekend to Winter Park.

The ski train was their favorite topic. "Remember the water cup on top of the swinging door?" Bert laughed. "We sat quietly giggling next to the vestibule, waiting for the unsuspecting victim to pull open the door!"

"We had to get to the station half an hour early to get that compartment. When the conductor came collecting tickets we'd be hiding on the long seat under piles of sweaters and sleeping bags, some girl perched on top, handing him one ticket instead of three or four."

Bert laughed. "Or crowding into the women's toilet behind the door with the same girl perched on the john to hand the conductor her ticket."

"Yeah, and she didn't mind since she still had her long johns on."

"Who was she? Did we ever give her a cut?"

"Probably Naughty Sue, and nah, we never cut her in; she just got a kick out of doing it."

"Remember forging ski tow tickets? We'd fumble through our old ones for the right day's color and change the date stamped on top. Sometimes didn't pay anything since we brought our bag lunches."

"It never cost more than fourteen dollars even when we had to pay for the train and tow. Today that'd be two or three hundred!"

"The guys checking the lift tickets knew. We were just kids, could get away with anything."

"Like sneaking into the basement of that ski lodge down the road."

"I remember that. Old Man Douglas coming down to check something and finding us instead. Not kicking us out, just leading us to a better place next to the furnace for our sleeping bags."

"Before sleep we'd casually wander upstairs for the ski movies. They never knew we weren't paying guests."

"Was that the time the four of us crowded into the Texas girls' bedroom, sat talking on their bed until midnight?"

"Yeah, dreaming about what could be but never would. Thirteen-year-olds condemned to remain virgin for another five years."

"Six in my case," said Bert. "Not until I was nineteen, in college, and spent so much time making up for lost time that I had to get married."

Edward nodded. "For me it wasn't until 22. But back to skiing--the bunkhouse. How much did it cost for those wooden bunks? And did they have mattresses?"

"A dollar a night. And yeah, they did. Sleeping bags but no pillows. After gobbling the extra sandwiches stashed outside in the snow, we'd steal a tray from the cafeteria and hike up Bradley's Bash. Come careening down on our butts."

"Here's to the good 'ol days," Edward said wistfully, holding up an imaginary glass.

CHAPTER SEVENTEEN: LOVING FRIEND

DEAR FRANKY BOY,

Guess what! I've finally started settling down. So listen up: it's time for you to come visit. I'll pay for the golf. Tell that beautiful Marsha she can shop her brains and your wallet out here. Even bring Trouble for Rowdy. Just come. Over 'n out. Bert

Dear Bertie Boy,

Do you like this stupid texting instead of talking like real humans?

Dear Franky Boy,

No, so I'm calling you in five minutes. Grab a chair.

"Hi Frank, Here I am, a real live human."

"Hi Bert, Good to hear your live human voice…."

They talked for twenty minutes. Before closing, Frank asked if he was still trying to find his destiny. Bert laughed and said he'd almost given up. As a kid his big question was whether there was purpose and meaning in life. He pondered that for forty years and decided it was too ambiguous. Then he tried to figure out whether he was in charge or nothing was.

Frank: Sounds like that's just a repeat of the first question.

Bert: I tweaked it a bit: is the big power sometimes in charge or always? And either way, am I supposed to surrender to it? And if so, how?

Frank: Did you ever figure out how?

Bert: You just take a deep breath and let go of trying to be in charge.

Frank: Meaning you blindly accept whatever comes along your way?

Bert: That's what people here call the answer. You just grit your teeth, or smile—whichever is the case—and mutter, 'Destiny.' Everyone here in la-la land says whatever happens was supposed to be...was meant to be.

Frank: And you can live with that nonsense?

Bert: Not really, I've never liked those words. But what the hell....?

Frank: You've been stuck on that merry-go-round too long, Bertie. Time to jump off!

Bert: I guess that's what I'm saying, I have. Look, it's simple. Letting go isn't losing, it's gaining. If something bigger is already living inside us, helping instead of hindering, than we just need to accept it-- stop fighting it. Tell our small ego to stop wanting to be in charge. That seems to be the big message. The Beatles kept singing, 'Let it be, let it be.'

Frank: It's easy to sing that song when you're higher'n a kite. Just smile your silly smile and chant, 'Here I am, I'm letting me be.' But in my profession, we try to get the person to take charge—admit to being a failure at something. People who can't accept responsibility can't change. You seem to be counseling irresponsibility.

Bert: That's what I thought for years. Now I see it all depends on *intention*. The difference between letting go to nothing or to something bigger, or just giving up.

Frank: How about letting go to a larger woman—say a big naked female?

Bert: Yeah, or a hippopotamus. You know what I mean.

Frank: I do. As usual, you mean God. Why not just say so instead of *Something Bigger*?

Bert: Because people like you always have their own ideas of God. I don't. I'm just saying when you have the intention in mind of something *other* than you, even if it's not some kind of religious image you've inherited along the way, then you're putting you behind the Other.

Frank: Much better! —*the Other*.

Bert: Stop heckling! Either you're intending something outside small you--something bigger than you—or not.

You're not adding something bigger that isn't really there, you're throwing away something in your head that *is* there that causes you to feel alienated from everything. That something, by the way, was probably put into your head by religion.

Frank: Convince me there's a difference between letting go and checking out—taking the path of least resistance.

Bert: How could I do that, Frank? Your mind doesn't appear to be very open.

Frank: At least not like a sieve.

Bert: Ok, let's stop going around and around.

Frank: I'd like to support you, buddy, but…."

Bert: Hey, I'm not trying to convince you or anybody. I was just saying I finally found *it*. Whatever *it* is.

Frank: I wish golf were as easy as finding the big *it*.

Bert: Hey, this isn't easy; it could be the hardest easy thing I've ever done.

Frank: Well, Bertie Boy, you haven't convinced me, probably never will. But you still haven't asked if I'm coming.

Bert: Are you?

Frank: I'm still trying to talk Marsha into it. Getting closer. I'll keep you posted. Over 'n out for now.

Bert decided late October was a good time for another visit to Mexico. Unlike his first two visits, where Jorge and Bert sat on the back porch getting to know each other, this time Jorge had planned a full week of activities. The first adventure involved climbing the famous tourist attraction, Tetakawi. Jorge said young bucks marched up in less than an hour but it would take them twice that long. They went slowly, stopping to rest and talk. On top they scanned the Sea of Cortez for whales. Going back down, Jorge showed Bert how to crab-walk and warned him about stepping on loose rocks. "Every year four or five hikers have to be hauled to the hospital for bad sprains or broken bones." Bert remembered his father's adage of long ago, "Step over not on, that's no fun." Once Jorge cautioned him about cactus thorns, but Bert reminded him he was no longer a stranger to the hostile desert.

The second day they drove up a canyon near Tetakawi to Mirador, another popular ocean-viewing spot. It was also a hefty climb, interrupted by two hikers cackling behind, "On your left, on your left." The view was as spectacular and Bert was again pleased he'd made the trip, knowing he'd never repeat it, and then asking how big the town was. Jorge pointed toward it, saying he guessed San Carlos stretched ten miles from end to end.

"How many people live here?" Bert asked.

"They tell me up to a hundred thousand come every Semana Santa—holy week. Hard to say whether they come to honor God or for the all-night beach parties...or just to cruise the main drag, stopping every block for another margarita."

Later in the afternoon after a brief siesta, Jorge took Bert to the pickleball courts, where he surprised himself by winning two out of four games. "I can't believe this place has six regulation courts. Back home we have only two. Tubac is the place everyone up in Green Valley calls the snobby rich place. Hell, this sleepy Mexican town has it all over us!" Then Bert went on to encourage his friend to take up the sport. Jorge said he used to play tennis back in Arizona but nowadays spent all his spare time painting.

"Plus your regular time," Bert corrected. "It's your job, after all."

"Well, sort of. The store pays the bills, though, so it takes up a lot of time. When our hardware went up on their house paint prices, I contacted a friend in Tucson to cut a deal for me with a warehouse. Now my house paint line pays for all my own art supplies, plus our food and gas. I raised prices a bit, but not much."

Bert asked if cutting prices hurt his local reputation and Jorge laughed. "Everyone does it; we've taken a lesson from up north. Live and let live."

The three sat under a wide umbrella on the white sands of Los Algodones beach at one of San Carlos' popular landmarks. "Why do they call it the Soggy Peso?" Bert asked.

Sophia laughed while Jorge pointed toward the boats offshore. "They swim in to eat and party…so, soggy pesos." It was late afternoon with the usual mix of nationals and gringos. "Marina San Carlos, where you could have taken Leticia to eat, is bigger. That marina also has the popular Shots and Hammerheads restaurant, but I like this quiet place best." He smiled. "I'm no longer trying to stay young. After watching the sun set, I'm ready to quit. Peso closes early and so do I. If you want dancing on the tables you have to wait until after nine for the locals to show up at one of the all-night places."

While he was listening, Bert kept track of the sun's slow disappearance, remembering the outdoor bar he and his college buddies had gone to every Friday to cheer the sun on its slow voyage over the hill. That sunset watch usually took four or five beers and a lot of shouting. "It's absolutely beautiful," he whispered to Sophia. "I thought the sunsets up in Arizona were spectacular, but these are better."

Jorge interrupted his friend's reverie by pointing out the banana boat. "They rent it or jet skis and kayaks at the San Carlos Plaza. I don't mind the banana boat but wish the jet skis would find another place to zip around." Bert nodded, remembering the way they'd set Brie's EMS head to buzzing when they camped back on Penland Island.

427

Watching a fishing boat head out, Bert asked if the fishing was good. "Used to be, but not so much anymore," Jorge replied. "Maybe you heard that Cousteau called this Sea of Cortez the world's best aquarium. Then overfishing and commercial development took over. Pollution. But sometimes the ocean's still that clear blue, and you can sometimes see flying manta rays and sea lions...plus the crazy dolphins off San Francisco beach."

For their last night together, Sophia made a batch of tamales, Bert walked to the market for a mixed salad, Jorge poured three glasses of red wine and two of orange cool-aid, and the five of them sat down to eat on the back porch. When the adults seemed ready to settle into talking, the kids jumped up and ran for the swing-set. Bert knew the time was right for his announcement. But first he'd ask about their financial situation.

"You told me about the store, Jorge, but I know that couldn't cover all your expenses. How many times do people down here repaint their houses?"

"Everything's fine, my friend, things are looking up."

"How far up?"

"Far enough. Every now and then I sell a few paintings, and we don't need much. The old Ford I got up in Arizona still runs, and we bike most everywhere anyway. The house is paid for, and food is cheap down here. Like I told you, the store pays for gas and food.

Everything's ok. Especially with that new refrigerator you brought us!"

"But there will come a day when the kids need more." Bert looked knowingly toward Sophia.

Jorge nodded while Bert continued: "How many paintings do you sell a month?" Jorge held up two, then three fingers.

"Not enough. You need a bigger market. Like up north." Jorge nodded again.

"Before coming down this time I visited with Richard--you remember, the guy who owns the store where you exhibited in back in Tubac. I showed him some of your recent paintings I'd taken pictures of on my cell phone. He was interested."

"Excellent. I appreciate that, but...."

"No buts, I think you need to be a regular there. And here's how it will work." Bert reached in his pocket for an envelope to hand to him.

"Thirty thousand pesos! What's this?"

"A down payment. He wants you to give me all you can unload now and keep painting more. Says people like your stuff, and he also has a friend up in Tucson with a gallery. So maybe you're ready for the big time."

While he was explaining, Bert glanced toward Sophia, hiding tears. Jorge sat quietly, trying to take it in, then finally spoke: "Well, you've done it again, my very good friend. I don't know how to thank you."

"You already have," Bert said smiling. "Just coming down here to visit with real people of the world is enough for me."

Before falling asleep Bert smiled again. The good part was not telling Jorge where the down payment really came from. The hard part would be serving as his invisible agent; painters were a dime a dozen up in his town, all scratching to make a living. But it would give him something to do. Even if he ended up with all the paintings hidden away in his small adobe, it was ok.

One late morning in mid-December of his second winter Bert found himself getting bored. He'd already ridden his bike the usual two miles; had played pickleball for two hours; had swept and mopped the floors and even washed the front windows. Golf was two days away. It was still only 11:30 with nothing written in his day planner for the afternoon or evening. He couldn't think of new local sites to explore and wasn't up to tackling unknown parts of Tucson. Didn't want to have a beer; one would just lead to another. So he did what he usually did in situations like these-- opened a book—not another novel but a local history book, and settled down in the hammock under the giant mesquite in his front yard, his dog jumping up to sit between his legs.

The book elaborated what he'd learned in the Presidio museum. He'd been reading for almost an hour when Rowdy suddenly leaped off to investigate an incoming delivery truck. The book fell off his lap, and when he stretched to reach it, he ended up on the ground. What the hell, he muttered, deciding it was time for an afternoon walk anyway. He'd start at the Resort side of the Anza Trail and return in time to say hello to the Presidio's director, who had shown him a 1774 map picturing building sites around the fortress. He'd been overjoyed to see his own adobe on the map. He picked up the book and went inside to pack drinks, a sandwich, and doggy cookies.

Rowdy always knew his way down Burrell Street. Four times a week they'd bike it to the Resort to ride the cart path alongside the course appropriately named the Anza. When no golfers appeared Bert could ignore the sign prohibiting walkers, bikers, and pets.

Before getting to the Resort, Rowdy and he had to pass the old Mexican cemetery with its brightly colored plastic flowers and metal sign that everyone laughed at, "Cementary." Burrell Street used to be the dirt road from Tucson to Sonoran Nogales, part of the Camino Real from Mexico City that soldiers and friars used in the eighteenth century to venture to Spanish settlements in California.

The book he'd been reading claimed the Indians loved Father Kino, who'd come not just to convert them, but more importantly to improve their quality of life. They appreciated his efforts to keep them from slavery and forced labor at the mines. Maybe also his better ways of planting, like the rural priest in the 1986 "Mission" movie who taught his natives to enjoy simple songs of joy while working their fields. The priest who was slaughtered like all the peasants by the war created by his own church.

Kino had brought with him horses, sheep, mules, and cattle. The animals proved a mixed blessing for local inhabitants busy with their subsistence farming, since they later became the basis for wide-scale ranching-- something that eventually brought wealth to a few but damaged the whole area, including the Santa Cruz River. That was to be a while in the future, however.

Still walking Burrell Street, Bert figured that Kino must have taken his own walking orders seriously since the book said he walked 75,000 miles to establish twenty other missions. But now Bert's thoughts turned to a later Spaniard, the famous soldier he'd just read about who preferred riding to walking.

Juan Baptista de Anza had become commander of the new Tubac Presidio fortress in 1759. In 1774 he volunteered to open a route from Sonora to California to help Spanish settlements in desperate condition. After returning to Arizona, two years later Mexico City ordered him to mount a second thousand-mile expedition to Monterrey, California to see about possible Russian colonization in San Francisco. This expedition cost only one life, something that in those days was unheard of. Then it was back to Arizona, New Mexico, and Colorado to round up fearless Apaches and Comanches. Somehow he managed to survive it all, ending up a quieter Tucson commander and living until 1788.

After de Anza left the Tubac Presidio, another Spaniard kept a garrison of Pima Indian soldiers near the old fort. They tried to stave off Apache attacks that continued to plague the area until Geronimo was captured a century later. While Bert was walking the Anza trail one day, he pictured the Pima soldiers shooting wild turkeys that flocked to the river to drink...plus wolves howling all night. He saw the soldiers strip off their sweaty uniforms to jump into the river for a swim during the hot afternoons. Back then it was a real river, not just a struggling creek fed by effluent from the treatment center.

For hundreds of centuries a dense mesquite bosque of Arizona walnut, Mexican elder, hackberry, and mesquite trees bordered both sides of the Santa Cruz flowing north from Mexico. By the time of Kino and de Anza, the area had changed into a cottonwood-willow forest. Even as recent as the early twentieth century, tall cottonwoods grew trunks eight to ten feet across, and like all cottonwoods, were brittle and littered the ground with limbs too thick to be swept downstream by monsoon floods.

The Santa Cruz got mortally wounded less than half a century after the Anglos started depending on it for mining and cattle. It didn't die immediately, was still flowing strong when an Eastern land surveyor was sent west in the mid-nineteenth century to settle boundary disputes. On his way to Nogales, John Bartlett came through Tucson to Arizona's first European settlement,

Tubac, where he found and rescued a fourteen-year old Mexican girl that Indians had captured and sold to gringos to be a slave. This story had recently been told by Bert's landlady, who was trying to get Hollywood interested in her novel, not for personal financial gain, but to draw attention to the border issues that so many citizens in southwest Arizona were fighting to correct.

That story was thrilling, but maybe even more captivating was Larcena Pennington's. Traveling west from Texas, this pretty young pioneer managed to survive a severe bout with malaria only to be captured in 1860 by Apaches just north of Tubac. They hauled her up to Madera Canyon, where one young "brave" tore off most of her clothes, plunged his lance deep into her back, and then stabbed her repeatedly. She fell unconscious 16 feet over a ledge, where he pummeled her with large stones for good measure and left her covered in blood to die in a snow bank. Days later her husband John came close to finding her, but she was too weak to yell. For the next two weeks all she had to eat was wild onions, seeds, and grass. Unbelievably, she survived and fully recovered—unlike John, who was killed the following year by Apaches. Larcena even lived to see Arizona become the 48th state in 1912.

Bert stopped mentally replaying that story to study the colorful headstones in the Mexican cemetery. The rest of the town, with the exception of the small Old Town area across from the Presidio where he lived, was occupied by wealthy Anglos either in the Resort or the Barrio or up in the hills west and east of town. Most of them tended to vanish during the hot summer months.

Bert debated turning east down Bridge Street to pick up the Anza Trail on the other side of the community center and pickleball court, but decided instead to keep going straight ahead toward the lush grass of the Resort. Tired of brown, dusty winter, he needed to feel wet, green summer.

The golf course was alive back in the early twentieth century but didn't become a destination spot until later in the century. Every time he played one of its three courses or walked or biked its trails, he applauded its desert oasis of pure greenery. Non-golfers could grouse all they wanted about the waste of precious water, but he knew a good part of it seeped back where it belonged—and how many of the grousers complained about the hundred-fold water waste up north in Green Valley's huge pecan groves?

Bert slipped off his Tevas to pad barefoot in the fairway grass, checking every few minutes to make sure no golfers or wardens were coming. Once he'd get to the nine-hole course called Rancho, he'd have to step carefully because resort owners had wisely chosen to let a dozen beefy cattle graze its fairways next to the river. He wondered how many of his fellow golfers appreciated the bucolic bovine touch that slowed them down. He thought most of them, being older and retired, didn't mind...were in fact used to deer, horses, oversized rabbits, and even families of javelinas strolling across fairways.

After stopping for a quick beer outside the bar with Rowdy leashed beside him, he got up to cross the Rancho fairway for entrance to the Anza Trail. Now the wilderness part of his walk was to begin—for every time he walked the trail, he pretended he was back in Colorado, Wisconsin, or North Carolina experiencing true wilderness. Better yet, Alaska, where he'd never been and probably never would.

He'd stumbled on the trail the day after getting settled into his new adobe home. That was two and a half years ago, back in July, too hot for most people to go outside walking. Someone had made a path in the lush grass with a lawn mower, of all things. On both sides everything was green: deep untrammeled grass, ninety-foot tall cottonwoods bearing light green leaves, an isolated green bamboo stand, dark green bushes, and no doubt lurking somewhere, tiny green frogs. Hopefully not poisonous Sonoran toads or hemlock plants disguised as wild carrots—the most poisonous plant in North America, someone had told him.

Now, in the middle of December, everything had turned brown. The trail was grassless dirt. The shrubs, bushes, and dead flowers wore a drab tan, dark or light brown. Half the remaining cottonwood leaves were brown--still beautiful, but monochromatic. Even the tamarisks, an invasive exotic that grow into tall salt cedars crowding out native vegetation and making the soil salty, had lost their pink plumes and turned into coppery-tan feather bushes.

He would have called the landscape drab except for the memory of what Suzanne had told him thirty years ago up on their Colorado mountain top: "Look, it's all wonderful shades of brown. He showed me—He taught me--to look carefully to see how all the shades are so very different." Suzanne had never been one to talk about her religious experiences, but he'd noticed the way she had switched from parroting what she'd been taught by a remote minister about an equally remote deity to what she actually experienced as a close Presence.

Rowdy used his nose, not eyes, to experience the place--no doubt indifferent to the particular season, but totally into everything he encountered. Bert tried to let his own nose call forth memories of fallen leaves. He couldn't smell anything until he reached down for a handful of brown leaves to crush next to his nose. That brought back lazy afternoons jumping off roofs into deep piles of leaves or driving through miles of red maples in Wisconsin.

Then the smells of decaying leaves and winter heat carried him farther back to Boulder, Colorado where the cottonwoods at the local park lost their leaves earlier. He used to run laps around the park and drive to the high mountains to watch quaking aspens turn yellow, gold, and rose during his favorite month, September. Mountain aspens, he remembered, were as thirsty as their bigger cousins five thousand feet lower but had to settle down for their winter sleep a lot earlier.

Like many older humans, Bert inhabited several worlds past and present, sometimes getting confused about which he was currently in.

The Anza was strangely quiet today. He couldn't hear any birds, though he knew birders would be around somewhere. He'd already seen most of the ones they spent hours looking for--vermillion flycatchers, yellow billed cuckoos, orioles, tanagers, phainopeplas, and high-flying black hawks in March. He'd never seen the crazy whistling duck that perches in trees, not to mention a rare mountain lion, mysterious coati, or elusive jaguar some claimed to have seen.

Today he found himself concentrating on the cottonwoods. Half the trees had brown leaves, the other half kept their beautiful yellow ones. Apparently, the unusual weather had produced two frosts this winter, a mild one in mid-November followed by a warming spell, and then another colder frost in late December. Maybe the milder frost had killed some leaves, but not ones which hadn't fully turned. That was his feeble reasoning, but he still couldn't understand why some trees succumbed early, whereas others right next to them tightly held their bright colors of yellow. One giant that he studied for five minutes quaked and shimmered golden, issuing a strong challenge to January.

The temperature being in the high seventies, it felt more like September than December. He still had a half-mile to go before reaching Bridge Road at the edge of Old Town. As he walked southwest toward the sun low in the sky, the brown leaves scattered on the dirt turned into giant snowflakes, shimmering silver and white until he put his sunglasses back on.

Before he got to the place where the Santa Cruz winds back to the Anza Trail, he felt something happening inside that brought him to a standstill. He found a giant cottonwood stump to sit on and turned off his mental motor. Even stopped admiring the tall cottonwoods. Stopped looking up to the puffy clouds floating through the blue. For no reason, he just wanted to sit quietly and taste the very ordinary moment. Everything had become overwhelmingly satisfying. More than enough.

I could be experiencing some kind of epiphany, he thought. He sat looking at the end of the log, feeling a goofy smile form over his face. He didn't know how long he sat there—an hour or a few minutes—but life was utterly ok. He was right with the world. Thinking of nothing, just enjoying silence and beauty.

This must be what true relationship is all about. With nature, with infinite Mystery, with himself. Sitting quietly without knowing, wanting, or needing to know, he felt bedazzled by absolute freedom. It wasn't just the beautiful cottonwoods, mild winter temperature, or pure silence, but simply sitting in some deep and spacious place. Sustained by something else. Being an empty nothing…and everything.

He looked down at the ants marching resolutely on a trail of their own to a destination of their own. Another world before his very eyes, a world always there but never understood. He laughed at how unimportant he was to them, this monster from another world, an obstacle to maneuver past on their way to somewhere important to them.

Then he slowly came back to his own world, the world of yellow, brown, and gold cottonwoods in a precious narrow riparian area in the middle of an endless desert stretching far into Mexico.

Rowdy barked, telling him it was time to go. Time to trod the trail a gentle priest and fearless soldier had trod. To head back to his pink adobe built two and a half centuries ago by Presidio soldiers. Life was certainly pleasant in this strange place.

Dear Frank,

Here it is, the start of the new year and I just got your e-mail. I'm texting my reply, if the battery lasts that long. In three weeks, we'll be banging balls! Sorry Marsha can't make it, but this means no guilt for you for being on the course. I think I told you I'll pay for the first three rounds, then we can average handicaps and take on match play for $20. I should double all my expenses in no time! Unless, of course, you've somehow managed to correct that outside-in swing. And I think I told you, we have eight courses here to choose from—we'll probably play all.

In between rounds we can sit on my porch looking for coyotes and javelinas and settling all the world problems we didn't before. Hey, remember to bring your passport. I want to introduce you to my favorite people down in Mexico, and you might want to make a visit to the cheap dentists there. Crowns are only $450, or you can change your smile for under $400. (Which of course is a good idea.)

Right now, I'm sitting on a rock 3,000-feet above my desert home. The Santa Rita Mountains reach 3,000 feet above me here, all the way up to 9,000 feet, and remind me a little of Colorado. Well, maybe not the strange Alligator Junipers or Elegant Trogon that's supposed to be here in Madera Canyon. It's a tropical looking metallic-green and rosy bird that breeds in only four U.S. mountain ranges, all here in southern Arizona. He didn't sing for me but couldn't have sounded as cheery as the finches that serenade me every morning while I'm sipping coffee outside my house.

Anyway, you are coming soon, and January and February are perfect months: lots of activity and usually good weather. I've already grown to love the desert but still need my fix of mountains, cool air, and pine trees, which is why I come up here every now and again, even in mid-winter. Today it's probably 70 degrees down where I live.

If the two mountain ranges didn't hug my Santa Cruz valley, or if the river weren't there with all its tall cottonwoods, I certainly wouldn't stay. It's taken me a year to decide I really need to stay. I've discovered a nice mix of people I've never found elsewhere, even though as you know, I've lived all over the U.S. It's hard to explain why they're so unusual; maybe you'll understand when you come. Most have left their professional mindsets behind. They seem intent on staying happily active in small ways, not on impressing others about their former importance. They love to socialize, and most paint or do something creative…at the very least, bird-watch (our area being one of the best in the country for that sort of activity). Sure, many throw their money away on cruises and extravagant clothing and household furnishings like a lot of bored retirees, and don't throw enough of it toward people who desperately need it, like our neighbors down south, but that's life here in the states.

Do you remember how we used to grouse about all the rednecks in western North Carolina? Arizona's also the land of conservatives, still immersed in the frontier take what you can while you can mentality. You know how that goes: 'Don't tell me what to do with my hard-earned money; life's a struggle where the fittest survive.' But my area is a liberal enclave where most people volunteer and give back at least nominal amounts of time and money. Half the people I've come to know donate big chunks of their time to some civic cause.

What about your golf community--are the people stereotyped wealthy retirees dressed to kill who always talk about cruises and touring the world? Or are some like my friend Edward who travels light, living on $40 a day? Now he could be in Guatemala, Sri Lanka, or Iceland...he just likes to meet new people and see new sights, has no interest in storing memories to brag about. And me? I guess I'm just too lazy to want to travel any more.

Hey, a strange big black bird just flew by. From here I can see miles and miles, like that old song. It reminds me of the view from the turnoff we always stopped at on our way back from Asheville. Looking down into the valley below, pretending we could see two old farts hitting balls at the Ridges...which of course could have been us. I miss all that, hanging out with you, and look forward to your visit. Remember your passport!

Bert

p.s. You can leave that stupid baseball hat behind but bring your tennis shoes. You, the ex-tennis champion, will love pickleball. Too bad you can't bring Trouble; I'm sure he'd remember Rowdy. We named our men's talk group after him, and he always falls asleep at my feet while we ramble on about matters of supreme importance. Well, enough for now. See you soon.

p.s. number two:

Hey Frank, I forgot to tell you I just learned a new word—*fingerspitzengefuehl*--The a-ha moment everyone's had at least one of. I had one last week...but won't bore you with it here.

A few days before Frank's visit for their three-year reunion, Bert received one text and two phone calls. Frank's text was brief: "Hi Berty, got your rambling message...birds, mountains, fingersomethings. I'm just texting to say I'll be there in three days; flight AA arrives at 5:20 p.m. Be home and remember to put some cold ones in the fridge."

The first phone call came from Gerald, saying he was finally getting around to sending him new information he'd found about EMS. Bert listened patiently, didn't tell him he'd heard it all before. Then unexpectedly Gerald's monologue took a new direction. For a long time, he explained excitedly, high-flying U.S. Air Force jets had been salting clouds to artificially modify climate change. When Bert asked why our government would want to do that at such a great expense the prompt answer was to convince the country climate change hadn't happened...or maybe to help control it.

Spraying aluminum mixture to prevent or cause rain, what the hell? Some kind of aluminum that falls to earth, polluting gardens and human airways? Come on, our government can't be that devious, Bert mumbled, trying to interject but not getting a word in edgewise to all the "blatantly obvious assaults" that kept tumbling out. He finally found an opening: "You must be reading different newspapers. I've never run into anything like that." Then, while his friend continued citing internet blogs, Bert slowly understood. He'd always heard about conspiracy theory but never encountered it head on, even though he knew many friends considered Brie's EMS scenario to be far-fetched. Here it was blasting out from the man he knew to be independent of any political affiliation, obviously well-informed about global affairs, and intelligent as hell. To all evidence, he appeared to be very normal, rational, reasonable, cautious—and Bert liked him a lot.

But he didn't know what to think about this. He had to conclude Gerald was just marshalling his facts to fit his preconceived ideas. "Ideology gone viral! Almost as bad as the idiotic ideology that kept Trump in office." Gerald's tirade intensified, turning to another case of governmental manipulation involving 911 and the World Trade Center's Twin Towers. "The news reported what it was ordered to, foreign airplanes bringing them down…but the truth is they were destroyed from within by strategically placed bombs."

"What about the videos showing planes crashing into the towers?" Bert asked in outrage.

"Those television shots were created by a giant hologram. It's all…."

Bert had to stop him, shouted into the phone that he needed to be somewhere soon, they could discuss this later. But he wanted to end on a different note, so he told Gerald to hold on a minute while he turned off the coffee that was starting to boil. He pretended to walk away while cooling off, and then asked Gerald if he'd ever met his friend Jorge in San Carlos.

Gerald took a long pause to clear his throat, and Bert heard his tone return to his everyday conversational voice. "Sure, everyone knows Jorge, even gringos like me. He's a painter who sells house paint. Nice guy."

"I'm thinking of acting as some kind of agent for him up here."

"Good luck. Doesn't your town have enough painters already?"

"Well, I…."

"Here's a tip. If you do, don't bother with the galleries. Skip Tubac, go up to Tucson and Phoenix. Find some furniture stores up there. He's much more likely to sell his kind of art in them than in galleries. And if possible, avoid consignment. Sometimes the store will buy at half the consignment price if the wholesale price is right."

"Thanks. Next time I come to visit Jorge I'll be sure to buy you a beer or two. Or three. Bye for now."

The second phone call an hour later was from Rhonda, saying she and Bob were thinking about coming west for a short visit. Bert encouraged her, saying he had a special pass they could use at the Resort. Well, he could buy them one. Before closing, Rhonda reported on all the church members, including Brie.

"How's she doing?" Bert asked.

"She's a little better," Rhonda replied. "Nowhere near fully recovered, still can't come to church or go anywhere, but she does get out to her safe places."

"I guess that's good news."

"She swims every day when it's not storming. Out to Penland Island, around it and back—almost four miles! Locals call her the Penland Mermaid."

Bert smiled. He hoped she'd taken his advice about tying a helium balloon to her swim suit to warn passing boats about the creature with big green flippers.

Rhonda continued. "After she's done swimming, she walks the dam road, talking to people. She calls it her Dam Ministry."

Bert pondered asking if she'd found any special friends, when Rhonda second-guessed his question: "I think she's found someone new. He doesn't come to church, but Margaret met him when she went to knit with her; she said he's quiet and very nice. I don't know if you wanted to hear that but thought you should know."

Bert said *that* news also pleased him; it was welcomed closure.

He woke an hour past midnight. Six hours to go. The music had stopped; he clicked on the clock radio next to his bed.

Who was the woman he'd been snuggling with? Already he couldn't recall the color of her hair, whether she had high cheekbones. Couldn't remember her smell. But he did remember his head cradled in her arms, almost as if she'd been nursing him. Not uncommon; breasts figure in his romantic dreams.

He told himself he didn't need to remember who she is or could be. Just another pretty woman in a happy dream. But he would like to hear her banging pots and pans in the kitchen. Then the world would return to normal.

Instead, he played back her presence, wondering whose face he should give her, hoping she might return again tomorrow night.

The following day Frank appeared. He'd called from the airport telling him not to come pick him up, he'd rent a car at the Tucson airport. He showed up unexpectedly an hour before midnight. "I see you've gotten so old you have to hit the sack by 6:00," he said cheerily.

"Well, you're not doing bad yourself. It's been what—three years—and you haven't aged more than ten."

They laughed and grabbed each other by the shoulders. Frank dragged his suitcase and golf clubs inside while Bert set up the day bed and put the leftover quiche in the oven. They ate quickly and saved catching up for the morning.

After a breakfast of coffee, rolls, and fruit, Bert talked about his new town, while Frank silently stewed. Now he had two dark secrets: one with her and another with him. Knowing how things needed to be kept perfectly clear between the two of them, he figured the first dark secret was the one to break. He waited for a quiet moment, then put on his serious face and announced there was something he'd been keeping from him. "It needs to come out in the open, Bert. There's not a good time, so we might as well get it over now."

Bert's eyebrows raised. "What—you've been taking golf lessons and have finally mastered an inside-out swing?"

Frank laughed, then paused. "This is going to be hard. I'm afraid you're not going to like it."

448

"Can anything be that hard between two good friends?"

"Yes, when it involves women."

"Uh, oh," Bert said, recognizing the change in tone of voice. "Well, go ahead, ruin my day."

Frank thought hard about backing away. He could make up something. But couldn't lie to his best friend. He finally spoke, slowly and deliberately.

"Here goes, Bert. I'm afraid the woman involved is one you know very well."

Bert's face fell. "Brie? What's up with her?"

Frank told him how it started with him getting a kayak and Brie suddenly jumping out of her car next to him with hers.

Bert interrupted. "So you kayaked together? What's wrong with that?"

"That's not all we did. I'm afraid there's more." He paused, looking for a good way to continue. "Well, that day we just kayaked." He paused again. "Want me to go on?" Bert nodded. "Two days later we kayaked to a specific place—Penland. With our tents and sleeping bags."

Bert bolted, scowling. "And….?

"And you can guess the rest, no need to go into details. It's just something that happened, beyond our control."

449

Bert grabbed his arm, shaking it. "'Beyond your control'! Don't bullshit me, Frank! Have balls enough to come out and say it straight. You fucked her!"

Frank shook his arm free. "Hang on there, it's not *I* did something to *her*, we both were in it together. In fact, she initiated it more than me."

Neither spoke. Then Bert sat back. "Ok, I'm trying to keep my cool. These things happen, I know. But *you*...my best friend? How could you have betrayed me, Frank?"

Frank rubbed his neck. "Don't think I haven't asked myself that a dozen times. But while we were quietly talking in that tent, you never came into my mind. Only her, right there in front of me."

Bert still hadn't calmed down, said he needed to visit he men's room, and went outside for a long walk. When he returned, he sat down, avoiding looking Frank in the eye, then finally spoke. "Ok, so you two got it on. I can understand how you'd have a hard time resisting her charms. She's a very attractive woman. But...."

Frank interrupted. "Believe me, at the time it was just lust that overcame me. Lust, not love. You've got to believe that."

Bert started to relax. "I *can* believe that. She's very attractive. Especially when she's wearing her sexy pjs, which I suppose she was."

Frank nodded, saying nothing.

"So you two made love that night and came home the following day?"

Frank hesitated. He didn't think it was necessary to say there was a second day. "Yes, that's it. We had dinner at her place after barely escaping a horrendous storm. And then I went home."

"What did Marsha say? Wasn't that a bit unusual for you to be gone?"

"I forgot to tell you, she was with her sister in Montana. We'd gone there together to help her recover from her husband's suicide, and she stayed a couple of weeks longer. That's where I got the kayak, by the way. They gave it to me for helping."

Bert absently massaged his arm. "I can see how it happened. Not deliberate; that's not like you. Yeah, how could you resist? But...." He faltered. "But what about *her*? Doesn't this make her look a little tawdry?"

"Don't be foolish. She's what--in her fifties, married twice, with a lot of boyfriends. Women like sex also."

Bert shook his head. "Yeah, sorry, that was stupid. I guess I was confused why it took us three months to connect and you only two days."

Frank resisted the wise-crack that would have come so easily on a different occasion. "Remember what I just said, it just happened, wasn't planned or anything. What you and Brie had was loving. That takes a long time to ripen. What she and I had was just sex. Period."

Bert sat back, not knowing what to say. Frank waited and then decided he had to continue with the rest. "I guess you don't know, Bert, but I should probably tell you. She did have several boyfriends after coming to North Carolina. Three or four, not counting you."

"Who said that?"

"Someone who knows her a lot better than you and I. Apparently a year or so after you left, she thought she'd found the right one to marry. They went together for two years and then set the date—after breaking up and reconnecting as many times as you two. That date came and went not long ago; I don't know who pulled the plug."

Bert frowned. "What the hell...? But I guess I should thank you for being honest and telling me what I never could have guessed. What do you think—she's in love with the idea of being in love but never with a real person? Is that what keeps her from a lasting relationship?"

"Maybe. But look through her eyes. Her life is totally governed by her condition. It's caused her untold amounts of grief, confusion, despair...not to mention fear. Think how hard it would be on anyone knowing what she knows, that there might be no light at the end of the tunnel. Wouldn't that prevent anyone from committing? Doesn't she deserve to grab on to whatever love or sex she can?"

Bert nodded. "Yeah, what you say makes sense. I came close to understanding it, although at the time I thought

I was to be the magic man, not this newer guy. Anyway, I feel pretty stupid thinking a while ago that I had to forgive you—or her. That makes no sense. I've been blind and pretty foolish."

Frank remained silent. They looked at each other and shook their heads. It was time to go outside and take a walk, not keep talking.

After a quiet fifteen-minute walk, they decided they had time for a round of golf. The air between them being cleared, Frank asked the question he couldn't before. "When did you two break up? Before or after your New England trip?"

"Before. In fact, that's what caused the trip."

"Before? Shit, why didn't I know that? It would have saved me a hell of a lot of guilt!"

Bert grinned. "Guilt's good for a person—especially you; you've always shucked it off too easily."

Frank grimaced. "Shit, you say! Ok, now we're even! I was just enjoying another woman—not *your* woman."

"You can look at it that way. Most people probably would. But you're smarter than most. You know the turmoil she put me through. Now I'm learning this woman I thought was mine—the woman I put up on a pedestal for all those months—might belong instead on a barstool." He paused, then added, "I'm thinking not just of you, but all the others you told me about."

"Come on, as I said before, she's just a normal, healthy person with strong drives, and sex is one of them. That hardly makes her a strumpet. Besides, we both know it was you who crossed a big line with her and suffered the consequences. My brief encounter with her had nothing at all to do with what you and she had."

On their way to the golf course, a pickup truck headed for Mexico loaded with old mattresses, tables, and chairs jumped the highway to come barreling straight toward them. Bert yanked the wheel right, hoping no one was there because that was his only option. The truck missed them by inches. They pulled off and looked back. The driver managed to get control of his truck—one wheel running on its rim—and pulled off the road before hitting anyone. They called 911 and started back to see if they could help, but the driver waved that he was all right.

"Phew! Glad that doesn't happen often!" Frank said, trying to sound casual.

"Makes you wonder, doesn't it! One second more and we'd be on the wrong side of the grass. He must have been going 80!"

They continued to sit talking until the police car arrived. "A short time ago we were discussing Brie's misfortune, and if you hadn't had the presence of mind to yank hard right, we'd never be talking again!"

Bert agreed. "This might confirm your philosophy—accidents happen or don't happen; nothing's destined."

"Or," Frank replied, "It could prove you right—after all, here we are. Maybe someone's looking out for us."

Bert smiled. "Either way, I give thanks. If it's just chance, giving thanks to nothing still makes me feel good, and if it's the other way...."

"Has this ever happened to you before?"

"Yeah, about forty years ago, with my first wife. We were motoring down that classic highway—Route 6...."

"Sixty-six, go on."

"This old beater came along and did the same thing, jumped the median. Missed us by a foot. But that guy wasn't so lucky; he crashed into the guardrail and flipped over. Everything in his car spilled over the highway."

"He died?"

"No, wasn't hurt. Just a kid, scared shitless. We helped him pick up everything and pile it next to his car...what was left of it. And we were just kids ourselves, maybe twenty-two."

They were an hour late getting to the course but the marshal let them on. It was threatening to rain, unusual for January, and on the fourth hole the wind picked up. They braved it until the thirteenth, then headed for the bar, joking about the golf gods having it in for them. Frank admitted he didn't mind, as he hadn't played for three months.

Two beers and more small talk later, Bert had relaxed enough to ask Frank if the bugs got him on his camping trip a few months back.

"Bugs?"

"Yeah, chiggers. On Penland; it's crawling with 'em."

Frank snorted. "The fuckers! All over my legs, even up my back. And I'd sprayed myself good."

"Penland. It's a dangerous place."

Next Frank asked if Bert was still seeing Becky.

"Charlene, not Becky. No, I gave up on her. She's a player, not in it for the long haul."

Bert asked about Marsha. Frank said things had improved. She had her female friends with activities five days a week, which left him free to go fishing.

"Still have that beater?" Frank explained he'd sold it before leaving and bought an ocean-worthy vessel. "Don't ask me to tag along, if I ever come to visit," Bert said, "I can't stand being in or on top of water. Deep water is just something to look at off in the distance."

Frank smiled and changed the subject. "There's still one thing we haven't come to conclusion on."

"The importance of sex in a person's life."

"We agreed on that a long time ago. No, after you and I moved our different ways, I kept returning to our talk about the end of the human race." He paused, noting that Bert wasn't registering.

Bert finally spoke. "Global warming, species loss, icecaps melting, population explosion...."

"Hold on a minute!" Frank countered. "We know all that, can't do anything about it. It just keeps getting worse and worse."

"Yeah, we *can* do something. We can stay alert, try to convince others. You know, education."

Frank smiled. "Agreed. Anyway, I was thinking of something different, maybe manageable." He waited for his friend to catch up. "You know, the whole EMS scare." Bert nodded absently as Frank continued: "Robert Becker, a famous scientist twice nominated for the Nobel Peace Prize has called it a greater threat than global warming." Bert nodded absently.

"I spent a month researching it again," Frank continued, "and before coming out here found studies that made their way past the eagle eyes of the telecommunications industry."

Bert's eyes jumped. "One of the country's biggest lobby groups! It automatically refutes everything about EMS."

"I read that more than six thousand reputable studies have already been published, and I guess you know that Europe takes it seriously."

"Now you're going to tell me our doomsday scenario has some basis in truth?" Bert didn't want to think about the possibility that his closest friend might start talking like Gerald, so he asked if the whole subject couldn't possibly fall into the category of conspiracy theory.

"You know me, if there's one thing that makes my hackles bristle, it's conspiracy talk." Frank reached in his daypack for a spiral notebook. "But the evidence looks bad. I'm no neurologist, don't know the difference between ionizing and microwave radiation, but right here it says the ionizing type comes from things like chest x-rays, and the other from wi-fi. Continuous versus pulsing, or something. One study says two days on a smart phone equals 1600 chest x-rays!"

Frank snorted, then went on. "Doctors and dentists shield their patients from e-ray radiation, but no one's telling you not to put your iPad on your lap, hold your cell phone next to your brain, or carry it all day long in your pocket next to your gonads. Hell, we do know that there's a fifty percent decreased sperm count in western countries. It's got to come from somewhere!"

Bert motioned to the waitress to bring another round. "Most of what you're telling me I read three years ago with Brie. Did you find anything new?"

"Yeah, one of these studies that looked credible said prolonged exposure to electromagnetic radiation can permanently change DNA, maybe even alter the physical body's structure."

Bert shook his head. "I doubt it can change DNA. And as much as I'd like to believe, I'm still not convinced they've proven a definite correlation between wi-fi exposure and EMS."

"Not yet, but there hasn't been enough time."

"What do you mean?"

"The reason medical schools still haven't begun to recognize or teach EMS is because any scientist will tell you a new disease has to be around for ten years before serious research is started. You tell me how long we've had cell phones and wi-fi."

"Two decades. Now everyone's wired up, even in underdeveloped countries."

Frank flipped through pages in his notebook. "But like I just said, the research is starting to flow in. One study says children and fetuses are affected 100 times stronger. Smart phones, wi-fi routers, and cell towers aren't the only culprits. Smart Meters are already installed in almost every house in the country. They produce the same kind of pulse energy. Wait 'till you see the video on that!" He turned another page, then paused, looking at his notebook. "Want me to go on?"

Bert grabbed his arm. "Keep it short and simple; cut to what we can do."

"Can we do anything? Even if we were smart enough to beat the telecommunication lobby, we'd take five steps backward for every one forward. Listen to this: 'Today's cellular and wi-fi networks have microwaves with frequencies lower than 5 gigahertz, but now the industry's pushing for higher frequency ranges up to 100 gigahertz...which is what the new crowd-control weapons use.'"

Frank flipped another page and started to read when suddenly Bert shouted, "Stop! No more! We're supposed to be golfing, not gabbing. I appreciate your research, Frank, and I'll get around to reading it sometime, but right now our job is to bang balls! Straight down the fairway and into the cup."

They played three holes without incident. On the next, Frank sliced it out of sight and came back grumbling, announcing he wasn't going to take the penalty. "The damn fairway's only 30 yards wide!"

Four cigar-smoking young guys wearing expensive golf clothes butted in, urging the older guys to move along. Bert and Frank waved them on. The golf game wore on.

CHAPTER EIGHTEEN: NOT DEAD YET

AFTER FRANK LEFT, Bert had a hard time sleeping. He couldn't tell when fall turned into winter or winter into spring in southern Arizona but knew summer would be upon him all too soon. It was already March; the heat would drive him north and he didn't relish traveling alone. One night after thrashing around in bed trying to get to sleep, he counted three years on his fingers and decided it was time to take stock.

In the first year he'd immediately started looking for the perfect house he couldn't resist buying and the perfect woman who couldn't resist moving in with him. Before doing that, however, he'd taken a trip to Prescott. It was cooler and a lot bigger. With his buddy's help he found a delightful creature—crazy enough to follow him back to Tubac but not crazy enough to sign on the dotted line. "Oh well, you know Charlene wouldn't have worked out," a small voice inside said.

The second year was better. The steady diet of pickleball, golf, dog-walking, and becoming part of the new place helped. He found several female friends, some of whom wanted something more than friendship, but none of whom he couldn't resist. The relationship he formed with his landlord continued to puzzle him. Like Dante's Beatrice, she also led him on, emotionally, not physically. A few months after he moved into the old adobe next to her place, Beatrice would come over to his porch with a jug of wine. They'd weep over their deceased spouses and try to make sense of life. Eventually they took to spending Saturday nights dancing like wild monkeys at Mike's-- which invariably caused Bert to picture her driving young studs crazy back in the seventies dancing at New York's Club 45.

Probably because of her exercise and good diet, Beatrice retained her striking looks. She had grown up in Tubac, but in her late teens left for big cities back east, working for dozens of different causes. After moving back to Southern Arizona, she kept promoting the common good of border issues and preserving cultural heritage of the three different cultural groups that had always inhabited the area. Bert liked listening to her recount tales of former times and tried to talk her into selling him the adobe house he'd come to love. She tried to talk him into buying her beat-up Chevy van.

From the start, both were convinced they'd been brought together—though she had no trouble articulating that belief, whereas Bert did. They understood, respected, and yes, loved each other, knowing they'd both always be there for one another, no matter what else happened. And they tried not to ponder that something else. She had less trouble not trying than he.

Then his mind moved closer to the present. December brought the magical afternoon on the Trail, spontaneously convincing him it was right for him to spend the remainder of his days in this sunny but not too sunny place. He could venture north for a few months in the dead of summer, maybe buy an oversized camper to stay in at his son's, or better yet, a condo he could rent out during off-ski season. He could visit Jorge and maybe even Leticia whenever he wanted. Now when people asked him if he lived in Tubac year-round, the predictable question after the one about where he came from, he simply said yes. Hell, he'd even changed his cell phone number to start with 520 so people wouldn't think his call was some advertisement from the east.

His decision to stay in the town 'where art and history meet' reduced his need to find a partner but didn't prevent him from wandering back in his mind when he went on long walks with Rowdy. The memories kept coming back. Sitting on the porch with Suzanne looking for faces in clouds. Watching boats go by with Brie on Lake Chatuge. Why, he kept asking himself, do memories keep intruding? Why, if they are good ones, do they hurt so much? Because he refused to let go of them? That suspicion sent his mind reeling, causing him to look back on his need to be with Jorge and his family. Was it destiny or just felicity that brought them together so unpredictably?

He immediately opted for the former, telling himself Jorge must have been in need of his great wisdom and generosity. But then distant laughter announced a competing inner voice. "Don't you realize that Jorge knew all along you were acting out of self-interest, not altruism?"

The laughter turned into cackling, telling him that peace and joy come not from some fuzzy spirituality but from an honest kind of selfishness. He tried to correct the voice but knew it spoke truth. Then it asked him if he'd learned the lesson about unlearning. He immediately countered that he'd learned that long ago. How can you learn about unlearning, he started to ask, and concluded he was getting a bit confused.

He needed to talk to his good friend Jorge. He'd been wanting to share his magical moment on the Anza trail with someone, and Jorge was the rare person he could get that personal with. He'd tried to discuss it with Frank on the phone, yet Frank obviously didn't want to listen. Bert knew Jorge would, and probably even needed to hear it. On his next visit he'd bring it up. He'd scrap all the big words like epiphany, and use the most elemental language. "I don't know why it happened," he'd tell him, "but there I was, sitting alone taking in the clouds, trees, ants…everything. I felt myself participating in their life, allowing everything around me to give me its dignity. I met reality face to face, not me to it—out there." Bert chuckled. "What am I trying to tell you, Jorge? It's hard to explain because it's so simple. I just allowed it to happen, and it did by my not trying to hold it or understand it…let alone interfere with it. It was something completely outside and beyond me."

He knew Jorge would understand, could even supply Jorge's answer. "That's wonderful what you share with me, Mr. Bert. I *do* understand. I too have felt it. I feel it whenever I disappear inside my painting. I become the horse and it becomes me. Isn't that what you're telling me?"

It's nice knowing someone well enough to predict his conversation, Bert thought, smiling. Then he went on to picture pretty young Carla rushing up to both of them, asking them to join her for a pony ride.

He replayed the imaginary conversation twice to get it fixed in his mind for their next visit. Then went on to finish taking stock. The main thing he accomplished in the first two years, he told himself, was getting out of his pet beliefs and mental habits.

Well, not entirely; the ones focused on women were hard to let go of, especially the mysterious and beautiful woman who might turn out to be the next and last love of his life. What about Chloe? She was so different from him that he guessed they'd butt heads if they ever did connect. The more he thought about it, he realized he'd been flycasting incorrectly…tossing the line out randomly and repeatedly without much attention to where the fish might be or might want. Maybe it would be better to play the wise Indian sitting immobile next to the pool, waiting for the right one to come investigate him.

He didn't know, would have to wait to see what would happen. To his surprise, the inner voice didn't return telling him he was right by not trying to control the situation. Maybe the Arizona desert had taught him something after all.

As he started drifting to sleep, the childhood refrain he'd hated for the first forty years of his life floated in—*que sera, sera.*

Dear Lynn,

Here it is May already! How can I thank you for dropping everything in your busy life to come attend your dying father? For dying was what I thought I was doing. Fortunately, I always keep my cell phone in my pocket; I couldn't have crawled over to get it to call Dan. He answered it in the middle of the night and rushed over to take me to the hospital.

Needless to say, I remember nothing of this; he pieced it together for me later. My memory starts with looking up to see this lovely face peering down at me. How long had you been awaiting my come-back? I guess I must have been out for two or three days.

Anyway, it's over now. The worst thing about being single is facing things like that alone. So many other people have to do it; I'm just lucky I haven't most of my life.

You must have been the one who arranged for the day nurse. She's been very helpful, and now needs to be here only a few hours a day. I can't believe all this has come and gone in only a few weeks; it seems like forever. I'm enclosing a check to cover your expenses, and don't you even think about refusing it. Heaven knows you and Freddy will be getting a lot more one day.

But it now looks like that day will be a little farther in the future than you must have thought while taking the taxi here from the airport. I know you must have been scared.

So that's enough carrying on! Now I'm able to walk around the house, and in a month or two will be back to pickleball and golf. There's not much happening around here these days; everyone's left. But how I hate the heat! You know me, I have to be outside, if only sitting on the porch—which, thankfully, I can do all morning until 11. Then it's creeping up to 90 and past 100, and I'm inside for a siesta. As you know, the nights cool down; I sleep with doors and windows open and by morning the house has cooled off. I rarely watch tv, spend most of my idle time reading or keeping in touch with friends—distant and close-by.

This accident did scare me a bit. Once again, I thank you for everything. I'll be visiting your brother Jed next month and seeing you and everyone in the not too distant future for Thanksgiving at your lake house. Worry no more about me! Give Freddy a hug. Love you. Dad.

Bert sat on his porch planning the months ahead. Aside from his accident, he'd just enjoyed another Southern Arizona winter. December and January mornings are what bring people here, abandoning their homes in

New England, Wisconsin, Colorado. Leaving behind bone-chilling cold that pushes them into cold garages seeking engine-block heaters or storage closets for long johns. Trading freezing winters for sitting on a porch in a light sweater listening to plump mourning doves sing their endless, monotonous songs: hutda-da de do… hutda-da de do… hutda-da de do.

Now in May, people in Southern Arizona who can afford to, venture back north to escape the heat… except for brave souls who tough out June and await the August monsoons that cool things off. This would be Bert's first June here. He thought he could last most of the summer. Then maybe he'd escape to Colorado briefly to see the aspens turn and be with his son and grandkids.

Early spring mornings in Southern Arizona encourage a person to walk the Anza. Bert went down with Rowdy, surprised to find it looking a lot like the trail back in January…so long as he kept looking down toward hard-packed dirt path or brownish underbrush. When he looked up, everything changed to different shades of green. Young mesquites with eight-inch drooping pods and leaves of light green; bushes and trees decked in varying shades of darker green. No sycamores, Bert's favorites, which he'd seen up in Madera Canyon, but interesting warty gray hackberries, and most of all, towering over everything, the giant cottonwoods.

Despite a two-day soaking rain last week, the first in months, the Santa Cruz was barely flowing. Enough for Rowdy to drink, search for tasty grass on its banks, and then jump in. As he watched the dog, Bert tried to figure out what he loved so much about the Trail. It wasn't its wildness, for every day dozens of people walked it. But they left it fairly pristine—no cigarette butts, wrappers, dog poop. Maybe he loved the way its dense undergrowth and trail disappearing around mysterious corners reminded him of truly wild places up in the Colorado mountains, Wisconsin lakes, or North Carolina woods.

He liked pretending he was alone in a wilderness, but also liked talking to people when they suddenly appeared—invariably accompanied by dogs. He knew most of them, especially now when few tourists came. They'd exchange tales of rattlesnakes, valley fever, good restaurants, or upcoming events. The last person he met before climbing the river bank to his parked car was Lincoln, telling him his dog needed to have his front leg removed because of valley fever, not cancer. Bert told him about his first dog, Bo, who'd gone blind but, like Lincoln's Labrador, didn't seem to mind. He hoped Rowdy would last another ten years, would stay away from javelinas.

Bert drove slowly back to his small adobe, looking forward to the evening's activity—this time not a penny-ante poker game at the Goods or a fund-raiser at one of the galleries but a poetry event next door. He always found it heart-warming to walk into a restaurant, bar, library, or deli and look around to see someone he knew. They always exchanged warm greetings, as if they hadn't been playing pickleball or eating out together the week before.

After getting home, he checked his day planner, found it filled for the week. Small things, but good things with the people he'd come to know and love.

He patted Rowdy on the seat next to him and told him to get ready for something very special...an afternoon nap. Rowdy smiled—or maybe just licked his paw again.

Bert wondered if it would be cool enough for another hour of sitting outside. From time to time he looked up from his book to watch small birds attack the feeder or splash in the birdbath. He enjoyed sitting in his comfortable wicker chair imported from Mexico. He hated to admit it, but he liked sitting more than walking.

A breeze blew from right to left, north to south, activating the wind chimes Suzanne had given him thirty years ago and setting the rope hammock in the yard to swinging. It also was thirty years old. Rowdy stirred, looking up from the yellow ball between his paws. He looked around to see if anything had changed. It hadn't, so he slipped back into his perfect doggy dream of whatever perfect doggy dreams are all about--winter, summer, spring and fall.

# #

INTERVIEW WITH THE AUTHOR

*What do you think about this puzzling EMS situation, and why did you include it in your novel?

It should be obvious I take it seriously, as I do all of our national problems—global warming, obesity, a sharp increase in autism and Alzheimer's not to mention undiagnosed chronic illnesses, computer hacking, nuclear war, social inequalities, and everything else so scientifically documented, for instance, in Thomas Friedman's books and media appearances--for which we should be thankful. I think solving national problems should be a personal job that starts close to home, which means people need to be led by facts, not opinions based on hearsay. Especially here in America we're quick to alarm but slow to respond. People think it's the government's job to solve problems but our government seems to be controlled by wealthy businessmen, big industry and special interest groups. Anyway, I've made EMS part of this novel because I've known people whose lives have been devastated by it, and hope the book may help raise public awareness. No one knows how many people are presently affected or could become affected. Many suffer silently for years and finally yield to suicide. To be very frank, I still don't know what I think about it. Since I didn't want to interrupt the narrative flow, I had Bert stop his friend's tirade toward the end of the novel. Researching the subject on the internet is still difficult, but one place to start is with an older U-Tube video, Dr. Magda Havas, "The Truth about Wired and Wireless Technology," or Dr. Pall's or Dr. Klinghart's videos. Even if it's too early to know what to conclude about EMS, we should try to learn more about it.

*Are you really Bert?

Everyone knows novelists write out of their own life experiences. Three examples here being my Yampa River trips, the Anza Trail epiphany, and the long New England trip (which in this novel wasn't just filler, but had to happen to give Bert's head time to clear). But characters? Some of mine are based on real people, although three-fourths are totally made up, and the others changed so much as to be pretty unrecognizable. All novelists issue caveats about their characters being fictional products of their imagination, and I'm no different. My task in this novel was to create a believable older guy who gradually gets to know himself. At the beginning he looks a little like me, but he starts becoming his own person half-way through. I like to think he gets a little wiser.

*What led you to become a novelist?

After teaching college literature for decades, I finally worked up enough courage to try my hand at creative writing instead of scholarly articles and books. Being involved in writing groups and leading workshops helped, but the most important thing was retiring with enough time to spend five or six hours a day writing. I especially enjoy rewriting. I rewrote my memoir about caregiving for my wife of thirty-four years at least forty times over a period of six years.

*Many say today's novels aren't as good as the classics you used to teach. What do you think, and what books can you recommend for beginning novelists?

I can't believe how good today's novelists are. Recently I tried to reread E.M. Forester's *Passage to India* and had to put it down. Same for Fitzgerald, though I wouldn't say this in public (oops). But I still reread many classics and continue to learn from carefully crafted works like Graham Greene's *The End of the Affair*. I think the best instructional book on writing is John Gardner's *The Art of Fiction*—though he doesn't get into the important distinction between memoir and novel, and poo-poos genre fiction, which I no longer do. (A genre book like *Harvest Home* (1973) by Thomas Tryon holds up very well.) Tim Gautreaux and Brian Hall are as good as any living novelist and I think better than many famous deceased ones, yet their names still aren't widely known. How many people applaud Jerome Charyn, called by a noted critic "one of the most important writers in American literature"? How well known are John Griesemer, Mark Helprin, Debra Magpie Earling, Jeffrey Lent, Elizabeth Kostova, Brian Hall, or Freddy Galvin? When I got depressed about my own mediocre prose, I turn to Goodreads to be reminded of people's radically different tastes—some terrible. And publishing practices have changed quite a bit. For several years now, the big national presses have admitted they no longer look first for quality. They publish only what they know is timely enough to sell. Literary agents are difficult to reach, and self-publishing is no longer frowned upon. People who moan and groan about books losing out to electronic entertainment don't seem to be aware of all of our book clubs. People still like the feel of an actual book, plus arguing about what's in it. And I think readers still go for quality, even if the big presses don't always.

*What's unique about this book?

I'm glad you asked. Most humans, unlike snakes, have a hard time shedding their skin. Some don't know it needs to be done; others don't want the suffering that usually accompanies it. People who grew up in the very different twentieth century sometimes look backward, repeating how much better everything used to be. Unlike them, writers like Richard Rohr in today's contemplative spiritual tradition discuss how to shed the "false" self that probably took half a lifetime to create, and might have served it well, but needs to be left behind. My novel is in that tradition of growing a more authentic self. Bert and Frank have to let go of personal baggage, much of which came from America's history of tribal and harmful thinking. "Stumbling" isn't an accidental title but expresses the difficulty of achieving positive transformation. If it's true that the opposite of love isn't just hate, but also fear, that opposition has been acted out daily in the lives of most of us in America since its beginning. Apathy and ignorance generally drive it on the personal level, and ideology on the national. The New Age movement has tried to help us choose love over hate and fear, but even it carries its own ideological demands.

*In addition to focusing on love, Bert talks a lot about purpose and destiny. Why?

Once you get older, what else is there that's important? This being a novel of relationship, a lot of what happens occurs inside somebody's head—mainly Bert's and Frank's. In my men's study group, we've discussed different types of love—platonic, romantic, married, friendship. All of the guys are retired from the workplace, organized religion, and two or more marriages, so our talk rambles on for some time. There must be many older readers, male and female, who talk about love, God, purpose, destiny, truth, and aging instead of sports, politics, sex, travel, clothes, and cars.

*The first and second half of the work have a different sound. Was that intentional?

Very much so, that was my challenge here. The first, in the format of a memoir, reads as truth, not fiction. I can't say it is a memoir proper, because memoirs must be by and about the author and tell the whole truth, whereas this book fudges. It's supposed to sound like a memoir but parts are fictional. (I'd fallen in love with the genre while writing my memoir about life with Marilyn and wanted to write a second one but had run out of personal talk.) That's why I call this book a novel. The second half should read more obviously like fiction--stuff made up. Hence the work is an intentional hybrid; I enjoyed trying to marry these two different novelistic forms. At the start we hear Bert in first person stumbling *in* love, and then in third person stumbling *away* from love, and finally *toward* a different understanding of love. I couldn't work all three directional adverbs into the title.

*Are you going to write a sequel?

No, my third work is about the real hero of this one— Rowdy. He's saved me in many ways, as he saved himself in the raging Yampa River. *Rowdy and the Javelinas* is almost finished. I've already started researching an historical novel about several interesting early-twentieth century people of my home state, Colorado: Enos Mills, Isabella Byrd, Chief Little Raven, my distant cousin Farrington Carpenter, and others. That time period marks the beginning of our national environmental awareness—which had to wait until we'd killed off half of our most precious legacy, but hopefully we'll wake up and stop finishing the horrible job.

*I've always wanted to ask a writer why he writes. Why do you?

Not because *it's there*; that's a mountain climber's unimaginative cop out. For me, like probably most artists, because it's enjoyable, therapeutic, and addictive. I can't say that about my earlier academic writing, which was mostly grind. As for mountain climbing, I once led a climb up a short but steep rock wall and it scared me to death. Like Bert and Frank, I'd rather play golf. It's the most difficult sport to master, but emotionally and physically rewarding as well as addictive. But the simplest answer to your question is because I have to—probably another unimaginative cop out.

Made in the
USA
Columbia, SC